## Love by Drowning

Magnificent in its conception and precisely detailed in its execution, *Love By Drowning* is a disquietingly obsessive psychological mystery of two brothers, Val and Davis, whose fates, set in motion early by their father, are tragically altered by their involvement with Lee Anne, a mysterious and charismatic woman. Poverman is a writer of such range and power, and of such oneiric strangeness and metamorphosis that at times the writing carries the force of myth. I disappeared into the world of the novel right from the beginning, and I haven't had that experience in a long while.

—MICHAEL COLLIER, Director, Bread Loaf Writers' Conference

C. E. Poverman's *Love by Drowning* is a wonderful novel. The first few pages will stun you (go ahead, read them now), and it never lets up. The characters are complex and compelling. Lee Anne Wilder is tragic and frightening, and Val Martin is a terrific, complicated character. C. E. Poverman is a superb writer. Read this book.

—THOMAS COBB, author of *Crazy Heart* and *With Blood in Their Eyes*

C. E. Poverman's great subject, memorably rendered in his 1989 novel *My Father in Dreams,* is fathers and sons. In *Love by Drowning* he gives us two brothers, each the secret sharer of the other's troubled life, whose fates play out in palimpsests of father–son dynamics. Enter Lee Anne, the woman who binds and divides them. She's a shimmering Cubist vision of asymmetrical angles and planes that don't quite fit, a major confusion in the atmosphere whose promise of ruin and death proves irresistible to them both. *Love by Drowning* is a noir thriller on its surface, but that reflective boundary of light and shadow offers sudden transparencies, glimpses of a sea bottom far below where the outlines of what has floated down stand revealed in microscopic, heartbreaking clarity. This novel lives in its bravura oceanic style that immerses the reader sentence by sentence, paragraph by paragraph, in the "secret rhythms of ceaseless tides"—not just of a sailor's Atlantic (Poverman's epic descriptions of marlin fishing will make you forget Hemingway) but the tangled undertow of human relationships in all their confounding mystery.

—VICTORIA NELSON, author of *Gothika* and *The Secret Life of Puppets*

In this powerful, beautifully written, and haunting novel, C. E. Poverman explores the murky and alluring waters where past and present merge, taking down life's sailors as they fight for air and offering salvation when the storm subsides. Who is left standing and how did that happen? Those are the questions posed here, and

Poverman's ability to tell a story in unexpected ways and get inside his characters—male and female alike—make *Love by Drowning* an irresistible siren call.

—DEANNE STILLMAN, author of *Twentynine Palms* and *Desert Reckoning*

## Solomon's Daughter

An extremely powerful book...staggeringly effective.

—*THE NEW YORK TIMES BOOK REVIEW*

Poverman writes brilliantly of adolescents, of parents, of the way we all change and compromise and come to grips with reality. His story rings so true, is so skillfully drawn, and deals with so much that matters that readers may not be able to put it down. A dazzling performance.

—*PUBLISHERS WEEKLY*

The passages which break our heart are the very words which console.

—*THE WASHINGTON POST*

A finely crafted piece of work, subtly controlled, emotionally taut...so well observed, and so moving.

—*THE NEW REPUBLIC*

...a striking abstract of all circular domestic communications, of souls bred to need but not to deliver...mesmerizing: a bright and highly original experiment.

—*KIRKUS REVIEWS*

This is a gripping, absolutely convincing, marvelous book, the best novel about American family life I've read. Solomon's daughter—and his wife—are great additions to literature's gallery of female characters...the Jewish Princess and her mother as they really are, not as they've been made to seem in jokes. A lot of readers will recognize their own family life in *Solomon's Daughter.*

—PHYLLIS ROSE, author of *Woman of Letters: A Life of Virginia Woolf*

## On the Edge

Has all the elements of classic noir.... Poverman is a fine writer with a suitably brisk style and a good ear for courthouse jargon.

—*THE NEW YORK TIMES BOOK REVIEW*

C. E. Poverman's gritty, utterly realistic *On the Edge* makes most suspense-mystery novels seem, by contrast, conventional and superficial. His portrait of a man in motion, attempting to keep his life from shattering even as he pursues an elusive "mystery," is memorable and exciting.

—JOYCE CAROL OATES

## Skin

*Skin* is a smart and moving and immensely brave collection.

—FRANCINE PROSE, author of *The Turning* and *Blue Angel*

Poverman's fifth book is a dazzler: Wide-ranging—from sexual abuse to psychosis, Vietnam nightmares, and the inner lives of drag queens—Poverman consistently holds anguished lives up to the light and unsentimentally offers the possibility of redemption.

—*KIRKUS REVIEWS*

## My Father in Dreams

In contrast to the spare and oblique language of much contemporary fiction, Poverman's prose is generous and rich.

—*PUBLISHERS WEEKLY*

I've read C. E. Poverman's novel *My Father in Dreams* with great admiration, wonder, and respect. It seems to me to be a major American novel of its time, admirably open and intense, poised, beautifully written. It's a book about fathering, about being a son, about a man's life, which is neither cynical nor leering, but is rich with incident and scene, with interaction, dramatization, and a Tolstoyan feel for intimacies. C. E. Poverman is a writer of honesty and vision.

—RICHARD ELMAN

## The Black Velvet Girl

Poverman takes us to new places, new cities in the imagination. He is adept, surprising, sometimes harsh and frequently very funny—a real discovery.

—DONALD BARTHELME, Judge's Citation: The Iowa School of Letters Award for Short Fiction

# LOVE BY DROWNING

# LOVE BY DROWNING

## C. E. Poverman

EL LEÓN LITERARY ARTS

Berkeley, California

Four chapters of this book were previously published online
by failbetter.com. *Marlin:* Issue 26, March 2008; *Held Under:*
Issue 39, May 24, 2011; *Still No Call?:* Issue 39, June 7, 2011;
*A Woman in Shades:* Issue 40, June 28, 2011.

*Love by Drowning* is published by El León Literary Arts,
a private foundation established to extend the array of
voices essential to a democracy's arts and education.

Publisher: Thomas Farber
Managing editor: Kit Duane
Book Design: Sara Glaser
Cover Design: Elizabeth Sisco

El León Literary Arts is distributed by
Small Press Distribution, Inc.
800-869-7533
www.spdbooks.org

El León books are also available on Amazon.com

El León website: www.elleonliteraryarts.org

ISBN  978-0-9833919-6-8
LCCN  2012951346

*For*
Linda
Dana and Marisa
*for*
Mike Fawcett
*and*
In memory of my father

# CONTENTS

# MARLIN

VAL SHIFTED HIS EYES from the bait riding just beyond the wake and glanced back toward his brother. Davis surveyed the horizon, arms crossed, a white sun visor shading his eyes, wireman's gloves tucked into the back pocket of his shorts. Last night Val had been as terrified of Davis as he had of anyone or anything in his life.

It had been over Lee Anne.

Face half-hidden by wild, bleached blond hair, her eyes averted, she had obsessed Val from that first moment weeks ago when she had stumbled in with Davis, something concealed in her gaze. And then, last night, her suddenly stepping into him, fitting her mouth to his.

Now sixty-five miles off the North Carolina coast, nostrils packed with blood-stiffened cotton, Val felt his broken nose throb. Davis wasn't talking to him.

With none of the sometime cat-and-mouse stalking of the blue marlin, the strike came without warning. Magnus, jerked off balance, recovered and braced himself in the fighting chair, the reel screaming as the marlin ran. Voice breathless and tightening with adrenaline, he yelled, "Crash strike!"

Val looked up at the bridge. The captain nodded that he'd seen it, the marlin stripping off line.

Val checked the cockpit. The wash-down hose was coiled and hung up, gaff ropes, leaders, baits, everything put away, the deck cleared for safe footing.

Davis adjusted the brim of his visor, then reached into his back pocket and pulled on his gloves. Val swung Magnus' chair in the direction of the fish, waiting for its first spectacular leaps. Surprisingly, the marlin didn't jump, but, fighting like a tuna, dogged it. Magnus quickly worked it closer to the boat. The swivel reached the rod tip. Davis took hold of the thirty-foot leader, and, wrapping the piano wire around his gloved hands—two wraps on each hand—he braced himself against the gunwale and began to raise the fish to the surface. Val divided his attention between Davis and the water, waiting for the fish to appear. He marveled at Davis' strength, the pole-vaulter's powerful hands and the massive, deeply cut forearm muscles. He'd felt those hands close on his throat last night before he found himself on the ground.

Now it was like watching a great athlete climb a rope, only the rope was a wire—slippery, razor thin, almost impossible to grip. With each pull, Davis retrieved more leader, then passed it behind himself and wrapped each hand twice more, bringing the fish toward the surface. No matter how many times he'd done this, Val never got over the sense of wonder and beauty he felt when he saw a marlin rising from below. Now he could see its pectoral fins, each the iridescent neon-blue of anger, a color you never saw on a tired or beaten marlin. The mackerel bait was on the fish's back, right behind the highest part of the dorsal fin.

Gary, the captain, yelled down to Val. "Too small. That's definitely no keeper. Cut it loose now, or do you want to tag it? You make the call. Only take a couple of minutes to tag."

Val picked up the pole with the barbed tag in place. This marlin was nowhere near as big as the one Magnus had taken yesterday, and probably weighed less than the tournament's three-hundred-pound minimum. Either way, it wasn't a keeper. Most everyone, conservation-minded, tagged the smaller ones before letting them go. "We'll tag it!" he called. "Can you handle that, Davis?"

Davis didn't answer. As Val extended the barbed tag toward the fish's back, he saw the round, black eye move; the marlin turned quickly and darted away from the transom. Davis pointed his hands toward the fish and let go of the leader, the wire wraps falling cleanly and freely off his gloves.

Magnus said, "We can cut him loose now, save everyone time and trouble. With that hook in his back, he's battling like a much bigger fish."

Val asked Davis, "Can you bring him up one time? We'll get that tag in him quick." Davis didn't answer. Val shouted above the engines and sudden scream of the reel: "Davis!"

Davis reached out and grabbed the wire leader to him. Wrap by wrap, pull by pull, he brought the marlin back to the surface and close to the boat. Val leaned overboard and pushed the tagging pole toward the fish. The marlin darted forward and turned, sending up an explosion of spray. This time Davis didn't let go of the wire, but held on as the marlin shot away from the stern.

Val yelled, "We'll cut him loose!"

Val dropped the pole on the deck behind him. He was surprised to see Davis keep hold of the leader, knees braced against the gunwale. He yelled at Davis to let go. Davis shouted something back but Val couldn't make it out. "Let him go, Davis! Let go of the leader!" Val unsheathed his wire cutters. As he extended their open mouth toward the wire, there was a sudden squeal of deck shoes—the sound of someone pivoting on a basketball court. Davis staggered against the board that covered the transom. There was a loud crack. Davis went headfirst into the water.

He surfaced, pushed the sun visor back from his eyes, started to turn toward the boat. Suddenly, he was pulled down. Val rushed to the transom. Davis was just below the surface with his hands together, outstretched. Neither panicked nor struggling, he seemed to be swimming.

But when he didn't surface in another moment, Gary yelled from the bridge, "Magnus, pull him back up!"

Gary threw the boat into reverse, water boiling under the transom as Magnus pumped the rod—once, twice. The blue marlin was just below Davis, rose with him toward the surface. Frantic, Val grabbed the rod and helped Magnus pull it upward, Magnus cranking the reel.

Davis and the fish were right beneath them.

"Stop!" Val yelled. "Neutral, neutral! Watch the propellers! You'll back over them!" Val heard the engines go into neutral. Val and Magnus pulled up on the rod, which suddenly lost tension and threw them backward. The wire leader had snapped at a kink a few feet below the swivel. Val staggered forward and looked into the water, expecting to see Davis rise to the surface. Davis and the marlin were free of the rod. But the hook was still in the marlin's back and Davis was still wired to the fish.

Val dove, and swimming awkwardly—shoes on, clothes on—he moved five, ten feet below the surface, driving his legs. Reaching out, he grabbed for Davis, gathered a handful of his shirt, but suddenly his grip was ripped open as Davis was yanked away....

Val broke the surface with a painful gasp for air, took another deep breath. Below him, he could see Davis and the marlin glowing iridescent in the sunlight where the clear blue water gave way to black. He stripped off his shoes and took another enormous breath, and driving his legs harder, pulling with his arms, he dove. He swam deeper this time, ears and sinuses aching, lungs starting to burn. He swam deeper. Beneath him, Davis and the marlin got smaller and smaller, shimmering into a deeper twilight blue, then disappeared into the black. Lungs bursting, Val looked up, surface distant, the sun huge and undulating....

# VAL

## *Held Under*

Val was running out of time—was it already too late? Should he try to reach his father in Connecticut again? The sun huge, white and undulating overhead, Val was stabbed by a sudden burning need for air. He pushed up and burst the surface of the water—his backyard swimming pool. Before he could take a breath, he was grabbed from behind, and, a forearm crushing his Adam's apple, legs locked around his waist, Val lost his balance and was pulled over backward, submerged. Still trying to draw breath, he sucked in water instead of air, gasped sharply. Suffocating and grabbing the man-sized forearms of his son with both hands, Val yanked frantically at Michael's locked arms and tried to slip beneath his grip. Michael held on. Val felt a stinging sensation against his shoulder, and the two of them sank to the bottom of the pool. Val sucked in yet another convulsing mouthful of water, desperately drove his legs against the bottom, burst the surface, pushed as hard as he could against Michael, and jabbed his elbows into Michael's stomach. With Michael's grip releasing, Val escaped to the shallow end. Doubled over, hoarsely, ludicrously gasping in loud, whistling inhalations like a seal, Val struggled to get his breath.

Michael surfaced beside him, rubbing his arms and stomach, eyes hurt and enraged. "Jesus Christ, Dad! I was just kidding around! You almost killed me!"

Still gasping for air, Val shook his head no, coughing and half-puking out pool water. In another few moments, he drew a smaller, less frantic breath, another. As he started to calm down, his throat opened and he could finally draw in air and smell the sweet orange blossoms and honeysuckle of late May; he became aware of the deep penetration of the desert sun on the skin of his back, tenderly probed his bruised Adam's apple.

"I had no idea you were out here!" Val gasped and coughed. "And if that's your idea of kidding, then I was kidding, too!"

"Dad! You're, like, always so fucking serious! Get your butt chapped!"

Val coughed, managed to whistle out, "You can use that four letter word—"

"Seven letters, Dad! *Fuck-ing.*"

"—you really can, if that's the way you want to talk—but just don't do it around me, Michael."

At fourteen, Michael was as tall as Val, had Davis' fierce strength. Val rubbed at a stinging place somewhere high on his back at the same moment Michael noticed and started probing a cut on his own chest; he looked at a diluted flow of blood on his fingertips. "Look what you did to me, Dad!"

Val took Michael's medallion between his fingertips, felt the jagged sharp edges. It was a quarter that Michael had placed on the railroad tracks; his knee and elbow skinned and oozing blood from a hard fall, he'd come home riding his mountain bike. He produced the perfectly flattened coin from his pocket, the eagle and George Washington obliterated, faint traces of letters like ghostly smoke. Refusing all attempts at first aid, he'd gone into his bedroom, and, crouched intently on the floor, long blond hair hanging in his eyes, he'd taken an electric inscribing tool and etched the symbol for anarchy—a squashed-looking capital A, a wild slash of lines—and then encircled the jagged circumference with the words *Crashing Sucks!* He wore the coin, a hole drilled through the middle, on a chain around his neck.

Now, Val dropped the medallion against Michael's chest.

"I've told you the edges on this are dangerous, Michael. It's like a jagged razor blade. Must have gotten caught between us."

"Must have been you! The way you just tried to hammer me!" He rubbed at the scratches on his forearm. "Look what you did to me!"

Val heard the push of the sliding glass door and saw Kazzie moving in the shadows of the porch. Having heard the tones rising from the pool, without knowing what it was about, she pushed the flat of her hand down toward the ground, a gesture to diminish sound, volume, pitch, emotion; she stopped abruptly as Michael turned, but before he could see the gesture.

"Little humor here, boys!"

Seeing her walking toward them, Val felt buffered, reassured. Fit from walking and hiking, Kazzie had an easy, athletic grace, which, Val had come to realize, was an extension of a belief she had in herself. She had large, beautiful, smooth hands, tapered fingers, a lovely way of handling and touching things.

Michael pulled himself out of the pool in a cascade of splashing water, and glaring one last time at Val, grabbed a towel. "Little humor for Dad! Butthead! God, I hate him! And he's all, like, such a hypocrite. He's always telling me not to use that dumb word. Fuck. *Fuck!* Don't use the word *fuck!* But I hear him! He uses that word!" Michael stalked across the grass.

"Don't walk into the house wet, Michael! I just did the floor!" Kazzie shouted. Michael slammed open the sliding glass door with a loud bang and, dripping, walked in. "Michael!"

Val shrugged. "You're yelling at him, Kazz."

Kazzie shook her head. "He's the one who's fourteen. You can't both be fourteen. Humor is the only way with him right now. The only way. I know it's hard, but you have to remember that. Why do you let it reach this pitch?"

"God, Kazzie. Why do I let it reach this pitch? I was taking a swim and next thing Michael's got me in a choke hold!"

Kazz sighed. She knelt beside the pool, half turned him around, touched a place on his back. "What's this? You're cut."

"The flattened quarter Michael wears got caught between us."

She smoothed the edges of the cut with her fingertips. She half turned him and kissed his wet lips, regarded him. Her face softened, became thoughtful. Her eyes filled with water-light, green, speckled.

"What?"

"That streak of silver in your hair, wet like this, the way the sun's catching it, is beautiful."

Val shrugged. "Forty-three in a week."

"Whatever else being forty is, it's kind of a privilege to get there," Kazzie mused as she stared into the water. "And at least you've got a full head of hair."

She smoothed his water-slick hair with her hand, kissed him, found his lips and kissed him again.

She started to rise. He took her hand. "Kazz, my mother hasn't called while I've been out here?"

"No, still nothing."

"I don't want to miss her."

"If we don't hear the phone, the machine will pick it up."

"If she's at the hospital with my father, it can be hard to get through to her."

"Take your swim. Just try to relax for a few minutes. I can get to the phone. It's okay."

"I know she hasn't been telling me everything."

Kazz squeezed his shoulder and stood, her knee clicking. She dropped a stack of mail enclosed within a folded *New Yorker* onto a chair in the shade beneath the olive tree and drifted over to pluck dried leaves from the flowering red hibiscus.

Val pushed into the deeper end of the small pool, its sixties decking starting to crumble, cracks in the bottom, several tiles fallen out along the waterline. A hummingbird, the green-throated female, hovered at the feeder hanging from the porch, needle beak extended to the red sugar-water flower; above the roof, a male, his ruby throat afire, soared for her, his cry an arid *tsk*. High beyond a Mexican fan palm, a rare streak of white cloud was spun thin by a silent wind. Val drifted with that invisible wind across sixty miles of desert to the south, to Mexico, curled like a sleeping animal dreaming strange, hieroglyphic dreams. Eyes at water level, he took in the enclosed yard, the phantasmagoria of gas grill in the shadows of the porch, the washer and dryer, assorted mountain bikes, Michael's trampoline by the brick wall. From beyond the wall, he heard his neighbor's boom box: the bombast of mariachi music, a flourish of trumpets; and, rising above it all, repeated attempts to start an engine. Long hair fanning out around his face, Val sank into the silence at the bottom of the pool, laced his fingers into the black holes of the drain grating, and knew, though the phone call hadn't come yet, that he was running out of time.

When he surfaced again, Kazzie was sitting in a lawn chair in the dappled shade beneath the olive tree; she sorted the mail on her lap, then stopped. She frowned, thrust a card in Val's direction.

"Can you just read it to me?" he asked. She vigorously shook her head no.

"Do I have to look at it right this second, Kazz?" She continued to extend the card and looked beyond him. "Guess that means I do."

Val pulled his top half out of the pool in a flood of water, leaned across the burning deck. His outstretched hand trembled short of the card. Kazzie stood and thrust it at him. Val pinched the corner between his wet fingers, and, sliding back into the pool, turned it over. The card didn't carry a salutation—none of them ever did—but just began as if something once started had never stopped. The lack of beginning implied a greater intimacy. The cards were never signed, also as if to say they were beyond that necessity. This one simply said:

*Dreamed of you again, you were coming to visit me, you came in a boat, then you were standing in my house. It was night. You stood in front of the window and even though it was dark, I could see the ocean behind you.*

She had added in the lower right hand corner in smaller writing:

*I forgive you nothing.*

The cards had come in flurries over the years, with irregular intervals in between. They were always postcards, never signed, and they carried a simple PO box as a return address. They had been cancelled in North Cove, New York. The messages were simple, cryptic, often enigmatic, like fragments of a dream; there might be three or four cards for several days, weeks or months, and then nothing for years, and then again, like a seismograph recording movement on a fault line, the cards would start again. They both fascinated Val and filled him with a kind of dread. At times he had the feeling that a picture was starting to emerge, the sense of which just eluded him. He remembered Davis had once said, "Lee Anne never lets anything go—and she never lets anyone get away with anything."

Val reread the card: *You were coming to visit. You were standing in my house.* There'd never been a card like this one before. *Standing in my house.* It seemed to bring something too near. And: *I forgive you nothing.* What *was* that? But without being able to put it into words, in a way he knew. There'd been a card several weeks ago with the single word *damage.*

That, too, had stayed with him for days: *damage.* The word had turned over and over, slipped in and out of his fingers. Damage. Damage coming to him? Damage in her own life? What damage? Val carefully composed his face and glanced at Kazz, who watched him with uncharacteristic resentment.

"I don't get it. I have never gotten it. Whatever your life was before, we've been married fifteen years. You have a son, a whole other life. Isn't there some way to put a stop to this? Who *is* she, Val?"

"I've told you. She was a girlfriend. And that's all. There's nothing more."

"What does she want?" Kazz stared at him.

"I don't know." Val shook his head. "I honestly don't know."

"Somehow, somewhere, you have to know. A person doesn't keep writing to someone without his having an idea why. She must want something. Even I can see—and I know nothing about her—that she wants you standing in her house. That means she wants me pushed out."

"Forget it."

"I might if I felt you could."

Val shook his head. Everything he'd said was true. Lee Anne had been a girlfriend. Kind of. He hadn't gone into detail. No one really wanted to hear about previous lovers. Kazzie had been with other men before they'd gotten together, and Val didn't want to know the particulars.

Kazzie slapped through the rest of the mail. She gathered her hair, pulled it back from her forehead and said with a touch of contempt and a country twang, "Whatd'ya think, Val, I'd be more interesting to you if I dyed my hair black, cut it short like KD Lang?" She sang, "'Catherine, Catherine, why do you...'"

Val said, "Please stop. I love you the way you are. And I've never once answered her, Kazz."

"How would you like it if I'd been getting postcards from some old boyfriend the whole time we'd been married? Someone you'd never met." She mimed the blankness of his face. "Somehow, she knows she's got something—some hold on you—because she hasn't given up!"

Val pushed off the side of the pool, swam across, hoping to break the momentum of Kazzie's angry mood. He knew Lee Anne's postcards were meant to disrupt. And they did, preoccupying him for days; it was as if she were saying, *if I'm not free of something, then you won't be, either.*

Still, he'd told Kazzie the truth when he said he hadn't spoken to Lee Anne since they were married, that he hadn't said a word to her, though one day several years ago, someone, a woman, had called to renew magazine subscriptions, and the moment he'd heard her Southern accent he'd barely been able to follow her words. "...a special rate of twenty-six dollars for two years, and if you renew now for three years, we throw in a blow job." Val had been stunned for a moment before he burst out laughing and the person hung up. Lee Anne?

As Val surfaced on the other side of the pool, he heard Kazz saying "... and you know something else, Val? If someone kept knocking on my door, sooner or later, I might just open it to find out why." She stood. "What I mean to say here, Val, is that if I were trying to sabotage someone's marriage, this is exactly the way I'd do it."

She was right. Perhaps the lie wasn't that he'd done anything or even omitted anything, but that he wasn't indifferent. The lie was that without his understanding it, Lee Anne was always somehow there, and he couldn't say that to Kazz. He didn't understand it himself.

## Still No Call?

In a sweat, Val entered the shadowy coolness of the fifties ranch house, and looking down at Michael's large, watery footprints across the tiles, he shook his head. What a mess. Well, it was, finally, just water, it could be wiped up, but he knew Michael wouldn't do it. Val sighed. Michael's attitude; that was the worst part. Fuck you, I'll do what I want. Don't like it? Clean it up or live with it. But Val couldn't split hairs with everyone about every little thing—postcards from people who were too distant and too far away in the past to worry about, Michael's tracking up the tiles.... Though the room was empty, the TV was on loud; Val, registering this, still didn't turn it off. He glanced at the *Arizona Daily Star* on the counter without interest: May 6, 2001. *Illegal Border Crossers...cause of major wildfires....* Outside, Michael rocketed triumphantly off the trampoline against the blue sky. God, he was going to break his neck. Knowing he couldn't stop him, Val, suddenly frightened, turned away.

With Lee Anne's postcard pinched between his fingers and on the lookout for Kazzie—Val could feel her anger permeating the house—Val walked down the shadowy hall into the bedroom, pulled a large manila envelope out from where it was hidden behind a row of oversized art books, and dropped the card inside with the others. He thought suddenly: do it, do it now, just throw them out, all of them. Kazz was right. Her sending them, his keeping them, they were divisive. He decided he would wait until Kazz and Michael were out of the house, look over the cards one last time, maybe tonight, then toss them out once and for all. Were they just random moods...or was there something she was trying to tell him? And if so, was she even aware of it? Was it a kind of game? He sensed a stubborn concealment within the cards. Maybe not. Angry, dreamlike, at times frightening, a broken puzzle, they roiled like smoke in the bedroom.

Val dropped the envelope back into its hiding place. Without thinking, he turned toward the framed picture of Davis on the dresser. Today it lay face down. Years ago he had put the print away for good. Then, several weeks ago, he'd retrieved it. He'd been wandering the house that night, thinking not of Davis but of their father, who was back in the hospital, and of wanting to fly East to see him, yet being held back by his mother's voice on the telephone—"Don't come now, stay where you are for the time being."

Upset, he'd ended up at his desk, turned on a light, dug through the bottom of a desk drawer. He saw an amnio photo of Michael at three months, a shadow sketch, the paper now curling, the color of dried blood. A sprinkling of Michael's baby teeth, which Val held tenderly in his fingers. Then, yes, here they were, a box of family snapshots. He took them to the sofa: Davis and himself when they were kids, pictures he hadn't allowed himself to look at in years; he'd gone back into the desk drawer and retrieved a framed 8" x 10" black-and-white picture. It had been taken of Davis at night, Davis caught and isolated in the burst of a flash. He was crouched behind the windshield of a boat, hands on the wheel, the boat hot and full of muscle, maybe an Aronow; a wall of spray flew at his elbow, a white wake boiling behind. Beyond the edges of the flash, there was a sense of huge, black ocean. Davis' long hair was blown flat behind him in the wind, his eyes slit by the rush of speed. He was looking over at the camera with a look of joy and triumph, perhaps contempt.

In the short time they'd been together in Brooklyn, Lee Anne and Val had never spoken Davis' name between them or referred to him directly in any way. But on what would turn out to be their last day together, Lee Anne, lying on the bed, her face webbed with pain, directed him to a suitcase. When he took out the picture, she said, "Davis." It was the first time she'd said his name in Val's presence; she pronounced it as if to say, the sum total, the essence of him, who he was. That night was the last time he'd ever seen Lee Anne.

Unable to make anything of the picture, he'd had to put it away and keep it put away. Part of him had thought it was a bluff on Lee Anne's part, that there was something to figure out, a final attempt to get to him. For what? For that last day, for the fading fall twilight, for all of Brooklyn, for an attitude she'd had toward him even before they'd met, for Davis, for whatever her part in it, for something in her which he'd felt but never understood....

He'd fallen asleep on the sofa staring at this picture of Davis, awakened the next morning with a sudden fearful intake of breath, heard Davis, the anger in his voice; he raised his head and saw him across the living room eating a bowl of cereal, snapshots spread on the table.

"...you can ask your father."

As Val stirred, Michael held up the framed picture of Davis and grinned. "Davis, Dad. Like, the bomb! What a dude! I've never seen this before. Did you take it?"

"No!"

"Who did?"

"No idea!"

"What's the matter with you?"

"Nothing. I just woke up."

"And like where's he going?"

"I said I don't know!"

"*Chala.* No! You said you didn't take it! Like all I did was ask a question. You *don't* know. Sure you don't, Dad! *Qué gabacho* asshole. *Qué jodida.*" Lately, Michael had taken to using pachuco slang he had most likely picked up from his friend, Chuy. What a gringo asshole. What a fucked up situation. Michael turned to Kazz for support. "*Chingado.* Like whenever you ask him about Davis it gets like all so weird, and I'm really supposed to believe you, Dad, you've got the picture, but you don't know anything..."

"I don't know! I'd like to be able to tell you! I don't know!"

"You've gotten very hard on your father lately!"

"Me hard on him! He's gotten very weird lately! And like you always defend him no matter what. All I did was ask a question and he jumped on my shit!"

"God, Michael, I hate it when you talk like that."

"Mom!"

Michael pushed back from the table abruptly, knocking over his chair, and swept the dozens of snapshots off the table toward Val. Snatching up the framed picture of Davis, he stormed out of the room.

Val lurched to his feet. "Davis, pick up the pictures!" Val took off after Michael before Kazz caught his arm.

"Val. Stop!" Michael's bedroom door slammed. "You just called him Davis. Don't give me that blank look. You did."

Val knelt and started gathering the scattered snapshots up off the floor. "Michael suddenly starts failing in school, cutting his classes, hanging out with weird kids, and I'm the bad guy." He placed a handful of pictures on the table, crabbed across the floor, went on gathering. "He comes home with a stud, wants to put it in his tongue—sure, why not? wants to pierce it himself, sure why not?—you think he smells of weed—" Val reached under the table, "—and you ask me to talk to him, but quietly, so I try to talk to him, but quietly, and he stonewalls me, tells me to get out of his room, and when I don't, he tells me to fuck myself, which I also don't, and then you and I talk about how it's all normal adolescent behavior and we just have to find a way…" Val stretched for a picture. "He should be picking up these pictures now, but I don't have the time to make it happen and probably can't make it happen and I don't want them wrecked so I'm doing it and that's my fault that I'm not disciplining him…"

Kazz walked from the room. What Val couldn't seem to say was that everything that had happened to Davis was starting to happen to Michael— his suddenly failing in school, the breakdown in trust, the anger. And that Val didn't want to do whatever his father had done to make things so bad for Davis. All, really, his father had wanted for Davis was for him to succeed where he couldn't. He'd loved Davis too much. Val raised his head too soon and banged it hard on the underside of the table and punched hard straight up, bruising his knuckles.

After several days, Val would go into Michael's room and quietly retrieve the framed picture. Unable to put the picture away, unable to look at it, he had left the photo face down on the dresser. That had been several weeks ago. Now he turned abruptly away and walked out of the bedroom.

In the living room, he looked out and saw the trampoline abandoned, the yard deserted beyond the sliding glass door, the surface of the pool taut and motionless. From next door, he heard a motor running loud and rough, missing. He slowed as the motion on the TV screen caught his attention. In an ad for something, Tiger Woods putted to victory in the Masters, dropped his putter. Walking directly to his father, he closed his eyes and buried himself in his father's embrace. Val felt his chest tighten, his throat constrict, and was astonished to feel his eyes fill with tears. He turned to hide his face as Kazz passed through the room, and then, wiping his eyes, he followed her up the hall into the guest bedroom.

She remained cool, distant: Lee Anne's goddamned postcard. He considered Kazzie. Tightness around her mouth. Too soon to approach her? He glanced at the bed, the door. And even if now was a possible moment, Michael was somewhere around. Nettled by Kazzie's anger and distance, Val licked his suddenly dry lips. But with the electric charge from Lee Anne's presence still permeating the house, Val couldn't move toward her.

"Kazz, you're mad about the card.... Look, really, I don't write Lee Anne. I don't put any conscious or unconscious vibes into the air which call out to her through the atmosphere, *send me a card.*"

"If they were unconscious, you wouldn't know, would you—by definition?" She said it dryly. "Okay, sure, Val. I imagine you're faultless and blameless. That's the hard part. You literally are. But there's so much you've never told me. Choose not to. And won't. Always have. You pretend all of this was nothing—is nothing—and I can see or feel some kind of pull from her. It comes through you—are you even aware of it?"

"Why are you starting it all up again?" He debated. Say something to her? Finally? But what? It was just too much, too complicated. "Kazz, are we going to keep this up? She's got you playing into her hands." He was surprised to hear an edge in his voice. His words were literally true, but the lie was just, well, what? It wasn't.

Val's voice softened. He took a step toward Kazz, put his arms around her. "Come on, Kazz. We're together." He kissed her. She let him, but didn't kiss him back. He found her lips, kissed her again, she turned her face away, but he felt something go out of her, she relaxed against him, he slid his hands down her back, pulled up her shirt and smoothed her skin, kissed her hair, her face, she drew him to her, Val felt a heat start to spread in him— relief, fear, anger, just desire for her, Kazzie. The front door slammed hard, shaking the house, and they stiffened and pulled apart as Michael came up the hall on a skateboard.

"Dad! Dad! Listen to me! Dad, we've got to act fast. I've got like a great deal for us if we, like, move on it. Celestino Hernandez is selling his boat. He's got about five guys in line ready to buy it and he hasn't even put it in the paper yet. He's just kind of detailing it up. But, he's all like, you know, he likes you, Dad, he thinks you're a cool neighbor, even for a *gabacho,* and if you're interested, he'll give you the first look at it. *Fíjate." Fíjate*: Check this out. "Just look at it, Dad. *Ésta bien.*"

"But, Michael...I don't want a boat so why should I pretend? We're three hundred miles from water here in the middle of the Sonoran desert!"

"Two hundred and thirty miles to Rocky Point, Dad. The Sea of Cortez. Sucker's sixty, seventy miles across. Fish. Deep-water canyons. Four hundred miles to San Diego. The whole Pacific. Not to mention the lakes—Powell, Mead, Roosevelt."

Kazz squeezed Val's arm. "It means so much to him, Just go look, Val," she said softly. Michael smiled and pivoted the skateboard. Placing hands flat on each wall, he shot himself toward the front door.

Entering through Celestino's side yard, the mariachi music louder, Val saw Celestino leaning against a buffing wheel as he waxed a hull under his carport. Val approached the boat, which rested on a trailer, noted it was a Mako, a center console, that she'd been run hard up onto too many rocky beaches—the fiberglass of her bow was chewed, as were her strakes and chines. The bow was tilted up slightly and the outboard motor's prop and shaft disappeared down into a fifty-five-gallon oil drum filled with water oozing oily rainbows. That, Val realized, was the engine he'd heard earlier.

Val nodded at Celestino, who switched off the buffer, turned down the music. "Selling it, Celestino?"

"Yeah, hate to, but it's time." He wiped the sweat from his forehead. Celestino had a full salt-and-pepper beard, mostly gone gray-white. Val glanced around the yard. Flowers. Cactus. A lemon tree in flower, the air heavy with its sweet fragrance in the heat. Close by, a knee-high statue of the Virgin of Guadalupe. The lovely gentle incline of her head. "The last few times I was out—I was in the Sea of Cortez—I didn't feel like I was getting around too good on the boat. Then I went out fishing for dorado—I'm too old to be going out by myself. I'm maybe six, eight miles off shore, can't get the motor started—I took off the engine cover to have a look, lost my balance, slipped and hit my head on the gunwale.

"Next thing I'm lying in the bottom, no idea where I am, or how long, but from the angle of the sun it's a lot later. I couldn't stand. There was blood all over. I knew I had drinking water, but I couldn't get to it. I inched over to some smoke flares in a locker, got hold of one of them with my teeth, pulled the ring and clouds of orange smoke started billowing up.

"I kept looking up and seeing my VHF on the center console, but I couldn't stand and get to it. The sun set and the stars came out and I still couldn't get up. Maybe a day and a night before Mexican shrimpers came over and looked in the boat, found me miles offshore burning up in the sun. So I'm done with it." Celestino showed Val the scar in his scalp. "Michael says you want the boat."

"This is the first I'm hearing about it. I'd never said anything to Michael."

"I'll give you a deal; worth it to me not to have people coming by." He pointed at a pile of life jackets, and overhead in the carport, an assortment of rods and reels. "I'll throw in the equipment. Those are good Penn reels. Anchor. Line. Fire extinguisher. Lot of extras."

Michael climbed up into the boat and looked down at Val, turned the wheel, walked from bow to stern. "Just look, Dad."

Val glanced at the knee-high plaster statue of the Virgin of Guadalupe. Gold stars sprinkling her sky-blue robe, she stood on a quarter moon just visible beneath the hem of her robe, a can of WD-40 beside her. Val gently smoothed the curve of her shoulder. He climbed up into the boat. He smelled the unforgotten odors of gas and oil, bilge, the brack of seawater. He looked the boat over. Center console. Lockers. VHF. GPS. He suddenly felt his father close; Davis, too, standing by his side. Michael watched his face from the bow, smiled and nodded quickly: yeah, Dad. He went through the motions of looking the boat over while Celestino showed him a few items. "You want it, Val, I'll stop detailing it, you take it as is, six thousand."

Val heard him out, nodded. "Very generous, Celestino. I'll have to think about it. For now, I guess just go ahead and do what you were going to do." Val climbed out of the boat. "Come on, Michael."

As Michael went ahead, Val called, "I'll be there in a second."

At the back gate, Michael looked back, gave Val a thumbs-up sign. Once Michael was out of the backyard, Val spent a minute thanking Celestino, but told him he had no real interest in the boat and not to wait for him, just to go ahead and sell it as he'd intended.

Michael was waiting in the back alley between the houses in the shade of a mesquite tree. "Did you make an offer, Dad?"

"No, I didn't."

"Are you going to?"

"No."

"Why not? If you don't move on it, it's gonna be sold!"

Val shrugged. "Michael...it's a nice boat, but it's old...chewed up. And you don't buy and sell things that way, quick, before someone else can buy them, looking over your shoulder...."

"It's a great boat! It's our chance."

"Mako is a sturdy boat, but it's just not...it's not right for me...."

"Nothing's right for you, Dad! What would be right for you? I mean, I wasn't fooled by you; you were faking it, but, like, I wasn't fooled, I saw you didn't really look like you were interested or gonna buy it!"

"Michael, we're three hundred miles from water. That's the simple truth."

"Lots of people have boats! Celestino took that boat down to Mexico all the time. We can't have a boat because of Davis!"

Val felt stopped by this. Then he managed to say. "That's all very dramatic, 'We can't have a boat because of Davis,' but Davis has nothing to do with it, and what happened with Davis happened a long time ago...."

"Yeah, but that doesn't matter to you! It's not like seventeen years or whatever it was. It's like it just happened yesterday! Mom says you've never set foot in a boat again since Davis."

"That's not true."

"Well, have you?"

"No, but not because of Davis."

"Why not?"

"I moved here after I finished my life in the East...."

"Yeah, and that was after Davis. You moved here to get away. You never cop to anything. *Qué jodida!*"

"Your mom's from this area and she feels comfortable here. And that's why we came. And we wanted to get away from the East."

"Yeah, and you don't feel comfortable anywhere!"

"Why do you say that?"

"Because I've heard you and Mom talking and I just know it."

"That's not completely true, either."

"Oh, yeah, not completely, like not completely, is like it *is!*"

"Never mind me. About this boat, we're hours from water here and I've just gone on to other things."

"Because of Davis! Mom said, don't talk to you about boats or Davis. She warned me not to, but I'm not afraid!"

"Good, don't be afraid. We've talked about boats and Davis before, Michael."

"Not much. And there's always something funny. You freaked out when I asked you about that picture of Davis."

"I just didn't know the answers to your questions."

"I'm not fooled by you. You don't wanna talk about boats or Davis. And that's why we live in a fucking desert!"

"I've told you about using that word. And we do lots of things. We hike. We go camping in the Chiricahuas. Why are you picking quarrels with me? We…" Val wanted to say, we love each other, but knew Michael couldn't stand hearing that.

"You don't even like the desert. You stopped being a lawyer and now you're—" Michael narrowed his eyes and pushed ahead, "a wimpy, middle-school art teacher, and make hardly any money when you could be making real money as a lawyer, and I don't even think you like that, either, being an art teacher."

"I do. For now."

"An art teacher. Jesus, Dad…"

"And if I want, I can go back to being a lawyer. I know you're disappointed about the boat…."

"I've got two hundred and fifty dollars of my own money saved up I could put in, Dad! We could fish, water-ski…"

"Michael, I don't want to be on boats!"

"It's not fair. You had a whole life on boats before me. Mom says you were great on boats—that you almost had your captain's license. You had boats but now you won't give them to me."

"It was all different, I lived somewhere else, my life was different, everything was different, it was a different time."

"I just fucking knew it would be this way with you, Dad, before I asked! Just knew it!"

Val glanced at his watch, suddenly wondered if he had missed his mother's call, and fought off a rising wave of panic; it was getting later, getting late, it was too late; he knew he was running out of time with his father. He restrained himself from grabbing Michael and shaking him.

Michael said, "You know something, Dad? Davis would have bought the boat and we would have gone water-skiing and fishing!"

Val was so startled by the wildness of this from Michael that he remained silent, then burst out laughing. "You never met Davis. He was gone before you were born."

"Doesn't matter!"

"How do you know what he would have done?"

"I just know! I saw that picture of him—that grin on his face. Davis knew how to be happy. He was a winner. He would have made a much better father to me than you have. He knew how to enjoy life. Davis and I would have had fun, man! And without you!"

This was so startling and such an obvious attempt to wound him that Val laughed again. Yet, Val knew Davis probably would have bought Michael the boat if he'd liked it, made up his mind right then and there, paid cash, hitched her up the same day, trailered her south to Puerto Peñasco, put her in the water, had a great time, been drinking *cervezas* with the Mexican fishermen by sunset, arm wrestling, teaching them funny English words.

"Michael...I can't be someone I'm not."

"You say I always have to be right about everything when we all like disagree. But that's not true.... Hey, you know, if I'm wrong, I just say now, like, you have to prove me wrong! If I'm not right now, prove me wrong!"

Confused, Val heard the familiar echo. Davis had once said, almost word for word, the exact same thing.

"That's not the way life is. That the world has to prove you wrong when something you want doesn't go your way! And what could I do to convince you? I'd have to buy the boat to prove you wrong. You can't do that to people."

Michael placed his hands on his hips. "If you'd had a different look on your face when you checked it out, I would have seen it and known. That would have proved me wrong!"

Suddenly, exhausted, Val said, "Okay, Michael, you're right. I wasn't really open to buying the boat. If that's what my face seemed to show, that's the truth. I just wasn't. Please forgive me."

Michael, pained by what he saw in Val's face—surrender, the truth, the pain beneath—blurted, "I don't want to be right! I just wanted you to want it so we could get it together and have some fun!"

Shaky, Val reached out a hand to Michael, said softly, "Michael...Michael... please.... I want us to have some fun, too. We do have some fun. I just can't have a boat."

Michael turned and slammed through the back gate.

Following Michael into the house, Val heard Michael and Kazzie in the bedroom, Michael's voice at an urgent pitch, a rant. Val hesitated outside the door. Kazzie caught a glimpse of him through the opening, pushed Michael inside, slipped out; she closed the door behind her. "Just a minute, Michael."

She said in a hushed voice, "Might be a good idea if you just disappear for a few minutes until he cools down. We're out of toothpaste anyway. Could you make a run to Walgreens? And why not pick up some Popsicles, too?"

Kazzie walked Val toward the front door. Val stopped and said in a hushed voice. "What is going on with Michael? He's frantic today."

"Well, could be he's picking up on your agitation about your father—the calls that went back and forth between you and your mother…"

"Did she call while I was out?"

"Val, I'd tell you if she had. He picks up on your fears. Maybe he's taking on some of your negativity, Val."

Val jerked open the front door. "Once you put my 'negativity' on the table, what can I say? It's like Michael's ranting *I don't have to be right; you have to prove me wrong.* So what can anyone ever reply to something like that?"

Kazzie's voice hushed. "All I'm saying is kids pick up attitudes. He's heard you talk about your father. Bits and pieces. Tones. He knows something's happening back East that you're upset about. We send kids all kinds of messages—good, bad. They get things we don't know we send." She pulled Val to her and kissed him. "It's just one of those days. Let's go to the movies tonight, relax. For now, just get some toothpaste, okay, and I'll try to calm him down. Toothpaste and Popsicles."

## *A Woman in Shades*

Val walked toward the car, still caught by the glint of the dime. Several years ago, Val tried to pick it up from the curb for several perplexed moments before noticing Michael crouched behind a tree and laughing at him; Michael had epoxied the coin to the cement. Since then, dozens of passers-by had done the same thing.

Val opened the car door, glanced up at the blazing blue sky of late May, and squinting against the white desert glare, he slammed the door and started walking. God, he hated it when Kazz threw his "negativity" at him. What could he ever say when she did that? Still, he couldn't help but wonder if there weren't something he carried which transmitted itself to Michael and which Michael translated into blind rage. Or, if Michael weren't incubating what had shown up in Davis, though so far standard school tests had revealed nothing definitive one way or other. Maybe it was Val's fears that enraged Michael, fears which Val himself could no longer name or define.

After half a block, he cut down an alley—white dust, prickly pear cactus in bloom, profusions of purple bougainvillea and oleander along walls and back houses, glimpses of the blue of backyard swimming pools. Along the way, dogs threw themselves against their back fences, barked under gates—paws and snuffling noses, bared teeth—Val talking calmly to each as he passed. A startled moment of pleasure when he saw a thin coyote silently cross at the far end of an alley, disappear through the undergrowth of a vacant lot and down into the sandy traces of an arroyo. In the distance, the mountains to the north were flat, purple-brown as they burned up in the sun, almost as if airbrushed against the blue sky. By the time he reached Walgreens several blocks away, he was sweating, calm and blank.

He sighed as he stepped into the huge drugstore and felt the cool, dry air envelop his moist skin. What was he here for? He started vacantly up a row, remembered: toothpaste. He puzzled over the choices, and picked a box. He walked a center aisle the length of the drugstore until he came to the glass doors of the dairy case. Ice cream. The frosted metal of the shelves. He opened the glass door; a profusion of milky, freezing moisture rose and curled around his arm and chest as he reached in, chose a box of Popsicles.

He started back down the center aisle toward the cash registers in the front, slowing to watch an old man reach for an Ace bandage with trembling hands, the skin mottled dark brown. The man brought the bandage close to his eyes, turned it over in a microscopic investigation. Val noticed purple-black streaks, bruises, on his arms, perhaps from a recent IV. The man went to replace the bandage on the shelf and, trembling, knocked several more down, the bandages rolling at his feet. Kneeling, Val picked them up and replaced them. The old man thanked him in a thin, quavering voice; Val touched the man's brittle shoulder, watched him shuffle toward the prescription counter.

Val turned toward the cashiers in front. As he passed an aisle, he noticed a woman at the other end. Large dark sunglasses, which didn't quite conceal a bruise, perhaps a black eye. From a boyfriend? Something about the woman. She turned and looked in his direction. She seemed to stiffen. Val felt a sudden burn of adrenaline push through his stomach, constrict his chest, felt his heart pound hard up into his neck, his ears.

The woman had several items in her hands. Suddenly, she turned away from him and thrust all of them onto the shelf in front of her, a number falling to the floor. She disappeared from the aisle.

Unable to move, Val looked to where she'd been standing.

Then he came to life and walked quickly to the next aisle—she wasn't there—and the next; he jogged the length of the aisle in time to see the woman walk through the Rapid Checkout, raising her hands to show they were empty, and rush out. She walked quickly to a white car. Val trotted to the front of the store, flung himself toward the doors when a clerk in a red vest suddenly stepped before him.

"Excuse me, sir!"

Confused, Val glanced at the man, who indicated the obvious, Val's hands. He looked down, then handed the clerk the toothpaste and Popsicles. The man shook his head and stepped aside. Val pushed out into the heat and glare, squinted as the car bounced over a speed bump and sped toward the parking lot exit and street. White. Late model. Indistinct. Maybe a Chevy or Ford. The glass tinted dark black. Still walking quickly toward the car, Val felt someone or something suddenly jerk him back hard, spin him around. The tail of his shirt had caught on the handlebars of a bicycle in its rack. He reached back and freed his shirt, which had torn, and rubbed his neck where the collar had cinched him.

Val shaded his eyes and thought he saw a sticker on the bumper. Maybe a rental car? He caught several numbers of the license plate. He stared after the car as it turned into traffic. In a moment it was gone. He re-entered the drugstore. The clerk still held the Popsicles and toothpaste. He seemed to have an attitude as he watched Val.

"Sorry. You've seen me in here before. You know I'm not a thief. I thought I saw someone I knew."

The clerk reluctantly surrendered the items to Val, who looked around, drew a pen from a display, tore a piece of paper from a spiral notebook, and wrote down the license numbers he'd been able to get. His hand was shaking.

Catching his breath, he made his way to where he'd seen Lee Anne—it was her, wasn't it? Or was he completely losing it? What would she be doing here? And at a drugstore eight blocks from his house? She wouldn't be. Impossible.

But if it weren't Lee Anne, who was it? Why would a stranger have run from him once she saw—and seemed to recognize—him? No, the woman—it had to have been Lee Anne—must have recognized him. And been surprised. Val stopped where she'd been standing and looked at the things she'd pushed back onto the shelves. Shampoo. Aleve. Nail polish. Personal things. They might have been anyone's.

Another possibility occurred to Val. If it had been Lee Anne, maybe he was supposed to have seen her—maybe she'd been waiting for him to leave his house, then gone into the drugstore by another door, gone to an aisle where he'd see her. But why would she do that? That was too paranoid.

She had sent him postcards for the entire time he'd been married. And he had no idea, really, why she did that either. But she had a reason. And perhaps she had a reason for doing what she'd just done, letting him catch sight of her; perhaps it was part of the same reason. Her card: *dreamed of you. You were standing in my house. I forgive you nothing.*

Val walked to the cashier, paid him, and stepping outside into the heat, walked home through the same dusty alleys; though the same barking dogs threw themselves at the same back fences, Val barely heard them.

Kazz fingered the rip in his shirt, stretched it out. "What happened to your shirt?" She took the bag.

"Oh, just stupid of me, caught it on the handlebars of a bicycle as I was walking by the drugstore."

"And here, your neck. You're raw and bruised."

"It's where the shirt pulled."

"Lately, I think you need a bodyguard."

Kazzie disappeared, returned with Michael and passed out Popsicles. Then she was drawn to sit and watch Julia Child. With his huge feet on the floor beside her, a head taller, Michael sat incongruously beside Kazz, just as he had as a three-year-old, quietly watching Julia Child burble on, taking it all in with subdued attention, the close-ups of sautéing onions, now the adding of chicken stock.... He seemed miles away and like a completely different person than he'd been half an hour ago. The three of them quietly ate their Popsicles.

Kazz came out of her absence long enough to say, "Your mother still hasn't called."

He went down the hall to the den, closed the door, slumped in an easy chair. Val saw the woman in the drugstore. He'd had a second before she'd turned and looked his way. The shape of the head. The black eye. And then the way she'd moved—was it Lee Anne? Or had he just been primed by the postcard? Would he have thought she were Lee Anne if there'd been no card? Or if the woman hadn't bolted out of the store?

Val reached into his pocket and brought out the crumpled paper with the license numbers. Four out of six. Not much good. He pulled the phone book to him and looked in the yellow pages under rental cars. In the next room, he could hear Julia Child's muffled laugh.

He went to the first one listed, dialed and said, "Uh, hi, I'm a waiter here at La Ventana…a woman forgot her purse at lunch…I ran out to tell her, but she drove off. I got a few of her license plate numbers. I thought the car was one your rentals." He ticked off the numbers, gave Lee Anne's last name.

There was the sound of computer keys clicking and then the voice came back, no, there was nobody by that name renting a car from them…. Val called several rental car companies—National, Avis and Hertz—but there were no cars rented by anyone with that name; maybe she was married, had used her husband's last name. Which he didn't know.

He circled the den. He was running out of time. Maybe Kazz was right. Maybe he was losing it a little, waiting for his mother's call, imagining whatever might be happening to his father. Maybe he *was* putting something into the air he wasn't aware of—and had upset the house. Michael. Kazz. Both of them. Negativity? Was he any more positive or negative than the next person? How could a person know something like that about himself?

He sat back down, opened the yellow pages to resorts, and called several hotels, simply asking if there were a Lee Anne Wilder registered. He was in the midst of his eighth call when he pressed down the button and swept the phone book onto the floor in a crumpling of pages.

He dialed his mother at home and let it ring for a long time, but there was no answer.

Seated between Michael and Kazz in the cool of the movie theater, his body a showered essence, Val held Kazz's hand, the tart sweetness of a hard candy lingering in his mouth. On screen, something big was happening, but Val, through the narcotic payoff of sun and heat and running exhaustion, the vast glaring space of afternoon light filling him from within, allowed himself the pleasure of fitfully abandoning the movie, let himself drift in and out of its sound and images, let it become something else altogether. He gave himself over to the pleasure of feeling Kazz and Michael on either side of him, the momentary safety of their enveloping presences.

———

Kazz pushed open the front door, took several steps and then stopped in the front hall. She listened. She held her hand out for Val and Michael to stop behind her.

"What?"

She took another step forward.

"Mom…"

"Sssh." She listened. In a hushed voice, she said, "Someone's been in here."

Michael brushed by her. "Suuuure, Mom. ¿Qué traes tu?" He went down the hall to his room.

"Someone's been in here," she repeated and circled through the living room, the kitchen, bedrooms, pausing, picking things up, putting them down. Val followed her.

"How do you know?"

"I can just feel it. Something's different." She sniffed the air, picked up the perfume bottle. "Don't you smell it?"

"No, I don't."

"Someone's been in this," she pulled the glass stem from the bottle. "It's still in the air."

Val sniffed. He shrugged.

She looked down at the folded laundry. Most of it had toppled to the floor. "These clothes…they were stacked on the chair."

"How can you remember where every little thing was?"

"Because I folded them earlier."

"Maybe the pile just fell."

"No, it didn't just fall. Someone knocked it over."

Val decided to humor her, and checking from room to room, he returned. "Nothing missing. And there are no forced doors or windows."

Kazz said flatly, "Someone's been in here," and began folding and re-stacking the laundry. Val started to ask if she wanted him to call the cops, but what was there to say? Again he walked slowly through the house. The woman with the sunglasses and bruise this afternoon in Walgreens…. He felt something pushing at the edge of him. Too unreal. Something else going on which had nothing to do with him. Had to be.

It was just one of those Kazzie things. Let it go.

Sleeping fitfully, restless, Val turned onto his back, felt the darkness thicken. He stood. He went into the other room, sat at the kitchen counter and dialed his mother. Remembering the time difference, and realizing it was too late to be calling anyway, he abruptly hung up, walked into the bathroom, peed. Recoiled. Some kind of twisted, dark animal—a mouse?—had fallen into the water, drowned trying to claw out. Val saw it was Kazz's used tampon, supersaturated with blood, the string tailing out. He quickly flushed the toilet.

In the living room, he turned on the pool light; radiant, nerve-white, it burst into the underside branches of the olive tree. Someone in here earlier? Val walked down the hall to Michael's room, panicked at his empty bed. Michael? The moon and stars and planets glowed pale on the ceiling where they'd been since Michael was a toddler. A blade of hall light hit Scully and Mulder, who stared out from an *X-Files* poster. Beneath them in small letters: *the truth is out there.* A second poster caught a skateboarder, arms outspread, in midair: stamped diagonally, it said: *Destroy Everything.*

Resuming his search, Val glanced onto the back porch, but no, Michael's bicycle was still there. He paced frantically back and forth through the house several times within a spiral of panic before he was jolted to realize that he was looking at a foot, it was Michael's, he was sleeping on the sofa, half-buried in cushions. Something let go in him, anger, relief; he looked down at Michael flung into sleep. For years, Val, too, had done this, slept on sofas, under tables, curled up in corners, as if to avoid being who he was, to experience the disorientation and temporary release of waking up strange to himself. For now, Michael had created the perfect obstacle between them: a boat.

Val walked quietly into their dark bedroom, looked Kazz's way, and reaching behind the art books, found the manila envelope. He inched closed their bedroom door. In the living room, he switched on an overhead spot, which fell in a circle on the dining table.

He spread Lee Anne's postcards on the table. Fitful fragments. Days, weeks, months, years between. He sank to one knee on a chair, placed his elbows on the table, and scanned them. Across the room, Michael breathed thick and deep from the sofa. Val watched him uneasily for an instant. Michael murmured something, sighed and swallowed, rolled over.

Val picked up a card and read:

> *those first moments when I walk out from the riverbank I kneel I put my eyes to the ice look down below feel something moving know I don't have to stay here any longer*

It ended abruptly as did all of the cards, leaving him now, as when he'd first received it, to wonder, what ice? And where? And did she mean that literally, *ice*? And what was moving?

Where was *here*? He read a succession of cards:

> *that empty bottle of Clairol in the trash was a mistake the only one or else maybe not something is always moving one part of me always in disguise from another, that part scares me, which one meant to leave the Clairol, I know but don't know*

Two days later, she'd written:

> *you know, too, but don't know.*

At the time Val had been sure that she referred to the picture she'd given him of Davis.

Had it been a taunt? What did she think he knew?

He picked up several more cards:

> *I was driving and pulled over onto the shoulder then I knew you had a son*

That postcard was postmarked five weeks after Michael had been born; it had shaken Val for days afterward, that she had somehow known.

Another card:

> *in all fairness to you, let me say I think you saw it, the truth of something about me right away*

> *I leave him, but I can't stay away, I come back everyone asks me why, after all is said and done, I am the last to know, it is because he is exactly wrong, I don't know, someday I'll know*

Val sifted through a dozen more which made little sense, read:

> *Moira's piano came a few weeks ago already it came out of the back of a truck it was wrapped in a quilt I told him I couldn't have it in the house and it didn't matter because it came in anyway it's been weeks of nightmares it just sits there on the other side of the room Moira's Steinway*
>
> *&*
>
> *Once I thought you were my way out. I still think*

And it had abruptly stopped, though she had still mailed the card. Out of what? To what?

Some weeks ago there'd been a card with one word:

*damage*

And then the card, today.

To each card, Val had shaped and reshaped a dozen explanations, enlarged a theory, felt each slip through his fingers. Together, the cards seemed to cover a time from when she'd left some frozen place and gone somewhere; there was something inside—or was it outside her?—that followed her or stayed with her. From what he could understand, she seemed to be with, or perhaps had even married a man she detested and who somehow frightened her; maybe she'd left and come back to him several times. And she appeared to resent Val long past any reasonable period of time. There were cryptic references to things he just didn't understand. What, for instance, was the big deal about a piano in the house? Or why was an empty bottle of Clairol a mistake? And what damage was she talking about? Beyond everything, never mentioned but always there, was Davis.

Of course he had thought of writing her back, but something always abruptly warned him: whatever you do, don't contact her. It was as if all the fragile boundaries that he had carefully constructed within himself would dissolve in an instant if he did. And even if he wrote, he didn't believe he could trust anything she'd answer. And what was his response? Why do you write me these cards? What do they mean?

He picked up one of her cards:

*someday you'll have to answer me, meantime, your silence is a connection between us impossible to break*

Michael suddenly sat up, opened his eyes wide, stared right at Val, but looked through him, and said something. Val swept the cards into a pile…. Michael mumbled, swung a foot to the floor, brushed his chest, and, eyes still open, fell back and rolled over. A cushion fell to the floor. His breath deepened into a long sigh.

Tomorrow, after Kazz left for work in the morning, he'd burn the cards, be done with this.

Val cut off the shower, dried himself, and, wrapping the towel around his waist, stepped out of the bathroom into the droning high seriousness of *All Things Considered*. The sofa was vacated, a pile of cushions on the floor beside it. Kazz had finally succeeded in getting Michael up, and somewhere he was dressing for school. Or, more likely, he'd reappear in the clothes he'd slept in.

Val looked down at his folder and notes. He had an in-service to present at school today—developing trust in the classroom. He turned as he felt Kazzie behind him, sensed what was coming even before she spoke.

"Your mother called while you were in the shower...." She reached for his hand. Her voice went tight. "She's moved your father from the hospital to a hospice." She took a breath.

"A hospice, Kazz?"

"A hospice. She's sorry to have been out of touch, but she's just been overwhelmed the last few days."

A wave of cold nausea went through Val. A hospice? Somehow he'd imagined the call might come as it had so many times before, *he's doing okay, the doctors are amazed*.... He heard himself say, "How'd she sound?"

"You know your mother. Just doing whatever has to be done, being tough about it."

Val gazed across the table. "Where is she? Does she want me to call her back?"

"Well, there kind of is no back right now. She's in and out, taking care of a lot of things while she looks after your father."

"Where's the hospice?"

"I wrote down the details and directions."

"And what did she say about him?"

"He's spiking high fevers and suddenly much worse. They've got him dosed heavily with morphine."

"Did she have any idea how much time was left?"

"She wouldn't say, but I have the feeling it's only a few days."

Again, Val pushed back nausea. He looked at the clock. "I'll get this meeting over with and then book a flight to New York. Did she say she wanted me to come?"

"Not directly. But she did say, 'The hospice is open twenty-four hours.' I think that means she wants you there. Why else would she say that?"

Val walked around the table, straightening his things. "She didn't mention if he—if my father—asked for me—or wanted me to come?"

The silence lengthened between them.

"No, Val, she didn't." Kazz said softly. "I get the idea—I mean, he's on morphine, how aware can he be?" She hesitated. "But whatever was wrong between you, I'm sure he'd want to see you now."

As if replying positively to her own statement, she nodded. Whatever was wrong, Val didn't know the answer to that. He wanted to know his father had asked for him.

Val pulled out the phone book, sat at the counter, and turned to the yellow pages. Airlines. He went back and forth through them, but couldn't bring the words into focus. Kazz gently placed her hand on his shoulder and slid the book to her. "I'll take care of that for you—why don't you get dressed? Did you get some coffee?" He shook his head no. She placed a cup in front of him. He peered into the grain in the counter, lost to himself.

Michael came in, lank hair darkened with water, parted in the middle and combed out full length so it almost touched at his chin and hid his face. He went to the cabinet, got a bowl, filled it to the top with cereal, and, managing not to look at anyone, poured so the rising milk forced cereal to overflow and sprinkle the counter and floor; then, dumping two heaping teaspoons of sugar on top, he walked to the TV and turned on *Bobby's World*. His neck was burnished dark from dirt and the metallic green from his neck chain, and he had resisted all attempts by Kazz to get him to bring a washcloth into contact with it.

Receiver to her ear, Kazz looked up. "Maybe you'd be more comfortable in a white shirt, Michael. It's supposed to be 103° today."

Never taking his eyes from the TV screen, Michael went on eating his cereal.

Val stood before the closet, stared blankly at several shirts, put his hand on one. He drew it out, looked at it, put it back. Took another, pulled it off the hanger and, no happier than he'd been than with the first, put it on. Slacks. Socks. He was pulling on the second sock before he noticed a hole in it. He slid into his shoes and stood, changed his mind and took off one shoe. He looked across the room at the picture of Davis. One shoe on and one off, he rose and walked over to the picture. Davis. His hair blown back in the wind. The smile. Triumph and contempt. The spray smoking up around him and Davis bursting out of the dark for a single moment in the flash, the ocean huge and black beyond. Val raised the picture and looked at it. When he turned, Kazz and Michael were standing there.

Kazz said, "Michael's leaving for school."

Val walked toward Michael, tried to kiss him.

Michael ducked his head.

Kazz said, "Kiss your father. He won't be here when you get back."

"Why not?"

"He's flying East to see his father."

Michael didn't say anything.

Val said, "He's sick."

"Yeah, I know. He's got cancer. Is he going to die?"

Val nodded, said softly, "He's going to die."

"Soon?"

"Very soon, I'm afraid."

Standing, absurdly, one shoe on, one shoe off, Val took a step toward Michael; as Val leaned over to kiss him, Michael averted his face.

Val gazed down at the sock with a hole in it, slid his shoe back on. Michael started out of the room. He stopped and looked back at Val. Val said "It's okay, Michael. I love you whether you kiss me or not."

Michael looked pained. Kazz shook her head and followed him into the front hall—Val felt the suction of the front door opening, heard and felt its slam. From the window, Val watched Michael walk toward the street. He stopped in front of Celestino's house and looked down into the carport at the boat, a great naked longing on his face, and then he turned and, shouldering his backpack, he cut diagonally across the street for the opposite corner where he would wait for the school bus.

Val said, "I can't bring myself to get that boat for him."

"I don't think it's really just about the boat, what he wants. He's been asking me a lot of questions about you and Davis. I did the best I could. I never knew Davis. It's not about Davis so much, either. He just wants something from you."

She reached up and touched her hand to his cheek. "Listen to me a second. I have a reservation for you on an America West flight at 1:15. You'll pick up the ticket at the counter. Gets into New York around 10:00. That okay?"

"That's fine. Thank you. I'm going to drop off my lesson plans for a substitute. Matter of fact, I'd better make that call now."

"I'll leave work and meet you back here after eleven and help you pack and get yourself together."

"You don't have to."

"I know I don't have to. I want to…I'll drive you to the airport." She put her arms around him and hugged him and he felt shaky and then forced himself to pull back.

He was sitting in the chair when Kazz pushed open the front door. She brought a sense of expectation and freshness, her movement through the world, which Val always loved. She dropped her purse on the table, walked past him. "Val?" She turned and saw him, stopped. "Packing going okay?"

Val nodded. "Pretty much done."

Kazz picked up his shirts and walked into the other room. Val heard the ironing board squeak and ratchet. In the bathroom, Val dropped toiletries into a plastic bag, wrapped them up, and tossed them into a carry-on bag. He stuffed socks, underwear, a light jacket into the duffle, running shoes. Running? All he could think of was the word *hospice*.

Suddenly, he returned to his closet and pushed his clothes down the length of the bar with a screech of hangers. A filing cabinet. He opened the drawer, groped under several files, and pulled out a videotape. Printed in block capital letters, the label read: June 11, 1984, MARLIN.

On top, there was a note from the wife of Magnus, the boat-owner. She had been standing right behind Val when Davis had gone over.

> *I've thought about you every day for the last ten years and struggled with whether or not I should send this. I know you blamed yourself for what happened to Davis, but I think the tape shows something else. You have been in my prayers.*

It had come five years ago, and Val had thrust it out of sight, had not been able to bring himself to look at it, knew that no matter what it did or did not show, she was wrong.

Kazz walked past him with the shirts. She stopped when she saw the tape in his hand. "Val. What are you doing with that? You're not taking it with you?"

"I think so."

"Why?" She held the ironed shirts in front of her. Her voice was soft, intense, pained.

"I don't know."

Kazz shook her head in disbelief, extended her hand for the tape. "That should have been thrown out the day it came. However well intentioned, she never should have sent you something like this ten years later. God, if there's one thing that's been in the middle of my life with you...." She came to him and put her arms around him. "I'm sorry."

She went to the bed, cleared a space, and with her lips tight, she started expertly folding his shirts. The sight filled him with tenderness and self-reproach. When she finished, she said, "Okay. Pants, shoes.... You've got most everything packed?"

He nodded.

She tucked his shirts into the duffle, went out. He heard the ironing board creak. He looked into the kitchen. She was ironing one more shirt. He reached behind the art books on the shelf, drew out the manila envelope—Lee Anne's cards—and pushed it down toward the bottom of the duffle. Then he reached over and took the picture of Davis off the dresser and carefully laid it in on top of his shirts. From the other room, she called, "Let me make you something quick—you can eat on the way to the airport."

Val took several bites of the sandwich, then gave up trying to eat and folded it back into its bag. Kazz glanced at his face. The air conditioning rushed into the car as she drove, neither of them speaking; trailers, industrial parks, low-income housing passed by as they left the center of the city behind and drove south. When they could just begin to make out the silvery drift of planes flashing in the sun far ahead, Kazz said, "Are you going to go see her, Val?"

"Who?"

"The woman who writes the postcards and never signs them. The ones that are in the manila envelope in your duffle."

"I'm going to see my father, Kazz."

"I was just trying to pack your shirts so they wouldn't crush and I found it." Val looked ahead. She said, "I know that you've kept that envelope behind the books. There was really no need for secrecy. You never hid the cards when they came and she made sure to write on cards so that I could read them, too. Somehow what she wanted. Disruption. Really, there's no secret there."

"No, there isn't."

"You're the one who knows her, Val. The only question is, why did you feel a need to save them and keep them hidden?"

"I just didn't want you to worry about..."

"That was really considerate of you. They're all postmarked North Cove, Long Island—it's not far from where you're going."

"You know why I'm going East, Kazz. There's only one reason. That's all."

Kazz slowed as she entered the airport complex, eased over for Departures, made her way up the slowly ascending ramp, pulled to a stop. She turned to Val. She was silent, then said with difficulty, "I know this may sound odd, but are you with Michael and me anymore?"

He looked into her face. What was she seeing in him that he didn't see about himself? "Why would you even ask me a question like that?"

"I have this dreadful feeling."

"Kazz—"

"There was someone in our house last night."

He said nothing.

"I really don't feel safe. Michael and I alone in there, you gone."

"Kazzie—"

"And now your taking out that videotape and those terrible cards.... I know the last few days have been hard, stress, your father, waiting, not knowing. But I've felt you pulling so far back."

"Kazz...I'm going to see my father and do whatever I can for him and my mother, and I'm coming back to finish the school year."

She leaned across the front seat and kissed him. He hugged her. She said, "Oh, God, your body is just so tense."

"I'll call you when..." he hesitated, "...I know something."

They pulled apart. She opened her purse and drew out a small box, gift-wrapped, and handed it to him. "What's this?"

"It's for your birthday...you're not going to be here. Open it now." Val peeled off the wrapping, opened the box. She smiled. "It was Michael's idea."

Val fit his thumb to the hole in the blade, pushed it open—the serrated blade snapped into place. He pressed the release and closed it. "It's a boat knife. I guess he hasn't given up." He opened his bag, carefully wrapped the knife in a sock, and closed the duffle.

"Tell me you love me."

"I *do* love you." He kissed her stiffly. "Thank you so much for the present. Tell Michael I love him. Thank him." Val kissed Kazz again and then stepped out of the car into the heat.

# LEE ANNE

## *Is This Me?*

Middle of the afternoon, dead silent, dead silent, I turn onto Val's street, but see no one…. Here is a car at the curb, I go around the block, once, notice an alley, turn in and, my rental car raising white dust, I slowly pass a high brick wall that matches his house, it's just one in from the corner with a high back gate, Ford pickup truck, cactus in flower, and still I see no one as I turn back out into the street, the road shimmering.

I pass a park, palm trees, tennis courts, soccer goals, a library, several playgrounds. Yesterday evening as the sun was slanting down, the heat breaking, people came out, played Frisbee, walked their dogs, Val came walking toward me, close enough to touch, straw hat and shades on, I kept my head down as he went by with Michael, that's his name, I heard Val saying, *Michael, just hold on a second…*and I looked after them and saw that the boy was as big as Val, with long blond hair, the same beautiful blond hair as Davis, first time he sat in the barber chair, his hair in my fingers, and when I came around a second time from a different direction, I looked right up and got a good look, sun angling into his eyes, and he was the image of Davis, moved like Davis, he said, *so, like, will you let me say something, Dad,* his voice Davis'…. He really should be ours, would be just about the same age, and I heard them talking as they passed, Val's voice all tender and frustrated as it was when he'd try to reason with Davis, I aimed my camera, and as the sun was splintering through the palm fronds and olive tree branches, I shot, and when they'd passed again, I followed at a distance, shooting, they walked back to the street, side by side out of the park and back toward their house, and I watched them.

Now as I drive away from Val's house, the street empty, I feel a stab of pain behind my eyes, it's this desert light, I fumble open my purse, feel into the Aleve bottle, empty. I remember passing a drugstore not far from here....

I am in the drugstore, freezing cold, fluorescent lights here, too, sun glaring outside the windows, and then I am in the aisles, pain relievers in hand, I'm slitting the plastic seal with my car key and remembering shampoo and nail polish, and I'm caught by the polish, maybe do my nails and feel better, still working the key under the plastic, is there a drinking fountain in here? I'll just take them right now, I press down the childproof lid, pluck out the cotton, I feel something and I turn and look down the aisle and there is someone at the end staring at me, and, fluorescent light? I see the silver streak in his hair, he's staring right at me, I reach up, sunglasses on, I keep my hand there to cover my face, am I completely losing it? It is him, a box in his hands, what is this? The thing that comes into focus is the bright colors, Popsicles, and he's just staring at me and then I look into his face, his mouth has fallen open, he looks as if he has been slapped, and I see it all, the moment when he first saw me, coming in at four in the morning with Davis after a fight and a roadside fuck, and the moment he came back off the water without Davis, and the seventeen years since, and it is all there in his face when he sees me, surprise, amazement, terror, and I see that he is still looking at the world as if he were underwater, since that day he has never trusted anyone or anything, or how things are or are supposed to be, least of all himself, and that he's never stopping thinking about me, and though he's never once answered me, his silence has been his daily answer, how much it matters, how afraid he is, we are still wired together, and suddenly I realize I can't be seen by him, not now, not yet, not here, I shove the things I have back into the shelves, all of them, and even as I turn I see him take a step toward me, and I run for the front of the store, past the cashier, and out to my car.

I drive blind in the glare for some time. I pass a Cineplex, black asphalt shimmering silver in the heat, pull in. Buy a ticket. Anything to get away from the knife edge of this desert light behind my eyes. In the theater, a wet paper towel on my forehead, I sink into the darkness, the movie, huge, loud, swims into my blinding headache, and I see nothing but flashing light and color. I hear music, voices. I watch the last three weeks, then…everything I've been trying not to remember:

…how I'm coming back from turning cards and dice, that Indian place, Mohegan Sun, the Connecticut shore falling behind me, Orient Point ahead; I'm standing at the ferry rail and looking down into the water, milky green, Block Island Sound, Atlantic Ocean, engines moaning below, wake boiling up under the stern, I know I dreamed something about Val, Val and Davis the night before, though I can't remember it, just that I jerk awake and feel them standing in the dark room beside my bed.

I'm thinking about what couldn't hold in me, three weeks already, first it started with the pain and then things blurred and there I was in the middle of the night, clots and lumps half-formed and blood, and then afterward the doctor taking care of the rest, and later by my bed I heard him use the word *damage*, it was a third miscarriage, but the first time a doctor's ever used that actual word *damage*, and then he said something, could not, would not, will never hold, there is *damage* from an earlier time, and the moment he said that I knew exactly when that was, I waited for Val and he did not come and so I went out and had it taken care of, went by myself, in Brooklyn, seventeen years ago, Val and I had Davis together, we still have Davis together, he never leaves us, even at our distance we're together, and then the doctor was gone, all of it was gone, and it was just me and I was emptied out from inside…

The movie boils on the screen. I can't make it out. I'm still on the ferry, still looking down into the water. I come in off the deck and stop to look at myself in a mirror on the bulkhead, thin smoke from the stack blowing down in the wind, curling over the deck, disappearing into the air, the boat's moving under me, engine making the boat shake and rumble, she's churning across that cold green water, I look in the mirror, it's one of these cracked mirrors where the silver is tarnished underneath and speckled with black spots like burn holes at the edge, what I see behind me is white light, clouds, and the water rising up to the horizon the way it does, all of it in the mirror, and me, me, too in the mirror, me in one half, the water and clouds in one half, and it kind of hits me all at once, my knees get soft and I turn slow and look out the window, water, the water is reflected there beside me, I reach out and actually touch the mirror like I forgot and expected something to be there, it's just glass, and then it hits me, water is the way it happens, everything all at once though I don't yet know how it will be or even what it is, just that I have to get out now once and for all and that it happens by water....

A week later I have the dream. I look out across the water, it's night, I see the boat drifts silent out of the dark, before I can make out his face, I'm sure who it is, it's Val, he moves down the dock through the trees, up across the grass toward the porch, I rise silent from my bed, step by step, I sink down the stairs, lights off, Val stands in front of the window, the ocean black behind him.

I wake thrashing, walk to the place where Val stood in the dream. Beyond is the dock, Brent's boat tied up out there.

In the morning, I write Val a postcard telling him about the dream, how he comes by boat, stands in my house.

I put on large dark sunglasses to cover my black eye—Brent may or may not remember hitting me before he passed out—and stand by the mailbox in front of the post office.

Just before I drop the card in the mailbox, I think of Davis, the first time I saw him I was cutting hair in Miami, 1982, dollar twenty-five, the *Allure College of Beauty,* he came in for a haircut, he was so beautiful I felt like I'd been hit in the chest with a hammer, I went on cutting, scissors whispering between my fingers, Davis waiting in the mirror behind me.... I think of Davis overboard, going far down below the sunlight. And.

Remembering Val, the way he left me in Brooklyn—if Val had stayed his son would have been our son, I lay the postcard on the mailbox and write small and hard at the bottom: *I forgive you nothing.*

I push the card through the slot, hold it a second more between my fingers. Once in Brooklyn I asked Val what it looked like, the marlin. When I was sure he wouldn't answer he said in a voice so dry and far away I could barely hear him, *it looked like something swimming out of the sunlight itself...*

I hold open the mailbox, the hangover of last night's dream rising on the wedge of black, Val drifting out of the dark, and then I let the card drop from my fingers. As it is still falling in the metal box, I feel my stomach flutter, turn over and over...

Then it suddenly hits me for the first time, and I wonder why I never thought of it before, that I can actually just go see Val, Val with his wife and son. That was last week.

I am here now. Yesterday I caught sight of Val and Michael for the first time. That's his name. Michael.

This afternoon I'm in this dark theater. In a while, I don't know what.

...and when the sun is slanting down and the shadows are long and purple across the sidewalks and streets, I get out of the car and step into the heat, air thick with the smell of orange blossoms and honeysuckle and tar...I walk a long diagonal through the park but today of course they are not there and then I walk the two blocks toward their house, nervous, he has seen me this afternoon, and though it was there in his face that he has never quite believed anything the same since, though he knows it is impossible, still he's seen me. I stop at the corner and his car is not in front, and then I pass the street, walk on by until I come to the alley, Ford pickup still here, I turn in and walk quietly in the fading light, the dust softly rising with each step until I come to the high brick wall at the back of his lot, and here I stop and look at the top of the olive tree growing on the other side, the branches already filling up with darkness and shadows, and then checking both ways and listening, what am I doing? I walk toward the back gate, notice the cactus flowers folding for the night, I stop and listen, hear nothing but my heart suddenly pounding, I reach up over the double gate—it is over my head—and looking at the brick wall and the gate, I realize, well, this is no accident, this is just the rest of it for Val, wrapped in the desert, in the middle of nowhere, this deep silence—which makes me think, what would you call being married to a man like Brent? a desert? I don't know—but here is the brick wall and gate between himself and that thing that's always with him. I stand on my tiptoes—notice a security floodlight under the eaves of the carport—and feel around above the top of the redwood pickets, find a metal fitting, a latch, push it, pull it, jiggle the gate, try again, and feel the gate release and swing free...I hold the gate open a few inches and peer inside, but there is no snarling dog...and there are no people that I can see, not yet...

I keep listening, then open the gate wider...a trampoline to one side of the enclosed yard and an old pool deck and pool, the water dark and breathless in the fading light, I hesitate, think, *that's all now, stop, take a step back, close the gate...* I look into the shadows of the porch, bicycles, a dryer, a gas grill, and then I am startled to see that I am looking through sliding glass doors which open into the back of the house. I catch my breath, but see no one moving inside, I see a reading light on, a sofa, a coffee table buried in magazines, books, a high-top sneaker, huge…

…checking the alley once more behind me, I step inside quickly and close the gate, the latch as it falls in the stillness making me jump, I drift across the thick grass to the pool, stand on the deck gazing into the darkness gathering in the water, the black holes in the drain…

When I can collect myself, I walk into the back porch, suddenly dark as I approach the doors. I walk right up to the glass and look inside. I listen and then I reach down and pull the handle, but the door doesn't give, and I feel a kind of relief, I step back and take a deep breath, here are the bicycles chained together, three mountain bikes, I run my hands over the seats, caress the smooth, worn contours, spot a skateboard with tagger script on the grip paper, can't make it out, toe it lightly with my foot, it runs smooth over the cement slab, bearings ticking in the stillness, it glides toward the back gate, *Michael,* I say, *Michael's skateboard,* and then I notice a side door and walk over and try it, but that is locked, too, and again I am relieved, now I can go, I start back toward the gate, and then I feel myself turned once more and I kneel and tip several flowerpots, circles of moisture and grit, round potato bugs, swirl of ants and sifting of tunneled sand, and under the fourth one, there is a key, I smooth the grit from its grooves and notches, walk to the side door and fit the key to the lock…the bolt snaps back and the door silently swings open…

…listening a moment, is this me, Lee Anne? I step inside and pull the door closed behind me. What am I doing? I am waiting to see, a little part of me wants to stop, but I just walk into the small kitchen and stop at the counter, turn slowly, spot a stack of grocery store coupons on the window-sill, a school lunch schedule on the refrigerator, papers on the counters, bills, school announcements, letters, invitations, I read an envelope, Ms. Kazz Martin, Kazz…his wife. Martin. She took his last name…I weigh that, taking his last name, to lose yourself, disappear, or be smothered, or start over, go free, reappear as someone else…. And Kazz, what's that? Catherine, Cassandra, Karen… I slide the letter out of the envelope, blur of writing, read a sentence, but then the rest of the house pulls me and I drop it on the counter…

In the middle of the living room, I look out through the sliding glass doors at the pool, the trampoline, its black drumhead stretched within dozens of gleaming springs, I pick up a dirty Nike high-top from the middle of the coffee table, Michael's, size twelve on the tongue, rank close smell of feet, of sweat, I walk down the hall to a bedroom, pause in the doorway, a double bed, unmade, I smooth my hands over the wrinkles in the sheets, the mounds of the pillows tumbled here and there, pick one up and smell it, close secret perfume of hair and sleep, I notice a black bra hanging over the arm of a chair, slide its satiny smoothness between my fingers....

What am I feeling? Nothing that I can name, yet...I'm like someone falling in this dense geological silence, this ancient silence, someone who sees the lightning on the horizon, but hasn't yet heard the report of thunder, do I hear it yet? I pick up an oversized folder from the floor, open it, some kind of grade book, Rivera Middle School, Val's name across the top, it's student work, art projects, I flip through them, beautiful colors, and then it hits me, I had been imagining Val as a lawyer in a well-appointed office, but he's not a lawyer, at least not now, or no longer, something about this makes me feel almost weak with what? pity? tenderness? I hold the folder with its art and realize that this is the rest of the silence he brought up from under water, it is the silence of this dry desert, this pre-human silence, these enclosed brick walls, silence within which he has remained enfolded as if inside one of these cactus flowers closed against the night, and it makes me feel a different kind of love I don't want to feel, a surprise, or does it just seem so in this fading light, and I start to wonder is it a self-deception, mine...? And Val, an art teacher, is that a movement toward his truest self.... Suddenly, it's all too much, and I drop the folders and move out of the bedroom...

As I drift up the hallway, I see myself in the house and know how it would look if a neighbor had spotted me at the back gate, had called the cops, if I were caught, I suppose I could put on my wide brimmed straw hat and shades and say they had just obstructed my vision and how in the world did I ever wind up in here, I do know I'm not crazy, though that would be my best defense, and maybe even until just a few week ago I wouldn't have done this, at least not exactly this, would I? I do know what I'm doing—and is this really any worse than what people do at parties, a quick sortie into someone's bedroom, a look in a drawer or closet, a search through a medicine chest...a little part of me wants to stop, or wants it to stop, but I can't seem to make it...

...I am standing before a framed black and white photograph, Val and Kazz walking on either side of Michael somewhere out in the desert, each holding one of his hands at their knees, Michael in overalls, and leaning in closer, I find my way into the woman's face, Kazz, Catherine? Karen? pretty enough I suppose, the boy's hand in hers, she's turning to look at Val, I realize that this picture, in years, couldn't really have been so long after Val left me or made it impossible for us to be together, my fault, too, he knew something was hidden there, and I kept trying to tell him, but I just couldn't let it go, or it wouldn't let me go, I got so close a few times, I think if only I could have told him…. I just stand there looking and then I realize I am shaking my head, pushing my feelings somewhere…. Isn't this everything he took from me on that last day? If he'd said yes, if he'd been there…*damage*.

I glance into a darkening room, see a glowing screen-saver design unfolding endlessly on a computer monitor, and then, I turn suddenly and face the darkened room across the hall. Michael's room. I breathe in the same rank smell of the Nike, his room, almost a wet dog smell, I fumble for the light switch, think better of it, I sit on his bed, smooth the sheet, unbelievable that I'm here and that I'm doing this, that I've done this, and standing, I ask myself, okay, is it over now? and I get no answer…. I look around and then a silver ring on the night table catches my eye and I slide a finger through it, huge, I drop it into my pocket….

…and back in their bedroom, something here, what? dresser, I raise a bottle of perfume, dab a drop on the inside of my wrist, a breath, quite lovely, I stand in the middle of the room, close my eyes, when I open them, I brush against a pile of laundry folded on a chair, it topples, I reach down to pick the clothes up, but see something in window light, I freeze—feeling that I am still falling, now is then, the same—I pick up the picture, Davis, boat running wide open, hair swept back, grin on his face, I turn the picture toward the light, and know that for Val, wherever he's gone, whatever he's done, this picture has remained and not gone away, that he has had seventeen years to think about this and the night I gave it to him, and for all that time, he has tried to do the impossible, ignore it yet at the same time figure it out, tried not to know what he has always really known about Davis and hasn't ever wanted to face, I put the picture back on the dresser and I know that whatever else happens, this is just beginning, and I stand suddenly—am I forgetting something?—I walk out of the bedroom, down the hall, through the kitchen and out the back door, locking it and hiding the key back under the flowerpot as I go. I stop to look down into the still-darkening pool…

Then I push open the back gate. Looking both ways and stopping to listen, I step outside and close the gate behind me. I freeze, arrested in mid-step, white lights, the Ford pickup leaps out of the dark. Squinting, hand shading my eyes, I find the floodlights in the eave of the carport, notice the motion detector photo cells, and, heart racing, again looking around, no one I can see, I step out into the dark and walking quickly down the alley, it hits me, that I might know nothing at all about what I'm doing, just that here I am, it's a surprise to me, I look back toward the house, the security lights go off, and I am gone back the way I came.

# VAL

### *Blameless...*

Val twisted sideways and cupped his palms between his eyes and the chill glass concavity of the window. Beyond the pulse of the wingtip strobe, Val thought he could make out the vast oceanic loom of New York City below the horizon. He sank back in his seat, dozed, but at a restless stirring among the passengers, Val sat up to see the horizon ablaze, and then the lights of New York City engulfed the airplane in all directions, and Val could pick out Manhattan, the twin towers of the World Trade Center, the Empire State Building, the Chrysler Building; he found the rivers by their absences, the East River, the Hudson, and their convergence in Upper New York Bay and The Narrows; he found the soar and swoop of the great bridges, their towers and lights, George Washington, Brooklyn, Manhattan; the plane passed out into the infinite blackness of the Atlantic south of Long Island, and banking, lower still, began the turn into its approach....

And then the interminable limousine ride up the New England thruway to Sound View, Connecticut, a coastal town settled by Puritans, three churches on its center green, where Val and Davis had grown up—he turned his head, but could make out none of it in the dark, could just smell the tidal brack of fuel oil and the harbor somewhere near, and then the lull of a taxi in motion from the limo station, now a long drive down a densely wooded, country road, patches of fog enveloping low-lying fields, glimpses of old New

England houses, porches, columns, faint and white; finally the cab slowed and the driver turned up a slight rise beside a recently cut meadow, and there, ordinary, was a low, single-story, red brick building, like an elementary school, lights from several windows, pale, falling onto the lawn. Val paid and thanked the driver, who looked at the hospice, but didn't say anything and didn't drive off. Val said, "My father."

The cab turned and went back down to the road, Val envying the driver his escape; alone in the parking area, he became aware of the faint sound of running water, perhaps a brook nearby, of crickets, of stars overhead, a deep earth smell of freshly cut grass. Now having arrived, Val put off for one last moment going inside; he looked around: meadow up to the wide lawn, the grass stretching away to the trees....

At the outermost edge of the silvery light, where the lawn reached darkness and woods, there was something, a shadow? Val held his breath. The deer raised its head. Its perfect black eye caught a point of light and remained motionless watching Val and then without sound or haste, it turned and delicately picked its way back into the woods and disappeared. Val walked across the thick lawn until he reached where the deer had been standing, and, kneeling in the faint light, he made out its tracks. He placed a fingertip in the deep indentation of a hoof. Unable to put off any longer the thing he had come so urgently and desperately to do—to be with his father one last time—he started across the lawn for the hospice.

The door from the hallway was half-open, the light low, and Val made out a man far too old to be his father in a bed by the window. The mattress was elevated so he was raised to a half-upright position. His hair was white and thin, the dome of his head fragile. A chair was pulled up next to the bed, its high back facing the hall. Val studied the man, whose body barely raised the sheet; he seemed to have no physical mass. Val double-checked the number on the door. He'd have to find a nurse to get directions. As he turned, something familiar registered at the edge of his vision: auburn hair. Barely discernible in the low light, a lock of his mother's hair, which had, improbably, remained dyed this color for years. Val walked with uncertain steps into the room, peered around the chair.

Shrouded within a thin sheet as if spun into a web, his mother dozed in her chair; a folded washcloth had fallen from her fingers onto the floor beside her. Her mouth fell slack. Val quietly picked up the cloth, which was still moist, and now he looked into the old man and saw his father, noticed his forehead glistening with perspiration. Val dipped the washcloth into a shallow basin of cool water, wrung it out, and circling to the other side of the bed he gently sponged his father's burning forehead. He took in the rest with a glance, an IV in one forearm and a circular morphine patch on the other. His father sighed as Val pressed the cloth to his neck and chest, the skin of which was almost transparent, and light and thin to the touch like silken paper. Across from him, his mother, tiny, dozed in her chair.

Val listened to the soft rush of air as his father labored to breathe. Should he say something now? Try to tell him he was here? Or just let him be? He looked at his father, his temples thin and concave; the hair, once thick and beautiful, black, then gray, now wispy and white; the closed eyes in which Val had seen so much—love, fury, pleasure, curiosity, tenderness, and the worst thing he'd ever seen in anyone's eyes, the pain of Davis' loss—the eyes now sunken, the lids brittle and thin. Val whispered, "...Dad?"

His father's lids fluttered, a thin white space opening at the bottom; Val had the sensation that he couldn't surface from wherever he was.

Val again whispered, "Dad...."

His mother stirred, opened her eyes, felt for the washcloth and then saw Val standing on the other side of the bed. She pointed behind her, and sorting herself out of the sheet, she touched her husband's arm before leaving his bedside.

In the hall, they hugged each other. Then, suddenly overwhelmed and unable to speak, Val remembered the snapshot, dug it out of his chest pocket: A picture of Val with his arm around Michael. She settled her glasses on her nose. "He is your height! Oh, that would please your father!"

Val looked toward him. "He didn't say anything about me...ask for me?"

"Val, he's just been in so much pain."

They returned to the bedside, where his father suddenly opened his eyes, looked ahead, and then, eyes drunkenly rolling, he searched out Val's mother, who said quietly, "I'm right here," and squeezed his hand, and then he found Val, steadied his gaze, seemed to figure him out, and Val, unable to raise his voice above a whisper, said, "Hi, Dad... it's me, Val," and his father nodded slightly and his lips shaped his name.

His father's eyes steadied; he looked into some place distant beyond the foot of the bed, and Val had the sensation of looking to windward, the thudding explosion of a sea against the bow of a boat, but now there was just the wall and the foot of the bed and his father's body, barely raising the sheet.

He squeezed his father's hand, said more urgently, "Dad," but couldn't raise his voice above a whisper, and was surprised to feel his father squeeze his hand back, hard, with strength, though his body had been eaten from within.

His father nodded slightly, his eyes wandering, forehead again shining with sweat. Val heard the rush of air in his nostrils, his breath coming hard, saw his body superheated and turned in on itself. He stood, and gently put an arm around his father's shoulders. He couldn't remember the last time he'd kissed his father, or his father, him.

His father groaned with a spasm of pain and his mother looked at her watch and opened a drawer. She peeled off the morphine patch on his forearm, unsealed a package, and placed the new dose on his skin.

Val pulled a chair up to the bed and sank down, and, taking his father's hand, he rested his forehead against the mattress; when he turned, the darkness had drained from the window, and the lawn had silently gone gray with a dilute light, though as yet the sun had not risen. Seized with fear, Val squeezed his father's hand. Now turning, he saw that the deer had come soundlessly to the window, was about to impart something crucial to him with the intelligence in his eyes…

Val jerked awake, the lawn a deep green, the woods slanting with sunlight, individual trunks and branches golden, green; and again, at this silent change of light, Val felt a deep fear go through his body, became aware of his father's hand still in his; he looked up quickly to see his chest rise beneath the gown. Val whispered, "I've been sleeping…how long?"

"Maybe a few minutes. Go ahead and sleep if you like."

"No, no." It was too late, too late….

His mother handed him a cup of coffee and he took a swallow and placed it on the windowsill. He looked at his father, who lay in a half-raised position on the bed, his breath coming hard. Finally, what he'd been feeling came into words. "Do you think he'll come awake enough so that we can talk?" Why couldn't he raise his voice above this hushed whisper?

"I can't say, Val."

His father suddenly opened his eyes. His mother said, "I'm right here, dear." He turned to her.

Val said, "Dad…I'm here. I love you."

His father worked his lips slightly. With the rapid darting movements

Val had seen earlier, the panicked eyes of someone cornered—or was it the morphine?—his gaze slipped past Val to the window.

Val glanced at the half-eaten sandwich on the plate—when had he eaten that? He couldn't remember, and what about this Coke? Everything was just the same, so ordinary, crushingly ordinary, the same, yet not the same. And dying, dying itself was work, pedestrian physical work, like labor, it was pain, a struggle, like being caught in a tight opening and trying to pull free.

Val gazed out at the late afternoon sun slanting across the lawn, the beginnings of evening already starting to flow into the light, and massed beyond that, night, another night; when had it gotten to be so late? There'd been people in and out, a doctor, a nurse; Val shifted his numb, sleepless body on the hard chair. He glanced out the window at the sunlight, every blade of grass casting a minute sliver of shadow; when had it gotten to be so late?

Again the sound of the morphine patch being peeled...

Now, the windows massed black with night behind him, Val continued. "Dad, listen, there's not much time. What happened, the way it happened..." His mother straightened the sheet. "Mom, were Dad and I talking?"

"About what?"

"Davis."

She shook her head, "No, no, I don't think so. No one's said a thing."

He looked at his father, whose eyes had now opened. Val stood. "Dad." Val took the snapshot out of his chest pocket. Would he be able to make it out in this low light? "I want to show you this picture of Michael." Val held it in front of his father. "Can you see it?" He thought his eyes struggled to focus. "Can you see he's as tall as I am now?"

His father made a hoarse sound. Val leaned close to his father, heard him whisper hoarsely, "Davis..."

Val looked at the picture closely: Michael and himself side by side, Michael's blond hair blazing white in the desert sunlight.

The window still dark, his mother dozing across from him, Val could feel his body chilled with fatigue and wanting to curl up into a depth within itself. He heard the hard panting of his father's breath, like a runner coming to the top of a hill. His father's eyes opened and he gasped. His eyes darted around the room. Val followed his glance. With the fierce hoarse rush of air, Val stayed silent.

His mother stirred, woke, took his father's hand again. He heard his father digging deep into himself, gasping for air. Another gasp. Val looked at his mother, and they stood up on opposite sides of the bed, Val stabbed with adrenaline. "Mom!"

"We're not going to do anything, Val," she said in a firm voice. "This is the only way left now."

His father heaved out another huge gasp, still coming to the top of that enormous hill, his mother holding his hand tight. Val gripped his father's hand, his father opened his eyes, looked up, looked down, as if starting to fall, as if to grab hold of something; Val squeezed his hand tight, "Dad!" His father's body gave a spasm, a sudden gasp, his eyes rolled up, and he sank back. Val became aware of himself squeezing his father's hand with both of his hands as hard as he could. His father's chest did not rise again. Val looked from his father—his eyes huge, open and dilated—across the bed to his mother. She stared back at him. They remained motionless.

Then he gently worked his hand free of his father's hand and walked around to his mother's side of the bed and put his arms around her. Still holding his father's hand, she put an arm around Val. She patted him consolingly, absently. She said softly, "Please, I think, just leave me alone for a few minutes." Yet they remained holding each other. Then Val walked numbly to the door, stopped. She was still holding his father's hand and looking at him; his head had fallen to one side. Val groped for the door, and stepping outside, he pulled it closed behind him.

Outside, he stepped onto the grass. Behind him, in a deeply luminous blue-black sky, the stars were shining. Ahead, the horizon—a massed dark line of treetops—was lightening, white, gold. He had come to be with his father, perhaps to have him finally pronounce him blameless in Davis' death, to have him forgive Val for something Val was sure he hadn't done, but had come to believe—perhaps through his father's unchanging view of him— that he had. Yet Val hadn't even been able to pronounce Davis' name. Instead, he'd shown his father the photo of Michael, perhaps as a kind of offering or proof of partial amends. Isn't that what Lee Anne and he had been attempting in Brooklyn? He'd heard his father's hoarse whisper: *Davis.*

Ironic, perhaps, that his last word was a misapprehension of whom he was seeing. Davis. Michael. Or maybe not. Maybe it was exactly to the point. Val's deeper point. He didn't know. Val sensed that he was again obsessing, was startled to see the knife in his hand. How had it gotten there? He fit the ball of his thumb to the hole in the stainless steel and snapped the serrated blade open. Stars still shining at his back, the sky rapidly lightening in the east before him, he breathed in the morning's air—grass, coolness—and teased the blade across his skin.

## *The Plainest Coffin*

She remained motionless, looking up into the rising green spiral of the linden tree, gently fragrant on this late spring morning. Then, she stepped over the large pile of unread papers in the vestibule and opened the front door. Suddenly embarrassed to speak of his father as dead, Val said, "What's planned for Dad now?" His voice was hushed.

"It's all been arranged, Val. I've set the funeral for two days from now. I debated whether there should be a minister. You know, your father wasn't religious. But somehow I'm going to have one." She walked to the sideboard and poured herself a glass of sherry.

"Did he know Dad, the minister?" Val had the feeling that they were speaking lines in a play that had gone far enough.

"No. He's someone who was recommended to me. Your father hadn't set foot in a church in years."

Val was surprised to hear himself speak again, "If he didn't know Dad, how can he talk about him?"

"I've given him some notes about your father's life."

He surprised himself. "May I speak?" His mother had raised the glass to her lips. She lowered it. Val said, "I can't let someone who didn't know Dad speak about him." He was surprised to hear his own fervor.

She said, "It could be very difficult for you." She took a swallow of the sherry. "I'm going upstairs to lie down for a while. You think it over."

On the second floor, Davis' bedroom; the morning sun streamed in the corner windows and angled across the floor, motes of dust spinning in the white light. A half-dozen plastic models on Davis' bookshelf had escaped childhood dousings in lighter fluid. A glorious array of trophies and plaques.

Every conceivable award. Team Captain. Best All-Around Athlete. All City. All State. On every wall, framed, still hanging, were pictures of his succession of teams—football, wrestling, baseball, track—through high school and college. Dozens of action pictures taken of Davis by his father. Clearing the bar in the pole vault. Sliding into home plate. Gathering in a pass. And framed newspaper clippings: "Martin Has Bright Future"… "Davis Martin Wreaks Havoc"… "Martin Stars Again"…

Val sank onto the mattress.

He awoke with a start on Davis' bed. It was early afternoon. His mother repeated his name, said that she'd spoken to Kazz an hour ago, that she'd be coming with Michael on the first available flight. The doorbell rang and she broke off and went down, and then he heard the murmur of voices, and Val knew that the house was lost to him, that he was just another visitor. Overhead, he noticed the phosphorescent stars still faint on the ceiling from when they'd been placed there, Davis a child.

Late the next morning, Kazz phoned from the limousine service, and Val went to pick them up, Kazzie and Michael. In the waiting room, he saw them sitting on the other side, Kazz reading a magazine and Michael playing his Game Boy with rapt concentration. Neither had yet seen him. They seemed to be someone else's wife and child. As Val walked toward them, he looked at Kazz's downturned face and was surprised at how pretty she was, her reddish-blond hair catching the sun as it slanted in the window, her beautiful hands, her dark lashes, the strength in her face. Did she belong with him? When he had almost reached her, she looked up and dropped the magazine on the chair. In that moment before they hugged, Val saw that in the time—was it just a few days of absence?—a thin mask of unfamiliarity had layered her face.

Kazz appeared at the screen door. Game Boy in hand, Michael followed her into the back hall in his oversized baggy pants and extra large T-shirt. Val's mother turned as Michael came into the kitchen. Val saw her intake of breath. She hadn't seen Michael since well before his last huge growth spurt. And now, with his height, long blond hair, blue eyes, and in his bearing…. Kazz exchanged a quick glance with Val. His mother too-carefully placed the teacup on the counter and said softly, tenderly, "Michael…" She opened her arms. "Michael, do you remember me?"

For Val, it was as if she were greeting Davis for the first time in seventeen years. His fractured dreams in which Davis wandered through the family house were no different than this moment. Staring self-consciously ahead, Michael shuffled toward her and shyly embraced her, his body stiff. "Of course I remember you, Grandma." She came to his shoulder, and he bent himself slightly so she could reach his face and kiss him. She pulled back and reached up and cupped his chin in her two hands and looked at Michael and said, "Oh, my god. Look at you. Look at you. My sweet boy." And Val had to turn away from the pained tenderness in her face.

In the upstairs den, a yellow pad resting on one knee, Val sat looking out over the front walk. If he was going to speak at the funeral, he'd have to get something written. He'd left Kazz and his mother spreading a white linen cloth on the dining-room table, currents of muffled voices flowing through the house.

Earlier, Michael had brought his bag up to Davis' room. "Do you remember visiting here a few years ago...you were maybe six or seven?"

"Kind of..." Michael dropped his bag on the bed and walked from picture to picture, trophy to trophy, asking about each.

Val answered, "That was Davis running back a punt for thirty yards... he'd just made an interception and was coming down the sidelines—that one was in the newspaper. Dad took these pictures. He never missed any of Davis' games."

"And this one?"

They looked at Davis' body balanced vertical on the downward thrust of his arms, chest clearing the bar against the sky.

"That's Davis pole vaulting. He's over thirteen feet there, thirteen-nine or ten, almost fourteen, I think it was."

Val was surprised to feel himself caught up in speaking. "Davis was on the baseball team and when we were at bat, for home track meets, he'd run down to the pole vault pit, pull off his baseball uniform—he had his track shorts and shirt underneath—and he'd jump into his spikes and vault, then sprint back...he'd be buttoning his shirt and tucking in his pants and running into the outfield and everyone would be laughing and cheering, 'Davis! Davis! He's our man.' It was funny. If the timing broke right in other innings, he'd run the hundred or two-twenty, book it back to the game again."

Picture to picture, trophy to trophy until suddenly Val couldn't speak, realized—how had he forgotten?—this also was why he'd found it impossible to come back. Michael pulled open a desk drawer, and there was a stack of Davis' baseball cards still twisted into a dried elastic band, a tangle of beaded key chains, a spark plug, hot rod magazines, a picture ID of Davis in eighth grade....

Now, the yellow pad on his knee, Val looked into the green elms and realized that he always saw them as they had been once they had reached the Bahamas—his father, Davis, his mother—an instant before sunrise, tropical water, coral heads and sand under the boat. He sensed that this moment had been a time to which he and Davis, separately, had been trying to return, Val in North Carolina, Davis working in a boatyard in Miami. In fact, in one of Davis' letters, he'd written, "Whenever I see the Gulf Stream it reminds me of the first time we crossed over...." Had each of them been trying to go back to a time before Davis' fury had split the house?

Just months before his anger had erupted, his father had started taking their boat south for the first time. Val saw the boat in freezing, green New England water, milky water, black water, his father and Davis in gloves, navy blue watch hats, heavy parkas, a long weekend toward the end of November, the sun low on the horizon, nothing but a lone barge or tanker on the brilliant horizon. Their mother had stayed behind on this first frozen trip. He saw just the three of them sailing all night, the red light of the navigation table through the companionway, saw the boat coming out of the dark, the decks and lifelines and cabin top white and sparkling with frost as they slid through the East River on the tide, opening out onto the Jersey Coast, then he and Davis leaving the boat a couple of days later and going back to school. Their father, taking Val aside before he put them on a bus, said, as he always did, "Take care of Davis. Don't let him out of your sight."

"Geez, Dad, he's thirteen. He's not a baby. He's as big as I am. And stronger. Just don't tell him."

"That he's stronger? He already knows. And I don't care. Just don't let him out of your sight.

His father continued on down the inland waterway: Delaware, Chesapeake, North and South Carolina, Georgia, Florida, and on to Fort Lauderdale, beyond snow, ice, and winter, beyond seasons—and into sun and clear water.

And to where they had returned over a Christmas break, sailed across the

Gulf Stream to the Bahamas—how amazed he'd been to see the light blue water off Florida where it had met the deep blue of the Gulf Stream in a sharply demarcated line of powerfully flowing northward current. Sailing from island to island, he and Davis had entered a kind of paradise, swimming, fishing, diving in water so clear it was like hanging suspended in a silvery-blue, sunlit room, where you could look sixty or eighty feet below and see the force of vast silent currents, sharks and rays lying motionless above the bottom, and schools of silvery fish eddying around the towering coral heads, and where at night, when the boat hung at the occasional, out-island dock under lights, the water clear and motionless, the hull seemed to float in midair above the sand.

Davis and he would sleep in the cockpit beneath the stars—Val had never seen the stars like this before, blazing and sweeping down to the black horizon on all sides, the constellations of the celestial equator and Milky Way burning bright with a terrifying and beautiful fire—and you knew in a way you'd never known before that the stars were pure fire. With no shore lights visible anywhere, and the boat swinging on its anchor line in the dark, the water black below, it was literally like being adrift among the stars. Mornings, he came awake in the first light to the sound of water against the hull and looked across the cockpit to see Davis motionless, loose rick-rack of blond hair spilling across the seat, that beautiful hair, sleeping bag dark with dew and sea mist, lines, sheets, and mainsail furled above, everything gleaming with condensation.

Val doodled on the yellow pad. Is this what he was going to tell people about his father? He saw himself in the cockpit; he opened his eyes to the stars fading, one by one, and in a heartbeat, the sky went a watery gray and the stars were gone, and then the smell of coffee, his father came up from below, and Davis stirred and sat up and rubbed his eyes as the horizon started to burn. Val looked down into the gray water where he could just make out the sandy bottom; silently, the first long slanting rays of the sun lit the water gold, and Val could see each coral head come out of the dark and cast an elongated shadow across the bottom, see the sand glow, the anchor, half-buried, shining like a quarter, and then his mother appeared and no one said anything as they could feel the Earth turning.

Val had been fifteen, Davis thirteen. They'd gone back to school in January and then, strangely, mysteriously, and, so it seemed, willfully and insistently, perversely, Davis, bright, funny, popular, had started to fail in school and that was when things began between Davis and his father. Ironic, because Val didn't think anyone had ever loved Davis more than his father had.

South—is that what he and Davis had been pursuing—a return to that time before Davis had started failing? Val wrote: "From the time I was a kid, I always knew that when you were on the water with him, you were safe." He felt his father's face come close. "Take care of Davis. Don't let him out of your sight." He said that to Val every time he and Davis went anywhere. "Take care of Davis." From the time they were kids. Val had always taken care of Davis until the last time he'd come back off the water without him....

Now, sometime after dinner, as Val looked up the dark stairs, the ancient dread he'd often felt as a child rose in him. He turned on the light, climbed to the second floor den. Unable to settle, he went down to the kitchen. Then, outside, he stood alone in the yard. Much later, after everyone had gone to bed, Val reread what he'd written earlier and started writing in fits and starts. He described his father as a self-made man who, through iron self-discipline, will and force of character, had worked his way up from poverty, often holding two jobs at once as he put himself through college and law school; like Davis, he'd been a gifted athlete—baseball, football—but hadn't had time to participate in team sports. He had been too busy with jobs and school. He knew how working people struggled in the world, never forgot where he came from, and always had sympathy for their situations. Val praised him for his unswerving loyalty and love for his mother. For his honesty, for dealing with all people the same, big people, important people; and little people, people with no power. And for appreciating people, taking them on their own terms. He wrote that he had always loved a good story— to tell one or hear one. He praised him for his avid curiosity and openness to the world, the way he never stopped asking questions, reading, the way he paused to talk to everyone, his easy open laugh, and that people knew they could trust him for his honesty and good judgment, trust him to care.

When he finished, he realized there was something huge missing: mention of Davis. It was just too big to leave out. His father's life divided sharply; when Davis was alive and his father's assumptions about the world were intact; and when Davis went into the water, after which there was always a piece missing, a remoteness, an absence in his look. He wrote this, then stopped. He couldn't say that. Not tomorrow. He crossed it all out.

Val wrote that his father was terribly wounded by Davis' loss, that he'd seemed to age almost overnight, and then shortly after, at the first signs of cancer—Val stopped at the word: cancer. He felt a thought start to form, but it slipped away from him. Cancer....

Val crossed out everything and wrote simply how much his father had loved Davis, and how fiercely they'd fought over something that had its origins in a profound misunderstanding, yet even while they'd fought, his father had always been proud of Davis, and that though his father was wounded by Davis' loss, he had carried on his life with admirable dignity. That's what he wanted to say. As he wrote, he'd stop and cry and then write more.

He slid into bed beside Kazz; it was the single bed he'd slept on when growing up, too narrow for two; he wanted to be close to Kazz, but neither of them could get comfortable, and Val felt none of the pleasure and comfort he usually took in their nakedness; rather, they were merely two bodies tangled and intruding on each other. He found a blanket in a hall closet and then returned to the sofa in the den, his nervous system numb and humming, his ears ringing...

Val jerked upright up at the loud jangling, flung his arms out as if he were falling, lunged for the phone. Blurted something. Listened. His father! *Help me! Come get me, Val!* No, it was Davis, wasn't it?! Confused, Val looked around. Where was he? He blurted something again, pushed himself up on one elbow, saw Lee Anne's postcard lying on the pool deck. A little more awake, he listened into the silence of the receiver. Someone listening? He couldn't tell if he heard breathing or if it were his heart pounding. Gasping, he slammed the receiver down, sat up. He knew there were creeps who read obituaries, harassed people. Someone had done that to his parents after Davis had died. Maybe it was just a wrong number. He saw the woman in sunglasses, felt the sudden blurred rush through the aisles and then the white car, windows tinted black, disappearing into the silvery glare. Small letters at the bottom of the water-stained card: *I forgive you nothing.*

At the kitchen table, Val's mother sipped her coffee, read what Val had written. He saw her hands working slightly as she held the pages, her lips compress once or twice; she flushed and walked quietly out of the room. When she returned, she said, "Val, I'd appreciate it if you'd cross out all references to your father and Davis—what you say about Dad's carrying on with dignity and so on." He started to protest, but then pushed her the pencil. "Just make the changes you want." She crossed out the lines referring to Davis, how much his father had loved him and how they'd fought and yet how proud he was of him. "Mom, I thought that I had to say something about Davis...."

Without looking up, his mother nodded. "I know. But... Please. Not today."

Upstairs, Val took out the blue suit and started to dress. When he finished, he was startled as he caught sight of himself in the mirror, a forty-three-year-old man—he'd had a birthday several days ago, hadn't even noticed until Kazz and then his mother reminded him—in a suit, dark tie, black shoes. Kazz came in, eyes fragile with circles beneath. She put her arm around him. "You didn't sleep..."

"I'm okay.

"Were you able to write something last night?"

He nodded. "My mother cut any references I made to Dad and Davis." Kazz searched his eyes. He shrugged. He looked at Kazz, slender, beautiful in her dark suit, her blond hair falling across the shoulders, her speckled green eyes. It seemed incidental that she would want to be with him, care about him.

He went down the stairs and was swept up into a series of hugs and kisses from friends and relatives, all the time fighting a choking sensation in his chest, and then Kazz and his mother and Michael came down, Michael clearly uncomfortable in slacks and a white shirt with a collar. They stood there in the front hall, no one saying anything or moving, twenty people, and finally Val said quietly to his mother, "Should we go?"

"I'm waiting for Mrs. Murphy—our neighbor. Last year, when Mrs. Douglas died around the corner, they came back from the cemetery to find the windows smashed and the house burglarized."

Val suddenly felt the jangled terror of the phone's ringing last night go through his body.

Within a few minutes Mrs. Murphy came walking quickly up the front walk and his mother let her in with a hug. Then, drawing herself up straight and squaring her shoulders, she turned to Val and said without looking at him, "I'm ready."

As they walked up the drive toward the funeral home—a turn-of-the century house set back from the street by a green lawn—his mother said quietly, "It's a plain coffin." She added in an absent voice, "It's what your father wanted. He said Davis had nothing at all—and so he would have nothing better for himself than Davis had. It's the plainest coffin."

They rang the bell as if they were invited dinner guests and were met at the door by an older couple, who led them into a front hall; they faced a long parlor with chairs set in rows, and there, silently, at the front was the coffin, a closed coffin, as Val had promised Michael; the fact of its being a coffin, his father's, and its being made of some kind of greenish synthetic material, made Val recoil. His father's wish: nothing better for himself than Davis, who had nothing. Beside him, he felt his mother draw herself up straighter. Michael stared with determination at the floor.

Val took Michael's hand—was surprised when Michael let him—and led him over to where his mother and Kazz were standing and then people started to come, to hug them, to introduce themselves. A man stepped forward, mid-fifties, salt-and-pepper hair, dark suit, thick glasses, introduced himself as the minister and offered his hand and a few words to each of them.

Then someone came toward Val who was familiar yet out of focus, pleasant-looking, well-dressed and comfortable in a suit, and he hugged Val's mother, turned to Val and shook his hand, and Val recognized him through his middle-aged demeanor, realized he hadn't seen him since senior year in high school.

"Val. Stan Miller. I'm sorry about your dad. Saw it in the paper. I always liked your father."

Val introduced him to Kazz and Michael. As Stan turned to Michael, Val could see he was confused; he had momentarily mistaken Michael for Davis.

The minister went to the lectern and started the service with a prayer and then several brief remarks about his father, which annoyed Val; he'd gotten the simplest things about his life wrong. When he finished, he nodded at Val. As Val stood, he saw his mother suddenly flush.

Averting his eyes as he passed the coffin, Val walked to the lectern and looked down into the long room, which was filled to the back and beyond, where people overflowed out into the front hall. Taking a deep breath and reaching down to find his voice, he began to read what he'd written, tentatively, until the words gathered momentum, each flowing into the next until the space between the words and his next breath suddenly fractured…

And then a blur, in and out of cars, the graveyard, the drift of the coffin across the grass in the grip of pallbearers, the air thick with the sweet smell of broken earth and grass, and the dreaded darkness of a hole, a grave; the pressure of his mother's hand in his as the coffin sank; in and out of cars again; the smell of coffee breaking the stunned preoccupied silence as each person came into the family house from the cemetery, and then Val's suddenly leaving the house as his mother came down sometime later and started giving away his father's jackets and winter coats to friends and relatives.

## Something to Hide?

Val drove without speaking. Michael punched the station buttons, bursts of rap exploding into the car. They made their way through the close shore houses and finally turned into the yacht club where Val pulled under a tree. Beyond, the river forested with masts, boats at their moorings. As they walked onto the dock, Val noted that the tide was high and covered the narrow beach, thin spears of brilliant green sea grass—just the tips—showing. At the end, he looked down into the opaque green water, out to where the river passed the town dock and then opened into the Sound, the red and green nuns and cans following through the rocks, which were all but covered by the tide. It was still early enough in the season that a faint chill rose off the water.

Val leaned against the railing, the sun-warmed wood calming to the touch, the air thick with the pungent, familiar smells of creosote, tar, tide. For years his father had kept his boat here, but the boat in front of them was unfamiliar—an Alden 45, riding high over the dock on the flood tide. Though they'd never spoken about it directly, his father had often said, "When the boat is yours, Val…" The understanding was that he'd sell the boat to Val when he was ready to pass it on. Good for Val, good for his father. It would remain between them.

"Where are we?"

"Your grandfather used to keep his boat here." Val indicated the slip.

Squinting against the glare of water light, Michael said, "This is the life we were supposed to be living, isn't it, Dad?"

Val shrugged. "We're just living the life we're living, Michael. I don't know anything else."

On the other dock, the flying red horse of the old Texaco sign swayed slightly in the wind. Michael said, "What happened to his boat?"

"He sold it."

"After Davis?"

"If you want to put it that way. Not right away. A few years after. But the boat just sat. He didn't go out on it. No one did. Yes, after Davis."

Val listened to the ringing slap of a halyard against the aluminum mast, then realized it was coming from the Alden. He yanked the bowline of the boat and climbed up onto the deck. In slippery leather-soled street shoes, still wearing his dark blue suit and tie, he made his way aft. In one of the cockpit lockers, he found a rust-stained sail stop, and returning to the main mast, he stretched the halyard away from the mast, looped the sail stop around it and the stay, and cinched the stop tight. The mast remained silent. He pulled the bowline and climbed off.

Michael watched him. "What'd you do?"

"I tied up the halyard so it wouldn't slap."

"How'd you know to do that?"

"It's something I've always known."

"He sold it—his boat—after Davis? And never had another?"

"That's right."

"Did you want it, Dad? His boat?"

Val was surprised by the question, more surprised that he couldn't find his voice. He said, "I would have been happy to have it." Even as he replied, he didn't say what they both knew, that he couldn't be on boats anymore, nor did Michael bring that up. Maybe Val wanted the boat or the person he'd been before. Or they were inseparable. Again he had the fleeting sense of once having moved with ease and certainty through the world. Maybe he wished that his father hadn't sold it without ever saying a word to him, never asking him what he'd wanted. But of course he hadn't. It was part of their impossibility. Neither had ever mentioned it again. The boat had just disappeared.

Michael said, "All of this is because of Davis…you and Davis, isn't it, that everything turned out different?"

Val said, "Let's not start again about Davis."

"Something happened between you and Davis."

Val looked at Michael. "Who said that?"

"No one. I just know it."

"Why would you just come out with that now?"

"I feel it from you. It's always all, like, there whenever anything comes up about Davis…you pretend not to, but you get all nervous and weird, Dad. ¿Qué pues? Like when I asked you about the picture of Davis the other day—who took it, where he was going in that boat—you flipped."

"I told you, I'd just awakened. And I didn't—don't—know the answers to your questions."

"Sure, whatever. It's just the way people are when they're hiding something."

"I've got nothing to hide."

Michael shrugged, "Like, I don't expect you to ever, ya know, cop to anything with me. You know something? When you're straight with me, I'll be straight with you. Even now you have that look on your face." Michael looked out to where the river opened into the sound. "No one ever wants to talk about Davis."

The wind silently darkened the water and Val watched the chop spring up. He remembered Kazz's saying he'd adopted his father's unforgiving attitude toward himself. True? Was that what Michael read in him? Or *did* he have something to hide? He thought he didn't. For the first time in several days, he remembered what he had come to think of as *the marlin tape* in his bag.

He started up the dock, the gust swirling his tie and billowing his suit jacket. He turned toward Michael. "Coming?"

Michael remained with his back to Val, staring out to where the river opened through the rocks. The gust freshened, caught his long, beautiful blond hair, shining in the sun, and stood it straight up over his head.

At home, the mourners were gone. In his room, he saw that the manila envelope with Lee Anne's cards was visible through the zippered opening of his duffle, and he slid it out of sight under his socks and underwear. He felt inside until he found the marlin tape, reassured that it was still there. Unable to take another step, he sank onto his bed.

Val woke to Kazz easing him out of his jacket and tie, and drifting back toward sleep he followed the slant of sunlight down to where it disappeared into the water.

———

In the morning, Kazz reminded Val that the show she'd been curating at the Arizona State Museum was opening in two days and that she and Michael had to fly back tomorrow. Failing in three subjects, Michael had tests coming up and she'd have to get him to study. Was Val coming with them? He couldn't answer.

Michael seemed to reflect his impasse, stumbling in and out of the house awkwardly. He had changed back into oversized baggy pants hanging down to reveal half his boxer shorts. Sometimes he'd just laugh or mumble, a distant look on his face, and more than once Val noticed him reach down to pat his pocket as if making sure something were still there.

Val sank down into the chair at the foot of Michael's bed, breathed in the cool night air wafting in the raised window. Michael never just went to bed; rather, fighting sleep, still reading, still watching TV, fighting it, he faded; he slept as though he'd been shot and fallen in mid-stride; Val would get up in the middle of the night to turn off Michael's bedroom lights, the radio, turn off the TV. Now, fully dressed, he slept with the Game Boy still in hand, the bedside light on.

What had been going on today? He'd been so goofy, stumbling around, his hair hanging over his face. Val picked up Michael's hand. Faded phone numbers and names. He gently pried open the fingers. More on the palm. Still there from last week. Val thought it funny and touching the way Michael wrote on his hands with markers and ballpoint pens, phone numbers, names, faces, doodles. Just so goofy. He had to have been stoned. Val remembered Michael dialing a number written on his hand, then overhearing a secretive phone call made with a friend, how they kept talking about getting *the thing*. The thing. What was the thing? It seemed so pretentious, self-important, silly. And yet, ominous. The thing.

Now Val remembered the way Michael kept patting his pockets today, and standing, he reached over and touched Michael's pocket lightly. Felt nothing. God, he hated doing this. Kazz seemed to have no compunctions. The first time she'd suspected that Michael was smoking dope, she'd just gone right into his room and said, "Do you have anything you shouldn't have? First and last chance to tell the truth."

When Michael didn't say anything, without further ado, she picked up his backpack and started going through the zippered compartments and in ten seconds she'd found a plastic baggie filled with marijuana and a pipe, which had started days of yelling and screaming, most of it on Kazz's part. *Now it's clear to me why you're getting D's in school! Why it's so hard for you to get up in the morning!* Perhaps the very worst aspect of it since had been that whenever Val saw Michael smile, he wondered if he were stoned. Suspicion. That was the worst of it.

Val came around the other side of the bed, reached down, patted his pocket. Michael pushed at his hand, smacked his lips, and mumbling, rolled onto his side. Val hesitated, rolled him onto his back, waited for him to settle. He tried again; this time he felt something. Keeping his eyes on Michael's face, he worked his hand into his pocket, drew out a plastic baggie. He held it up to the light. Pills. He pulled one out, studied it. No emblems or markings. What were they? And were these *the thing*? Were they Quaaludes? Ecstasy? Some kind of downer? *The thing.*

Val fought to restrain himself from jerking Michael awake and shoving the pills into his face, demanding an explanation. But that approach was hopeless with Michael. When they'd confronted him about the dope, he hadn't cried or apologized or lied or explained or alibied. He'd done something much more chilling. After a few minutes of raving and cursing, he'd gone stone cold and just stared through them and had responded to nothing they'd said or done for days. Stone wall.

Pills in hand, Val was repelled, then outraged. Had Michael been on these things at his father's funeral? Already, he felt the spread of suspicion and doubt. Val reconstructed dozens of Michael's looks and glances of the last few days. His posture. His gaze. No, he couldn't have been. Could he? Where was Kazz? He'd find her and talk to her. But no, not now. Whatever he was going to do, it couldn't be a knee-jerk angry response. Not the least of it, he also didn't want to risk a loud, out-of-control confrontation in his mother's house, and certainly not at a time like this. And Michael would have tests when he got back. Val didn't want to drive him away, risk completely severing their connection. Because that's what would happen. Stone wall.

Michael turned on his side and mumbled something. No, the response to finding pills wasn't as simple as punishing him, the problem being that it wouldn't work. Michael was like Davis—and little had worked with Davis. His father had pushed too hard and lost him. Val would have to do something different. But what? When he reached down into himself, he felt a sense of not knowing. How had Davis been driven away? And into what?

Miami. Lee Anne. Then his sudden reappearance in North Carolina where he'd needed something, perhaps desperately, from Val. But before he'd been able to give it, Lee Anne had shown up. His loss of certainty seemed to start with Lee Anne. He was sure that if she hadn't come, Davis would still be alive.

Val decided not to say anything about the pills to anyone—not Kazz, not Michael. Not now. Instead, he'd take them. And Michael would know that he'd been found out, and have to live with it, and look inside himself. That was all Val could do for now. Send the message silently until he could figure something out.

In the morning, Val's mother reassured Val that she'd be all right by herself, that she had lots of friends to look in on her; practically speaking, everything had been neglected in the last eight weeks—bills, the house, dozens of other details—and she was going to stay busy. She urged Val to go back to work, to be with his family, that it would be the best thing for him. He knew she was right. Yet, he wasn't going. He called the school—he had accumulated sick days—and made arrangements for substitutes to cover his classes.

He loaded Kazz's bag into the car for the drive to pick up the limo to the airport. From the time he'd gotten up, Michael hadn't looked at Val or said a word to him, and Val knew that he'd discovered the pills missing from his pocket. A terrible silence hung between them, the silence a kind of provisional lie, a failure, a tactic, an accusation, and through the silence, Val could feel Michael's anger and fear. He heard Michael's voice at the boat dock. *You're hiding something. When you're straight with me, I'll be straight with you.* Michael was wrong. Val had nothing to hide. But until he knew something more, he couldn't break that silence, couldn't reply to Michael.

Holding Kazz's hand, Val waited at the station for the limo, Michael sitting across from them, hair covering his face, the hum of his Game Boy endless. And Michael close behind them, Val walked Kazz to the limo when it arrived. They'd already gone through things: *Sure you'll be all right here?* A kind of silent reproach and disapproval from Kazz mixed with guarded understanding. She turned to kiss him, said "See you in a few days…" It was half question, half statement.

He nodded. A few days. Val tried to read her face to see if he was telling her the truth, but she ducked into the car before he could. Without looking at him, Michael got in on the other side. Val peered into the shadowed interior. "Bye, Michael." Michael said nothing.

Kazz shook her head. "Say goodbye to your father." Michael still said nothing. Val reached in and hugged Kazz awkwardly, blurted, "Bye, Kazz. I love you. You're so beautiful." Michael made a sound of disgust. Val had never imagined playing out his love for Kazz close up before a contemptuous fourteen-year-old. The driver finished counting heads, called, "Careful, there. Step back from the limo please."

Val stepped back, and they were gone. The sudden emptiness of the parking lot in the sunlight stabbed him, and he knew that it was a mistake to lose sight of them, that he should be with them. As he walked toward the car, he became aware of the sour brackish smell of the harbor, its dreamer's secret rhythms of ceaseless tides. And turning onto the frontage road, he caught sight of the water, shining like a blue mirror in the sun.

# DAVIS

## *Spook*

Val remained unmoving in the front hall, the memorial candle throwing up a soft light on the ceiling, the silence monumental.

And in the next day, the silence lengthened, deepened, grew into an uneasiness between himself and his mother; it was all of the questions he wanted to ask her: what had Dad been thinking—really thinking—and had his feelings ever changed about him?—and still couldn't ask. Val's mother sat quietly going through a stack of mail at her desk in the bedroom. Val offered several times to help her with things. Oh, she answered, that was sweet of him, but really, she was okay here alone and he needed to go back to work and his family…. He recognized that her return to the daily and mundane was her way of distracting herself.

But in the morning she said that if he really wanted to do something, there was the cedar closet in the attic; all the clothes were to go to Good-will…one just had to be realistic.

Each stair creaking under his weight, Val climbed to the third-floor attic. The deep tub with its claw feet, the tiny sink, streaked orange beneath the hot and cold faucets, and the ancient toilet. Beyond, in the window, the green top of the elm. Davis' fading The Who poster was still taped to the wall, Pete Townshend smashing his guitar, the poster concealing the hole that Davis had once actually punched in the wall.

Opening the closet, Val pulled the string to a hanging bulb, revealing neatly stored clothes on hangers, many in dry cleaners' plastic bags: his father's topcoat, winter jackets Val had worn in high school, his father's outdated suits. Gathering them into his arms, Val spent the morning taking three full carloads of clothing to Goodwill. Returning once more to pick up the tangle of plastic wrappers and bent hangers, he noticed a cardboard box shoved into the corner. He dragged it toward him. Davis' schoolbooks. Algebra. Geometry. French. Science. English. A black plastic case: Tangoes. A puzzle game. Geometric plastic pieces: a selection of triangles, squares, parallelograms. Here they were. Val slid out the cards. Each card had a two dimensional, geometric, black shape, which one player tried to duplicate with his pieces before the other could; the solution was on the reverse side, the reduced black shape broken up with thin white lines to show how its separate parts went together.

Val sank onto the floor of the closet, began to work the pieces. He remembered watching Davis play, wondering how he could make such weird inept assemblages. And then Davis, a determined look on his face, first trying one puzzle, then, unable to complete that, pulling out a new card and starting over with a look of blind anger and frustration—as if he were being slapped across the face.

Sitting cross-legged, Val pulled out an algebra book. Davis' name was written in block capital letters across the vertical edges of the closed pages, with a little lumpen-nosed Kilroy peering—just curled hands and eyes and nose—over the top of the stylized *D* of Davis. A loose-leaf notebook, the cover scrawled with inky, faded doodles. Val flipped open the cover, and at the sight of Davis' handwriting and numbers, felt his stomach tighten, felt a weight—so much time gone—pull on his body. February 20, 1973, Davis' math assignment covered with red ink and rows of X's. "F" scrawled across the top. Underneath: "Do over!" The initials underneath were R. M., for Richard Metraux. The paper had once been crumpled and then smoothed out. Studying the handwriting, Val was further unnerved at how much it was Michael's writing—snarled, idiosyncratic, a mix of capitals and lower-case, but with Davis' distinct left handed hook to it. In the pages, he found several notes from Richard Metraux, heard his father's voice: "No, you tell me, Davis…because I want to know…I mean it, I sincerely want to know… how does someone who's been at the top of his class go—overnight—liter-ally, overnight, to the bottom."

Davis sat motionless, staring at his plate.

"Davis? Is this what you want?" Davis still didn't answer. "Just a simple yes or no will do it. Davis? Yes or no?"

Davis exploded. "Fuck you!"

Davis snatched the paper out of his father's hand and crumpled it. He flung the test at his father, who stood suddenly, and Val stepped between them. Davis shoved Val into his father and stalked out of the room.

His mother said, "I've talked to you before, Ted, about backing Davis into corners by demanding yes-or-no answers. It's never worked. It never will."

"Davis also has to learn that raising his voice isn't going to change things."

Val reached down to pick up the overturned chair. His father said, "Leave it. Davis will pick it up when he comes back to the table. And we're going to do algebra until he gets A's."

And so they sat down night after night, Davis and his father, to do math. They'd pull up their chairs side by side at the dining-room table after the dishes had been cleared away, the splintered white light from the crystal chandelier speckling their hands and faces like rain, book and paper between them. Dreading this, Val would retreat to do his homework at the kitchen table, to his room, to the TV, to some other part of the house. Within a short time, their voices would rise.

"No...no...are you paying attention?"

"I'm paying attention!"

"You're going to sit in that chair until you get it!"

Sometimes Val would rush out onto the second-floor landing. Sometimes he'd meet his mother there. And sometimes the voices would quiet and Val and his mother would return to what they had been doing. More often the voices rose. Often Val would have to rush in and separate his father and Davis, throw his arms around Davis from behind, pull him back, knocking over dining-room chairs, a blind, enraged look on Davis' face. His father would say, "Let him go, Val. He can't intimidate me. Davis, this won't solve your math problems, or anything else in life! You could learn if you took the time and wanted to learn!"

This would send a resurgence of rage through Davis, and he would drag Val forward, often lifting him off the floor as Val hung on. Val's mother would suddenly appear, pushing their father out of the room. "This is just enough for one night." His parents' voices would trail through the house, rising, falling, in their own sharpening quarrel.

Then Davis would wordlessly plunge from the room, and Val would hear the bang of the basement door thrown open, the jangle of steel plates being loaded onto the bar, the stereo exploding with The Who, The Rolling Stones, Led Zeppelin, ass-kicking music thudding through the floor, the bass cranked up; he'd hear a sudden crash as a dumbbell would come down hard on the mat surrounding the weight bench. Sometimes Val descended into the close, sweet smell of laundry detergent, the pungent cloy of fuel oil and sweat, to find Davis on a last set of curls, legs braced, the corners of his mouth down-turned with pain and effort like the caricature of a baby about to burst out crying, his face blood-red, blond hair matted with sweat, the bar rising for one final, impossible pump; Davis would gasp, the weeping groan suddenly filling the room as if torn from muscle and cartilage and bone, itself.

Docked, grounded, shamed, stuck at home, Davis spent hours across the street in the garage of a neighbor, George. There he worked on engines, George often reeking of alcohol, but sweetly, quietly, patiently instructing Davis, taking off his thick glasses and resting them on a radiator so that he could thrust his myopic eyes inches from a carburetor under the glare of a light bulb hanging in its cage. Blinking, he'd say, "Okay, Davis, this is lookin' like good work here. Let's start 'er up and see what's what. Now these Rochester two-barrels are a piece of cake, but you gotta watch out for a couple of things…" Over at George's, his hard and increasingly wary look would slip away, and the Davis Val had always known, open and easy, would resurface.

When Davis wasn't at George's, he was often at a garage a few miles away, which was on the edge of a poor, black section of town, and which belonged to Biggie, a friend of George's; here, too, Davis seemed to find a place; he worked on engines, talking cars or motorcycles with the guys who came around the shop, and was employed there part-time summers, perfectly at home with everyone; with Biggie, easy-going, affable, with his hair short on top, long and curly down the back, reminding Val of a dog's nape stiffening before a dog fight; with Mickey D., an iron freak like Davis, slicked hair, tight-muscled, neat, with a single, finely-etched, grinning death's head on his forearm, tumbling red dice for eyes; and a number of other guys. Val recollected that most of them were heavily tattooed, wore gold crucifixes or gold horns, or both, and came and went on chopped Harleys and in cars that were in a perpetual state of evolution. They had panels covered with flat gray primer paint, and doors that disappeared and reappeared mysteriously.

Here, in the dark caverns of the garage bays, would be the deafening sound of engines being revved; the squealing whine of a compressed air hose driving a socket wrench; rock and roll hammering out of two oversized speakers; the added noise of the phone ringing; and the penetrating vapors of solvents, primer, gasoline, combustible smells which Davis would carry home with him in his clothes and hair; here, Davis continued his hands-on tutorial in the art of the combustion engine under a calendar and poster pantheon—Snap-on, Mac Tools—of big-titted girls writhing out of their bikinis across the gleaming fenders of muscle cars.

Davis came home talking ignorant and tough. "...so I told 'em, I didn't order them parts, Biggie didn't order them parts..." And though Val knew that Davis could more or less turn his *dese, dems* and *doses* on and off at will, and that it was mostly Davis' sense of humor at work, his parents—particularly his mother—were disturbed by it. She would just shake her head or look away, occasionally saying, "That's enough, Davis. You're educated, you come from a good home, everyone here loves you, and no matter what else you may think about things, you know how to speak properly." Davis would ignore her—or sometimes, just laugh. His dress mirrored his speech. Wild, clashing sports shirts, always weird shoes, with buckles, pointed toes, woven patterns, anything.

One night Davis came home late from Biggie's and seemed bugged all night. Later, Val and Davis wandered away from the house, and Davis told Val in a lowered voice that someone had been breaking into the cars parked overnight behind the garage. Biggie had finally caught a kid, maybe seventeen, with a stereo, a couple of speakers, a car battery, other stuff. Cornering him in the back of the building, Biggie never raised his voice. "'Okay, fucker, you're a thief, and you've been stealing from me—I just caught you—and you ain't gonna deny it, are you?'

"The kid shook his head no. Hey, there was the stuff right on the floor, like, what's to deny?

"Biggie said, 'I'm gonna give you your choice. I'll call the cops and you take what they give you. Or,' Biggie picked up a heavy steel wrench, 'you put out your arm and you take what's coming to you from me.'

"The kid said, 'You can't call the cops. My old man'll kill me.'

"Biggie shrugged. 'I been there, man. Your choice. Put out your arm.'

"So, like, the kid put out his arm and Biggie smashed him with the wrench—this huge thing, two feet long—across the forearm, and the kid started to scream and cry. Biggie dropped the wrench and walked the kid over to his car, the kid's just about passing out, and opened the door and helped him in—we drove him over to the emergency room—and dropped him off maybe fifty yards from the entrance; Biggie said to the kid, 'Hey, it ain't nothing personal, but I can't let you—or no one else—make an asshole out of me. You understand?' And the kid nodded. 'Go on, get out and go in there and get help, and don't steal no more.' And the kid got out and staggered in."

"Bad, Davis...."

"Yeah, so, like, we drove away and then Biggie said to me, 'You can't let people make an asshole out of you or you're dead. The kid knew that. Them's the rules. You gotta play by the rules. You break 'em, and you get caught, you fuck up, you gotta pay.'"

"He could have just called the cops, Davis."

They walked on, still talking in hushed voices, "Yeah, but Biggie said, 'The cops ain't gonna do nothing, man. Little this, few days of that, just ain't gonna come to nothing. Kid's out stealing again. Hey, that kid cost me a lot of dough, that's my work, man, my reputation, that's fuckin' with me.'"

Davis was quiet, looking down the street. "I know one thing. That kid'll never steal from Biggie again."

"You don't know anything. Maybe he'll come back and blow Biggie's head off."

They walked on. "Tell you, man. I for sure didn't like hearing the sound of his bone breaking. Matter of fact, I keep hearing it. Just like, suddenly, crack, I hear it. Like breaking a big stick over a knee: snap."

They walked in silence back toward the house, the lights of the second floor shining through the trees and above the high evergreen hedge. Just before they went in, Davis gave a sudden derisive laugh. "Well, Val, you just go on being the good guy, Mr. Wonderful, Mr. Easy, and I'll be the asshole for both of us."

Val would think of this exchange over and over the next few years. He would think of it when Davis started calling him from Miami.

Davis went on having trouble in school, and the war between Davis and their father seemed inescapable for everyone. But then, something else happened. Davis started playing football—serious football. He was the only freshman not only to make the team, but to start on the varsity, and so was held in silent awe by his classmates, who behaved with deference, feigned nonchalance, and restrained jealousy in his presence at this singular feat; and it was not just his classmates, but the upperclassmen as well. For what Davis had beside his uncanny feel for the game—knowing where to be and when—were exceptional athleticism and strength, furthered by his obsessive weightlifting; his precocious size, which had somehow skipped adolescent awkwardness; and explosive speed—his speed a pure gift—as well as great balance; and, ironically enough, great vision. For whatever he couldn't seem to find on his math and French papers, he saw coming across a football field at the very edge of his vision—and what he couldn't see, he just seemed to know was there. As a freshman, at six feet and a hundred seventy-seven pounds, he played wide receiver or halfback, and he played safety. On offense, you would suddenly see him, there he was, a step, two steps behind the linebacker, and the ball already in the air, another moment, the ball in his hands, and just when you thought he had no more speed or was staggering off balance, within a heartbeat he was back at full stride, had yet another burst of acceleration.

And, if it were possible, Davis seemed to come even more to life in a special, almost terrifying way on defense at free safety, roaming center field, or perhaps stalking might be the word; from his position, he would be all over the field, blitzing the quarterback, breaking up passes and making interceptions or tackles with unbelievable force, with the precipitous, explosive clatter of a car crash. He would range from sideline to sideline, his blue eyes burning with a trance-like brilliance above the blacking on his cheekbones. His shirt would streak with lime from the markers, his numerals obliterate with mud, his helmet clot with turf, and his face mask and shirt were often streaked with blood from a nosebleed, a spiked hand, the single gash across the bridge of his nose where his helmet had slammed down in one of his ferocious head-on tackles. On defense, he was called *Headhunter*. His other nickname, taken from his trance-like game face, was *Spook*. With his long blond hair streaming out from under his helmet and across the back of his shoulder pads, with his powerful calves tapering like hooves into his low cuts, Davis was loved by the crowd, the students often chanting in unison, *Spoo-ok! Spook!*

There was one ongoing problem: eligibility. For a student to remain eligible for sports, he had to maintain a C average and could not be failing a subject. And Davis' grades were often on the brink, with most of his teachers, who liked him, giving him the benefit of the doubt, but his antagonists, mainly Metraux, giving him D's and F's. And this always put their father in a tough position. On the one hand, as Davis was on the verge of losing his eligibility, their father would say to Val, to Val's mother, to the air itself, *Okay, let it go down the drain. I mean it, don't let him play. As a matter of fact, I think it might be good for him. If he's forced to sit there on the sidelines every Saturday and watch, it will bring him to his senses once and for all. Life's not going to be a football game.*

And Val would say, "You know something, Dad? Let them bench Davis and you've taken everything from him. Is that what you want?"

And his father couldn't bring himself to reply.

His father, right or wrong about his analysis of Davis' academic failures being a deficiency of character or a lack of discipline, and right or wrong about the salutary effects of not letting him play, in the end, would quietly talk to the headmaster—they were friends—and whatever didn't seem to work for him in the classroom, they did make work for Davis, blurring the lines, the grades, to restore his threatened eligibility and get him back onto the playing field, where he wanted to be, and where they wanted him to be, and where he could shine.

Davis' friends, too, his non-school friends, often showed up for the games; George, moochie drunk walk at eleven in the morning, two in the afternoon, whenever, peering at the world through his glasses, thick and silvery like chunks of clear, shattered ice—he would straggle across the playing fields to the stands, coat open on freezing days, puffing on a cigarette, occasionally coughing out his cheer, "Way to go, kid!" And doing his own little shuffle and dance, disappearing at halftime for a few pulls on his bottle.

And his buddies from the garage, Biggie, Mickey D., came wearing studded and zippered leather jackets, their girls with black eyeliner and ratted hair piled high, other guys Val had only seen or been briefly introduced to around the garage, guys with tattoos, heavy chains wound twice around their waists for locking up their choppers; you could see them as they came up a back road through the woods, snaking through the bare trees, appearing and disappearing, the ratchet and snap of their changing gears and winding engines rising and falling as they followed the contours of the unpaved road until they came bouncing out with a roar right onto the asphalt which circled the end zone. Here, they'd take up their places on the blacktop, four or five abreast, roll them back onto their stands, drape themselves over their high bars, and perch on their seats, big-haired girls on the back. They'd remain apart, emanating a palpable sense of menace. The preppies loved it. No one said anything about who they were or what they were doing there, no one asked them to move off, but it was understood that they were Davis' friends. No one else in the entire school had friends like these. They weren't what Ridgefield Prep was about. They were being tolerated, noblesse oblige; that, too, was what Ridgefield Prep believed it was about. His buddies loved Davis' ferocious play, reacting the same way his father did, taking each blow, leaping to their feet, exploding into tackles with their bodies, applauding, punching the air. *Way to go, Davis! Kick ass! Yeah!* After a game, people rushed out onto the field, friends surrounding him, touching him, staying close to him as he walked—and Val knew that whatever Davis' problems with school, with people he was charmed, magnetic, that people always lit up when Davis was around.

Later that day when Davis returned home, his father, still wearing his game-day transformation into a much younger man, the street-fighter he'd had to be growing up, would say, "You played a great game today, Davis. Just great." And then add, "But like it or not, in this world a man is known by the company he keeps."

The gash over the bridge of his nose raw and swollen, Davis would reply, "I got a lot of friends."

"You know what I mean. And you can speak correctly. 'I have a lot of friends.'"

Davis, with a snort of contempt, would shrug and walk away.

Spring of his senior year, a droning PBS documentary caught Val's ear, the narrator's voice suddenly drawing his attention. It seemed to be describing Davis exactly. Students who had often done well in school and were intelligent, almost overnight, mysteriously started to fail. They had several things in common. Students said they couldn't seem to see numbers or letters on the page, saw them reversed or juxtaposed. They had problems learning foreign languages, seeing spatial relationships. Val had noticed all of these in trying to help Davis—disastrous attempts to do geometry, algebra, the simple diagramming of sentences. Not that much was known about the condition's causes. Maybe it was brain related. There were terrible consequences: the causes were misunderstood and students who exhibited these

qualities were considered slow or even retarded…they developed a pattern
of low self-esteem and a poor image of themselves, became defensive and
angry, and this in turn escalated into discipline problems at home and at
school…. The whole thing was called *dyslexia*.

The narrator gave an address to contact for more information. Val copied
it down. He was almost relieved. There was a word for Davis' condition.
It wasn't some dark failure of the spirit, of character, a will to defy the
authorities, defy his father, the manifest destiny offered to each individual
by Ridgefield, which everyone believed to be the case. The school, his father,
had thought the worst about Davis—hadn't they all, really? How could his
father have given in so quickly to others' worst opinions of Davis? Val knew
that Davis did not forgive his father for that betrayal. Val gave the dyslexia
information to his mother; she, too, thought she recognized this as Davis.
He *wasn't* stupid; he had a disorder. Still, their father couldn't quite bring
himself to accept that Davis' problem wasn't one of character. Character
was everything to their father, who ate only half a chocolate as an act of
discipline. Character was destiny. Davis. If only he wanted it badly enough,
he could find a way!

And so renewed steps were taken to help Davis—counseling, more talks
with teachers. It became a personal crusade of his mother's. No possible
solution was too outlandish. His mother heard or read somewhere that
visual perception might be helped by wearing special glasses, one lens red,
the other blue; Val remembered Davis looking like some mad scientist in
these weird things; when Val tried them, they made him feel off balance,
nauseated and confused. His mother spent hours making phone calls to
experts and counselors and psychologists and brain researchers with her
own growing library of books, research, articles, clippings. Added to Davis'
possible dyslexia was another possibility, of a condition that was beginning
to be known as Attention Deficit Disorder. That would explain why he could
never be still. There was the remorseful feeling of a wrong and transgres-
sion in the house.

After one of her conferences with an expert, Val asked his mother why he
thought it had taken so long for Davis' dyslexia to show up. Why at twelve
or thirteen? Why not in first or second grade when everyone first started
learning to read and do arithmetic?

She said, "I asked him that exact question and he told me that there were many different kinds and manifestation of dyslexia—and that it's almost always misunderstood. Teachers just aren't trained to see it. They take it as a lack of motivation, defiance, stupidity." She shook her head in frustration. "He said quite honestly that at this time, there's just a great deal about dyslexia that even experts don't understand. If it doesn't show up until adolescence, it is particularly insidious because it's taken to be," she shrugged, "well, we hardly need to draw a picture of that now, do we, what it's taken to be?"

His father, their case in point. While he now acknowledged that Davis had a problem, something not of Davis' making, he still couldn't seem to change his attitude, that it was all a goddamned excuse, really, and if Davis just wanted it badly enough, he could get A's, or at the very least, B's, go on to a good college, maybe not Yale, Harvard or Princeton, but someplace he could hold his head up about.

Val said, "You don't have to be an expert to see you're just not making it better for Davis."

"Should I give up, tell Davis everything is okay, work in a gas station, be a mechanic, hang out with a bunch of ignorant guys going nowhere? Is that what you want for your brother?"

"If it makes him happy."

"Don't give me that."

But Val understood his father's point of view, his frustration, his love for Davis—and the way it was coming out wrong.

"You know something, Val?"

"No."

"You have always taken special pleasure in defying me through Davis."

Where had that come from?

His junior and senior years, Davis was captain of the football team—he was six-two, over two hundred pounds. And on the football field, he was feared. Val would come down from Harvard and watch him. Now it was Davis' picture in the paper week after week: *Prep Star Wreaks Havoc; Explosive Speedster....* It was Davis, handsome as a movie star with his long blond hair and hero's profile; Davis, as he'd snap on his chin strap with that thousand-yard stare: *Spook... Spook!*

Davis was recruited by many of the big football powers: Penn State, Ohio State, Syracuse, Clemson. It was hard to believe that with grades and

College Board scores like his he could go to any college, but somehow such fundamentals were irrelevant. Wherever he would end up going to school, Val knew that, in some deeper, much more devastating way, beyond schools or sports or boards or grades, an incalculable harm had already been done to Davis—class clown, *Spook*, *Headhunter*, and, behind his back, along with the admiration and affection, *dumb fuck*. Val remembered the last football game of his senior year, a homecoming, sleet under a stunned black and gray sky, Davis' team down by a field goal; the other team with the ball and, forty seconds left, just trying to run out the clock, their quarterback handed off to their big fullback who had been pounding Ridgefield all day; as he hit him, Davis stripped the ball and twisted from the tangle of bodies; he staggered once, spun away and, exploding into his stride, the crowd coming to its feet in disbelief, Davis burst down the sideline, the crowd surging forward and screaming; in another moment he was in the end zone, the game, lost, now won; turning, he dodged his teammates who ran toward him, and, nose spurting blood, he pushed into the crowd until he reached his father. He thrust the ball in his face. Blood splashing off his face mask with each breath, he stared at his father with those spooky blue eyes. *"Huh? Huh?"* His father turned and walked away.

Val knew the damage had already been done to Davis.

Davis ended up going to Clemson. Both Davis and his father believed he would be helped and tutored, that academics—and graduating—were important. Everyone was thrilled. Davis going to Clemson. Big time football. The coach thought there was a very real possibility Davis would get to play, maybe early on. Speed. They needed his speed. Though Val knew better, he was still caught up in the excitement: football. It *was* thrilling, Davis, after all of his setbacks in school, all of the put-downs, actually being recruited. Ironic, too, Val thought, after all of the carefully modulated condescension about Davis' being so stupid. Val had always been convinced that Davis was the most inventive and intuitive person he'd ever known, street-smart, quick on his feet, always making the unexpected come out of the moment. He would do it again and again in sports, where the stage was set for such moments. But out of the monotony of every day, of lived life, Davis brought forth amazing surprises. The summer before he left for Clemson, he and Val were in someone's ski boat just inside a breakwater—July, sunny, hot; they looked up to see another ski boat coming straight at them.

Heeling hard into a turn, it was running wide open and throwing up a sheet of spray. Without hesitation, Davis yanked their wheel, jerking them into a yawing swerve and just avoiding the collision. In that moment, they saw the boat was empty—the driver had been thrown out; the wheel was locked and the boat was making a wide circle inside the breakwater and headed back toward a beach crowded with hundreds of swimmers who as yet had no idea what was happening. Val froze in horror. Pushing the throttle forward, Davis reached for the spare tow rope heaped on the floor. What was he doing? Val was still imagining a hopeless attempt to corral the runaway, when Davis ran their boat across the bow of the oncoming ski boat and flung the towrope into its path. The outboard jolted to a stop and died, its prop tangled in the line. The move was so quick, decisive and brilliant that Val was stunned. If he'd had an hour to think calmly of a solution, he knew this would never have occurred to him. Davis was cited by the Coast Guard, his picture appearing in the paper: "Sports Star a Hero. Quick Thinking by Athlete Saves Untold Lives…"

The summer after Davis graduated, he worked as a boatyard mechanic and started going out with serious sports fishermen on weekends to Montauk and the open Atlantic. Davis was always in demand. He was big and strong and could handle the wire leader on marlin and tuna; he was a great guy, funny, jiving, fast talking; he could troubleshoot and fix an engine, and when your motor was dead and you were forty miles off shore, that was someone you were glad to have aboard. The day had passed when he'd sail with his father—said he couldn't stand to sail, too slow, too dumb, too fucked, said that he couldn't stand to be with the old man on his damned boat. He brought Val into powerboating, taught him a few of the basics about engines and maintenance, and they went out on butt-kicking muscle boats and came home with the cockpits filled with huge marlin and tuna, silver and blue, iridescent as jewels. There were pictures of Davis grinning with sports fishermen at weigh stations, marlin hanging from cross beams, sometimes a huge shark stretched out on the dock at Montauk, pig-eyed, monster-faced.

Val and Davis would talk on and off about their doing something together with boats—chartering, delivering, something real. Daydream talk. Maybe. Maybe not. Davis would conclude, "Yeah, money talks and bullshit walks, dude, but you'll probably wimp out and do the safe thing and go to law school." Val always laughed, but it stung him. Secretly, he had always wanted to design or build boats. Several times he'd mentioned this to his father, and always his father shook his head. "Leave it to others. It's a hell of a chancy business and nine out of ten of these guys go broke, end up in debt." Val said if that was so and everyone felt that way then he wouldn't have had any of his boats—nor would anyone else for that matter. His father repeated, "I love boats as much as the next guy—you know I do, but I'm just telling you, when it comes right down to it, leave it to others." Did that mean his father thought others were better or had something Val didn't and that Val wasn't up to it? It pissed him off. Yeah, somewhere inside, without ever having even thought about it, he knew that he would probably finish Harvard and go to law school. Strangely, for Val it seemed the coward's road. Any plodding dullard could go to law school. Grubby. Ambitious in a pedestrian way. And buried beneath his awareness, Val saw his father's relentless ambition, which he both hugely admired and detested. He saw it in his classmates, grade-grubbing to get into the best law, medical and business schools. Boats. Water. They were the real magic.

Val remembered one winter when Val and Davis had been kids. They'd sent for a boat kit, a thirteen-foot plywood skiff. They'd spend the winter building it in the garage, an old wood stove stoked up in one corner, snow piled on the windowsills, icicles hanging. They'd worked on it after school and evenings, finished in late spring, and bought an old, second-hand motor; they put the boat in the water and spent hours that summer exploring tidal creeks and estuaries, salt ponds and rivers, and it had been great. But you were supposed to know that you couldn't do things like that when you were an adult. Yet around Davis, Val had the feeling that maybe he could—they could. He remembered that winter just before Davis went to Clemson to play football and Val headed back to Harvard.

Two-a-day football practices in the sweltering heat and humidity. There had been some talk of Davis red-shirting, but when the coaches noticed how quickly he learned the playbook and actually saw his speed and slashing running style up close, they immediately reconsidered. He consistently ran back punts and kickoffs for long gains, made great catches, and once he had a half step on his man in the open field, he was gone. He had amazing speed and power. The papers started describing him as a slashing runner, a burner, a possible game-breaker, someone to watch. A week before the first game, Davis wrote that there might be a chance that he could see limited playing time, which did not happen in the first two games. Well, what did you expect? He was only a freshman; whether or not Davis was playing, they'd gone down for their third game, Clemson-Georgia in their home stadium, also known as "Death Valley," and still Davis did not play; Clemson fell behind on an early Georgia scoring drive, another quick Georgia touchdown on an interception; there were several key Clemson injuries and suddenly Davis was in toward the middle of the second quarter to take the kickoff.

Val, heart pounding, stood with the rest of the crowd as the ball sailed high and deep, too long in the air to allow a return: Val was half-hoping the ball would go to the other back, and when he saw it was coming to Davis, he could only think *don't let him bobble it, don't let him fumble.* Davis took the ball two steps back in the end zone, and Val thought he saw the other back instantly turn toward Davis to signal that he kneel and take the touchback. Either Davis didn't see or he ignored the signal—in baseball he'd had a nasty habit of defying the coach and swinging when he was supposed to take. Val swore, dry-mouthed, as Davis ran out of the end zone, got maybe ten to twelve yards upfield before he met what seemed to be most of the Georgia defense, and for a second Davis disappeared, and Val thought, God, why couldn't Davis ever, once, do what he was supposed to do, just take the touchback; getting into the game at all and handling the ball for the first time under game conditions was enough. He watched for the play to be whistled dead, hoping Davis hadn't fumbled, saw motion, spotted Davis breaking through the tangled wedge—Val couldn't see how he had gotten free—and suddenly he had that half-step in the open field, another, he broke toward the near sideline, slipped a tackle, another, Val heard a wall of cheering roll down through the stadium, Davis was still coming down the sideline, two Georgia tacklers angled up to drive him out of bounds at midfield, and Davis cut back in toward them, spun, and with another burst, caught them going the other way and blew by both, a vast expanse of green now opened as Davis angled diagonally back across the field, slipped by several more tacklers, and then was suddenly caught from behind on a diving desperation shoestring tackle by a lone defensive back; he fumbled the ball as he hit the ground and quickly gathered it in. Val glanced back upfield, sideline to sideline. There were no yellow flags for clipping or holding or personal fouls, nothing to call the play back. The play stood. Val looked at his father as they slapped each other's shoulders. Davis! His father's lips were trembling and there were tears in his eyes. Val had never seen him so alive. Even his mother, who hated the violence of football, was grinning. The ball was on the Georgia seventeen and the crowd remained on its feet cheering Davis as the Clemson offense went in and scored three plays later. When the game was over, Davis was an up-and-coming star. He was all over the sports page on Sunday. The next week, dispelling the possibility that it might have been a fluke, Davis did it again, and then again for the rest of the season and on into his sophomore year and the beginning of his third year. And then, just as suddenly, it was over.

Davis had been involved in a series of minor incidents—small infractions, several fights, some team rules broken—all of which had been smoothed over. Then one Saturday night there had been an incident in a bar, and Davis and several other players had been charged with aggravated assault. Caught in the glare of publicity, the coach had to kick three of them off the team. There was nothing he could do about it given the circumstances. When the legal situation was sorted out, Davis was given a year's probation. Shortly after that, Davis left school in the middle of his junior year. Their father was sick. Pro ball, school, all of it seemed to be gone for good. Not to mention the disgrace. Val spent hours talking to his father about this on the phone. His father despaired, "What's he going to do now?"

Val didn't answer what his father probably already knew. He would be a mechanic. What was so wrong with that? Davis was already good—a wizard. Nor did Val venture that maybe Davis might make a terrific salesman. He could jive his way in and out of situations. And people loved him. In the meantime, NFL football scouts were still showing interest in Davis. They invited him to mini-camps in spring—the Raiders, the Jets, the Giants—as safety, wide-receiver, punt returner—but somehow nothing more came of it, and Davis started drifting south.

Val would get a postcard from him, a middle-of-the-night phone call, Davis slurring his words, the sound of noise and music, a girl's sudden laugh or insistent, "Honey, let me talk to him…" in the background. She would tell Val how much she loved Davis even though she'd just met him two hours ago and…Davis grabbed back the receiver; sometimes the phone disconnected, dial tone, and then no word for two months. Sometimes Davis called to ask for money. There might be urgent reasons: a fight, a DUI or a job that Davis had either lost or just quit; it was never quite clear, the details, the pieces.

By now Val had started law school. Why couldn't Davis just stay in touch with any of them? But Val knew. The message: this *isn't* what we do. Cars. Work with our hands. Hang out with these people. Davis, intuitive, and, ironically, a quick study, had gotten it loud and clear. After hearing nothing from Davis for months, Val started calling some of his old school friends. Had anyone heard from Davis? None had. Val was wondering what he should do next when, out of the blue, a letter, with its distinct left-handed hook, mix of uppercase and lowercase letters. Postmarked Miami. Without bothering to tell Val where he was or how he'd gotten there, he wrote simply, "Found a '33 Ford." What was that about?

Then, more letters. Davis had talked his way in as a mechanic in a boat-yard in Miami; there were a lot of big-money muscle boats: Aronows, Fountains, monster engines. Beautiful boats everywhere you looked. He was crewing on sport fishermen—Hatterases, Bertrams. He wrote clear-eyed, beautiful and naively lyrical descriptions snared within a net of tangled syntax, misspellings, and touchingly odd attempts at punctuation. The people on boats. Crawling down into engine compartments to work on engines. Wind and sea conditions. He wrote, "Whenever, I see the Gulf Stream, it reminds me of, the first time we crossed, over to the Bahamas, with Mom, and Dad; it was gushing, North, like, blue ink, being poured into milky, green, water." Davis suddenly seemed to have money. Or at least he'd stopped asking Val for loans. He was rebuilding the '33 Ford. Doing the engine. The body. Turning it into a roadster. Chromed everywhere. He called it his beast.

Each time Val got a letter from Davis he would finish reading it and feel restless. Not exactly jealous, but more like there Davis had gone and done it again, somehow found the nerve center of life, and here was Val stuck in law school. Val's life was always going to happen somewhere in the future. Davis just went out and did things. It worked for him. Val couldn't quite put it into words. He didn't want to be in law school, wasn't exactly sure what he was doing there.

Davis started writing about a girl he'd met, Lee Anne. She was from some small backwater town in Florida, had a thick Southern accent. She was a huge pain in the ass, which, from Davis, could be the highest of compliments. Or not. Despite his snarled syntax, Davis had a guileless, arresting way of describing things.

Davis wrote about Lee Anne, a description of her sleeping:

*I look, over, and she looks, like someone else, totally different, from when she's awake, and something, kind of rises off her as she sleeps, you can feel, it there, hanging over her, in the room, all night, she tosses and turns, it's, fucking, creepy, when you come right, down, to it, the other night, she sat up with her eyes, wide, open and was talking, in whole, sentences, but it was all slurred, I was trying, to figure out, what she was saying, but I couldn't understand a word, but it was very weird–scary, actually–and I, finally, had to shake her awake, and then, she just looked, at me, like she'd never seen me, before, and fucking, started crying, and telling me, she loved me, and that I had to promise, never to leave her. I haven't, had a decent, nights sleep, since I've met her. Chicks are, more trouble, then their worth.*

Val couldn't get the description of the girl out of his mind. Something rises off her as she sleeps. You can feel it hanging in the air. And there seemed to be a kind of fearfulness in Davis. What was he seeing or feeling? Val realized that his writing about her with that intensity suggested that Davis loved her; maybe Davis feared loving her. Val didn't know, but there seemed to be something in his letters that Val hadn't seen in him before. Val read and reread them. In fact, he started waiting for them.

Davis wrote that he kept trying to get Lee Anne to go to the movies with him, but that she couldn't sit through one; she'd hyperventilate, bolt from the theater. Said she didn't know why. Davis thought she was having acid flashbacks, but wouldn't cop to it. At the very least, he was starting to think there was something she wasn't telling him, though he had no idea what. Davis wrote:

*She reads a book every couple of days. She's everything, I'm not, when it comes, to books. Loves 'em. Gone into, another world. It's like maybe, she's looking, for the answer to something. I mean, it's book after book. She's not your average, every, day, hair, dresser. I'm still trying, to figure out, how one day, I went in, to get a haircut, and the next, I'm living with her. Whether, I made it happen, or she made it happen. I'm not sure, where this goes from here. She could be, too weird, to stay with, but too weird, to leave. She's not, the kind of chick, you can just dump, that much, I do know.*

Val saw that Davis was fascinated by her, somehow in awe of her, and was a little afraid of something—maybe, at times, more than a little. It wasn't like Davis to show fear and definitely not about women. He seemed to know there was some big contradiction about her—a barber, a hairdresser, whatever you wanted to call her, and her reading tons of books. On the other hand, Davis didn't pay that much attention to books. Hairdressers—the stereotype—read Judith Krantz. Maybe. That's probably what she was reading. Really, when you came right down to it, Davis might be in awe of anyone who was reading a book not assigned in school.

Val came back to himself, started replacing the books and papers that had been spread all over the floor back in the cardboard box.... From somewhere he thought he heard someone calling. His mother. Telephone. He came down, picked up the receiver. It was Stan. Who? Stan Miller. He'd seen Val the other day at his father's funeral. Stan was in the neighborhood. Could he take Val to lunch? Val couldn't form an image of him. He didn't want to have lunch with a well-meaning classmate who'd come to his father's funeral, who he couldn't remember and who he hadn't seen since he was eighteen. But he couldn't find a way to say no without being abrupt or rude.

## *His Father's Secret Dream Life*

His mother answered the door, and from upstairs Val heard her starting to chat. Showered and cleaned up, he came down, and there was Stan in a suit and tie. Right. Stan. Stan Miller. He looked almost exactly as he had at Ridgefield—slender, tan, all of his hair, even the same glasses, with their heavy, tortoiseshell frames. He was pleasant enough as he turned to Val with a self-conscious nod and an offering of his hand. They shook hands awkwardly, and then Stan poked his glasses back up onto his nose with a simple, precise touch of a fingertip that suddenly brought back memories of his frowning over a trigonometry test, of Stan—where? standing on the sidelines with a clipboard and a look of concern during football games. He'd been manager of the football team, hadn't he?

Outside, the front walk dappled with shade, the sky blue, a lightness in the air. At the curb, a new silver Mercedes. Val slid in. Enveloped in the expensive smell of leather, unbidden and unwanted, envy rose in Val. Stan loosened his tie slightly. "Don't mind the suit. I'm just coming from a deposition." Added, as if in answer to Val's question, "I'm a lawyer."

Val, still pondering the Mercedes, the feeling of invulnerability once inside this car, and remembering with some discomfiture the sense of triumphant satisfaction he'd felt on getting into Harvard early admission, advanced placement, didn't reply. Stan, he knew, had gone to some small but decent college. Union? Hobart? Hamilton? He was distressed at the memory of his assumed superiority. Adolescent arrogance? The competitiveness fostered by Ridgefield? Or sports? Val's having been an outstanding soccer and baseball player, he knew that almost sexual flush of certainty that the world was yours in a special way, that everything was coming to you. Now he felt the unbidden rise of envy—a surprise—and, for Val, its first cousin, self-reproach. Given his opportunities, he'd made very little money—and really could have, should have, done much better as a lawyer than he had. Now as an art teacher in a public school for the last four years, he made next to nothing. Yet it had seemed to Val that he should not have things—and perhaps not even the relationship of a wife and child. Had it always been that way? He heard Michael at his father's old slip, "This is the life we were supposed to be living, isn't it, Dad?" He remembered how his father had sold the boat without ever saying anything to him. One day it was just gone, as if it had never existed.

Over lunch, stopping and starting, they talked a little about their wives, kids, but it was too formal to be interesting. They tried other things: Ridgefield. Classmates. Faculty. Val suddenly heard himself going on about his being unable to sleep last night, how the pictures of Davis were still in his bedroom, his weights in the basement. He lapsed into silence. "Sorry. I don't sleep when I'm back in the house. After Davis, I never could be there." Val stopped. He'd have to get through this interminable lunch. He had known that meeting Stan was a bad idea. Before he could check himself, he said, "I'm not ready to go home yet, but I just can't be in that house." Surprised by his outburst, he apologized.

Stan nodded sympathetically and started talking about something else. His voice came into focus. He'd been manager of the football team—Val *had* been right about that—and Stan had never forgotten Davis. His game face: *Spook. Headhunter.* He'd seen that look, once, off the field. "Do you remember Curt Brubaker in our class?"

"He was on the football team. With Davis. Big. A tackle, wasn't he? 230 or 240. Six-five. Just big. And mean, as I recall. I always avoided him."

Stan nodded, and for the first time they seemed to make a connection. "Mean. That was Curt. Since I was the manager, he thought I was supposed to be his personal gofer...." Stan told how Curt thought nothing of sending

Stan all the way back to the field house for a chin strap or replacement shoe-
lace. How he'd always yell from the showers, "Hey, Miller, get me a towel!"
And how Stan, afraid of Brubaker, would do it, each time vowing this time
would be the last as Brubaker splashed and laughed at him. One day Curt
kept hollering, "Miller, what are you, fucking deaf? Get me a towel!" Stan
didn't. Enraged, Brubaker burst naked and sopping wet out of the shower,
tracked Miller down in the now empty locker room, and, grabbing him
by the collar, dangled him above the floor. Next thing, Davis appeared out
of nowhere in just a jockstrap. He grabbed Brubaker by the throat and
slammed him against a locker so hard he stove it in and snapped it off its
foundation. He bent Brubaker down to his knees. Davis said, "Apologize,
fuckface!"

"Brubaker shook his head no, and Davis just squeezed and Brubaker
gagged and Davis knelt over him—Davis had those huge, powerful arms
and legs—and he squeezed harder and bent him down lower to the floor
and said, 'Apologize! You're fucking sorry! Say it! *Sorry!* Say it! You're sorry!
You're sorry! *I'm sorry, Mister Miller!* Say it! Say it!'"

"And I was amazed, but Brubaker kind of choked it out, 'I'm sorry.'"

"'No! Wrong! *I'm sorry, Mister Miller!* Say it!'"

"'I'm sorry, Mister Miller!'"

"And Davis let him go and stepped back in a crouch expecting Brubaker
to come at him. Brubaker just got up holding his throat, never raised his
eyes and walked out.

"And Davis turned to me and said, 'You okay?' I thanked him and he said,
'I saw the way he was pushing you. Should have done something about it
sooner. If he fucks with you again, tell me. I fucking hate bullies!'"

The waiter put down the check and Stan pulled it to him. Stan said, "I
loved Davis, the way he played with his shirttail hanging out in the fourth
quarter. I loved his head-on, open field tackles. I can still hear the sound of
those tackles."

They slid back into the Mercedes. Stan looked at his watch and pushed his
glasses back up onto his nose with the straight index finger, which made
Val smile—with amazement, too, that a gesture could last that long, could
be forgotten and remembered—and then Stan bit his fingernail, thrust his
hand back into his pocket and said, "Got time to take a ride? I need to check
out a property."

As they crossed the Sound View Harbor Bridge, both grew silent at the sight of the water, the boats below, the harbor, the breakwater, Long Island low in the distance on the horizon. More comfortable in their random comments and lapses into silence, they drove down several exits before Stan got off the thruway, turned toward the water.

In a few more minutes, he slowed and pulled onto thick grass—there was no sidewalk—in front of a gray-shingled garage. They walked through a narrow backyard, the grass uncut, toward a two-story beach house, a house proportioned like something a third-grader might painstakingly draw, tall, narrow, with a steeply pitched roof; it, too, was gray-shingled, with white, chalking paint on the moldings of the windows and doors. Up three back stairs, which were enveloped in a profusion of faintly sweet, pink, wild roses. Stan fit a key to the lock and pushed open the back door with a squeak. Inside, cool, the faint smell of wood and rankness of a closed house. The kitchen: mottled, yellowing sheet linoleum, narrow counters, cabinets. They walked into a long front room. Through the side windows, the other houses, one on each side, close: the front windows looked into a screened porch. Beyond, the water and horizon rose in the windows. Val followed Stan outside onto a cracked and crumbling cement deck, stopped where they stood on the seawall looking down at a rocky beach.

"I just acquired it over the winter. Came out of a settlement. Needs lots of work." Stan indicated the seawall's partial collapse onto the narrow rocky beach, a boat lift, pitted and flaking with rust, its gears frozen. "I've got three contractors bidding on the renovation. It's pretty run down, but, hey…you know, you could stay here if you want."

Stan, offering him this house out of the blue? They hadn't been close friends at school. And he hadn't seen him in twenty-five years. Val noticed Stan's posture in his suit and tie. He had the self-possessed air of command of a man who had worked hard, made money and was pleased with himself.

"Stan. Thank you. It's just too generous. Really."

Stan shrugged. "It's not the Hilton and it's easy for me. Just take it."

"Really, it's a great offer, but I should just fly back home tomorrow." He listened to the sound of that, trying to convince himself.

"I didn't mean to be presumptuous, but you just said that you hadn't slept last night in your family house. This is a tough time for you. I've got a place. You seem to need a breather. That's all."

Stan smiled wryly and pointed a hundred yards offshore at a number of outboards and day-sailers hanging on their buoys. "It even has a mooring."

For a moment, Val suddenly thought he understood that Stan needed to do this, perhaps even as vindication, the never-forgotten sting of not having gone to a first-rate school—here he was, a success. God, did Val only think of these things when he was back East?

Without waiting for a reply, Stan said, "I'll show you the rest." Inside, he led Val back into the kitchen. "There are pots and pans, dishes. Everything." He opened and closed cabinets. "It's all just as the owners left it." In the front room, he indicated a TV, a VCR, a rattan sofa, a Formica kitchen table and a banquette covered with fitted cushions beneath the window.

They climbed up the narrow wooden staircase to a second-floor landing, where two front bedrooms overlooked the seawall. Val could see a fiber-glass dinghy overturned on the deck and look down into an outside shower behind a lattice screen. He raised a window. The gentle sound of waves drifted in on cooler air. As he turned, he realized that the house had the narrow beam of a boat.

In the kitchen, a heavy old dial telephone—black. Val picked up the receiver, and, at the silence of the earpiece, felt the thickening of dread in his stomach.

Back at his parents' house, Val called Kazz and explained about Stan Miller and the shore house.

She seemed strangely silent. "What, Kazz?"

"Nothing."

Could he give her the phone number?

Oh, it was disconnected. He would just call her.

He went to look for a sleeping bag in the attic, then saw that he'd left the light on in the cedar closet. The closet itself was still a mess. He grabbed a broom and dustpan. Some of Davis' schoolbooks and papers were still scattered about on the floor. He knelt to replace them. A loose-leaf notebook fell open, an envelope dropping out. Something familiar in the handwriting. Frozen, he stared, then picked up the letter. He studied the scrawl in numb disbelief, already knowing whose it was. Yet, it couldn't be. These were Davis' schoolbooks and papers. Lee Anne had come into Davis' life much later. He ran his fingertip along the sealed flap. It had never been opened. He held it up to the bare bulb and studied the postmark:

May 31, 1984. Miami, Florida.

Twelve days before Davis had drowned. It had been sent between the time Davis had last called Val from Miami and when Lee Anne had actually shown up at Val's place in North Carolina. It was addressed to Davis. Why had Lee Anne sent a letter to his parents' home in Connecticut when Davis was on his way to visit Val in North Carolina? And how had it gotten in with these schoolbooks? Val could only imagine that the letter had come to the house and been held by his mother, and then in the days and weeks after Davis had drowned, perhaps his mother, respecting Davis' privacy even in death, or more likely just distraught, had placed it in with these books, which had gone into the closet. Whatever the circumstances, it had never reached Davis.

Squinting against the window light, Val opened the door to the tiny bedroom—the squeeze of the roof's slope—and sank down onto the unmade bed. Thin, city soot blackened the windowsill, green elm leaves brushed the panes. Val balanced the envelope gently between his fingertips, traced the serrated edges of the stamp. Postage in 1984: Twenty cents. He pried open the envelope, took a breath at the sight of her slashing handwriting, pulled out the first of two folded pieces of paper and opened it:

> I can't say I didn't know. I could feel something moving, starting to turn. Hoped I was wrong. But never am. Or it never is. Or wasn't. Woke. Before I opened my eyes, I knew. There's something in a room when someone's left you. The silence. How it's always been there. How you always come back to it.
>
> How could you just leave me like that? I know you do love me. I know we are the only ones for each other. Knew it the moment I saw you. Don't you know that? You know it, too. Just forgot it. Or don't want to believe it. How can you leave someone you love without a word? Is everything between everyone all lies? At least I know when I'm lying. My lies, I know, are also turning out to be my truth. Maybe my lies are my greatest truth. Someday, I hope, I will be able to explain that to you, and when I do, I hope you'll understand what I'm talking about—and forgive me if I need forgiving. And whatever else, I know my love for you is not, is never, a lie. Maybe that's what scares you most of all, to be loved so hard.
>
> I've finally stopped crying. Now I'm just fucking furious. I'm sending a copy of this letter to your parents' house in case you actually ran that far. But I'm betting you're on your way to find The Great Val. And after I mail this I'm

*taking the bus up to North Carolina. Sooner or later I'll find you. You can't just leave me. Disappear. Never. Right now I don't know which I want to do more. Kill you or fuck you. Maybe I'll fuck you first and then kill you. Won't know until I see you again. Won't rest until I do. See you again. Find you. Fuck you. Kill you. God, how could you! I just keep thinking, no, he couldn't have meant to leave me like that—no word, no note, no nothing! Panic I can understand. But just disappearing. And panic, that is not like you. Remember that day with the guy and the boat trailer in his driveway? That was the real you. Only you could have pulled that off. I understand being scared—they are scary—but why wouldn't you take me with you? And didn't you forget something? I know everything! And if I want I can take it to the right people. All of it. The wrong people for you could be the right ones for me. Did you forget that? Could you really be that desperate to get away from me? No, like it or not, you've got me. I know it all. I hate to hold that over your head, but I will. And even more, if it weren't for me, you would have gotten what Billy got. I figured out what was happening. You never saw any of it coming.*

*I've enclosed a reminder of something else. Me. Have you forgotten Lee Anne and her myriad charms? I'm sending this and then I'm getting on the Greyhound and coming to find you. When I find you, you're going to have to look me right in the eye and tell me you don't love me.*

Underneath it, a lipstick kiss pressed onto the paper.

Val could hear her voice in every syllable, the Southern accent, part plea, part threat, the intimidation. As it was with her postcards to Val, the letter carried no salutation and was unsigned, as though some part of her never could completely emerge or let herself be identified, say hello or goodbye, or maybe as though everything said were part of the same ongoing stream, whether to Davis or himself or anyone else. In fact, he heard the echo of some of the strange phrases that had been in her postcards to him: *I could feel something moving, starting to turn...it never is... It.* Something moving. Starting to turn. How could she be writing things like that to Davis? The letter was written several years before her first postcards to him. He'd thought that what she'd written in her cards was addressing something that had to do with only them—though there were those weird references to a riverbank and ice, an empty bottle of Clairol. Those phrases referred to a time and place before him, perhaps even an event, a place that had come to seem almost familiar, though he'd never been there.

He drew out the second sheet of paper. Inside, there was a photograph of Lee Anne, a self-portrait taken with a Polaroid camera and a timer; it was slightly blurred, but the colors still burned with a Jello-chemical brilliance. Naked from the waist up, Lee Anne cupped her breasts, thrust her chin slightly forward, and with lips puckered, she blew a mocking, pouting kiss at the camera. He heard her Southern accent: *Have you forgotten Lee Anne and her myriad charms?* Myriad charms. It was as if she were writing about some-one else, and at the same time satirizing that person. And myriad charms? That was no hairdresser. But the pouting kiss, the pose....

Val heard himself groan into the room. Though Davis was gone, though Val had been married to Kazz for fifteen years, though there was Michael, though he loved them both, he felt the wild rush of the intimacy between Davis and Lee Anne; he felt the ambush of the most unexpected of emo-tions in himself: jealousy. It was as if in a single undeniable moment, he had now lost all of the ground he'd been working to win back from some part of himself. Seventeen years. He couldn't take his eyes from the Polaroid. He looked at the lipstick kiss on the paper. So pathetic, so impossible...whether it was he, or the kiss, or the photograph, he couldn't decide. Perhaps all three.

He reread the letter, each phrase sending out a shock wave:

> *I know everything...if it weren't for me, you would have gotten exactly what Billy got...the wrong people for you could be the right ones for me.... Not like you to panic...*

Val remembered the fearful way Davis, after he'd arrived in North Caro-lina and was sitting with Val in this bar or that, kept watching as each person came through the door. And later in Brooklyn, Lee Anne's handing him the picture of Davis in the boat: "Davis." He'd never know what she meant by giving it to him or how the two might be connected: Davis in the boat, his fearfulness.

Val studied the black geometric pieces spread on the pink Formica table: Tangoes.

As he worked the puzzle, several items had arranged themselves around him in an uncertain order as if they, too, might be parts of the game. There were the postcards Lee Anne had sent him since he'd left her; the video cassette labeled in Regina's block capital letters, "June 11, 1984, MARLIN," which Val always thought of as *the marlin tape*; there was Lee Anne's letter—enraged, despairing, threatening—written to Davis after he had run out on her in Miami, and which Val discovered unopened two days ago, along with its Polaroid picture of Lee Anne naked.

Val slid two black plastic triangles together and studied the remaining pieces.

Distracted, he glanced over at the print Lee Anne had given Val the last time he'd seen her, Davis driving the boat at night, over which Michael had declared, "Davis! *Phat*, dude! The bomb!" along with his implication that Davis possessed precisely the qualities Val lacked.

He picked up a plastic rectangle, looked back to a handful of Stan's office letterhead stationery, which Stan had left behind one day while making remodel sketches. In the corner of his eye: the plastic baggie of pills that Val had taken from Michael, and which Val was acutely aware awaited his response.

Val rearranged a trapezoid; he studied the black shape on the Tangoes card, then flipped it over to check his solution, which matched. The pieces made a crane, the bird's wings outspread in flight. He stood and surveyed the items gathered around the black plastic figure in the middle of the table.

The hectoring cries of a gull, the scent of cut grass, sun-warmed shingles, and beach roses through the screens—the smells of his growing up—brought Val back to himself. A bag of groceries in hand, he'd come into Stan's beach house late yesterday afternoon. Unrolling his sleeping bag on the cot beneath the front window, he spent the night tossing and turning to the ebb and flow of tide sighing through the windows. He couldn't seem to sleep here, either. Now he stood.

Outside, he shaded his eyes. The water inshore, dead calm, had a delicate pewter sheen. Beyond, long shafts of late afternoon sunlight slanted, radiant, silvery-white, and Val felt as if he could walk into that great distance and come to a luminous city just below the horizon. Rocks and shells grinding under his shoes, the fetid reek of low tide filling his nostrils, he picked his way toward the water, now skidding on sheets of seaweed, now peering down into isolated tidal pools to discover the secret creep of snails and the dart of minnows, to hear the gasping whisper of barnacles waiting for the flood tide to return and revive them. When he looked back at the seawall, the high-water mark a horizontal black shadow on the concrete, only the second floor of the house and steep roof were visible above and beyond. He continued out among the tide pools until his shoes stopped at the water's edge, and here again he peered down into the shallows, the fine sand of the bottom etched with a pattern of delicate ripples as if it were breath being silently blown through the water.

Suddenly, he heard his father say, "If only you'd stayed where you were!" the voice so clear, Val actually turned around and looked across the empty beach. From what time in his life? Law school, wasn't it?

Law school. He could feel that time again on his skin: a summer internship in the prosecutor's office, San Francisco. A mentor—Craig Benoit—who'd taken him into his complete confidence, opened his eyes; Craig was street smart. They'd gone to ball games, drank together. Overnight, Val felt like an insider, suddenly knowing how things worked, was perhaps even a little drunk with power. It had been great. Val had wanted to impress Craig, to be perfect for him, to be diligent, to be beyond reproach. They'd been bringing Sonny Ramirez, a swaggering gang *vato,* to trial; he'd gotten off several years previous on a murder charge; he'd silenced his witnesses—no one had dared testify against him—and they'd had to drop the charges. When he walked, he had shown contempt for Craig. Craig had taken it personally; it *was* personal. But now they had a second crack at Ramirez. A year before Val's internship, word was that Sonny had gone up to the Mission to settle a score and killed a rival with a brick.

Charged by Craig to review the case and know it backward and forward, Val discovered a name in Work Product—the notes generated in a working case—that he couldn't account for in police reports or discovery, just a single name on a piece of paper—Caballo—with a phone number and question mark next to it. Panicked that he'd overlooked something—god, he just had to get everything right! Val started with the Criss-Cross directory and found the guy's address. He went up to his place on his own initiative, identified himself as from the prosecutor's office, but said nothing more. He didn't really know who this guy was or how he fit in the case. But Caballo, as he was called, started talking. *Hey, isn't our deal going to hold up? You said we had a deal.* Having no idea what he meant, Val nodded to keep him talking: *No, no, we have a deal, everything's cool....* Caballo went on. Val could see the guy was a young laborer just home from work; his clothes still spattered with mortar, he paced in the tiny basement apartment while his wife tried to shush a crying baby. Then, as Val went on listening, he came to understand that Caballo was a witness who'd seen Sonny attacked by the victim; seen that Sonny had only been defending himself. It wasn't murder. It was, at most, involuntary manslaughter. That's why the "murder weapon" had been a brick. It was the first thing Sonny had been able to pick up.

When, later, Val revealed that he'd found the witness who corroborated Sonny's version, Craig sat back in his desk chair and just stared at Val. Finally, he said, "I'm impressed. I thought from the start that you were a very smart guy." He paused; he leaned forward. "So you'll understand me now when I say that if you breathe a word of this to anyone—anyone! I will personally see to it that you will never practice law anywhere ever." Then Val fully realized what he hadn't previously allowed himself to understand. Craig's investigator had gotten to the witness before the defense's investigators could find him. This was exculpatory evidence, concealed exculpatory evidence. And it was going to stay concealed.

In trial, Craig had hammered the defendant, Sonny Ramirez, with the testimony of a jailhouse snitch who'd been paid off with the promise of an early release. Instead of involuntary manslaughter, Craig had gotten Sonny convicted of murder, and in the penalty phase, sentenced to life without parole, LWOP. To Craig, it was justice. One way or the other, Sonny had it coming. It had been incredible for Val to watch Craig and his snitch and two cops lie in trial. Fascinated, he couldn't stop watching their faces. People actually lied, lied under oath.

Later, he thought he would have the same sensation looking into Lee Anne's face.

Off-balance, confused and paralyzed, Val had drifted back to law school at the end of the summer without taking any action. Indeed, what action? Who would believe him, a lowly summer intern, or his story about a potential witness who'd subsequently disappeared when Val had tried to find him again. At times, Val had been so uncertain and depressed, he'd wondered if he had actually ever found and talked to Caballo.

Val thought of confiding in friends, faculty, but no one seemed right, and part of him didn't want other opinions now. His part in the story was too... ambiguous? As people spoke to him, he found himself looking too long and hard into their faces until they turned away—something alarming about his gaze. He was fascinated by his discovery that people lied—really lied, the depths of it—and acted on those lies. And got away with it. He started skipping classes. Two. Three. Then another.

One afternoon, there was a postcard from Davis: the cliffs of Miami's beachfront hotels shining white in the sun. And in Davis' left-handed, hooked writing, his tortured dyslexic mix of uppercase and lowercase letters:

*Val, This is the life. Come visit sunny Florida. Davis.*

A corner of the card had the whorls of Davis' fingerprint. Davis. Grease. Engines. And suddenly Val knew that Davis was the person who could help him understand San Francisco. Davis had been hammered and humiliated in school by bullies like Metraux, and though idolized, he had also endured the contempt of his classmates. He had found ways not only to cope but to strike back. Street smart, he would see what Val didn't, know what he should have done, still might do…. In fact, Davis' life, the way he was living it now, was a kind of repudiation of his tormentors, a reply to those who had tried to silence him. Living with his Southern girlfriend in a beautiful place. Building the '33 Ford. Doing not what other people wanted him to do, but what he wanted to do. Working on boats, something they'd both always wanted, had even talked about doing together. Something Val still wanted, he realized. Boats. Davis was living a real life.

Val wrote through the afternoon on a legal pad, page after page, the whole story, Craig, Sonny, the intimidated witness, the snitch, LWOP, and when he looked up and stopped, the light was fading gray, and he was exhausted. Though he knew Davis was out of touch with their father, he added, "Whatever you do, don't mention any of this to Dad." He stuffed the handwritten pages in a manila envelope and mailed it off.

Davis wrote back right away. A note on paper torn from a spiral notebook, and a postcard. Both stuffed into an envelope. The card was of ten girls smiling and waving as they were towed in formation behind a ski boat. Cypress Gardens. Davis had scrawled, *Up up up and a way!* God, did Davis have to make a joke out of everything? He read Davis' note. The spelling in this letter, so quickly scrawled and usually overlooked by Val seemed particularly egregious.

*Dear Fuckhead, you fucking, a maze me. Okay. Heres the name, and address, and phone, of a yaht broker, who just sold a used Hatteras, up in Portsmouth New Hampshare, the new ownar needs the boat, delivered to North Carolina, I've greased it for you, told the broker, you're a dude of high*

*morals, got good navygation skills (maybe) or at least, if you've got enough*
*fuel, you'll hit land, eventually and can hitch to a pay phone, and ask, where*
*the fuck you are, and can get the boat, down the ditch to NC, in one peece*
*more or less, (maybe) the boat has state, of art, electronics, radar, auto pilot, it*
*can run itself, the new ownar is, a marlin fisherman, also a plastick surgeon,*
*maybe heel he'll be so gratefull, he'll throw, in a face lift, tell him you allways*
*seecreately wanted, to look just like me.*

"But not punctuate or spell like you," Val said aloud.

Val picked up the postcard of the ten water skiers in formation, each
waving and smiling, reread Davis' "…up up and a way." Val heard Davis'
voice, droll, derisive; he laughed out loud in response. He read on:

> *What will Dickhed say?*
> *But I did, let Lee Anne read your letter, well, she got, into it, on her own,*
> *don't know if, I could have stoped her anyway. When she, finished, she laghed.*
> *Out loud. She said, "The Great Val." That is what, she started caling, you*
> *after my buildup, Harvard, all your advanced placment shit, this and that.*
> *I must have laid it on, too thick, cause that's what she started, calling you.*
> *Then she said. "He's so starry-eyed I could almost love a guy like this."*
> *Anyway, what the fuck. We always talked, doing some thing cool, with*
> *boats, so if you decide to baile, maybe we realy will. It'l make me have, to*
> *clean up, my act.*

What did that mean, clean up my act? It rankled him, Davis calling their
father *Dickhead*. The contempt in it. Though their father was impossible to
get along with, Val loved him, admired him. And Lee Anne…some cracker
chick with a second-hand attitude toward him and Harvard that she'd picked
up from Davis, laughing at Val. But then, some small part of Val thought
that he, himself, didn't get it, either. He couldn't tell if he was being honorable, a fool or a coward. Whatever it was, the bad feeling didn't leave him.
And, he realized, if he did what he wanted to do, which was to leave law
school and take the Hatteras south, things were going to get much more
complicated. There would be even more he couldn't explain to his father.

By now Val hadn't been to classes in weeks. He called the yacht broker
about the boat, the Amazing Grace, as she was called—they talked about
Val's boating experience, and the broker said he'd relay word to the owner
over in Charlotte: "He played tackle at LSU, imagine that, this huge guy,

huge hands, and you know, a plastic surgeon, and they say a very good one."

In a couple of days the broker called back and said that the owner was fine with having Val deliver the boat. They worked out details, payment for Val, a credit card for fuel, how and when to pick up the keys and the yacht—a map and directions would be sent to him there in Cambridge—and so on.

Val wrote Davis a short letter telling him that he had made arrangements and would be coming, and please to stop showing his letters to his girlfriend or leaving them where she could find them so that she could hold him up to ridicule. Maybe he was being sensitive right now, but he didn't feel like letting someone he didn't know have a good laugh over him. Val was pissed. *The Great Val.* What was that shit?

He mailed the letter to Davis and then he went to see the dean about taking a leave of absence. Late in the day he found himself walking along the Charles under a bloodless, white sky, Boston across the river, the water like cold gray steel flowing out toward the harbor. All the time he had a nagging feeling that there was something more at work, that maybe he had an agenda concealed even from himself. He noticed a flickering weave of movement on the horizon. Flocks of birds, probably ducks, a skein, forming and reforming as they flew. Flew south, he realized. He glanced at his watch. Almost three. When he looked up, the birds were already gone, leaving just the white sky. He watched a gust of wind darken the water across the river, suddenly became acutely aware of how little light and visibility were left in the day, that it was November and the days were short and getting cold. Dark soon. He turned and walked on.

Davis wrote back: *Youve gone, and done it. Stuped. Okay, go get the Hatteras.*

Val replied: *Thanks for the boat.*

His father had finished up at his office and was already home when Val came in. He was standing at the hall table sorting through the mail. Quiet, composed, he smiled at Val. "This is a pleasant surprise. I feel like I never get to see you."

Val took one look at his father and knew he couldn't tell him anything; he couldn't stand coming in here and shattering his well-being. Beyond that, Val realized his father would be neither sympathetic nor understanding of his justifications. His father had come down on the side of the school when Davis had started failing, always sided with the authorities. Like Davis, he had a sudden, unpredictable temper. No, it was out of the question, telling him what had really happened. Val would stick around for a couple of hours, make some excuse, get away. He'd write his father after he'd gotten started on the boat. By the time they could connect on the phone, his father might have cooled off a bit—and Val would be calling from some harbor on the way south, and just the fact of it, the momentum, would make it less arguable.

His father placed his hand on his shoulder and said, "You seem tired. Everything okay. School?" Val nodded. "You left a message with Mary Beth at the office that you wanted to talk to me about something."

"I've already taken care of it."

His father nodded. "But you're forgetting just one small thing."

"What's that, Dad?"

"I *know* you. What's really happening, Val?"

Val shook his head. "Nothing. Where's Mom? She home? Actually, I'm going to have to take off in a couple of hours; I didn't want to miss her, either."

"Should be back any time."

Val watched his father's face mask over—it was a look of feigned indifference, yet the gaze was carefully angled to tell Val that he didn't believe him and that he was waiting for something better from Val; it was a veiled challenge. Was Val up to it, up to doing something better?—that's what it said. Behind him, the afternoon November light was starting to dilute, a moment which had always filled Val with desolation, the thawed ground freezing, branches bare against the sky. Val thought of the Hatteras waiting up in Portsmouth. The days short, cold, the water freezing. An impossible time to start taking a boat south.

His father said quietly, "What's on your mind, Val?"

"Dad, I'm leaving law school—I already have. I know what you're going to say, but I just need some time to think things over."

"What things?"

"Dad, it's not one thing."

Exactly like Davis when angered or offended, his father had stiffened, his posture had changed, and a kind of blindness had come into his eyes. "Think about what things!? In my day I didn't take time off to think. I did my thinking between two jobs and my classes!"

"Right. You're right."

"What you need to do is complete what you've started! Davis' not finishing school is one thing, but I never would have expected this of you!"

Val shook his head. Hopeless to have ever tried to talk with his father about anything. Now he just had to find a way out of here. Quick.

His father lowered his voice slightly. "Val, what's happened with you? You seemed so interested in what you were doing in San Francisco when you wrote me at the beginning of the summer." His father shook his head in disbelief, crossed his arms over his chest. "And let's say for a second that you actually are leaving law school. What are you doing instead?"

This was pointless. He blundered on. What difference could it make now? Val told his father about the Hatteras, that he was taking it down the inland waterway to North Carolina for a new owner, and when that was done, he would deliver another boat, and that maybe he would start some kind of business involving boats, which was what he'd really wanted all along.

His father cut him off. "You're picking up a boat and you're starting south now!?" He held his hand toward the November light fading in the window. "Are you crazy?" Val didn't answer. "You have talent and ability and are just throwing them away." His father was shouting now. "This is great. It just amazes me how you two guys can just take the opportunities I had to fight so hard for and toss them aside as if they were nothing." Val saw the hurt in his face, that he was taking Val's decision personally—as a rejection of himself.

"I can't explain anymore." Val started for the door.

"You haven't explained a thing. Aren't you going to wait for your mother?"

"No. I'll call her."

"What did you want to accomplish by coming here and telling me this today?"

Val stopped. "I didn't want you to call Cambridge and find my phone disconnected. I didn't want to put it in a letter. I didn't want to pull a disappearing act on you."

"Honorable, I suppose, your intention. But not good enough for me!"

As Val reached the curb, the streetlights came on in the November twilight. He looked back at the house behind the hedge. He knew that his father was completely right about everything. If he had a son leaving law school midway through, he probably would say the same things. He drove half a block and then pulled over. Where was he going?

———————

Now on the beach in front of Stan's house, as Val stared down into a tidal pool, he realized he'd always meant to do something with boats and his father had discouraged him. *A very chancy business. Let others do it.* But that was what Val had wanted. He'd let his father silence him. More than anything else, Val realized that his father's attitude toward Davis pissed him off; no matter how much Davis fucked up, his father seemed to love Davis more. He had the same take on Davis' life on boats that he'd had about Davis and sports—a kind of despair, yet an admiration, a double standard. In fact, his father glowed whenever he spoke about Davis on boats in Florida, as if Davis were living out his father's secret dream life.

Peering down into the tidal pool, Val saw himself sitting in the idling car a block from his father's house. Where was he going? He slammed the car into drive. Portsmouth. If Davis could do what he wanted and get away with it, Val sure as hell could, too.

# THUNDER BAY

### *Send Him Back*

The trip to North Carolina would take longer than the three to four weeks he'd projected.

The first days out of Portsmouth were clear, bright, and bitter cold. He'd run through the Annisquam River, Gloucester, on to Marblehead, Plymouth, Boston, down through the Cape Cod Canal, Buzzards Bay, Newport, down through Long Island Sound, making decent time, making the most of his short daylight. The sooner he could get out of northern waters, the better off he'd be. Each day was time borrowed against severe weather—snow, sleet, ice, freezing temperatures. Each morning, up before first light, stove lit, thick socks, long underwear, a blue knit watch cap; the day's charts spread out at the navigation station, instruments switched on and reading, LORAN, radar, and a check of the engines and gauges—fuel, tachs, oil pressure, depth—the morning radio playing into the din of the idling engines; then, out onto the float or dock, white and slippery with frost, the sharp cry of a single gull staring at him from a piling, a bleak beautiful vista coming out of the pale predawn gray, a deserted marina; a boatyard—boats hauled and on their cradles and cocooned under tarps or plastic for winter storage; clearing the entrance of a harbor as the horizon separated from the dark sky.

Val continued to make decent time—New York, New Jersey–until he woke in the dark one morning in Delaware to hard rain beating on the cabin top and deck overhead, and gusts of wind shaking the boat and whining through the outriggers and tuna tower. Topside, he was met with freezing rain mixed with snow swirling across the windshield and zero visibility; he found a warm café ashore, and later in the day, at a Laundromat, noticed there were Christmas tree lights up. Several mornings afterward, he stepped into the cockpit, slipped and just managed to catch himself on the fighting chair. The boat was encased in a smooth, clear layer of glaze ice, icicles gleaming from the outriggers, the stainless steel tubing of the tuna tower, the lifelines and bow pulpit; he stared in wonder, laughed, his breath a frozen cloud. Nothing to do but go to the movies, go to the town library or a bookstore, go to the café, wait for a thaw.

Slowed by days of rain and poor visibility, by the shifting channels of the inland waterway and the inside speed limit, Val worked his way south, calling home less and less as his father maintained his disapproving silence. Now he felt released into a new life, a bigger life, his real life, one he'd been trying to reach, each day the sky huge, the water beautiful, but often—so empty of boats—foreboding.

Physically exhausted, weary, Val reached Thunder Bay, North Carolina, in late January, slept straight through until noon the next day and then called Magnus Johnson over in Charlotte, told him his boat was safe and in good condition. Magnus had a friend who was going to need a Grand Banks 40 brought over from Nassau to Fort Lauderdale toward the end of February, and if Val was interested, Magnus would be glad to recommend him.

By the first week of March, Val was in Lauderdale with the Grand Banks and had lined up a thirty-foot Bertram to take to Savannah in the next few days; the logical next move was to get on a bus and run down to see Davis, but Val realized that he didn't have his phone number. Information in Miami listed a number for a Davis Martin, but when Val called it, he got a recording: the number had been disconnected. Just like Davis. Disconnected. Val called Information for a new or recent listing. Nothing. But somehow Val didn't think Davis had left. He seemed to have come back to life in Miami—that's where he'd met Lee Anne, found the boatyard job he liked. But if he wanted to know for sure, there was nothing left to do but get on a bus and see if Davis was still living at his last return address.

Reaching Miami late in the day, Val walked through the Greyhound bus station to the street, caught a cab, and gave the driver Davis' last address. After some time, the taxi driver pulled up in front of a small duplex in the fading light. Art Deco. Whitewashed stucco. Glass brick and a border of blue tile. A painted red porch. A couple of ancient, chipped, iron porch chairs. Blinds drawn.

On his second ring, a young woman—maybe twenty—unlocked a deadbolt and pushed open the screen door. Took him in with a steady, relaxed gaze. As he said, "Lee Anne?" Val knew she couldn't be even before she shook her head no and said that she'd just moved in and had no idea who the previous occupants were or where they'd gone. He was surprised; he already knew that much about someone he'd never met, that this woman wasn't Lee Anne.

The driver called to him. "Are we waiting for her?"

Val shook his head no. The meter clicked. Time. Money. Time equals money. Something like that. The palms stirred, clicked in the breeze. A wild goose chase. In the end, he let the cab driver suggest a low-priced motel nearby where he went and collapsed onto the bed.

When he took a walk looking for a breakfast place in the morning, he saw that there were several boatyards in the area. Was it unfair to assume people often lived close to where they worked? He headed toward what appeared to be an industrial park on the water. Corrugated iron boat sheds, boats in storage. Boatyards. Repair. Boat building facilities. The scream of a power saw, air thick with lacquer, the dust of fiberglass. Muscle boats. Cigarettes. Long, lean, overpowered.

He angled across a parking lot toward an office, spotted a mechanic in a blue jumpsuit coming out of a shed, asked if he might know a Davis Martin. Looked at his hands. Fingernails black with grease, split. They could have been Davis' hands. Almost as if he were considering the idea of it, the guy was thoughtful, then seemed to blank his face. No, he didn't. Maybe he mistook Val for a bill collector, which wouldn't be an unlikely scenario for Davis. Val added, "I'm his brother. Just visiting from Lauderdale." The sound of an engine being tested rose to a deafening roar and the mechanic shrugged and walked away.

He went on to several more yards down the row. Air reeking of oil, gasoline, resin, these were exactly the kinds of places to which Davis had always gravitated. The yard workers didn't seem so much not to know Davis as to show a flicker of guarded recognition when he asked and then make a decision not to show anything. But maybe that wasn't so. Maybe Val was just tired and frustrated and it seemed that they were holding out on him when in fact they simply didn't know Davis. As he walked back toward his motel room, he realized it wasn't an accident that he couldn't find Davis, but rather that Davis didn't want to be found.

For the next few months, Val was on and off boats. The Bertram to Savannah. An Egg Harbor back down to Lauderdale. In and out of harbors where once again he would come back to the order and rhythm of the new boat being taken in on its course, the white compass needle on the heading, the blade of the black compass card silently suspended, the churn of the engines, the throw of spray exploding silver over the windshield.... Sometimes there would be a passing fling, a pleasant interlude that never came to anything. At times he felt that he had stumbled through a maze and now, for the first time in years, emerged to come back to his real self. How had it happened? Could it have been this easy? You just stepped out of an old life and that was the end of it?

Every few weeks, Val would try Information anyway, but no new listing appeared for Davis. He was sure Davis was still somewhere in Miami, the phone maybe in Lee Anne's name, but, he realized, he didn't know her last name. Instead of calling home and braving his father's charged silences, Val had taken to dropping three-sentence postcards along the way to reassure his parents he was all right. It was as much as he could do.

By early May, Val was back in touch with Magnus, who asked him if he could come up to run the Amazing Grace weekends, stay through the Atlantic Blue Marlin Tournament, which was starting in early June. There was maintenance that needed doing on the Hatteras if Val wanted to make some extra money.... Here he was in Thunder Bay, North Carolina. Not a bad place to be for a while.

Seeing the Amazing Grace in her slip at the end of the dock gave Val an affectionate feeling of belonging; he knew the sound of her engines, the rise and fall of her bow in a hard chop, her stainless steel bow pulpit and outriggers and tuna tower jagged with icicles. When Magnus came up the next morning, they finally met on the boat with big grins, pats on the shoulder; instant friends, if for no other reason than that Magnus had entrusted his boat to Val sight unseen, and Val had safely brought her hundreds of miles, made good on that trust. Magnus was just as he'd been described by Davis' yacht broker acquaintance, a former college defensive tackle, six-five, 250, yet with a quiet, almost scholarly manner, a thick Southern accent; he really was a plastic surgeon, and, as Val would repeatedly hear, a superb one; Val would study his huge hands and thick fingers and wonder how he carried out the minute intricacies of cosmetic and reconstructive surgery.

They'd driven over to a rented bungalow a few minutes from the yacht harbor, and, at the sight of it, Val realized how nice it would be to settle for a few weeks. He'd been living on boats for months, in tight bunks, cabins variously smelling of cold, bilge, engine oil and heat, of propane, sometimes the head, an icebox gone sour.... Here he had a small screened porch, the shingled roof furred a rust color with sun-dried pine needles; an old Grady-White sat on a boat trailer under a tree. Inside, Val picked a bedroom—each was simple, sparsely furnished—and dropped his duffle on the bed.

They loaded the Amazing Grace with heavy-duty rods, massive Penn reels, hooks, wire leaders, lures, spools of extra line, more tools, which Magnus had brought from home, and then headed for the grocery store to stock the Hatteras with staples. Val plucked a postcard from the rack beside the cash register—an aerial shot of the harbor and coastline, the Atlantic beyond: Thunder Bay. He wrote a message to his parents: *Back with the Hatteras—the Amazing Grace—for the next few weeks. Owner turns out to be a great guy.* As if to legitimize himself, he added. *He's a noted surgeon.* And: *Big marlin tournament coming up in early June.* As an afterthought, he wrote the phone number of the bungalow at the bottom. But at the mailbox, he decided, no, no way, and placed the card in his chest pocket. The next day, though, he mailed it.

Val jumped when the phone rang loud into the stillness, let it ring several times before answering. He recognized his father's voice. "I've been trying to reach you since noon." He said it with exasperation, as if it were Val's fault he hadn't been there for the call. "I need to know if you've heard from Davis."

"I haven't been in touch with him for months. Or more like he hasn't been in touch with me. His phone in Miami's disconnected." Val started to add that he'd gone to find him, but thought better of it. Instead: "I wrote him, but my letter came back." Not literally true, but close enough. "He has no forwarding address."

"And no new phone. I tried Information down there."

"When would I have heard from him?"

"Today. Because he called me this morning at my office."

"What did he want?"

"To know if I knew where you were. I gave him your number—this one. I told him you were in Thunder Bay, back on the Amazing Grace, and had a phone."

"But what did he want?"

"Wouldn't tell me." They were silent. His father said abruptly, "But I know Davis. He thinks I don't, but I know him like no one else does." Val heard a kind of tender, hurt pride and love in his father's voice: that only he really knew Davis. "I could tell there was something terribly wrong."

His father never spoke in such drastic terms. "Dad, it can't be anything too serious…"

"He's out of touch with everyone for months. Never calls me, anyway. And then he rings me at my office at ten o'clock this morning out of the blue. Wants your number." Val waited. "If he calls, I want you to get back to me, I don't care what time it is, day or night. If he asks or says he's coming up there, tell him no, absolutely not."

"Why would I do that? How am I even supposed to do that?"

"You never had any problem telling me no. I'm sure you can figure it out."

"Thanks."

"I want him to stay where he is and keep working at what he's doing. It's his best chance, maybe his only chance, to have a life. If he starts to drift again, he'll just get back into trouble.

"Get his phone number and address. I'll send you money for a plane ticket. I want you to fly down, spend some time with him, re-establish whatever you can, but down there."

"Dad, what if I tell Davis no and he still says he's coming?"

"Send him back."

"For me—or anyone else—to try to stop Davis physically is just impossible."

"Look, you've always known how to connect with him when no one else could. I'm counting on you." He added quickly, "If Davis asks you if I called, tell him no."

"Why?"

"I've always felt he's lived to defy me."

"Oh, Dad…"

"Go ahead, 'Oh-Dad' me, Val. Maybe I'll get on a plane and come down there myself, anyway." The thought hung. "Just call me the minute you hear from him." The line went dead.

A breeze stirred, brought the sun-heated smell of the estuary and tide through the screens, the scything sway of the reeds. Something alarming in his father's voice. Outside, Val looked back at the bungalow, light streaming from its window into the darkness. When the phone rang a few minutes later, sudden and loud, Val jumped, then answered it.

"Like, answer your phone much, asshole? I'll give you the benefit of the doubt and figure you were getting laid…"

"Lovely greeting. Where you calling from?"

"Miami, dude."

"Got a number there you can give me in case we get disconnected?"

"Don't worry, if we do, I'll call back. Dad call you?"

Val said too quickly, "No, he didn't call."

"Your voice always goes up half a fucking octave when you lie. Never could lie worth a shit. Okay, he called you and what?"

"Can I have your number there?"

"I told you if we get disconnected, I'll call you back. Don't you trust me?"

"Can you just cut the shit and tell me what's going on? Like why you have no phone number, no forwarding address for the last couple of months, where you've moved…

Davis said, "I want to come up there…" He lowered his voice. "I'll come up there and we'll talk."

Secretive Davis rarely volunteered anything about himself. Val decided he had to hold his father's line. "Davis, that won't work right now. We're headed north in a couple of days on the Amazing Grace."

"Bullshit."

"What do you know?"

"I know from the yacht broker that the doctor's a serious marlin fisherman and the biggest blue marlin tournament on the East Coast starts right there in North Carolina in two weeks. You're not headed north. He's going marlin fishing. Hey, I won't fuck with your gig. I got you the Amazing Grace to begin with, didn't I?"

"Give me your phone there and I'll call you back in half an hour." Davis didn't answer. Val said almost as afterthought, "And what about the girl?"

"Lee Anne. What about her?"

"Is she with you?"

"No, I don't think so. No." He sounded like he was trying to make up his mind about something. "I'm coming alone."

"Give me a place to meet you and I'll fly down there."

"Out of the question. Not down here. Gotta go. Now. Right now."

Davis hung up.

In the middle of the night, the phone rang, loud, once, into the silence, and Val sat up with a gasp, but then it didn't ring again, though Val remained tensed against the next ring until he started to wonder if he'd heard anything at all. Dreaming? He dozed the rest of the night within the feverish dread he'd heard in his father's voice, woke hung over from nightmares, and, trying to quiet his own fears, he called his father at home to reassure him. His mother answered, her voice distant. "I'm just calling to tell Dad I've heard from Davis, but I'm sure coming here was just one of his impulses. He'll stay in Miami…"

"Your father doesn't think so."

"Is Dad there?"

"He's gone to the office."

"It's only 7:30."

"He's working on a big case…. and he feels better when he's working."

"What's got him so worried about Davis?"

"His phone's been disconnected for the last couple of months. Maybe that's when his apprehension really started." She hesitated. "He's worried that Davis is in trouble. He just sleeps for about two hours and then comes wide awake and is up all night."

"How long's it been like this?"

"Weeks."

"I just wanted to tell him that I'm sure Davis won't show up."

His mother said dryly, "I'm sure he'll be so glad to hear that."

Val hesitated—it was pointless to go on like this. He started to hang up, but caught himself. "Mom," he said quietly, "I'll talk to you later." He hesitated. "Bye." He held off a moment. When she didn't say anything, he said, "Bye, Mom," and hung up.

Like his father, he did the only thing he could think to do. He went to work, not in an office, but on the Amazing Grace, opening her up, turning on the fan and radio. Was he waiting? He didn't know. Was Davis still in Miami? He had no idea.

Bent over his sanding, Val was refinishing the interior of the Hatteras when he looked up suddenly. A car had pulled into the parking lot. Val could see its thick, oversized black tires, its chromed engine, blinding in the sun. Several men had already gathered and were staring at the car from a respectful distance. As Val came up the dock, he could hear the engine idling with a deep loping rhythm. He made out someone behind the windshield in the dark cave of the interior. Chopped low and raked, body a blazing red, orange and yellow flames curling back from the firewall and engulfing the doors, the car was all sleek menace and beauty.

Without turning off the engine, Davis got out—Val caught a glimpse of crumpled speeding tickets on the floor and seat—and they embraced, Davis so thick and dense with muscle that Val could barely get his arms around him. Davis pulled back. "Okay, dude, I know it's the eighties, but don't get, like, all queer on me." Davis. Unshaven. Blood-shot eyes. Green slacks, a red and yellow rayon shirt, crushed and wrinkled in a hundred places; pointy-toed, pearl-colored shoes—tropical—delicately woven of plaited leather with two holes for the laces; no socks, the whole thing a kind of enormous, dyslexic clash. Val laughed. "You're here." Suddenly embarrassed, they faced the car. Val said, "The '33 Ford. Beautiful, man."

"She's not too shabby."

"What's in it?"

"Like, do we have to? You wouldn't know an Edelbrock carburetor from a butt crack...and, like, I could use a shower and something to eat." Davis feigned extreme patience. "Okay, Slick, listen up, you only get this once." A couple of the bystanders edged closer to hear. "A '33 Ford Standard Coupe, three windows, one two three, even you can see that, chopped her three inches.

"Small block Chevy 350—that's a mouse—bored out, 30 over TRW eleven-to-ones...lost already, right?"

"But keep going."

"Sig Erson high-lift cams with solid lifters. I'm doing this only because you're my brother, counselor. It's a 30-30. That's why it makes that long, deep, uneven sound, that's the cam."

Davis pointed, recited. "Holley 60 double pumper on a Victor Junior, 202 angle plug heads, T10 four-speed, rock-crusher tranny," Davis circled the car, Val momentarily distracted by something about the appearance of Davis' hand. "Everything chrome: valve covers, air cleaner, thermostat housing, timing cover, chrome, man, oil pan, water pump pulley, thermostat housing, timing cover, more chrome; those are Corvette-style side pipes, all chrome. And a '32 Ford straight axle dropped three inches—I'm a big fan of straight axles—leaf springs go across right under the frame, chrome shocks—even you know what chrome looks like, right, counselor? End of tour, I think. Suicide doors open front to back, the body's completely decked, handles are under the car...spun aluminum wheel covers—moons, dude."

This was what he loved most about Davis, that he could do something like this—would do it. He now knew what had caught his attention about Davis' hand; it was comparatively clean. His nails, knuckles didn't have that fine, indelible etching of grease Val always remembered. And there was something else Val sensed and couldn't identify.

A couple of the bystanders took this moment to step forward and ask Davis about the car and Davis smiled and started answering their questions. Val studied him. Blond stubble, long blond hair down the back of his neck. Brilliant blue eyes, a child's ingenuous smile layered over with a provocateur's glint of calculation, play and cunning. His physical presence, as always, overwhelming. That's what it was. From the tone of his father's call, Val had been expecting Davis to be hurt or injured, that there would be something conspicuously wrong with him. His father was having nightmares, but Davis looked great.

Davis broke off from the admiring cognoscenti. "Hey, guys, I'll catch you later, gotta take care of a few things now." He grinned, patted one on the shoulder, slapped hands with the other, and Val saw that there was something about Davis' recognition and friendship that made them feel pleased to be included. It had always been that way.

Val said as playfully as he could, "Hey, you're not supposed to be here. Remember. I'm the one who's getting off the plane in Miami...."

Davis gave Val an unreadable smile. "That the way we left it, counselor?" He looked around. "Which one is the Amazing Grace?"

Val pointed it out at the end of the dock as two women came walking up the ramp, smiled. Val recognized them from the supermarket, had a friendly flirtation going with both. They slowed to get a better look at Davis and neither seemed able to take their eyes from Davis or the Ford, which, driver-side door open, idled its lopsided lope. Val saw them exchange looks: Davis, of course.

Tires screeching, a black Corvette pulled into the lot, and Davis whipped around, flinched. In another moment, he seemed to recover.

Davis popped the lid of the car's tiny trunk: inside, a set of golf clubs, a couple of large tool boxes, and a cloth bag, unzipped and disgorging hand-fuls of clothes. Davis pulled out a nine iron and golf ball, handed the ball to Val. "Drop it. Anywhere on the grass."

"You're not going to hit that ball. Not here."

Davis snagged another ball from the golf bag, closed his eyes and dropped it onto the scrub grass. He took a couple of practice cuts with the wedge. He aimed toward the Amazing Grace at the end of the docks. People were in and out of boats, up and down the dock. Someone stopped to watch. "Don't. There are millions of dollars worth of boats in here. Glass. And people."

Davis' body stilled with concentration and he swung. The ball rose with a sharp crack, flew over thirty or forty boats—tuna towers, masts, radar masts, flying bridges, outriggers—a gull veering in his flight toward it, and then it descended above the Amazing Grace—windshields, cabin windows gleaming in the sun. The ball rocketed down. Just clearing the radar mast, it grazed the tip of the tower enough to feather the ball slightly as it dropped down on the far side into the water with a splash. In spite of himself, Val let out a sudden laugh—of horror, relief, maybe delight.

From behind, there was a smattering of applause. Pickup truck doors open, the girls from the supermarket had paused to watch. One put her fingers in her mouth and whistled.

"So, like, are we gonna stand around here all day or what?"

The inside of the car was elegant, the bench seat covered with tuck-and-roll upholstery: the interior of a jewel box. On the dash, five black gaug-es with white numbers set in burnished stainless steel. And the chromed engine, gleaming, was so massive that it seemed to be sitting in their laps. As they swung onto the road, and Val peered through the chopped wind-shield, he heard the loping sound of the cam even into a deep-throated roar as Davis stepped on it. The front end rose with the surge of raw horsepower through the seat. A beast. Val glanced down, noticed the *Miami Herald* on the floor. June 2, 1984. That had to have been at least a day old. When had it become June?

Nothing more was said about Davis' arrival, but it was there between Val and Davis—the fact that he'd ignored Val and done what he wanted. Their father called while Davis was in the shower, again wanting to know if Val had heard anything. "Because if you're lying to me now out of some misplaced loyalty to Davis, please don't. I have to know what's happening. He can't be there."

Hating himself, Val said, "He is not here, Dad!"

He needed just a little more time to figure out how to handle Davis. And when he stepped out of the shower, Val said, "You have to call Dad. I'll give you one more day to get it done." He had been going to say, "and then I'm kicking you out," but things only got worse when you gave Davis an ultimatum. Davis didn't answer now anyway.

They went to a driving range, and, matching drive for drive, they sent balls rocketing towards a dark line of woods beyond the chain-link barrier. Val remembered a goofy place called *Home Plate* outside of town, which had batting cages behind it. Next stop: ludicrous, the *thuck* of the pitching machines, aluminum bats ringing, line drives and foul balls ricocheting off the netting of the cages, hard balls raining down around them from every direction. Davis loved it; they teased each other about terrible pitches they'd chased in games, Davis playing his movie trivia quiz, a line of dialogue, or even a sound effect, his laugh spiraling into a high-pitched, whinnying cascade; they moved on to another place for beer and sandwiches.

Now, another drink, and then, circling the pool table, the two of them playing eight-ball in moody silence, the juke box booming, two guys suddenly coming in the door from the parking lot, and Val looking over to see Davis frozen over his cue in midshot with a look of fear, Davis holding the tip of the cue poised in front of the cue ball, just his eyes moving on the two guys, who were maybe local rednecks in their late twenties, early thirties, big guys in old football jerseys. They walked toward the bar, Davis never taking the shot, his eyes following them, abruptly sliding the pool cue onto the green felt.

"Let's boogie, counselor."

Davis still watching the bar door behind him out of the corner of his eye, he walked quickly toward the '33 Ford. Inside, he started the engine, groped under his seat, accelerating, until the broken white lines solidified into one white line, the road peeling up and flying right at them, a wall, Davis checking the rearview mirror. Suddenly, he relaxed and laughed about something and Val wondered, had he just seen something—or was it his own distrust? He looked at Davis, but could tell nothing from his face. Val dropped his sunglasses, and leaning forward to pick them up, he looked under the seat until he spotted what Davis had been feeling for. A gun. Davis saw him and shrugged. "Big world, lot of creeps. Nothing to worry about, counselor."

Another bar, air thick with smoke and music, Davis withdrawing into moody silence, several times freezing, as if struck by silent lightening, when someone walked into the bar or passed behind him. Val watched him. Where was the gun? Had he brought it in with him? If he couldn't actually feel the fear coming off Davis, then Val would have thought that all of this was just ridiculous, something out of a movie. He now remembered how he'd always been on edge with Davis when they'd been growing up or anytime he'd come into a room—impossible to be aware of anyone or anything but Davis.

And then suddenly the girls from the supermarket were joining them—they'd just gotten off work—and another round had been ordered and everyone was laughing about Davis' chip shot, one of the girls, Brenda, saying that it was just the bitchinest, scariest, wildest thing, though he probably could never do it again, and a few minutes later, she was leaning into Davis' shoulder and neck, talking and smiling, Val couldn't make out what she was saying, and Davis was nodding, still watching the whole room, and then they were getting up to dance. Val watched closely as she put her arm around Davis' waist and they came together in a slow dance; no, he couldn't have been carrying the gun. Though still watching the doors, Davis seemed to relax slightly. Val got up to dance with the other one, Denise. Dance by dance Brenda and Davis moved slower and slower until they were just standing in one spot holding each other, and when Val came back from the john, he looked around and didn't see them, and as if in confirmation, Denise joined him and said, "They've gone back to Brenda's place. I'll give you a ride home," and Val just laughed and said, "That didn't take long."

Within a couple of days, everyone on the docks seemed to know Davis—the guy who'd made that chip shot over the Amazing Grace. He turned up in the middle of the day after his disappearance with Brenda, checked on Val, who was refinishing the cabin, and went off to a poker game on someone's boat. When he came back several hours later, Val was still hard at work. Davis dropped into the cockpit. "Nice boat. How is she?"

Val said she was good, good in rough water, tracked and turned clean, rode and handled well and pretty dry, could take a big sea, just a good boat overall. "How'd you do in the game?"

Davis pulled a handful of crushed bills from each pocket, dropped the money on the table. Val could see it was a few hundred dollars. He put his brush in a jar of thinner, started putting things away. When he looked up, he was surprised that Davis looked exasperated. Val stopped. "What?"

"How much is he paying you for this?" He waved at the work in progress.

"Ten bucks an hour."

Davis shook his head with disgust.

"Hey, you know something, Davis, I've got my reasons."

Davis shrugged. "It's just like fucking everything else. Everyone lies and cheats; you just got caught in someone else's bullshit and they played a bigger and better game, dude." He didn't refer directly to the prosecutor, Craig Benoit, the concealed exculpatory evidence, the case—didn't have to.

As they started out of the cabin, Val picked up the poker money. "Don't fucking look at me like that, Val, you're so great, I'm such a hard case. Like, take your fucking ten dollars an hour. Maybe that's what you deserve after all, pussy."

Val handed him the crumpled bills. Without looking at them, Davis squeezed the money into a tight wad and tossed it overboard, climbed up onto the dock. The money floated intact. Val swore as he watched the bills slowly open in the water, but made no move to go after them as they sank, slid down. Fucking Davis. He climbed off the boat.

Brenda had been waiting for Davis and met him as she came down the dock. When she saw him, she smiled, eased her arm around his waist and fit herself against his side and under his arm with a shy searching smile, and Val saw again how pretty she was: soft, blue eyes, black hair, but more, she emanated softness and kindness. You just felt better in her presence. Beyond whatever else had been going on in the smoke and music of the bar last night, Davis seemed genuinely glad to see her in the light of day; almost, Val thought, relieved to see her, as he had when he'd arrived yesterday and greeted Val. He nuzzled the top of her head with his chin, brushed the hair back from her face and kissed her, and without saying anything more about what had just happened, the three of them went off to a local restaurant for dinner. Soon, Davis disappeared with her, again leaving Val with the sense of things unsaid and undone between them. "Hey, Val, we'll get to things." He wanted to spend this time with Brenda. She was going off tomorrow to see her aunt for a few days over in Greensboro.

The next day, a Friday, Magnus came up late in the afternoon to be ready for an early start fishing Saturday morning. Davis appeared and Val introduced them about the time they were warming up the engines, and within a few minutes, Davis was back from the Ford with a few tools, had the engine hatches open, and was all intensity and concentration adjusting the carburetors, talking head to head with Magnus about some obscure technical detail, Davis pointing out this and that, and of course Davis was coming out tomorrow, didn't have any place he had to be, did he? and even if he did....

...and Saturday after an hour in the Gulf Stream they tied into a decent-sized marlin and Davis swung the doctor's fighting chair and handled the leader perfectly, tagging and releasing the fish while Val ran the boat from the flying bridge. It was just assumed from the way Magnus was talking—*when we're out there next weekend*—that Davis would be on board during the marlin tournament, good luck and good timing because his regular wireman wasn't going to be able to make it, and now with Davis on board, there were the ongoing movie questions starting and stopping along with Davis' sound effects and the sudden, rising laugh, the trivia quiz.... All of his moody, watchful fearfulness was gone, left behind on shore; it was just the boat and the three of them. Out here Davis had this confidence, this optimism, this belief in himself and his luck; it was almost like being kids again when they'd felt invincible in everything—the long vistas to the horizon, the sky enormous overhead, the tuna tower swinging with the motion of the swells, and Davis laughing and turning the chair for Magnus.

Tanned and wind-burned, still moving around the kitchen with the motion of the boat, Val cooked while Davis tuned in a rock and roll station, and they talked happily about the fishing, the boat, the last couple of days, Davis easy and relaxed. Val was sure that this was the way it could be, that they could do something with boats—charter, sell, some kind of business—and that Val didn't have to go back to law school...he couldn't, anyway. And he saw the rest of it now, too. Davis was ready to open up tonight; they'd talk out whatever was bothering him—it couldn't be that bad. Afterward, he'd call his father, reassure him, and maybe, by so doing, get back into his good graces.

The phone rang loud into the room, and Val put down his fork, hesitated as it rang again, and then grabbed the receiver.

"You haven't been answering your phone." His father.

"Dad, I've been out on the boat."

"I'm calling to tell you I've realized that Davis is there now. You've been lying to me about it. Isn't that so?"

"I won't answer when you start like this."

"You've completely disregarded my wishes. You told me you would not let him come there. And that if he did, you'd send him back to Miami."

"God, it's impossible to make someone do something he doesn't want to do. Most of all Davis. Don't you see that?"

"The point is that you've lied, he's there and you can't deny it, and I want you to put him on. Now. Right now!"

Val extended the receiver to Davis, who had stopped eating. Davis shook his head no. Val put his hand over the mouthpiece. "What, you're never going to talk to him again?" Davis pushed back from the table and walked out onto the porch. The screen door slammed. Val said, "He won't talk to you."

His father said, "Make him talk to me!" Again Val heard the desperation in his father's voice. "Why can't you understand me?"

It unnerved him that his father, who was always in control about everything, was completely helpless now. "Dad...I can't get this done for you. I'm sorry. If you want, come down here and talk to him yourself. I just don't know what else to say." When his father still didn't answer, Val said, "If you don't say something, I'm hanging up." There wasn't a sound. "Dad? Please. Say something.... Okay, I'm hanging up." Val hung up.

Davis was outside in the dark. Val started toward the door, changed his mind, took a bite of his half-eaten dinner and slid his plate away. Screen door slapping behind him, Davis came back to the table. "Davis, would you please call him now and just put an end to whatever weirdness is happening here? Please." Davis sat down and started to eat. Val felt the words coming out too fast. "Or, okay, here's another way. Either talk to me or talk to him—one or the other."

Davis stopped chewing. "I've been talking to you."

Val stood more suddenly than he'd intended. Outside, he reached under the front seat of Davis' car, found the gun, and came back into the kitchen. He read in a flat voice, "Beretta. Nine millimeter."

Davis said, "Yep. And ten in the clip."

Val placed it on the table between them. "Start talking to me about this. Why you had to come up here suddenly when no one's heard from you for months. Why you're freaked and watching everyone who comes and goes. What's happened down in Miami, Davis?"

Davis tipped his chair back and crossed his arms over his chest. "Nice try, but I've always kept a piece under my seat."

"A piece. Listen to you. A piece. And bullshit. Since when?"

"Since forever, Val. I'm not going around empty-handed, have some little shit shoot me in traffic."

"But even if it were so, that you have always had a 'piece,' which it isn't— this is the first time I've seen you scared shitless."

"And, like, why should you be the one I have to explain myself to, any-way, Mr. Wonderful? What do you know? You're the dude who's had it all coming to you on a silver platter—fucking Harvard—and then, Mr. Easy, like what, you got a little squeamish because the prosecutors set up some piece of crap beaner, who had it coming to him, anyway, and now you're here running boats up and down the ditch and doing Magnus' boat shit work when all you had to do was keep your mouth shut, your dick up, keep dancing and you could be sitting in an office making a shit pile of money moving paperclips from one side of the desk to the other...."

"You just can't get over that, can you? Like that money I'm not chasing was your money."

"Would if I could. I'm just, like telling you, it could be clean and simple for you, Slick, it was in your hand. Jesus, Val." Davis shook his head with genuine dismay and contempt.

Davis was right. Of course he was right about everything. But wrong. "Dad probably would have told me the same thing, only politer. Maybe not politer, either. I don't know why you can't make the phone call to the old man. You're exactly like him."

"Well, there's only room for one of us and he got there first."

They both laughed.

Val said, "You still haven't explained about the gun." Davis stared past him. "No? Since I went on a goose chase, you could at least tell me if you ever worked at Avenger Boat Works? Speed Marine Service? I went to all those places. No one seemed to know anything about you. Where'd you go after you left the house...glass brick...just one of the stops on my little snipe hunt looking for you?"

Davis stared past him, his face defiant, impenetrable. "I explained about the gun. Take it or leave it."

This was exactly what Val hadn't wanted to happen. You could never get anywhere banging heads with Davis. They sat in a lengthening, moody silence, the music playing, the gun on the table between them....

## *not pretty girl*

When the phone rang in the next moment, Val said, "I'm picking it up. If it's Dad, you're talking to him right now."

"Or what?'

"Or you're out of here."

"Do whatever you have to do, counselor."

The phone rang again and Val snatched it up. When no one spoke, Val said, "Speak. I'm counting to three and hanging up. One. Two...."

"Three!" someone said.

"Who's this?"

"Honey, paranoia's just oozing out of the receiver here," said a woman with a thick Southern accent. "Hey, I'm Davis' little friend who he ditched back in Miami. Lee Anne. Are you the Great Val?"

"Val will do."

"As you wish. Is Davis there?"

Davis mouthed, "Who is it?"

Val put his hand over the mouthpiece. "Lee Anne.... Are you here?"

Davis said to no one, "How in the fuck did she get this phone number?" He stood, the chair screeching.

She said, "I know he's there. Tell by your voice."

Davis shook his head from side to side—dismayed, he still seemed almost pleased. Rubbing the back of his neck, he sauntered over to the phone. As he picked up, his posture changed slightly, as though hollowing himself both to make a space for her and also to protect himself. "Uhhhh...hi...huh.... What? Am I surprised? Uuuuhhh.... I don't know. Do kind of wonder how you put it all together and got the number. Got to hand that to you.... I am glad to hear from you! ... I don't sound it? How do I sound?"

As he talked, he paced back and forth, the phone cord tethering him in a tight circle. "Hey, if you'd let me get a word in I would explain.... Anytime you're finished, just let me know. Finished? ... Finished yet? Okay, first I was not, like, running out on you. I know it looks that way, but.... I wasn't going to leave a phone number lying around...You know exactly why...no, I'm not making excuses.... I had to leave when I did.... You saw the newspaper, Lee Anne! ... I was going to contact you.... Like, you don't believe me...like, fine...then why are you calling me?"

His voice had a hectoring, counter-punching edge to it. Val was sure he was going to slam the phone down. Yet something held him. Perhaps he was locked into having the last word. Val laughed. She was getting to him. Good, let someone get to Davis for once.

"I'm not shouting at you. No... *No, I'm not shouting!* I. Am. Not. Shouting." Davis rubbed the back of his neck, yanked handfuls of his hair. The conversation seemed to twist on interminably.

Davis slumped against the wall and stared across the room. "No, Lee Anne, I have no idea how you got this number.... Why don't you tell me since you're, like, gonna, anyway." He turned, balanced his head against the wall, long blond hair hanging over his face. "Uh huh, cool.... I'm impressed. What do I have to say? What, you want a medal? I, like, sincerely hope you've taken a shower." He was silent a long time, then stood straight up. "You're kidding? Now? Where? You're kidding? Am I surprised? Fuck yeah, I am. Hello?" He laughed. "She hung up." His hair was in wild tangles, his blazing orange-and-yellow rayon shirt looking as if it had been gnawed and gummed.

"Do you wanna know how she says she found your phone number here. Cause like this isn't your place and all? I didn't tell her I was leaving, but she knew I had a brother on a boat somewhere up here. She figures I must have gone to see you. Then she decides she'll get on a bus and look for me. She's halfway to the bus station when it hits her I took out the garbage before I left. She stops the taxi driver and tells the guy to turn around and go back to the house.

"So this is, like, her thinking. If I never take out the garbage, and this time I did, then there must have been something there I didn't want her to find. I fucking ask you, is this a normal chick?

"She hauls ass back, goes to the curb and pulls four garbage bags out of the trash cans. The taxi driver is sitting there waiting. She starts going through each bag, pulling all this shit out right then and there. The whole time the meter is like running. She goes through all four bags." Davis stopped.

"So, what'd she find?"

"Your phone number. I'd written it on a grocery bag after I got it from Dad and left it on the table. She sees something in everything. Misses nothing."

Patting his pants pocket, Davis walked into the bedroom, fumbled around in there, came back out, searched along the counter.

"What're you looking for?"

"My car keys...."

Val pointed. "They're in your hand," Davis looked down. "Where're you going?"

"Where's the bus station in Jacksonville? I need directions. How far is it, anyway?"

"Maybe an hour. Half that, the way you drive, if you actually make it in one piece or don't get a ticket. Why?"

"Pick her up. That's where she called from," Davis had a bemused look on his face.

"Did you ditch her like she said you did?"

"Tell you like the flat ass truth, I'm not sure what I meant to do with her. I just left." Davis looked around, distracted.

"Well, Davis, did you figure on going back to her?"

"I don't know. Not to Miami. Can't. She knows that. No point asking, anyway. She's here now." Still distracted, Davis kept looking around the kitchen as though trying to remember something, but he couldn't seem to focus. "Directions, Val, give me directions...."

Val wrote them out.

Davis left, came back in. "Am I still kicked out of here?"

"Davis," Val said in a weary tone, "just go get her. We'll take it from there."

He turned and went out and the car headlights came on suddenly, brilliant, and the engine exploded, the windows and screens rattling. The screen door slammed once more as Davis burst into the kitchen. Not looking at Val, he grabbed the gun off the table and went out again, revved the Ford several times, and took off, the car's roar fading into silence.

———

Val settled on the old sofa, and, flipping through a magazine, he kept hearing snatches of Davis' conversation with Lee Anne. "You saw the newspaper…" If he could get a *Miami Herald* from the last couple of weeks, maybe he could figure out what had set Davis in motion. It had to have been something. He turned on his side and the print blurred, and the magazine slid to the floor, and Val drifted from room to room going through drawers and closets—he wasn't sure what he was looking for, just that he had to find it, and part of him didn't want to know….

A white light flashed. A roar. Val, with a sudden intake of breath, opened his eyes, headlights burning through the window above the sofa. He glanced at his watch—almost four—heard car doors slamming, the rise of a woman's laugh, the slap of the screen door. Val squinted against the glare of the lights still on, the sudden eddy of smells in the room—perfume, booze, the sweet thick smell of dope—someone leaned over and looked down at him, her face in shadow. She took his hand, a kind of handshake, and he was surprised by her strength, an ammonia quickness in the air, come, lovemaking, something else overpowering. Val mumbled, still half asleep, "Smell like gas in here?"

Voice hoarse and slurred, Davis said, "I tell her not to, but she's always gotta top off the tank and so, like, it all comes gushing up and I'm standing right there…ruined my shoes…." He raised one of the pointed, woven shoes that reeked of gasoline. Val said, "Take 'em off and put them outside," and Davis said, "Good idea, counselor," and he balanced first on one foot and then the other and pulled off his shoes, and Val saw that he had a deep scratch across his neck, something on his cheek. "Bathroom?" she said, Val pointed, noticed that the fly of her jeans was half-unzipped, the button still undone, in fact half torn off, dangling by a few threads, he saw her in isolated detail, as if frozen in a strobe—beautiful gray eyes—there was nothing else but *right now* in them, and yet they were remote, here, not here; one eye was slightly lazy, as if looking at something just beyond; and teeth so unbelievably white, they were beautiful in and of themselves; hair, grown out long and platinum blond, almost to her shoulders, an undercurrent running through it of a neon blue, an aborted dye job, like static electricity; her face seemed to be in pieces which didn't fit together, but that could have been anything—the light, the hour…. If asked, he couldn't have said whether or not she was beautiful. She seemed completely and overwhelmingly here, yet as if part of her were still coming down from a trip, as if most of her had been spent hard somewhere else. He noticed her T-shirt, which was torn—shredded—around the neck; it displayed three words in the blotchy, uneven letters of an old typewriter. As if to head off and settle the very question of her being beautiful, they said:

*not*

*pretty*

*girl*

Val was startled by his own soft laugh.

As Davis turned in the light, Val saw that his shirt was torn in the same way as hers, and Val realized that they'd gone on with their white-hot argument right where they'd left it when she'd hung up; they'd stopped for a bottle somewhere, driven on, her accusations, his denials, she'd maybe grabbed his shirt or slapped at him, and Davis, who never let anyone hit him without hitting back, grabbed her.... When it sorted out, next thing, they were making love.

After his one hundred writhing telephone postures—head against the wall, hands twisted in his hair, cord winding and unwinding around his biceps, Val had expected Davis would not be happy to see Lee Anne. Yet now, except for his face thick with fatigue and stoniness, Davis seemed more completely himself than Val had seen him since he'd arrived.

Lee Anne suddenly came out of the bathroom. "Where we sleepin', Davis-butt?" Davis pointed toward his room, and glancing toward Val, but not quite finding him behind the fall of her hair, she waved, "Hey, sometime tomorrow, Sportin' Life...." He heard the whip of a kind of mockery in her voice. Without looking at Davis, she extended her arm back for him and waggled her fingertips. Barefoot, Davis followed her. "Hey, counselor, we'll pick it up in the morning..."

Val could see them in the bedroom as they shuffled back and forth, spreading out the futon, toeing Davis' scattered clothes aside. As Davis started unbuttoning his shirt, Lee Anne suddenly pulled up her T-shirt with one hand, exposing her naked breasts; with an arm around his waist, she smoothed her breasts against his chest. Val felt himself suddenly catch his breath as Davis kicked the door shut.

Val found himself completely unsettled, disappointed. To put some feeling or question to rest, he'd wanted to see her face, her eyes, just one more time. There was something about her gaze, as if startled, or suddenly struck by an object, and blinded. Now he'd have to wait until morning. The sickly sweet smell of gasoline lingered in the room.

Going into his bedroom, sinking onto the bed, still dressed, he switched off the light and lay in the dark. He turned on his stomach, then onto his side. Something hung in the air. From within, he heard his heartbeat rise loud, then thicken, a muffled cry, a sob; he listened into himself, the sound louder...it seemed to be rising in his ears. And then, from outside himself, he heard a hoarse startled cry, and Val felt himself flush...another cry, sharper. Moving quietly through the bungalow, he could still hear her as he walked outside, Davis' shoes reeking of gasoline beside the door. He left and spent the rest of the night on the Amazing Grace.

In the morning, he splashed water in his face, started coffee. He remembered he needed to wash the hull. Perfect. Something outdoors and mindless. Last night after Lee Anne had come out of the bathroom, there'd been one more thing he needed to put her in focus, something he had or hadn't seen in her face. Once he saw it, he'd know what was happening with Davis, and then what to do next, or maybe, how to do it—Davis, his father, himself—and the whole situation would fall into place. That plan had been interrupted by Lee Anne yanking up her shirt, her naked breasts against Davis' chest. Pushing the memory away, he went to find a bucket, cleanser and a scrub brush.

Standing half-crouched in the dinghy—always a risky business—and holding tight to the Hatteras' gunwale with one hand, Val scrubbed the hull overhead, rock and roll blasting down from a radio on the cabin top. When nothing came out of the hose, Val looked up to see Davis, his hair hanging in a blond corona around his face, the hose doubled in his fist. Davis was silently laughing. Val climbed into the cockpit.

Slumped in the fighting chair, Lee Anne turned, looked him up and down from head to foot. Val couldn't have said what it was in her look—indifference, perhaps mild curiosity or amusement, or was it quizzical disdain?—that made him feel self-conscious, ridiculous, somehow a fraud, and transparent to her gaze. At the same time, he thought that her look might be practiced, a mask, and that it was meant to make him feel diminished. He wiped his face, replaced his sunglasses to hide his eyes, smoothed his wet hair back from his face. He'd been sure that if he could get one more look at her—full-on—he'd know something, but her face revealed nothing, or not the thing he needed to know, and he suddenly felt slighted, wounded—and confused that he would—and quickly went in to change into dry shorts and a T-shirt.

Davis sat on the stern covering board where he could face Lee Anne and also keep an eye on each person coming down the dock. Val called in a voice that seemed forced, "Anyone want a drink?" He brought them out a couple of Cokes. Suddenly nervous, he busied himself, turning down the radio, hosing the sea grass and slime out of the dinghy before it dried.

Val sensed the undercurrent of their sharp quarrel and anger, which had been smoothed over by their lovemaking for the time being. When Davis leaned forward, Val saw the raw blush, a welt on his neck from her nails. Now he could study Lee Anne, her mannequin's platinum blond growing out, one side singed electric blue, as if she were a cartoon cat hit by a jolt of electricity, tail in a socket; the hair was an indecipherable tangle, a welter of half lengths, one section cut short as if someone had started to give her a haircut, and she'd abruptly changed her mind and stopped it; there was also an improbable streak of black like a smear of wet paint; it was an overlay of impulses—which had superseded which?—and reminded Val of a winter garden cut back, an embryo evolving, a bird molting; almost comical, it was not a style so much as a series of vacillations and disruptions and abrupt right turns. Yet the roots themselves glowed a honey color, and Val thought that if she'd just let her hair grow out, untouched, it might be beautiful.

Still not daring to sit, he stowed things away, cleaning up, observing her. The sunlight caught her nails, chipped, dark, metallic, like black-and-blue marks from a hammer, a slamming door. Davis picked up on his energy. *"Fer christsakes,* will you fucking just leave all this crap and sit down...you're wearing out my eyeballs."

"Yeah, just a second." He knew he couldn't sit, didn't dare. He kept moving, making suddenly awkward small talk with his own brother as he wiped out the dinghy, sneaking quick glances at Lee Anne, who didn't bother to look at him, and who, in fact, now seemed oblivious to him. Preoccupied, she pressed her index finger to her pursed lips, pushed them to one side, gnawed the inside of her cheek—repellent gesture! Davis had written that she was a hairdresser. Why would a hairdresser have a tangle of hair like this? Now, finding what he wanted, the last detail, Val made up his mind:

cheap, she was really cheap, another one of Davis' hit-and-run chicks; he furtively looked for Davis' eyes, a conspiratorial glance, an appeal to Davis; didn't he see what she was? Why had he let someone like this jerk him around the way she had on the phone last night; whatever else had happened in Miami—and like it or not, they *were* going to get back to that!—he'd been right to leave her behind. As if she had directly received that thought, Lee Anne looked at Val for the first time this morning, found his eyes with her own, which were a luminous gray. Held, he tried to look away, couldn't, and then managed to do so, shaken.

The eyes were completely immediate, and yet were, somehow… unreachable? Again, as in his first impression last night, he sensed she was consumed elsewhere, perhaps with a kind of petulant grief. And that there was something concealed or not even there in her gaze. He looked back at her to confirm and confront something, but she wouldn't return his look; she stared past him. She was just another one of Davis' cheapo numbers. She sipped her Coke and stared into the sun-splintered darkness under the dock, echoing and cavernous as the tide continued going out…. There was something he had to take care of for Davis, but he still couldn't remember it.

Lee Anne stood, popped the empty Coke can. "Where's the head on this thing? Never mind, I'll find it…." With an edge in her voice, she added, "If I may, please, and by your leave, sir." She walked toward the cabin.

"It's opposite the galley. Push the lever down, pump it, when you're done, pump it again and pull the lever back up. Make sure you remember that or we'll sink eventually."

Davis called after her, "Don't take anything." She didn't turn. "Joke," he called after her. She still didn't turn.

When she was gone, Val said in a hushed voice, "Davis! Who *is* she and what's going on?"

"Like, what?"

"There's something wrong about her."

"She's pissed. She thinks I tried to dump her."

"You did dump her. Said so yourself. But now I can see why."

"I love it, counselor. I really do. You've seen her all of thirty seconds and you can say shit like this." Davis continued to regard Val with cool amusement. "Well, one thing, I've gotta hand it to her. She figured it out and came up. Look, man, she's smart in ways that you can't even begin to imagine.

"If it weren't for her...." He dropped the thought, started again. "Thing is, she's not really a chick you say no to."

"What's that mean?"

"You say no to her, it gets funny. Things come back upside down and inside out." The head door opened. She reappeared in the cabin. "Anyway, it's like too late to leave her."

"Why?"

"Just the way things are between us. I can't go into it now. It wouldn't be too smart to leave her a second time. That would be pushing my luck."

She stepped into the cockpit and they pulled their heads apart and were silent. Now there was nothing veiled about her glance. She seemed to be weighing and balancing the two of them, one against the other. Davis said that she never missed anything.

"Make sure that lever is back in an upright position?"

Without answering, she walked to the other side of the cockpit. Davis followed her and put his arm around her shoulder, but she shrugged him off. They remained side by side looking out at the harbor.

Val and Davis launched ball after ball. Davis' idea: back to the driving range. "Nice try, counselor, but you're dropping your left shoulder. You've always done that. Why the ball's hooking left." Davis drove the ball like a rocket as if to show Val how, grinning at Lee Anne who sat in an old iron chair under a huge tree and couldn't have cared less. But Val became aware that he couldn't stop thinking about Lee Anne, who, lost in the deep shade of the tree, gnawed the inside of her cheek, kept her eyes fixed on Davis from out of her preoccupied distance. It wasn't as though she was interested, but more that she was afraid to let him out of her sight now that she'd caught up with him. When Val looked again, she had a folded page on one knee. She wrote, stopped, frowned, wrote again. A letter? A journal? She was so intensely focused, it had to be important, maybe related to whatever Davis wouldn't talk about back in Miami. Then he saw that it was a newspaper; she was doing the crossword puzzle, and in ink.

Still, when Val walked back to the drinking fountain, he sought her gaze—if he could see one more thing in her face, he could know or confirm something. Teasing several hairs so close she went almost cross-eyed checking for split ends, she was oblivious to him. And remained so as they moved on to the next stop, a bar. Just as they walked in, Davis remembered he'd left his sunglasses back on the counter at the driving range and swung around in the parking lot. Lee Anne shook her head no. "Just leave me here. I'm hot. I'll be here when you get back." They let her out.

Returning to the bar, they stood enfolded in sun-blinded darkness before Val found Lee Anne's platinum blond hair. Someone was sitting on a stool beside her. Close. Something too familiar in the way he leaned toward her, and something pliant in her position on the stool seemed to say it was okay. She had a slight smile and watched him with a coy sidelong glance that told Val she was encouraging the man's interest.

Val thought he saw by the turning of her head, the flash of her face in the back bar mirror, that she had caught sight of Davis, but still she didn't move away. More than anything, this struck Val as odd. She had known they would be coming back any minute. Why would she let a guy sit down and start coming on to her, some idiot in an Atlanta Braves T-shirt. She was just a cheap woman. Val put his arm out to grab Davis. Now was the time to make his point, get him to see what she really was, but Davis was already across the dark bar and sitting down on the other side of Lee Anne. The Atlanta man stiffened and swiveled on his stool. Now Lee Anne drew into herself between both men, her head slightly bowed, her long hair hiding her face. The man half-stood and said something across her to Davis. Val couldn't make out the words, but caught the anger; Davis stood and in the same movement, placed his hand, fingers spread, over the man's face and pushed him back hard; it was the gesture you might use to correct a dog who was about to get up onto the dining-room table. That Davis had done this and not hit him was an insult—as though he were beneath hitting— and was instantly seen that way by a table of men who laughed, suddenly, abruptly, as one. The man staggered backward a couple of steps, reached up and smoothed his face with his hand, as if to take it back, and gathered himself to come at Davis. Saw something in Davis' eyes. Stopped dead. Swearing loudly and trying to save his pride, sour with beer and cigarettes, he pushed roughly by Val, rushed down the length of the bar and slammed out. The men at the table laughed louder. In another moment, Val, Davis and Lee Anne were in the car, a charged silence between the three of them, and Val said, "Davis, I'll be staying on the boat again tonight. Just take me back there now."

———

Unable to break the hold of his fury, Davis dropped him off with a nod; as he backed up, Val heard Davis blurt to Lee Anne, "And you wonder why I left you in Miami…" The rest was lost in the revving engine. Val caught a glimpse of Lee Anne's face behind the gleam of the windshield. Inward. Tortured. Val heard the cam leveling out into a deep roar as Davis turned onto the main road, and as the sound faded, Val realized he'd been holding himself clenched.

In the galley, he opened a beer and slid into the fighting chair. He saw Davis' huge hand over that guy's face. Davis had a great ability for living in the present in ways that Val never could or would. He loved that in Davis. Envied it. Davis acted. Reacted. Maybe some of that was what Val had been looking for in himself…. But then, he wouldn't have wanted to live like Davis. And the wounded exasperation he had heard from Davis in the car…. It was something Val wished he hadn't seen. He almost wanted to believe in Davis' bravado. Davis could pull off the act with everyone else: The chip shot. The handful of money won in the poker game, then tossed on the cockpit floor, then flung overboard in a wad. The '33 Ford, elegant, beautiful, grotesque. And Lee Anne, herself…why would she do something like that in the bar—particularly after Davis had just left her and she'd been so clever and resourceful about finding him and coming so far to catch up with him? Had it been an attempt at a last bit of revenge, gone wrong?

Never mind. He'd send them on their way tomorrow. He thought about her face—there was something more he had to see. She did have, he had to admit, a kind of beauty. Something. Her T-shirt anticipating, deflecting, repudiating possible speculation: *not pretty girl* in misaligned type.

Then he realized with pleasure that by this time tomorrow night he'd be able to call his father and tell him that he'd sent Davis home to Miami. Earn something back from him. He watched a school of shiners dart off the stern, looked down into the water with a child's pleasure. The glint of sunlight, the secret orbit of fish. A dart and flash. Something dark uncoiling beneath. An eel. Without being aware of it, Val went on seeing Lee Anne's face behind the silvery windshield.

But by early afternoon of the next day, they still hadn't shown up, and when much later Val did finally see them sauntering down the dock, each with a hand in the other's back pocket, he already knew that it was Lee Anne who had in some way weakened Val's resolve. The moment had gotten away from him.

# OVERBOARD

## *Broken Glass*

And so they were there.

Magnus and his wife, Regina, came up late that afternoon, and Val helped them carry boxes of groceries, booze, what-have-you from their car to the boat. A short time later Davis and Lee Anne wandered down to the Amazing Grace, and Magnus and Davis slapped hands, old buddies, and here was his friend, Lee Anne, *welcome aboard, honey....*

For the next couple of days, everyone came and went from the Amazing Grace; there were dozens of other boats, people appearing and disappearing to make runs to the store, work on fishing tackle, go out to eat, Davis grease-blackened as he fine-tuned one of the *Grace*'s engines, a wad of cash tossed in the galley: *what was this?* Oh, Davis' poker winnings....

Regina had a new video camera that always seemed to be running in the background. Everyone played to or ignored it except for Lee Anne, who quickly turned from the lens. It was not coyness; it freaked her to be photographed. Strangely, Lee Anne seemed taken by something about Regina, who emanated kindness and acceptance; she would stare at her until it was awkward, embarrassing, almost as if she were childishly infatuated with her. Regina dealt with it as she did everything else, easily, gracefully, never at a loss. She would turn and smile at Lee Anne, who might look away, or ask *can you give me a hand with this*, or offer her a drink. Maybe, Val thought, Lee Anne lacked social graces, or perhaps, she willfully opted to do whatever she wanted. Maybe she was unaware of what she was doing. Sitting next to Regina in a large restaurant booth one night, Lee Anne—too much to drink?—lay her head on Regina's shoulder. Everyone else at first pretended not to notice, but Davis chided her. "What, Lee Anne, a coupla pops and beddy-bye?" And his laugh. But Lee Anne didn't answer or move her head, and Regina put her arm around Lee Anne, fit her head to her shoulder and let her be.

Everything she did seemed to come out of a premise that Val couldn't understand. Was it just him? At times she had a slightly crooked smile, secretive or ironic, which related to nothing going on around her, at least nothing that Val could see, the smile of someone who had a private joke or perhaps was keeping something to herself. Didn't Davis see this? Was Val the only one who noticed—or cared?

She spoke little or not at all, requiring only to stay close to Davis, keep him in sight. She reminded Val of a child in that way. He thought her whole thing was just weird. She slumped in a director's deck chair in the cockpit and did crossword after crossword, did them quickly, puckering her lips, gnawing the inside of her cheek, her gray eyes focused on the page, always working in pen—confidence? Ignorance? Occasionally, he'd hear her murmur, "Informed about…five letters." And then she'd dash off a word into the boxes. Right word? Wrong word? Would she even know? Care? She read a thick paperback folded over, what was it? and then another one, the pages water stained, curling from the sun. Supermarket trash, no doubt. When she said Davis' name, her voice would rise a little, expressing her vulnerability, her love, her desperation, which? Val thought, maybe all three, maybe the three were inseparable. Only half there, she seemed to be biding her time, waiting for Davis, waiting for what? For the threat of his having run from her to subside? To take him back? In the meantime, it seemed enough for her just to keep him in sight.

Recalling her moans of the first night, Val would secretly try to look beneath her face to find her sexual face, the face his brother had seen when she was making love with him. He could find nothing. Though she rarely looked at him, he knew that she was aware of his watching her, and that she was keeping herself a blank.

And still he couldn't stop thinking about or watching Lee Anne. When she ate, she inclined her head on a slight angle toward the table, and like some feral animal, she ate fast, ate a lot, and yet she never seemed nourished. Her cheeks and eyes were hollow, and in fact, she appeared starved, as though all she ate went to feed some inner thing driving her, devouring her. Though Val wanted to approach her, he couldn't find a way. Several times he caught her watching him with a look of quizzical interest, amused contempt, as if to say she knew that this wasn't really him, and that she saw that he was a fraud. How so? He tried to speak to her and each time what he said was exactly wrong. Once as she gnawed her cheek, he imagined the inside of her mouth raw and tasting of blood, impulsively said, "If you chew a hole through it, the thing won't hold water." He instantly regretted it.

Without looking at him or hesitating, she said in a low, even voice, her Southern accent thick, "Fuck off, honey. I'll do what I want." Though embarrassed by his remark, he knew she'd given him the only possible answer, loved its rude fierceness.

Sometimes as he looked at her, she slowly closed her eyes to shut out his gaze, and then it seemed that he had gained something—how, or over what, he didn't know—that strengthened his determination to understand how or why he felt that something wasn't right with Lee Anne, or that there was at least some kind of contradiction in her. She would open her eyes as if to say *I'm still here, go ahead and look.* Val realized that he was caught in some kind of contest with her that he hadn't invited, didn't want, and couldn't seem to exit. Or was he just reading into everything she did?

A sense of apprehension, of fear, hung over her. Didn't it? He recalled overhearing Davis' half of the conversation with her when she first called, one of them mentioning something that had been in the newspaper and connected to his leaving. But from his replies to her, it sounded as though she'd dismissed it as his excuse for his bailing out on her. If Val could get hold of Miami papers starting maybe two or three weeks ago, or farther back, maybe he'd get lucky, get a hit off something, be able to connect it to Davis' actions....

Whatever Davis or Lee Anne had spotted in the paper, Davis' fear was real enough. He still watched everyone who came and went, his face tightening with fear—the flinch Val had seen the first day. Davis wasn't someone who flinched. He obviously felt that the threat wasn't confined to Miami—that it could reach him here. But Lee Anne's fear seemed different. Davis was watching for someone who would come in the door, pull up behind him in a car, walk down the dock or come by boat.... Lee Anne, too, had a fear of someone or something. But it was almost as if it were coming up behind her from, well, from where? Out of the air. It was something Val saw in her eyes. Or was it just him?

He found himself standing in the bow one afternoon, his attention drawn to a purse—Lee Anne's purse—flung carelessly on the V berth. It was large, dark blue, carefully handmade of soft leather, perhaps even elegant, and he had never seen it away from her side. Everything she used went into that bag: her nail polish and remover, her doubled-over paperbacks, a deck of cards for solitaire, her wallet—in fact, he'd joked with Davis about Lee Anne's bottomless bag and Davis had just rolled his eyes. "Women are crazy, all that shit they carry around."

Now Val looked down at several of the items spilling onto the bunk. Touching nothing, he leaned closer and tipped his head sideways. Birth control pills, most of them gone. Two thick books of expert crosswords. He thumbed the pages. All filled. He checked the answers in back. Most right. He was stunned.

He glanced through the cabin into the cockpit. No one around. He could see the corner of a paperback, and he slid it out the rest of the way and looked at the cover. Again he was surprised. It was not the Judith Krantz or Sidney Sheldon novel he had expected. It was Céline's *Death on the Installment Plan*. He moved out of the cabin, listened. He thought he heard voices coming down the dock. They stopped, veered away. He felt himself drawn back for one more glance. Her wallet was half out of the bag—he flipped it open. He saw her driver's license in a smudged plastic holder. Lee Anne Wilder. DOB April 7, 1962. She had turned twenty-two almost two months ago. Blond hair in the picture. He flipped the next plastic frame. A University of Florida picture ID. Tiny picture. Also with blond hair. He looked closely. It was her. He quickly thrust it back into the wallet. This was more than enough. He hated even the smallest of deceits or invasions of privacy. Still, her things had been carelessly flung out in plain view—or, almost, he told himself.

But, unable to move, he remained. Again he felt something indefinable, an atmosphere, hanging over her. Or was it him? Here was this girl from a small Florida town—hadn't Davis written that? Or had he imagined it? He'd assumed from her hair, her presence, her accent, that she was ignorant, a lowlife. So many things seemed to confirm it. Always painting and repainting her nails, no sooner finishing than starting again, as if she were endlessly making and remaking herself, revising herself, trying to get it right. And that weird thing she'd done with Regina the other night, laying her head on Regina's shoulder, what was that? Unless she had been drunk, and Val thought she hadn't been that far gone. And her slouchy posture…something just didn't fit, either in the way he was seeing things or in the way he expected them to be—or else it was her—or both of them. Céline?

He noticed one of her T-shirts flung beside her bag and, without thinking, he reached for the shirt, weighed it in his hand, and then, raising it to his nose, he breathed in the thick scent of her perfume, skin, hair. He sensed people had come aboard. Shirt still pressed to his nose, he glanced into the cockpit and froze. She was staring at him. Their eyes met, and he knew he'd just given her something that he'd been fighting not to surrender.

Acutely embarrassed, Val made a show of busying himself—remaining inside the boat until he heard Davis and Lee Anne leaving again. He thought of the enclosed screened porch of the bungalow and how nice it had been in the afternoons before Davis and Lee Anne had shown up. Egrets and herons and ospreys in the estuary. That's where he'd go. Baseball hat pulled low over his eyes, sunglasses on, he eased quietly up the dock.

Ahead, Lee Anne and Davis were walking slowly, their backs to him. They sauntered, bouncing off each other in a playful rhythm, pushing each other. Lee Anne whispered something to Davis, and they laughed, and Val was sure she was joking about his smelling her shirt—it hadn't been what it looked like, just a moment's idle curiosity. Val slowed his pace and pretended an interest in one of the boats, waiting for them to get to Davis' car and drive off. He saw someone moving toward Davis and—how could he have forgotten?—this was what he'd been trying to remember: to warn Davis to call Brenda before she got back from her aunt's, tell her that things had changed, that Lee Anne was here. Davis hadn't yet noticed her, and Val saw her open look of softness and tenderness for Davis, then saw her realize that Davis was *with* that woman beside him; Brenda froze, looked for a retreat. Too late. Davis noticed her and suddenly stopped laughing. Lee Anne stiffened. She looked from Brenda's face to Davis', back to Brenda's, and then let out a sudden cry, slapped him hard, once, twice—his sunglasses flew off—flailed at him with both hands until Davis caught her wrists. He pushed her back once so hard that she staggered. Val thought, no, Lee Anne, don't hit him again, Davis never let anyone hit him without hitting back—in fact, this was the only time Val had ever seen Davis not do so. Lee Anne turned and walked quickly toward the road; Davis said something to Brenda, reached out his hand to her. She pushed it away and walked off. Davis picked up his sunglasses, straightened them. A number of people on the boats and dock had stopped to watch.

Now Davis spotted Val, and they walked toward each other. Davis shook his head. "Okay. Just don't say it." Davis rubbed several scratches on his wrist. "Hey, it wasn't my fault. There isn't time to talk now. I've got to go get her before she does something weird." Val saw Lee Anne walking toward the main road. "Look, can you do me a big favor? It's too soon to bullshit her, like, seriously, but I'm going to try to pick her up and drive her back to the bungalow. She'll fight it, but she'll go…. Hey, I didn't fool with Brenda to bust anyone's chops. I never thought Lee Anne would end up here. And it was over…."

"One day it was, next day it wasn't…."

"Will you please, like, shut the fuck up, please. I'm trying to talk to you. I said I'm going to drive her back." Davis remembered his sunglasses and slid them on. They were bent, crooked on his face. Ridiculous. Val tried not to laugh. Davis straightened them, tried again. "Just do me the favor now. Ride with me while I take her back."

"Davis, I don't want to be part of it. If you can work it out with her, go ahead."

"Your being there will keep her cooled out till I can do the next thing."

"What if she won't get in the car?"

"She'll get in the car! Hey, man, I'm telling you I, like, need this."

He started toward the car and Val swore and followed him. By now Lee Anne was out of the parking lot and walking toward the main road, her hair hiding her face. Davis jogged over to the roadster, gunned the engine as Val got in. They caught up to Lee Anne. He rolled slowly beside her. "Lee Anne…come on, babe…." She kept walking. "I can explain it." Val shook his head. "Just give me a chance." Val didn't know whether to laugh or what…. It was just so ludicrous, such a lowlife scene. The car was going slowly enough that Val contemplated stepping out. "Babe, just look at me." Lee Anne kept walking without looking at Davis—walked with a completely different posture than Val had seen before, her head high, arms swinging, as if she had momentarily regained some part of herself—and suddenly Davis pulled up, jumped out, dashed across the road and put his arms around her, tried to hug her. She pushed him away. Half-hugging her, half-dragging her, he pulled her over to the roadster. "Lee Anne, I love you!" He pushed her in on his side, the driver's side. Val yelled, "Davis, what are you doing?" Lee Anne struggled, then stopped and went almost limp, staring straight ahead in a show of contempt and resignation. Davis said in a pained and tender voice, which Val wished he wasn't hearing, "Lee Anne...babe...it's not like that...it's only you."

Disgusted, Val said, "Davis, I'm getting out."

Before he could, the car shot ahead; Davis tapped the brakes once as he came to an intersection, the light, already yellow, turning red; he blasted through oncoming cars to the sudden sound of horns. Then he was on the main road out of town, four or five cars and a pickup strung out ahead; Davis downshifted, almost touching the bumper in front of him, pulled to his right onto a loose shoulder. As Davis slammed into third, Val felt the power surge through the car. Fishtailing on the sandy shoulder, Davis shot by the right side of one car after another until they were up to the first car in the string, which had put on its right turn signal; they flew past the car, just missing it as it started to turn in front of them.

Davis smiled at Lee Anne. She wouldn't look at him, but defiantly crossed her arms in front of her chest. Val could feel her breath coming quickly. Davis had terrified her, was mocking both her and Val. Val felt her weight against him, became aware that he was holding his breath.

They pulled up in front of the bungalow, and Davis let Lee Anne out. Following her, he tried to take her hand. She pulled away, and again Val, watching from the car, wished he were someplace else, wished they were gone; Davis seemed to be pleading with her. She shook her head, wouldn't look at him; she walked onto the porch and gazed toward the estuary. Davis stood outside the screened porch staring at her back for some time, the 350 keeping up its tethered, loping rhythm. When she still didn't turn around, he got back in the car. "When she gets like this, I just leave her alone. She made her point. She's not going anywhere now."

Beers untouched, they'd been avoiding each other's eyes; Davis had again positioned himself with his back to a wall where he could watch people coming and going. Val kept fighting the urge to turn around. Why couldn't Davis just talk about whatever was bothering him? Davis took a gulp of his beer, replaced his glass, and spread his enormous hands carefully on the table, like a gymnast about to press up into a handstand. Val looked at Davis' fingers, etched in grease, nicked and cut, and remembered how their mother had once taken Davis' swollen hand between both of hers after a football game. Val felt an upwelling of love and admiration for Davis.

"Davis," he said softly, "Davis…listen to me…"

Without looking at Val, Davis said, "Hey, I know things are fucking up…." He lapsed into uncertain silence, then, as if to justify something, he started talking about meeting Lee Anne. Where? Getting a haircut at the Allure College of Beauty, in Miami. Val laughed. Davis said, "No, I'm serious. That's the name. The Allure College of Beauty. After they do the basic *yakkaty yak*, students get the rest of their shit together on live heads. Big sign up front says it all: 'We cut your hair at your own risk.' Dollar fifty.

"So I go in there one day and my regular dude's been graduated out and there are a couple of chicks I've never seen before, Lee Anne, someone else at the next chair…. I sit down to wait. The girl beside Lee Anne finishes up, instructor comes over, a snip here, a snip there and then, you know, nice job, she waves me over, and I sit in her chair and she excuses herself for a second, I'm kind of staring into space, *da de dah*, Lee Anne's—I don't know her name yet—she's cutting someone in the next chair and next thing she's like a blur…

"No time to think. She's falling. Later, when I looked, it's a linoleum floor covered with hair, and she was wearing these, you know, flat chick shoes worn down in the backs to where they're hard and slick on the sole…"

"She skidded?"

"Yeah. And she's falling backward…I kinda half–come up out of my chair and catch her. She lands, like, on her back in my arms, scissors just under my Adam's apple. She's looking straight up at me. She can't say a word. Hey, she would have split her head open on the arm of the chair or broken her neck. I'm talking, like, her feet out from under her, body horizontal and three feet of air between her and the floor. Falling body.

"First item is the scissors. I don't wanna startle her. I say, soft as I can, 'Okay. You're okay. Let's lower those scissors.' After a second, she remembers, oh yeah, the scissors, and she lowers them. Then I stood her up slowly on her feet. After she pulled herself together, she said, 'Least I can do is cut your hair.' Chick is shaking all over.

"I say, 'Okay, cut it short.' My hair was down to here." Davis touched his shoulders.

"She said, 'How short?'"

"I said, 'A buzz cut.'"

"And so, dig this. She stares at me in the mirror. She's not moving a muscle. I'm starting to think, did she hear me, does she understand?

"She hangs for about ten seconds. Then she shrugs and turns on the clippers. She brings them over to my scalp and then she stops."

"I'm waiting. I look at her in the mirror, like, what're you doing? She turns off the clippers and puts them down. She says, 'I'm not gonna do it.'

"I said, 'What do you mean, you won't do it?'

"She says, 'Can't. Won't. It's too beautiful to buzz.'

"I say, 'You do this with all your customers?'

"She says, 'Whadya want a haircut like that for?'" Davis laughed. "You *ever* have a barber ask you that one? Ever? She reaches down and starts to pull the sheet off me and I grab her hand. 'Maybe I should have let you fall.' She doesn't answer. I say, 'Like maybe I shouldn't have caught you.' She won't look at me. I let her hand go and start laughing. By now I really like this chick. I ask her what's her name and I say, 'Okay, Lee Anne, why don't you just give me the best haircut you think I should have. How's that?' And so she gives me the haircut she wants." Davis laughed.

"Was it any good?"

"Yeah, it was just fine. I thought that's that, but I went back to work and kept thinking about her and finally I swung by after she got off work. I'd just finished the '33 Ford and she starts laughing when she sees it in the parking lot. She goes to get in and then she stops. 'Now what?' I say.

"'I'm waiting for you to open my door.'

"God, this woman cracks me up. I said, 'I thought all the bullshit was about we weren't supposed to open your doors anymore.' She waited. I laughed and opened the door. But she doesn't get in. She walks around the car slowly. She gets all kind of dreamy. 'It's beautiful. It's a work of art.'" Davis derisively imitated her voice, but Val knew that Davis really did think of his car that way.

"Finally, she got in, and we took a ride up the coast and went back to her place, this hole in the wall, and next thing I knew it was two weeks later and I was living there with her." Still watching the doors, Davis dropped his chair forward, and Val came back from Davis' catching Lee Anne as she fell behind the barber chair, the look on her face and tone of her voice when she'd first seen Davis' car and told him it was beautiful, Val's sudden envy for when they went back to her place. He pushed the feeling away, but knew that this was why he had to get her to leave as soon as possible. As Val looked at Davis' face, he realized that despite what he said or how he acted, he really did love her, perhaps even more than he knew. Maybe, along with everything else in Miami, he'd been running from his love for her.

Davis said, "Val, about Miami...." He stopped. "Look, some things are happening there, stuff that's gotten way out of hand." He shook his head. "For your own good, it's safer for you not to know."

"Davis, just talk to me. We'll sort it out."

Davis emptied his glass, leaned forward, glanced around the room. Val could see he was trying to make up his mind. The waitress appeared. "Another beer?" Davis shook his head no. She walked away.

When he looked back at Davis, Val saw the mood had been broken. "Davis. Talk to me."

Davis slapped the table, looked around. He found the clock behind the bar, "I've gotta get back to Lee Anne." Davis dropped some change on the table and walked out ahead of Val.

They stopped behind the bungalow. The area outside the back door was covered with broken glass. Davis stepped gingerly over the shards, reached up and carefully extracted a large piece that hung precariously in the window frame. He pushed open the door. Calling Lee Anne's name softly, he went inside. Had she thrust her hand through the top half of the door by mistake? Looking for blood, Val followed. Davis pushed wide the doors to their bedrooms and the bathroom. She wasn't there. Val picked up the trash basket and broom.

Carefully, he extracted each remaining fragment of glass from the top half of the door, then picked up the largest pieces from the floor. Davis said, "I don't know."

Val said, "I do. That back door's always open. She slammed it so hard the glass shattered out of its frame. I can't have this. I'm not blaming her for everything—some of it's your fault. I mean, Brenda. Who wouldn't be mad?"

"I came alone. I thought I was going to be alone."

"She found you. You're half-glad she found you. You're pissed off. You love her. You don't. It's both of you." Val picked up another large chunk and dropped it in the basket. "Either she goes now by herself or you can both go. If you do decide to stay, you call the old man before you get on the boat in the morning." Davis didn't answer. "Davis? Call him or don't get on the boat with us. Lee Anne leaves no matter what."

But Davis wasn't listening. He was looking behind him. Val turned and saw Lee Anne watching them through the screen at the far end of the porch. She walked away. Val said in a lowered voice. "How long's she been standing there?"

"I don't know. Long enough to hear us." He shook his head.

## Cheating at Solitaire

When the sun was slanting green fire through the sea grass and bulrushes in the estuary, Val saw Lee Anne and Davis throwing long shadows across the sandy track as they walked toward the house. They were several steps apart and not looking at each other, and appeared not to be speaking. They came in and Lee Anne went into their room and closed the door. Davis walked to the refrigerator and poured two glasses of ice water, walked across the kitchen with the same kind of sullen menace with which he used to run the bases. He went into the bedroom and kicked the door shut, and then it was dead silent. Val quietly left and drove over to the Amazing Grace, where he had dinner with Regina and Magnus, and Gary, his captain, who had come in for the tournament; they talked over the moon and tide and wind direction, the water temperature and the movement of the Gulf Stream and fishing conditions, Gary and Magnus doing the talking, Val mostly listening, and then, suddenly tired, Val excused himself and climbed into one of the midship bunks. He read half a page of a magazine and then turned out the light; he listened to the water against the hull; the toneless drone of a marine radio carrying across the dock; the thrum of an idling engine; the rising high whine of an outboard boring through the water, a woman's sudden laugh.

Coffee cup warm in hand, Val stood alone in the predawn chill contemplating the Amazing Grace, her outriggers, the stainless steel ladder to the flying bridge, all streaming dew and night sea mist, the random sounds of people coming to life drifting across the water—the clatter of a plate, a weather band, the whine of a bilge pump....

He sipped his coffee, spotted Davis coming down the dock. Val climbed off the boat and walked toward him. Without looking at Lee Anne, he said,

"Excuse me," and lightly took hold of Davis' arm above the elbow to turn him in his direction. Davis shrugged him off, said something to Lee Anne, and then followed.

"You didn't take care of anything, did you? Obviously didn't send Lee Anne away. Didn't call Dad." Davis crossed his arms. "I see you think you're taking her on the boat today."

"Hey, counselor, Magnus invited her right from the get-go."

"It's not about Magnus. It's you and me. You said you'd take care of certain things."

Davis' face seemed to narrow when he angered and it did so now. He took a step to one side, and without thinking, Val moved back. He'd seen Davis knock a guy cold at a party, once, hit him so fast he'd never seen it coming.

Davis shook his head, "God, you're an even bigger dickhead than I thought."

"Right. Guess you never should have come up here looking for me." Val started for the boat. "You'd better give her some Dramamine. I don't think Magnus wants someone out there puking all over his boat."

Davis laughed. "She doesn't get seasick. You're too much, counselor. You really are."

A few minutes later, Davis and Lee Anne came aboard.

The Amazing Grace eased her way into a line of boats heading out through the channel as the sun came up out of the ocean, long flat rays burning the hulls orange, gleaming off their windows and brightwork, the smell of diesel and gas fumes pungent in the air. Davis wore a white sun visor, his long blond hair spilling down the back, hair reddish-gold in the sunrise where he stood beside Magnus and his captain, Gary, on the flying bridge, their faces lit by the sun clearing the horizon as everyone silently turned to watch it. Val thought of the time they'd been in the Bahamas, almost eleven years before, he and Davis still kids, and the moment he'd seen the water silently go from gray to golden, the turning of the Earth in a breath, coral heads and the hull itself casting shadows on the bottom. Davis turned back to Val, and Val was sure that Davis was remembering that time; for a second he felt how he had enfolded Davis within his protection when they were kids—skin–diving, or on a ball field, or a boat, or anywhere. As big and difficult as Davis had become, it was still there in Val, his awareness of that child presence.

———

As they cleared the last harbor buoy, they fell in behind other boats swinging onto their courses. Slowly increasing speed, the sound of their engines rising and drifting across the water, one after another they set off for the Gulf Stream. Val watched the bow of a Bertram come up out of the water, her wake widen and flatten out, a coppery sheet of spray rise from her midship chines.

They, too, the crew of the Amazing Grace, cleared off the flying bridge and went below, the engines rising to a roar as they opened up. Val felt the Hatteras' bow lift as she planed up to cruising speed—exploding a wall of spray through the Bertram's wake, the harbor and the shallow greenish-blue water of the coast falling behind them. Val glanced at his watch. It would be a while before they found the Gulf Stream. As if sinking into a trance, Magnus sat down beside Regina on the bank seat, Davis and Lee Anne on the other side, together, but separate, uneasy in their postures. Val could see the sharp undercurrent of Davis' quarrel with Lee Anne, that terrible moment for Lee Anne when she'd recognized the tenderness for Davis in Brenda's face…. Except for the few words on the dock and in the car, he hadn't seen Davis actually say anything to her, didn't know if she was speaking to him. Thinking of nothing, Val gave himself over to the motion of the boat, the drone of the big engines. No one spoke. When Val looked back again, the Carolina coast was a thin line on the horizon, and when he looked once more, it was gone and there was nothing but water in all directions and no boats visible.

Outriggers lowered to forty-five-degree angles, the water of the Gulf Stream clear and blue and moving in a soft, easy swell, Magnus, huge in the fighting chair, trolled a belly-rigged mackerel. Val watched the bait riding the wave just in front of the wake. Gary and Davis were out of sight overhead on the flying bridge. They'd been trolling maybe half an hour when Davis shouted, "Starboard side! Five yards behind the bait!" Val and Regina rushed to the stern.

Val saw it, pointed. He turned to Magnus. "Big!"

Gary shouted down. "He's hanging back. Magnus, make sure you've relaxed that drag."

Lee Anne looked up from her book in the general direction of the excitement, and Val thought he'd point the marlin out to her, but he saw from something in her face that she didn't really care, or perhaps it was almost as if she didn't want to see the fish; she actually seemed to avert her eyes, look the other way. He thought she might be uneasy in such a vastness.

Val watched the marlin, a slightly darker blue than the water. Swimming effortlessly, motionless, he hung behind the bait. Gary maintained speed and no one spoke.

Magnus yelled up. "What's he doing?"

Gary called, "I'm waiting to see. Looks like he's just window-shopping."

"What do you think he runs?"

"Gettin' up there. Six, maybe seven hundred pounds. He'd be a winner."

"Has he colored up?"

Before marlin attack, they light up like neon signs. When hungry, they are voracious, can eat a small sailfish or a thirty-pound dolphin. "No color, but let's just hang on. I don't want to spook him."

"What're my options here?"

"Options are slight turn, speed up, slow down, drop the bait back, or reel up."

Val watched the silent blue shape. It rolled up slightly with the swell, swam motionless.

Val glanced at his watch. It had been twenty minutes since Davis had spotted him.

"Let's do something."

Gary shouted, "I'm going to make a slow turn to starboard."

Regina raised her video camera. Gary brought the Amazing Grace into a gradual turn. When they looked back, the bait was alone in the water. Val felt something go out of him. No one spoke, each waiting for the marlin to reappear. When he didn't, Regina said, "Maybe he'll be back, Magnus."

But the fish was gone and didn't reappear, and after a few more minutes, Gary changed course; Magnus heaved a big sigh, drank some water and ate half a sandwich and a huge handful of cookies, and Val turned away and laughed at the cookies, a child's greedy handful. After that they tried a succession of weed lines, followed changes in water color, depths, spotted gulls working over a school of bait fish, all of which yielded nothing; they changed baits, tried artificial lures, which allowed them to troll at a faster speed, cover more ocean—important, as blue marlin are scarce. Nothing more appeared.

With the sun starting to slant down in the west, Magnus reeled in. They secured the outriggers, Gary came down from the flying bridge, and they swung around and started back. Again, everyone fell into the silent trance brought on by the motion and speed of the boat, the roar of the engines. When Val looked over at Davis, he saw he was staring off into the distance, his eyes very blue and clear, and Val realized that they had avoided each other all day; for Val it was like something stuck in his throat; he could barely speak or look at Davis. He wondered if it was the same for Davis, or if he really didn't give a damn as long as he got to do whatever he wanted whenever he wanted. He glanced across the cockpit at Lee Anne; their eyes met, and Val recognized the face that he'd seen through the porch screen yesterday when she'd overheard him talking to Davis; he realized that she blamed him for whatever wasn't working here with Davis. He was the one who'd said that she had to go. Out of the corner of his eye, he saw her slide her hand over toward Davis. Whether it was intentional or a coincidence at that moment, Davis got up and stood beside Gary at the helm. She stared at his back, bit the inside of her cheek. She looked both furious and frightened. Val stood and made his way back into the stern, watched the wake curling up. He tried not to think about her.

As they reached the dock, Magnus pointed over to the weigh station. There was a crowd and TV news people. They walked around in time to see a thick line noosed around the narrow tail section of a blue marlin; she was being stood up in the cockpit by four or five guys and hoisted on block and tackle under the supervision of the weighmaster. She rose in the air until her tail reached beneath the crossbeam and she was weighed in at 454 pounds, two pounds deducted for the weight of the line. A second marlin, bigger, was hoisted out of a second boat. Val felt the uneasiness he always felt when he saw something this big, this beautiful, out of its place. Long and powerful, supported by a dozen hands, she floated overhead, inched up to the crossbeam, and Val looked at her as if seeing a marlin for the first time, her sharp dorsal fin, long black rapier bill, the inky blue of her back, the dark vertical lines on her silver-white sides, and her slender tail, tapered, scythe-like, the source of her huge power: the marlin in black silhouette against the slanting sun.

The boat owner moved slowly, exhausted from his three-hour fight—he said his hands were still numb, his arms and legs tingling. He walked stiffly, but when the numbers went up on the board, 587 pounds, he pumped a fist overhead. This made him the leader. Other marlin brought up to a boat and appearing to be smaller than this one had to be released—tagged if crews could—rather then taken. It was the present standard for the tournament. Val noticed Lee Anne standing apart from the crowd, and as he'd seen earlier, she seemed to keep her eyes averted from the fish. Something about it seemed to terrify her.

They'd been trolling almost an hour. The sky was again clear and blue, the Gulf Stream calm, Davis on the flying bridge with Gary, Regina and Lee Anne in the shade beneath, Magnus in the fighting chair. Val made a couple of attempts to approach Davis, but Davis put up his hand. "Hey, I don't wanna hear it, counselor."

Now Val saw a white wake appear on the water behind the bait, heard Davis yell, and in the same instant, there was a huge boil. The line snapped from the end of the outrigger, and a hundred yards screamed off the reel in the intake of a breath. Magnus struck the fish, each time lowering the rod tip, then pulling it back up. There was a sudden thrashing on the surface and then nothing, and the line went slack. Magnus swore. Hands shaking with adrenaline, he reeled in. Gary crouched on the aft deck of the flying bridge, and they talked back and forth about remembering to hold off, letting the line drop back first.

They rerigged the line with a new swivel and wire leader and set another belly-rigged mackerel. Silence settled over the boat but for the low hum of the engines and sighing of water against the hull. Val watched the surface intently for several minutes. Just as he turned to go into the cabin, he sensed something, perhaps movement or a change in the color of the water. He shaded his eyes with the flat of his hand, looked back outside the wake.

A long slender form, darker blue than the water, had silently appeared behind the bait, perhaps a yard below the surface. It swam easily, but hung back, did not move closer. Then the bait disappeared with a sudden splash. Davis yelled from above, "He hit it with his bill."

The bait popped back up, and Gary slightly increased their speed. He shouted, "Magnus, free spool the reel! Let the bait fall back!"

Magnus released the drag, and keeping his thumb on the line to keep it from snarling, he let the forward motion of the boat strip line off his reel.

Gary yelled, "He's taken it now! Okay, put the drag back on!" As soon as Magnus engaged the drag, the line dropped from the outrigger.

Magnus yelled, "I feel his weight back there!"

"Keep the rod tip up, but don't strike it yet! Don't!"

Heart pounding, Val watched the line running steadily off the reel. It seemed to go on forever. God, he thought, strike it!

Gary yelled, "Don't strike!" The line kept running out. Gary shouted down, "Now!Strike him!"

Magnus spread his feet wide and braced them on the rest. He lowered the rod tip, and, putting his whole body behind it, he pulled back up hard. He did this three times in succession, the rod bowing. Then, nothing. Val looked at the line. Gone slack? He couldn't tell. Line broken? Or the hook thrown?

The marlin exploded out of the water, shaking his huge head, trying to throw the hook. The fish hung in the air, silhouetted against the brilliant blue water and lighter blue sky, his back inky blue, belly silver, sides stripped with vertical slashes. He plummeted back down like a block of concrete, throwing up a sheet of white spray. Davis whooped. In quick succession he exploded into half a dozen more spectacular leaps, each time writhing and throwing his head, each leap bowing Magnus' rod. The marlin came up once more, tail-walking an unbelievable distance against the horizon, water boiling white beneath him. Gary yelled, "He's hooked in the corner of his mouth!" which meant the fish was going to be much harder to control. The marlin crashed back down and then sounded, tearing off several hundred yards of line so fast that the reel turned hot—Val saw Magnus jerk his hand away.

Now Val reeled in the second line and went behind the fighting chair, turning it in the direction of the fish. For the next four hours, Magnus fought the fish, reeling in eighty—one hundred yards, the marlin suddenly taking back that much line and more, making run after run until half the line from the reel was gone and Magnus was completely drenched with sweat. As it was forbidden by tournament rules to have a second person assist, Val was careful not to touch the rod or reel in any way. Help would be allowed only when the swivel above the wire leader reached the tip of the rod; then someone could handle the wire to bring the fish into the boat for gaffing. That would be Davis' job—if they got that far.

As the marlin swam, Gary kept the boat behind the fish, and after some time he could angle up beside him, creating a belly of slack that dragged between the boat and the fish, helping to tire him more quickly. Meanwhile, Val and Regina talked to Magnus, and Regina applied a damp towel to his head and neck.

Now Gary started backing down on the fish. Each time, Magnus took in a little more line, and each time the fish ran again, but his runs were shorter, and Gary kept backing down, and Magnus kept reeling, and the marlin kept running. Twenty, thirty times Gary backed down on the fish until Val lost count, and Magnus' eyes were glazed and feverish, his mouth and cheeks slack with exhaustion. For a man of Magnus' size and strength. Val couldn't have imagined it possible.

Gary shouted from the flying bridge, "Watch it! Hang tight. Lots of them will try to sound about now, and then they die down there. It's almost impossible to get them back up when they do!"

With each new run, Val saw Magnus trembling, hanging on, trying not to give the marlin enough line to make that dive, but not to keep the drag so tight it could snap. Davis suddenly came down the ladder from the flying bridge and pulled on his padded wireman's gloves, stretched, swung his arms around to loosen up. Val surveyed the cockpit to make sure that everything was secured—boat hooks, tagging pole—that there was nothing anyone could slip on.

Now the marlin was closer, though the swivel wasn't yet anywhere near the rod tip, and Val could see the fish shimmering up out of the deeper water into the sunlight; closer still, just beneath the surface, he made a sudden spectacular leap, drenching everyone in the cockpit with water and releasing in each of them something between a howl and a laugh and a cheer for the fish. Davis shouted, "God, I love you!" and again he ran, and again Gary backed down on him, and Magnus reeled, and now the swivel came to the rod tip, and Davis stretched across the covering board beyond the tip and grabbed the wire leader and gathered it toward him, his face narrow and intent, his whole body flexed and alert; he took a wrap with one hand, then other, drawing the marlin closer to the boat. Val divided his attention between Davis, who never took his eyes from the fish, and the marlin, which was suddenly on his side: long, streamlined, shimmering, iridescent, its scythe-like tail moving slowly. Taking a wrap at a time with each gloved hand, Davis gathered the wire, each time pushing with his foot to make sure the wire already gathered was well clear of his body and behind him. Round black eye moving, the fish rolled back onto his stomach. Val yelled, "Watch it, Davis! He's going to run! Let him go! Let him go!"

Davis pointed his gloved hands and opened them in the direction of the marlin just as he flexed and the wire unwrapped cleanly and fell away. Davis stepped clear of the remaining wire leader which instantly disappeared off the deck; the fish ran, leapt again, splashing them, and without thinking, Val felt for his wire cutters on his belt to make sure they were there. He opened the tuna door and there was the water awash at the stern. There was no question that this fish was bigger than yesterday's leader and that they were going to boat it if they could.

Again, Magnus fought the swivel back to the tip of the rod and again Davis gathered it, and after several wraps, Val saw the fish again flex. Val shouted a warning, "He's running! Let him go!"

And again Davis opened his hands and stepped clear of the wire and the fish ran, and again Magnus fought him back to where the swivel was at the tip of the rod. Once more Davis gathered the wire leader in and wrapped, and now, pulling up, half crouched, braced with his whole body, wrap by wrap he drew the wire in, and the exhausted fish came alongside the boat. Val brought out the gaff, reached overboard, and had the gaff in the marlin's side. Blood clouded the water, and, Davis beside him, their arms entwined on the handle, wary, they guided the fish around to the stern, and suddenly had his head in front of the tuna door. Davis grabbed his bill with both hands, and Val and Davis heaved with everything they had. Magnus lowered the rod and dropped to the deck beside them. Slipping, falling to their knees, they heaved, and the marlin, huge and magnificent, slid aboard in a wash of seawater, tail hanging out of the tuna door. Drenched with sweat and seawater, on their knees, panting, the three of them stared at the fish in silence. Val fought back a sudden rise of uneasiness at taking something this beautiful from its place in the water.

When Val looked up, Regina's camera lens glinted hard and bright at him. Overhead, Gary was looking down from the flying bridge, and Val became aware of Lee Anne, her eyes darting back and forth from the fish to Davis, who was still on all fours beside it. Gills heaving, black eye still moving up at the sky, the marlin lay motionless, the only sound that of its gasping. No one spoke. No one moved. The marlin went on gasping.

When Val came back out of the cabin, Davis and Lee Anne had disappeared and Val saw them walking up the dock. The fish had been weighed in, 641 pounds, a new leader. Everyone exhausted, they could take a day off tomorrow, see what other boats brought in. As Val hosed blood and scales out of the cockpit, he realized he didn't want to see another marlin boated. Catch and release was one thing, but there was just something about taking these fish. It occurred to him that maybe he was finished here. If nothing else, at least a day off tomorrow seemed good. But then, at the last possible moment, someone had come in with another big marlin. Six hundred and forty-nine pounds. Magnus groaned, but then decided that if he was going to make a real run at the tournament, second place wasn't good enough, and though the odds were against it, he'd have to go out again in the morning. And that's where they left it. Val finished hosing off the boat and started up the dock.

Newspaper under his arm, he paid for the Coke and then looked around the café. He wanted to be alone, spread out the sports page, and forget everyone and everything. As he turned, he could still feel the boat lurch and roll beneath him and the café go airless after the motion of water and openness of sky all day. He looked for an empty table and saw Lee Anne alone in a booth. Sideways to him, she held a deck in her hand and was looking down at the cards spread on the table. Solitaire. She may or may not have seen him. Leave before she looked up? Find a table out of her line of sight?

He took a swallow of his Coke. This—just the way he was thinking, and ducking around corners—had gotten so convoluted and weird. Hey, he had always been able to talk to people. That's what he could do now, find a way to talk to her. But the thing with his smelling her shirt…. He'd get past that, too. He walked over to her booth.

She drew three new cards, studied the table, kept her eyes on the cards. Anyone else would have at least looked up. This was exactly what was wrong, the small courtesies weren't there with her. Were they deliberately withheld from just him or was it that she didn't have them? His certainty that he could talk to her evaporated. "New game?"

She didn't look up. "New?"

"Solitaire. Instead of crossword puzzles?" He heard his voice. So forced. What was wrong with him? "Solitaire. Crosswords. Games," he added, still self-conscious, his throat suddenly dry.

"Games. Oh, I get it now," she said ironically. "Thanks for explaining. I must be so dumb. But is a crossword puzzle a game?"

"Diversion. New diversion."

"Diversion. There's a fancy word. Harvard word?" Still not looking at him, she surveyed the cards.

"Don't think they've got a monopoly on it. That the problem? Harvard?"

"What problem?"

"Between you and me."

"Didn't know I was getting a grade for conduct. I keep to myself when I think that's the way to go." She kept playing.

"Right. Me, too. And you don't have an attitude, either, right?"

"What's that mean?"

"As in, if I looked up 'diversion' in the dictionary, I don't think the definition would include, 'Harvard word.'"

"This isn't going to be a legal argument, is it?"

"No legal argument. Just trying to talk to you."

She turned up another card. "Kind of person to person, heart to heart."

"Something like that. Anything wrong with it?" She didn't answer him. "You figure you know all about me, don't you? Harvard, whatever you think that makes me...."

"A fool, most likely, for running out on it—I hate it when people run..." Was that supposed to be an allusion to Davis? "...not staying put where you had it good—and didn't even know it."

"If only I had known *I* was getting a grade for conduct." She looked up at him for the first time—it was the look she'd given him the morning she'd first come down to the boat. Contempt. This time he was almost ready. "Your practiced look, Lee Anne?" She stared at him. "Why not package it?"

She smiled slightly. "This part of your heart-to-heart?"

He slapped the newspaper lightly against his leg. She glanced at it, raised an eyebrow. Everything he did seemed ridiculous to her. Suspect. She'd overheard him tell Davis she had to go...was that it? But it had been there before, her anger. Was it that Davis had run out on her? Run here? Maybe she thought he'd encouraged Davis to dump her. Maybe Val and Lee Anne just had bad chemistry.

Should he sit uninvited now? Walk away? With her, he could never find a balance. Something was always unfinished and unsaid, and no matter what he did—walk away and ignore her, or try to talk to her as he was doing now—he could always feel something pulling on him, something about her that didn't make sense, that made him feel that he was losing ground. He was sure it was a practiced trick on her part, something she was doing.

She went on playing her cards, pushing up three at a time from the top of the deck, playing them where she could. Now he became aware that she'd gone through the entire deck, but couldn't play anything. He saw her turn the deck over once more and push up two cards instead of three, play the second card.

"Guess that was your lucky card."

"Guess so."

"Except you pushed up two cards instead of three."

She went on playing. "Good eye. You *are* paying attention."

"Breaks the sequence."

"Right. Wouldn't have ordinarily, but I just wanted to see if you were on the ball."

"Cheating."

She shrugged. "Game was over if I didn't."

"Lose and start a new game."

"Maybe the thing you don't get is that cheating's part of the game."

"Yeah, I don't get it."

"Sometimes you've gotta want something bad enough first. Not everyone can cheat and make it work, either."

The way she said it, he suddenly felt that it was a weakness on his part to think otherwise.

"Only problem is you didn't make it work."

"Why not?"

"Because I just caught it."

She said, "You're on to Lee Anne, are you, counselor? We'll see what you're on to." She played several cards rapidly. "This is what it is about you."

"Right, what's that?"

"You think you're not down here in the shit with the rest of us."

"I never said that."

"Didn't have to say it. Written on your face." She played a card. Then as she snapped three, four, five cards in rapid succession onto the Ace of Clubs, she said in rhythm. "But. You. Are. Bubba. You are. Thing is, you just don't really know it yet."

She played a couple of more cards. Again she measured him with a look. "You playing to win or lose now, counselor?"

"Not playing."

She smiled slightly. "Not playing, huh? My ass. We'll see."

Angry and tired of the conversation with its undercurrent of veiled threat, the sense that he couldn't escape her control, he said, "I'll see you later."

"No doubt."

"Gee, you never did ask me to sit down and join you."

"I guess Lee Anne just isn't a lady. Or maybe she just forgot her manners today."

"Well, there's always next time."

"She'll try harder."

Lee Anne scooped up the cards, evened and rapped them hard on the table, shuffled, and started dealing a new hand as Val walked across the restaurant. He glanced up just as Davis came through the screen door. "Bird-dogging my chick while I'm not around, Val?"

Val couldn't read his tone, quickly held up his newspaper. "Just getting a paper. I'm going back to the bungalow and cool out."

Davis had a veiled way of looking to the side of someone when he didn't want to be read, and he did do so now. In fact, since Davis had come down to the boat yesterday morning, neither Val nor Davis had looked directly at each other. Now Davis shook his head. "No, you're not, counselor. You're going to a party with us."

## *A Kiss*

Davis drove, Val studying the hand-drawn map, Davis missing turn-offs and then backing up to check road signs—they were way out in the country somewhere. The radio played over the roar of the engine as they wound down the thickly overgrown, narrow roads, Lee Anne silent between them. Several times, Davis suddenly came up to a turn and cornered hard, throwing Lee Anne against Val. Eventually, they turned up a long wooded drive, which gave way to a rising lawn, an enormous house floating in the twilight.

It was massive, horseshoe-shaped, of whitewashed brick, with a steep slate roof, and high chimneys that looked almost like minarets. As they walked toward it, Val could see a brightly cobbled courtyard with Greek revival marble sculpture positioned like non-load-bearing columns along the walls of the house. And looking back across the wide expanse of lawn, he saw that there were ponds, ponds of all descriptions, large, small, like the watercourses of a golf course, each shining like coins in the twilight, and beautiful spreading trees among them, weeping willows, massive oaks, others Val couldn't identify, and that a stream actually ran through the court-yard—a clever engineering feat—and that there were fountains, a lot of them, of all kinds and shapes and descriptions, and that everywhere there was the sound of running water. Amazed, Val couldn't stop looking.

When he turned around, Davis and Lee Anne were gone, and Val became aware of music and the murmur of people talking and laughing. He noticed French doors ajar directly in front of him—this must have been where they'd gone. He stepped into a large, high-ceilinged room, darkened and crowded, air thick with the close heat of bodies, music coming from one end, and started making his way through the crowd—some people were dancing, others talking—occasionally recognizing someone from town, from the marina, from a boat. He saw Davis go by alone on the other side of the room, and a few moments later, Brenda walking in the same direction. She caught up with Davis, and Val wondered if it were coincidental that they went out a door together.

Suddenly, Lee Anne was beside Val. Without looking at him, she said, "Dance with me," and, not waiting for an answer, she stepped forward and fit herself to him, the inside of her leg sliding along the length of his thigh, one arm around his shoulder, a hand resting on the other; when he felt her breasts against him, he remembered her pulling up her top and smoothing her breasts against Davis' chest. Her smell overwhelmed him as it had when he buried his face in her shirt. He didn't dance with her so much as struggle to regain his balance. He tried to pull back to say something, but she held him to her, said, "Don't talk. Just dance with me now. Can you do that? Not talk. Dance?" Unable to speak, immersed in her smell and the pressure—not the pressure, but the fit of her body against his—he danced with her, unable to know if he was following the music or how he was moving, unable to separate anything out from her body against his.

When the song ended, he stepped back, tried to say something. She tipped her head slightly to one side and looked at him, as if to say, *uh huh, I'm waiting*, but he couldn't speak, just pointed toward the French doors alongside the room, finally said, "Excuse me," and stepped out onto a flagstone patio. He took a deep breath, walked to the edge and stopped, looked up at the half moon over the dark mass of a tree beside a pond. Where was this place? He didn't know. He stepped down onto the grass and took a deep breath. He couldn't think. He knew he had to get out of here.

"...close in there. Out for a little breather, counselor? I'm ready to continue our heart-to-heart talk." She stepped soundlessly down onto the grass, positioned herself to face the house behind him. "In a heart-to-heart talk people are supposed to tell the truth, aren't they?"

Sensing the challenge in her voice, he didn't answer.

"You were after the truth back there in the café. Trying to get things straight between us, wasn't that so? Didn't really cotton to my cheating at solitaire."

He still didn't answer.

"Actually what you've been trying to do is figure out something about me the whole time I've been here. Looking at me and looking at me. Can't make up your mind if I'm good lookin' or not, can't make up your mind if I'm trash or not, my hair, my nails, can't figure out what I am…."

He suddenly felt wary.

"You know, I've gotta give you credit for that much…. That you've just been looking so hard at Lee Anne and thinking so hard, even to the point of, like, going through my things—and then there was the little indiscretion with my shirt, but maybe that was just kinda human…we'll overlook that. The purse, that was just a little teeny weenie bit of your own cheating, wasn't it, Val? Just kinda human, too." She waited for him to answer. "You can jump in any time. Cat got your tongue? I did leave it more or less right out there in the open. How could even you resist? Maybe some little part of me, just the little part that might still be there, half the time I can't even be sure anymore, wanted you to know something.

"Your tuning in to me, it makes me kind of, I don't know how to put this without getting too corny, yearn maybe, kinda yearn for you, somehow. Surprises me, actually. Almost like wanting to be loved for your true self… now there's a real idea, isn't it? You sense things Davis doesn't…but then maybe he's just too close…. Whole thing kind of fascinates me, which is maybe why I've been looking so hard at you, too. You just know that, too, don't you…course you're pleased and surprised right now to hear me tell you, come right out and actually say it…wasn't supposed to do that, was I?"

As she spoke, he saw her glance back toward the house several times.

"You want the truth. But now, suddenly, here we are and you've just got nothing—absolutely nothing—to say."

Deliberately, consciously, he said to himself, take a step back. Walk away. Catch a ride with someone…

"Why is that?" She waited. "Always trying to do the right thing. Very touching and a pain in the ass all at once, isn't it? Most of all for you….

"But then, maybe I can't say I'm surprised you're not talking, cause the

café was your deal, and this one's mine, and you're not sure of the game....
But then you say you're not a player.... So let's see."

For just an instant he saw her attention again drift back behind him.
He started to turn. She took his hand suddenly and pulled him toward her
and fit herself to him as she had inside, fit herself and found his mouth
and kissed him—a kiss bittersweet from alcohol, hard and seeking—and
he managed to push her back to arm's length; she looked at him, and then,
determined, she shook her head, no, mumbled something more, he couldn't
quite make it all out, "...no more lies..." or maybe it was "...the truth, no
more lies..." and again she fit herself to him and kissed him hard, and now
a rush of feelings surged in him; later, he would wonder at his response,
which surprised him, his kissing her back hard, a reply to her challenge, to
her days of contempt, maybe also an effort to actually to find her—really
find her—in this kiss, and know something once and for all about her; or
would that be a rationalization? He kissed her hard, chaotically, felt her nodding as she followed the kiss, her tongue suddenly in his mouth. She fit her
body to his, and at the same moment, from far away, another part of him
was trying to call him back to himself. He felt a powerful jarring wrench,
he was looking at Davis, Davis' face almost touching his, his eyes filled with
a bewildered rage as he crushed Val's throat in his hands. Val felt a sudden
stab of pain, a flash of white...

...he was lying in the damp grass. When he reached up and touched his
face, he felt blood in the back of his throat. He raised his head and said,
"Davis...." the word gurgling slightly. He pushed himself up and spat out
blood, wiped blood from his nose.... He tipped his head back and groaned,
understanding what she'd done. "Davis, it wasn't like that..."

He rolled onto his side, pushed himself up onto one elbow, felt the
release of wet heat somewhere. He touched his jaw, gingerly probed his
nose; he tipped his head forward and felt his hands thicken with a gush of
blood, pushed up onto his hands and knees. Then stood, and, leaning forward to keep the blood from splashing over him, holding his hand below his
nose, face pounding, he looked toward the house. Where? Could he make
it to the darkened part of the house...maybe he could slip inside without
being seen, find a bathroom where he could clean up.

He closed and locked the door, flicked on the light, leaving streaks of blood where he'd felt for the switch. He stumbled toward the sink, looked at himself surrounded by white tile in the bright surgical light. His lips and chin were smeared with blood, hands, wrists and forearms, his chest and stomach. He took a deep breath and, trying to summon his courage, he said out loud, "Davis…"

He touched the swelling bridge of his nose—a stab of pain through the throbbing. Had to be broken. He looked at his neck. Already streaking black and blue from where Davis had grabbed him, lifted him off the ground? His lip, too, was split and swollen.

Val peeled off toilet paper, rolled it into tight wads, and, wincing, he packed it up into his nostrils. He sank back down onto the toilet, tipped his head back, and remained still for several minutes. He washed his face and arms and chest with warm water, dabbed at the splashes of blood on his jeans, and then washed out the sink and wiped the floor. Remembering the tiles around the light switch, he wiped down that area, as well.

He drifted. He'd been talking to Lee Anne. Suddenly, she was against him, kissing him. He'd kissed her. She'd been waiting for Davis to come out looking for her, knew he would, had waited for her moment.

Now, in the hall, Val came face to face with an older man—maybe fifty-five or sixty, gray, in reading half-glasses, his finger marking the place in a book; he was coming out of another room. When he saw Val, he stopped and looked him up and down. In a thick voice he didn't recognize, Val said, "I'm…I'm here for the party. I've had an accident… I'm okay now. I just had to clean up." He pointed toward the bathroom. "In there." Was he talking too much? Making sense? He stopped himself, then added, "I'm not a thief."

The man peered at him over his glasses and then took a step back without looking behind him and closed the door. Val thought he heard the click of a lock.

Outside, Val walked the line of cars until he came to where they'd parked. Davis' roadster was gone. Maybe he could get away with asking someone for a ride without raising questions if he kept his head downturned. Throat welling with blood, he coughed and spat, wiped his mouth, then approached several people he recognized from the marina. Val? That you? A ride? Sure….

Turning on lights as he went, he made for Davis' room. His bag and clothes still strewn about. Lee Anne's things. In the bathroom, he examined his face in the mirror. He went to the freezer for ice, which he packed into a plastic bag, then pulled off his blood-spattered pants and tossed them into a corner. He sponged himself off. He wrapped the ice in a towel and touched it to his nose, winced, held it for several minutes, and then flung the whole thing into the sink with a loud clatter. He dropped onto the sofa and lay with the lights on, staring up at the ceiling. He kept hearing the sound of the Ford, and then each time it would not be there, and he would sink to the darkness of the lawn, Lee Anne, Davis, and taste the salt, metallic brack of blood seeping in the back of his throat, and drift....

Val was squinting against the early morning glare of sunlight. He heard the sounds of voices; a marine engine idling; another starting, idling, dying, restarting; weather reports and ship-to-ship, ship-to-shore chatter coming from cockpits; VHF radios; music; morning news; the crying of gulls; all drifting up to him as he sipped a cup of coffee. Baseball hat low over his face, he stared out across the harbor. His stomach took a sudden queasy turn as he realized he wasn't doing anything other than listening for the sound of Davis' roadster, waiting for Davis. And if he came? When he came? What then? Then he'd start explaining himself...? And he was furious at Davis, that Davis always had to see things that way, not know better, not trust him, not figure something else had to be happening. But then what had been happening? Val was, he realized, furious not at Davis, but at himself—and that it was something Lee Anne had read in him. When? He suddenly knew. The moment she'd seen him smell her shirt. But really, he was certain, it had been from the first moment he'd seen her, something he hadn't been able to trust in himself.

Val started down for the Amazing Grace.

He groaned out loud just as Magnus, hair tousled, came out of the cabin with a steaming cup of coffee raised to his lips. He put down his cup. "What happened to you, Val?"

"I was getting into the car last night—leaving the party. Hit the door."

Magnus waved him into the cockpit and gently held Val's face between his hands. He lightly touched the bridge of Val's nose. "Broken." Magnus put his hat back on his head. "Soon as we can get to a medical facility, I'll check you out. You must be in a lot of pain."

"I took aspirin."

"I have codeine in the medicine chest."

"Where's Davis?"

"Don't know."

Magnus waited for more of an explanation, but Val shrugged.

Magnus said, "Is it like him to be late...or not show?"

"No, but I have the feeling we can't count on him this morning. I'll handle the wire today if he doesn't make it."

Val ate while Magnus and Gary studied charts. Every few minutes, Magnus would pause, look up toward the parking lot, glance at his watch, fidget. Finally, after a look from Gary, Magnus nodded with resignation, and Gary started the engines. Around them, boats continued to cast off, voices fading as the crews took in lines. Magnus paced in the cockpit, stopped and spread both hands squarely on the back of the fighting chair, squinted up at the lot, and then shook his head. "Gonna have to leave without Davis. Hate to do it. But it's time to go. Let's get the lines off."

Val and Gary released the bow and stern lines from their cleats, both spring lines, and Magnus eased the Hatteras out of the slip, a swirl of flotsam and jetsam in the silent whirlpool under the stern. Gary pointed, the Ford flashing into the parking lot, gleam of red, and suddenly Davis was out of the car, long blond hair blazing in the morning sun. His heart pounding, no idea what he was feeling, Val watched him as he heard the Hatteras go into reverse.

Davis walked quickly—not a run, but a walk, his hipster walk, fast, cool, his face neutral. It was an old posture Val knew well, explosive and dangerous, his cover, which said, in effect, always stand your ground. Almost without breaking his stride, Davis jumped onto the covering board, dropped down hard into the cockpit. Magnus put out his hand. Davis high-fived him with a slap.

"Another thirty seconds and we were gone without you."

"Never happen."

Val looked in his direction, a glance to show he had nothing to hide, that things could be straightened out, but Davis didn't turn his way. He smiled at Regina and Gary.

Gary eased the throttles forward once more, a soft rise of air through the cabin, portholes and vents bringing her to life; they eased out and turned her bow toward the channel. Val looked back. Motionless, Lee Anne stood beside the roadster, hand shading her eyes.

———

Aft of midship inside the cockpit combing, Val let himself fall under the spell of the boat's motion, the roar of the engines, the rainbow of sunlight caught in the spray rising from her chine. Looking around for Davis, Val saw him standing side by side with Magnus, hanging on to a grab rail, the two of them gesturing over the roar of the engines about something.

And then, a while later, glad to busy himself, he helped Magnus take out rods and reels. He glanced at Davis. Davis somehow always had his back to Val, which meant he was paying close attention to him, though he was always talking to Gary or Magnus, or having a laugh with Regina. Now Davis had Regina's video camera out: *this way; smile, Magnus!* Suddenly, Davis pointed the camera at Val; he walked across the cockpit, thrust it right in his face. "Got something to say, Val?" Val held his hand up, Davis pushed the camera closer, then abruptly turned away, handed the camera back to Regina and climbed the ladder to the flying bridge.

They'd been trolling for an hour when Davis plunged into the cabin for water. Val said, "Davis, we've got to talk." Davis stared past him. "I know what it looked like, but that's what she was after...." Davis started for the ladder. "You're the one who broke my nose, *I* shouldn't be talking to *you!*"

Davis walked to the stern and looked back at the bait. Val followed him, said in a lowered voice. "Just talk to me now. It wasn't what it looked like last night. Okay, if you won't talk, just listen to me now."

Davis crossed his arms in front of his chest, and then put up a hand and lightly pushed Val back. "Okay, Val, let me hear you. Just what the fuck do you have to tell me?" Suddenly, Val couldn't say anything. "Huh? Huh? I'm waiting, counselor."

Magnus glanced at them from the fighting chair. "What's happening? Is there something I can do here?" He kept his eye on his bait, trolling astern.

Without answering, Davis cut away and studied the horizon.

Val shifted his eyes, from the bait riding just beyond the wake to Magnus, relaxed but alert in the fighting chair beside him. It seemed unbelievable that the quarrel with his brother could be going on out here. Davis should have stayed ashore. Val should have stayed ashore. In all his time on the water, he'd never brought something like this onto someone's boat. He glanced over at Davis' broad, T-shirted back. Davis' arms were crossed; a sun visor shading his eyes; wireman's gloves tucked into the back pocket of his shorts. Eyes narrowed against the glare of the Gulf Stream, Davis watched the wake. Okay. Davis wasn't talking. This was his reply. Just to be here.

With none of the sometime cat-and-mouse stalking of the blue marlin, the strike came without warning as an explosion, and Magnus, jerked off balance, had just a moment to recover and brace himself in the fighting chair, the reel screaming as the marlin ran. Voice breathless and tightening with adrenaline, Magnus yelled, "Crash strike!"

Val looked up at Gary on the bridge, who shouted that he'd seen it. Regina raised the video camera to her eye and pushed the button; Magnus pumped the rod and began to crank the reel, the marlin still stripping off line on his run.

In a short time, as Magnus worked the fish closer to the boat, and the swivel reached the rod tip, Davis carefully took hold of the thirty-foot leader, and, methodically wrapping the piano wire around his gloved hands— always the same two wraps around each hand—he braced himself against the gunwale, and slowly began to raise the fish to the surface.

As Val saw the marlin still rising, he could see its pectoral fins were the iridescent neon-blue of anger, excitement, a color you never saw on a tired or beaten marlin; he spotted the mackerel bait on the fish's back, right behind the highest part of the dorsal fin.

Gary yelled down to Val. "Too small. That's definitely no keeper. Cut it loose now, or do you want to tag it? You make the call."

Val hesitated. Better to cut it loose now. Make it quick and clean and save time for Magnus to try to hook up with another marlin. But then, the marlin was already close to the boat. He picked up the pole with the barbed tag in place. "We'll tag it! Can you handle that, Davis?" Davis didn't answer. "Hey, I need you to talk to me now!"

Davis said nothing. As Val extended the barbed tag toward the fish's back, Val saw the round, black eye move; the marlin turned quickly and darted away from the transom. Davis pointed his hands toward the fish and let go of the leader, the wire wraps falling cleanly and freely off his gloves.

Magnus said, "With that hook in his back, he's battling like a much bigger fish—got a lot more fight in him."

Val said, "How about it, Davis? Cut him loose?"

Davis didn't look at Val. He reached out a gloved hand, gathered the wire leader to him and, wrap by wrap, pull by pull, brought the marlin back to the surface and close to the boat. Okay, if Davis wasn't talking, he'd follow through. Val leaned overboard and pushed the tagging pole toward the fish.

Again, the marlin darted forward, and again suddenly turned. This time Davis didn't let go of the wire, but held on as the marlin shot away from the stern.

Val yelled, "Let him go, Davis! I'm cutting him loose! Don't hold him!"

Val heard Davis yell something, couldn't make it out over the screaming of the reel. Val unsheathed his wire cutters. Davis yelled something again. Why was he hanging on? As Val extended his cutters toward the leader, there was a sudden squeal of deck shoes, the sound made by someone pivoting on a basketball court; Davis staggered against the transom covering board with a loud crack. Then he was in the water, head first.

And in another moment, Val was in the water diving down after him. Reaching out, he grabbed for Davis, gathered a handful of his shirt, caught his arm, yanked him…suddenly his grip was painfully torn open as Davis was jerked away….

Val broke the surface with a painful whistling gasp for air, took another deep breath. Below him, he could see Davis and the marlin glowing iridescent in the sunlight where the clear blue water gave way to black. He dove as deep as he could, ears and sinuses aching, broken nose pounding, lungs starting to burn. Still, he swam deeper. Beneath him, Davis and the marlin got smaller and smaller as they shimmered into a deeper twilight blue, then disappeared altogether into the black.

Lungs bursting, Val looked up, the surface distant, the sun huge and undulating, and drove his legs hard for the surface, and thighs burning, a scorching sword of breathlessness piercing his chest, he exploded to the surface, gasping, unaware of his nose, which was now streaming blood from the water pressure…. Again Val dove, turning his face this way and that, looking back behind him, looking down to where the sunlight glowed in long, electric-white shafts, fading down into twilight and black far below, and again he ran out of air, and again he surfaced with a gasp into faraway voices, shouts. He flailed, looking down into the water. Where was Davis!— he was running out of time!—Davis was running out of oxygen! Magnus shouted, "Stop, Val!"

And then Val heard a splash. Magnus was thrashing in the water, arms around him, face close, glasses off; Magnus held onto him as Val struggled to free himself and dive again: *let go, let me go!* Val thrust his hand into Magnus' face, jammed his feet against his thighs; tangled, the two of them flailed, Magnus holding him tight, and then, suddenly exhausted, Val felt everything go out of him; he went limp, and, both of them gasping hoarsely for air, Magnus pulled him over to the stern where Gary opened the tuna door in the transom, and reaching out he dragged Val into the cockpit. Val lay gasping on the deck in a pool of water, and then Gary pulled him up into the fighting chair and wrapped him in towels. Magnus heaved himself aboard through the tuna door on his chest and stomach in a huge sloshing of seawater. Magnus, too, lay gasping. Val heard Gary, who was holding Val's shoulders tightly from behind, "Don't go back in. Don't!"

Understanding nothing, Val shook his head no.

"I'm letting you go. Can I let you go?"

Gary let him go and hovered over him. Val saw the rod and big Penn reel fallen on the deck in a pool of water, the tagging pole where he'd dropped it, the wire leader, snapped....

He took a deep breath. Another. Became aware that he was breathing. He stared through the open transom door at the glassy surface of the water. Air. Davis was out of air by now, had to be. But maybe not! Val bolted out of the chair, but Magnus blocked his way to the water, and Gary encircled him from behind. "Where is he? There's still time!" As Magnus held him, Gary closed the transom door. Talking softly, Magnus took him in a sopping bear hug and backed him into the fighting chair.

"We'll find him, Val, we'll find him…"

Behind him he heard Gary on the VHF "…I repeat, Mayday! we are the Amazing Grace, we have a man overboard…." Gary broadcast their position, repeated the message, "…a man overboard, now lost from view, I repeat, he is not in sight, we have a man overboard, we are putting up a smoke flare and requesting assistance."

Val heard the VHF come alive with voices, the names of boats, positions. He looked down. A towel in his lap, his arms and chest and clothes stained with blood. Had he gotten into the prop blades? He saw no gashes, heard the engine still running in neutral. The propellers weren't turning. Around them the water remained silent and glassy, the surface like a silk curtain, Davis waiting for Val to reach through, pull him back up, shadows moving, orange smoke billowing into the blue sky from the flare. Motionless above them in the tuna tower, Gary held his binoculars on the water and slowly scanned the surface.

## *Together We Have Davis*

When he looked up again, Val saw the white V of a bow wave coming toward them from far off, and then others, heard their engines across the water. Val looked up to the *whump*ing thunder of a helicopter, its white underbelly etched with huge black letters—USCG: United States Coast Guard. The helicopter swept over and banked. Shortly after, a second helicopter and then a third arrived, and, still slumped in the fighting chair, Val watched them deploy into a low search pattern.

Val rose out of the chair, and, Magnus' hands locked on his belt and shoulder, he peered down into the water, his reflection rising toward him, the engines idling, the boat in a drift. Davis was in the water. Val looked up at the sun, looked in disbelief that it was still shining, that the sky was still blue. His father and mother were somewhere alive and breathing right now.

He remained standing at the stern staring down into the water, Magnus still holding him, and now Val glanced up and saw the sun lower, heard Gary say, "We're losing our light."

Then it was later still and Magnus, voice trembling, said, "It's getting too dark to see, Val. We have to go."

Val felt the vibration of the engines powering up, a stab of panic as he felt the bow rise. He watched the wake spreading out, hard, white, flat; felt the boat leveling off; saw water to the horizon, the white Coast Guard helicopters, like dragonflies golden in the last high rays of the slanting sun. He could see night bleeding down and rising in the water, the first stars in the east—night on the ocean, dark and endless, Davis out here alone.... He saw the running lights come on bright and startling, red, green. The first of the Coast Guard helicopters broke off its search and, lights strobing, came back low and thundering and disappeared far ahead, and then the second and third, and Davis was alone in the water....

Magnus had taken a block of rooms on the first floor of a motel: Lee Anne on one side, Val in the middle, Regina and Magnus on the other side, and Val didn't recall getting back to shore or going there, but suddenly he was standing in the middle of a motel room with all the lights on, and he had been answering questions from Coast Guard and police investigators. He had no idea what he was saying, simple answers, yes and no, people taking notes, and then there were sandwiches on the table that he couldn't eat, and when he looked up, he saw Lee Anne standing alone in the middle of the parking lot. She was talking to herself; she would walk and then stop and walk again, back and forth; once as she circled past he could hear her saying over and over, "…please, please, please…", almost as if she were pleading with someone, pleading or praying, her platinum hair silvery under the mercury-vapor street lamp, and when she turned, he could see that her eyes were funny, they weren't looking at anything, they were averted and refusing to see—that was it, refusing to see—the way they'd been at the weigh station, with the marlin hanging black against the sun. Maybe that's what it had been about her eyes the whole time, that there was always something she was refusing to see, and Val followed her gaze trying to see it, knowing that if he looked hard enough he could, knowing nothing….

And then it appeared the investigators were gone. Magnus was behind him with a glass of water and two capsules, tiny in his huge hand, a sedative or tranquillizer. Val placed the capsules untouched on the table, water beside them. He heard himself explaining that Davis wasn't supposed to have been here at all, in North Carolina, that his father had called Val and told him not to let him come, and that if he did, he was to send him away. How do you send someone away, much less your own brother? But, no matter, it was his job to send Davis back to Miami, and he had tried, and then, too, Lee Anne had showed up, and something had changed. Though Val could see Magnus nodding, he knew he couldn't really understand what Val was talking about. Val looked out the window and saw Lee Anne still walking back and forth in the parking lot, Regina's arm around her now. Val wanted to stop but went on; it was the dyslexia that had started it, though for a long time no one knew what it was, they didn't have a name for it, his father had thought Davis was lazy, or doing it on purpose, failing, and everyone else thought he was dumb. Their father thought it was lack of character, and even after they figured it out, their father still couldn't keep himself from believing it wasn't about Davis' character, that Davis was wrong, but the funny thing was that their father loved Davis more than he loved anyone else in the world— Magnus nodded, his hand on Val's shoulder, and though Val knew he didn't understand, he couldn't stop talking—their father made Davis what he was, who he was, the kinds of things that were always happening, the gun under Davis' seat, and whatever had happened down in Miami that Davis wouldn't talk about, all of that was what their father had put into Davis. He paused, trying to get this right, then went on: not directly, see, but indirectly, but still, it was as though his father had put it into Davis, and the really weird thing was that Val thought Davis got everything their father ever wanted him to get, his message, only it came out upside down and backward, in fact, it was exactly like dyslexia in that way, the thing went in one way, it scrambled, came out reversed, but that Davis got it, he stopped, surprised by his words, "...that's what I think and...who I was in it the whole time or am now," he faltered..."I never was sure..."

...Val noticed the door to the motel room was half open and got up and opened it wide, saying that the door had to stay open, he couldn't explain that Davis was out there, still out there in the water, the door had to stay open. He turned to Magnus and said that he had to call his father, and Magnus said again he would be just next door, right there, on the other side of the wall, that he was here for Val and that he would be keeping his door open, too, so Val could come in to him any time, and that Magnus would be calling Val's father and mother soon. Val dialed the family house and later would remember nothing about the conversation, not his words, not his father's words, but would always remember the sound of his father groaning as he'd come to understand about Davis, and with that groan Val felt himself in the water again, the light fading as he sank below the surface into his father's nightmare....

A while later Val was again aware of himself standing in the open door of the motel room looking into the parking lot, Davis, against all odds, with twenty-seven seconds on the clock, down by a field goal. Davis had once more somehow found a way, he'd been rescued and would come walking in the door, nonchalant and laconic, laughing at Val: *typical, you were worried, where the fuck did you think I was?* Val listened—there was a sound coming from far away, he didn't know what it was, watery, rhythmic, he couldn't figure out what it was or how long he had been hearing it, maybe it had been minutes, hours...

...then he couldn't stand any longer and, swaying from fatigue, he looked at the bed for a long time, as if pondering what it would mean to lie down, felt the boat moving under him as he took a step, another, reached the bed, and collapsed onto his hands and knees, rolled onto his side, then his back, became aware of his body, his skin encrusted with salt, his hair thick with salt, the room lights miles away...

...again he saw the marlin rising through the sunlight and water from below, became aware of pain in a hand—in both hands—and flexed his fingers, stiff and so sore he could barely move them. Davis was below him in the water, and the fish, shimmeringly iridescent, long and blue, just below Davis, the two of them wired together, and he reached down and grabbed Davis' shirt, white and trailing like a cloud, he gathered the folds in his fingers, and then felt a stab of pain in both hands. Davis and the fish were gone…

…he heard something, water running, a dog panting, it was someone in the next room, it was Lee Anne, wasn't it? He flexed his hands, each tendon wrenched and on fire. He raised a hand and looked at it. Why couldn't he have held on? Now he saw Davis and the marlin small and far below him where the sun met the blackness, Val descending on undulating rungs of white sunlight. Val could feel Davis and the blue marlin in the blackness, closer, and again he lunged for them as they disappeared into the black, and now, out of air, lungs burning, he looked up and saw the sun huge and white, and drove his legs for the surface….

When he looked up, Lee Anne was standing outside his door, and he might have heard himself say *don't come in, I don't want to see you!* He felt himself go light-headed as he swung his feet to the floor. He'd never hit a woman before…. The doorway was empty…

…and then he was back on the bed, and when he looked again, she was again standing motionless outside his door—how long had she been there? She was no longer crying. Her face was empty, and when he looked again she had stepped inside his room, where she again stood unmoving, like someone balancing on a sharpened stake, and too, like a child who'd been beaten and was pleading to be taken back. She seemed to be waiting for him to do something, but he said nothing, just watched her, and then she was sitting upright in a straight-backed chair by the dresser at the foot of the bed. She had something folded small in her hand. Later this would be crucial to Val, and he would repeatedly try to remember, try to recall those moments in the room when she had sat at the foot of the bed, no longer sobbing, just staring, and he would ask himself, was this when it started?—what *it* was he couldn't say—he would try to peel back the edges of those moments, but they would remain smoothed and indecipherable, like trying to remember a dream forgotten on waking; sometimes Val was sure she had actually said the words, *together we have him.* Or was it just that they both knew this with complete certainty beyond words, beyond everything else that had happened, but that the words had never been spoken? He could feel someone there—it was Davis, wasn't it? He didn't believe in things like this, but Davis was there with them, in each breath they took—Val, Lee Anne—they had Davis, but more, there was a promise now between them—had something actually been said? Or did they both just know it? He saw the first shimmering below, Lee Anne and himself wired together, Davis below…. Startled, he glimpsed Lee Anne's face to see her smiling toward Davis, and Val realized that whatever had happened, Lee Anne and Davis had loved each other….

When he looked again, she was gone, the chair was empty, and the piece of paper was resting on the dresser. He pushed himself up off the bed. The paper was folded into a tight wad the size of a credit card, molded by the pressure of Davis' body, and on it was written in Davis' left-handed, hooked printing, with its mix of lowercase and uppercase letters, "Dad," and it reminded Val of the way they used to fold their papers in elementary school to bring them home so their mother could put them on the refrigerator with magnets, and now Val unfolded the paper, the edges razor thin, folds stuck together, the pieces falling apart as he spread it on the dresser, and he recognized it as an article from five years ago about his father's winning one of his big cases, and Val understood that Davis had always kept it with him in his wallet…

…now the darkness had drained from the open door and there was a colorless light. He walked to the threshold, looked out and saw Davis' '33 Ford at the far end of the lot, its chromed engine and side pipes gleaming, body sleek and low, orange flames curling back along the door. Confused, he wondered how it had gotten there, if it had been there last night or if Davis himself had driven it over…. He stared at the car a long time, but it was impossible to figure out…

…and sometime later he heard Magnus on the phone, his voice coming through the open door…it was the next morning, wasn't it? the Coast Guard was just now resuming their search for Davis. Val looked up and saw white clouds, high, thin, stretched across the sky like an archipelago touched gold by sunlight, and Val, effortlessly, rose up to them and followed the curve of the Earth. From up high he saw the stars shining and Davis and the marlin wired together in the water below, which was endless and black, and he swooped low over the surface and reached down into the waves and wrapped his arms around Davis and brought him up out of the water, his long blond hair streaming, his cheek pressed to Davis' cheek, mouth to mouth as Val breathed air into his lungs…

...someone carried a bag out of a room, placed it in a car trunk, and went back into the room...

...and when Val looked down, he saw that Davis was no longer in his arms. He turned back, and swooping low over the waves, he looked down into the water for Davis. He'd just had him, but now he couldn't find him. He thought he saw his father searching for Davis, white sails tiny on the horizon, and Val flew on, trying to overtake his father and land on the deck and rest for a while, but the boat was always just a speck in the distance, and so he flew on looking for Davis. He was running out of time, the stars were shining above, he swooped down over the water, flew into the day...

...the food sat untouched on the table. Magnus in and out of the room, on the phone. Now Val recognized his duffle bag and realized that Magnus had brought over his clothes from the bungalow, and also brought a plastic bag filled with toiletries—toothbrush, toothpaste, razor and shampoo—and told him to go ahead and shower and wash his hair and get the salt off. Then Val felt the soft sweet water running over his skin, he washed his hair, water curling down the drain, noticed his face drift in and out of the fogged mirror, felt the razor on his cheeks...Davis was in the water, Val was running out of time...

...when he looked outside, he noticed the roadster was gone. No one but Davis and, sometimes, it seemed, maybe Lee Anne, drove the '33 Ford. He walked to the next room, saw the door was ajar, the TV loud. He pushed open the door. A maid was making the bed, and, except for her, the room was vacant. He said something to her, she shook her head, *all's I know is they said make it up,* and he looked around and knew that Lee Anne was gone, and he went back outside and looked at the empty parking space... she had taken the car, gone where? Back to Miami? The maid looked up at him again—and later, he would remember this moment as crucial to himself, that it was part of the moment when Lee Anne had sat in the chair with the clipping folded in her hand and they both knew that someone was there with them, and that together they had Davis, could keep Davis. This was something he knew he must never try to explain to anyone, that it was outside of time or comprehension, it was beyond explaining how he—they—knew, and that, as an extension of that moment, he now felt the pain of the empty room, of her absence. It seemed that now that she was gone she had Davis, or had taken him, the rest of him—but together, they had him, could keep him.

Later, too, he would have to face that moment when he knew she was gone, and that that was why the rest of it had to be; a promise, wasn't it? and that was why the postcards, and that it was beyond explaining—or was it revealing?—to himself or Kazz or anyone else, that they had their knowing and their promise, nothing could explain it away, and everything else was and would be a lie. Part of him knew it couldn't be so, would argue with himself, say, that was just the way it was right after, no one can be held to that, but part of him could never quite believe it, it was irreducible, incomprehensible, as were the sound of line stripping off the reel, the thud of his body against the covering board, Davis and the blue marlin iridescent in the water below him…

…Val followed the curve of the Earth, water below him, all that night and into the next morning even as Magnus steered him through the airport, handed him the plane ticket, explained he had arranged to have a driver meet him at the other end, he'd be holding up a card with his name, *he will drive you from Kennedy to your folks' house,* Val knew the Coast Guard was still looking for Davis. Regina's arms were around him; Magnus was saying *you did everything you could, you were heroic,* but Val knew the truth. And then the seat by the window, the sudden cabin pressurization, his gasp for breath, the plane rising; and when he looked out, he saw the ocean, endless in the tight windows, and, gasping for air, he closed his eyes and pressed his head against the seat in front of him.

…and then saw his name, VAL MARTIN, on a card, and thought if only he didn't have to move toward that card, but could walk in another direction, not look back, become someone else, the baggage claim, and then he followed the man through the parking lot, planes rising into the air, engines thundering, swirls of passengers moving here and there; he stopped and watched them, knowing they were silently being pulled in the same secret orbit as schools of fish, and Val wished he could be any one of them going anywhere else but where he was going…

…which was to the smell of his parents' house exactly as it had always been. He pushed the front door open wider, and now he knew he would surface at last to hear the thud of the Stones and the sudden clank and jangle of Davis' weights in the basement, to hear his mother calling *Davis, for the third and final time, please turn it down!* His father pushed himself up slowly off the living-room sofa, and Val saw that something that had always been there in his eyes—certainty, belief in himself, in his place in the world—was gone, in the same way it had been ebbing out of his voice when he'd first called Val in North Carolina. There was something else there instead—panic, nightmares—and though he looked the same, Val saw that he was someone else—he moved as though he were impaled—and Val couldn't help wonder at how he, himself, appeared: nose broken and swollen, sleepless, and who knew what else about him was showing through; his mother stood beside him. She always straightened when things were hard—she reminded him of the pictures of third-world women standing tall when they balanced impossibly huge loads on their heads—and she did so now. His father looked at his broken nose but didn't say anything; no one moved, then Val saw his mother touch the back of his father's hand, something he'd seen her do whenever he was about to lose his temper. His father took a step toward him, and Val felt certain that his father was going to hit him. He blinked and felt an involuntary ripple of tightening across his scalp and face, and may have flinched.

He had been preparing to explain every single thing going back to Davis' phone call and his trying to get him to stay in Miami, and Davis' just showing up anyway, but it was too big to grip. Words were slippery and would neither emerge nor adhere, and anything he might try to say about Davis evoked Lee Anne, if she hadn't come, and if he hadn't had to see her face one more time—yes, that was true—then he would have had the strength or authority to send Davis away, everything would have been different, and enfolded within that like a heart was the dark lawn, the sudden fit of her body to his, her mouth, a kiss, just a sudden kiss. If he hadn't kissed her, Davis would be alive; he knew Magnus had been in touch with them about everything, about the search for Davis' body—he'd already spoken to them on the phone—Val said nothing, instead, he reached into his chest pocket and found the carefully refolded newspaper clipping that Lee Anne had left on the dresser, looked at Davis' writing: "DaD," and then held it in front of him toward his father as if to prove to him that Davis had loved him in the same way his father had loved Davis—more than anyone, impossibly, beyond reason, which maybe was part or the rest of why it couldn't work—and that this was the proof. But he couldn't say anything, his father didn't say anything, nor did he move to take the clipping, but just stared at Val almost as if trying to figure out who he was; and Val could find nothing in his father's look he recognized as belonging to himself and placed the clipping on the mail table; and when he looked up his mother had come forward and was hugging him hard, and his father remained standing alone on the opposite side of the room.

...and calls from the Coast Guard, still searching, and then the call that said they were suspending the search. Val was still sleepless. Day and night the ocean was endless and black; nothing was in sight now, no boats, no birds, no fish, no people, no land, it was the primal ocean before or perhaps after, life. Sometimes as he flew above the water, the horizon was far ahead, sometimes so far below he could follow the curve of the Earth, the stars shining; sometimes he was so low he could feel the water massed, and, somewhere beneath, Davis, his long blond hair streaming.

...he looked up the at phosphorescent cluster of stars and streaking comets, the moon and Saturn with its rings as they had been above Davis' bed since they'd been kids watching them slowly fading in the dark after turning out the lights. Wandering the house, sleepless, Val met his father, sleepless, on the landing. His father just stared at Val coming out of Davis' room, and then, without looking at him, he said in a toneless voice, "....if you'd just stayed where you were supposed to have stayed in Cambridge and done what you were supposed to do..." He trailed off. "...if you'd taken care of things the way I asked when I called you down there..."
Val didn't listen to the rest of it.

But after that his father and he made sure they didn't meet anywhere in the house. Unable to sleep, not wanting to slide beneath sleep, wanting desperately to sleep, Val dozed fitfully, sitting in an old easy chair in his room with his desk light on—that much he could do—came awake suddenly looking up for the sun through the surface of the water, which way? He was running out of time...and then he would become aware of the room and the house, silent, and his father somewhere, sleepless, in another room.

A memorial service up on the football field at Ridgefield, Davis' friends and classmates standing in the thick, undisturbed grass of late June, and there were people Val hadn't seen in years, George and Biggie and some of the rag-tag retinue of guys and big-hair girls from who-knew-where who used to come to the games, and Bill the old maintenance man with his fading USMC bulldog tattoo on his forearm, who ran the mowers and laid the white lines on the football fields and dragged the infield smooth before baseball games, and his coaches, and the big silver trophies and cups brought out from their glass cases—Team Captain, Best All-Around Athlete, and the Jack Donovan Memorial Award for most inspired leadership—Jack had been a baseball and football player, class of 1938, and then a carrier pilot killed at the Battle of Midway in 1942. His framed picture was in the field house, Jack grinning, one leg on the wing, the other straddling the cockpit of his plane, Pacific sun glinting off the fuselage. All of the trophies with Davis' name inscribed and shining lay on the thick grass. The headmaster spoke first: whenever he thought of Davis, he always saw him moving at high speed, no, not just high speed, explosive speed...

...the smell of grass and earth rising warm and sweet, the sky blue and clear, and the sun on their faces, Val looked over and saw his father, his cheeks hollow, unseeing, somehow grown smaller and colorless, almost as if he had been drained of blood and you might see his organs within. And then no one spoke as people walked back across the field in twos and threes, Val heard just the threshing of shoes through the grass with each step, Val apart from everyone, one of his classmates falling in beside him but not talking until they reached the dark shade of elms in the parking lot...Val's plans? Val shook his head; he didn't know, but didn't think he could stay in the family house much longer. Keith nodded, that's what he wanted to talk to him about. The bank was sending him to be trained in Belgium for a year, his place in Brooklyn was in the middle of being remodeled, but if Val wanted, he could rent it. Low rent. "I'll call you with the details." Around them, doors slamming, cars starting, people hugging and saying goodbye, Val envying each person as he or she drove away; and then he turned and walked over toward his mother and father, who stood beside their car, none of them looking at each other...

...and handed the Brooklyn phone number to his mother, who hugged Val and indicated with a nod that he should try to connect with his father, who stood with his back to them at the window. Val approached him from the side, stopped, placed his hand on his father's shoulder and tried to fit himself into the narrow space between his father and the windowsill to hug him, but his father stepped away without looking at him, and Val picked up his bag just inside the front door and walked out to the waiting cab.

# VINEGAR HILL

## *Three in a Picture Frame*

Still following the rise of sound, Val was sure he'd heard it, the loping cam flattening into its hard acceleration; he'd been hearing it for days. He gazed across the flat warehouse roof, the wind-whipped East River gleaming in the slant of afternoon sun, the bridges—Manhattan, Brooklyn—soaring up and away into the air. Manhattan massed on the other bank, the Statue of Liberty lost in the lemon-silvery, August humidity beyond the Battery, a thousand things seen and unseen in motion....

Val suddenly doubled over with a hard, wracking cough, and, gasping, ribs aching, he pulled a flat pint bottle from his waistband and took a hard swallow, the alcohol easing his burning chest; as soon as he could get rid of the cough, he'd get rid of the bottle.

He looked across the rooftop at Per, who stood with his back to him staring out at the river. Keith's neighbor two doors down, Per had been the first person to whom Val had spoken in Brooklyn, six or seven weeks ago. He answered his door: *Oh yeah, sure, Keith called about you*; and went to get the house key. He spoke with a slight foreign accent and a gentle courtesy—too gentle? Val understood that Keith had to have told him about Davis. Val took the key, thanked him and quickly started across the narrow street, Per calling, "Hey, I'm here, if there's anything you need."

Just as Keith had described it, his place, set on a street corner, was a one-story, whitewashed house; it looked as if someone had taken a knife and sliced off the corner of the house and set the front door within that diagonal face. After a last look through the cobblestone streets leading back to the subway station—a fitful, downhill maze of warehouses, industrial buildings, turn-of-the century houses and old trolley tracks—he worked the key into the lock.

Inside, barred windows let in a dilute, tea-colored light that seeped through the curtains. A short sofa set in an alcove and a couple of crammed bookshelves made a reader's nook. A day's gathered heat and stillness enveloped him. Only half of the long, narrow main room had been tiled; the tile had not yet been grouted. Two partition walls—one with a doorway—had been erected, but the work had gotten no farther than the studs; instead of Sheetrock, opaque plastic, its chemical smell thick in the heat, had been stapled onto the two-by-fours, probably to control construction dust. Val made out a brass double bed, tarnished green, and beyond, a section of plaster had been cut away like skin peeled back in an anatomy diagram to expose a run of plumbing pipe. Low rent.

Val dropped his bag, flicked on a floor fan. The plastic rippled softly. He stared at the bed, couldn't remember the last time he'd slept...the mattress, so inviting.... And waiting just below the surface of sleep, electric-white rungs of sunlight reaching down into black water. He opened his bag and changed into shorts and running shoes.

Approaching the middle of the Brooklyn Bridge, he felt the stitch in his side ease into a second wind. As he avoided casual strollers and other runners, he glanced through the suspension cables and towers, saw a tug pushing barges hard against the current; off to his left, the Statue of Liberty; the Staten Island Ferry; large and small boats, each tracing a sinew in the water; the sun slanting across the surface, which was whorled like a fingerprint, rippled as if with breath; and ahead the World Trade Center towers. Last December, the water steel gray, he'd brought the Amazing Grace through here on a freezing day: Hell Gate, the East River. He felt himself getting light-headed, as if the bridge were giving way under him, and, forcing his eyes away from the water, he fixed them on the World Trade Center and ran toward Manhattan.

...later, Val couldn't remember the rest of June, little of July, couldn't remember settling into Keith's, shopping to buy food, nor eating. Always, he seemed to awaken to his coming onto the Brooklyn Bridge, the river spread below him, lower Manhattan ahead. Sometime later a wheeze caught in his throat and chest, and he drank whiskey he found in Keith's kitchen cabinet to ease the tightness. As he pulled off his sweat-soaked shirt, he caught a glimpse of his ribs, which were starting to show.

He called home several times, always getting his mother. No matter when he phoned, his father never answered—had he completely stopped taking calls? *His* calls? If only he would say something to Val.... Val saw him bloodless white in the June sun against the blazing green of the football field, the goal posts stark, pure and beautiful and white against the grass and sky. His mother said he'd returned to work, that it was the best thing for him, adding quietly, "...just give him some time." She hoped he was thinking of getting back into... She avoided saying *law school*. She said *his old routines*. Her voice was distant. Muted. Exactly how was he spending his days?

He mentioned that he was doing odd jobs with the guy who lived across the street, to which she was silent, and then said, "I see."

He started to elaborate, "Just small things. House painting. We replaced someone's water heater the other day..."

She said, "Odd jobs," and he heard it for what it was and let it go.

Just before hanging up, he added, "I'm not going to keep asking for Dad. If he wants to talk to me, he has my number."

"I'll tell him what you said."

Odd jobs. He'd seen Per coming and going in a battered pickup, and one day Per dropped by and asked Val if he might give him a hand unloading lumber not far from here, a couple of hours, a few bucks. Val was glad to have the work and company, needed the money, and later they went for a beer. To Val's relief, Per never asked him about Davis. After that Per called Val to help him with his projects repairing and renovating houses in the neighborhood, plumbing, tiling, Sheetrocking, framing, digging a garden, cutting down a tree and slicing it into firewood, anything. For Val, the work kept him busy. There was comfort in a handle—hammer, shovel, axe—shaping itself to his grip.

Per was a Swede—the slight accent Val had heard the first day—who had gotten into some kind of trouble with the law as a teenager, fled Sweden, and joined the US Marines. He'd been wounded in Vietnam—once he said in passing, *I'm paid for the steel in me,* the steel being shrapnel and several rods and plates in his bones. He had one-hundred-percent disability, which made it illegal for him to work; he was paid cash under the table. As the day went on and he tired, he limped, at first a little and then a little more. Val would look up to see Per, lean, six-four, sometimes careening slightly as he balanced several four-by-fours on a shoulder, all angles, face composed. He disappeared once every week or two for post-traumatic stress counseling at the VA hospital. After one session Per said, "They told me what happened to me. I know the facts, but I can't remember the thing itself." And since he'd volunteered nothing more except that he was lucky to be alive—that he shouldn't be alive—Val let it drop. One other time Per mentioned a Marine sniper in their PTS group who'd been at a ball game a couple of years ago and stepped into a Porta-Potty between innings. Cops had finally managed to take him a couple of days later barricaded under a house. He'd been holding down the street with a rifle. The smell of the Porta-Potty had flashed him back to human shit in rice paddies and the rest was a blackout. Aside from these few isolated things, Per said nothing more about the VA hospital.

Val tried to tell Per about Davis, but after a few minutes, he trailed off. It was too big. He didn't have words. He just kept seeing the flashes of broken images, the cockpit, the marlin rising, the sound of the reel, but none of the pieces fit, and he couldn't force them together, and when he tried, he went blank, and maybe there was something he had or hadn't done to make it happen. His father thought so. And then, Lee Anne, something she'd brought with her and put between him and Davis, an edge, the twist and pull of something, and that kiss, and lately he thought that Davis had been shouting at him in those last moments, what? he heard the rev of the engines and the reel, but nothing else....

When he could concentrate, Val read, walked through the neighborhood up to the cul-de-sac above the old Brooklyn Navy Yard, gazed at the abandoned white houses of Admirals' Row. He walked everywhere. He noticed there was a huge white building on the East River waterfront where Jehovah's Witnesses came for a year-long mission. They did something inside, though exactly what, he didn't know. At lunchtime, he'd see them walking two by two in a long line; they wore uniforms of white shirts and blue pants and looked into a distance; it was a while more before he discovered that they were marching down to a communal lunchroom by the river. Sometimes he wished he could be one of them.

His wheeze had developed into a chronic cough, and often he coughed so long and hard that his ribs and diaphragm ached, as if he were taking body punches. He didn't recall sleeping; he would leave the lights on and then become aware of them still on and the windows dark in the middle of the night, become aware of himself lying in the brass bed, which was placed haphazardly, almost as if flung down in the middle of that framed-in space; in a trance he followed the Jehovah's Witnesses appearing and disappearing between the buildings down into the water.

He'd dream that Davis' body had come in on the tide. He'd jerk awake, heart pounding, to the phone ringing…it was Davis, it was his father, it was the Coast Guard, they had found Davis…. Other times he'd wake knowing that the steel leader had snapped, that Davis had gotten free of the marlin and surfaced, had been missed by all of them, and was now living somewhere. Hadn't he been running from something in Miami? He'd made the ultimate escape to a tropical paradise. One night Val woke, saw someone suspended motionless just beneath the surface of the water, the opaque plastic moving with the turning of the fan; he stared, holding his breath.

He stopped trying to reach his father and stopped asking about him, and his mother didn't mention him as she had earlier. His father had said, "…if only you'd done what you were supposed to do…." Val held endless, unceasing conversations with him in which he explained what had happened on the Amazing Grace and the days going back to their first calls. He waited for his father to phone, but he never did. He understood his father's feelings. Then, overnight, Val felt his heart harden into an unforgiving anger, and his father's anger toward him seemed to bend, circle back, hover and charge the air.

The next afternoon, as he reached the middle of the Brooklyn Bridge, he felt the water, far below, starting to rise. Was he awake? Dreaming? Slipping through a crack between the two? The water was rushing up. Had he jumped? Was he already in the air? He stopped running and grabbed the railing hard. Hanging on tight and keeping his eyes averted from the water, step by step, he walked back toward Brooklyn. He had stayed off the bridge since.

Now on the warehouse roof, Val coughed again, took another quick swallow from the bottle, put it away. Per would think he was a drunk, which was not the case. He straightened, massaged his ribs. Per studied him. He had a deeply seamed face, roughly handsome; long brown hair that looked as if the wind had just caught and settled it; dark blue eyes speckled with shadows; and a gently ironic smile. At times Val sensed that Per had traveled a long way from some starting point to reach that smile. Val never looked at himself in the mirror except to shave, and then, with his broken nose, he barely recognized himself—remembering Per's smile, he had attempted one, but his reflection had just appeared distant and lopsided.

Val said, "Did you hear an engine, a kind of loping cam?" He imitated the sound. "*Da—DAAH, da-DAAH*. I told you that I'd been hearing it for the last few weeks."

Per searched Val's face, then shook his head no.

"Hey, I'm not crazy. I *heard* it."

Per said, "I didn't say you were crazy. I didn't hear it. But I hear that cough of yours for the last few weeks. I have a friend who's a doctor. I'm taking you to him."

Val shook his head no. He'd be okay. He'd picked up the cough jogging in that bad air, end of July. He didn't have the money for a doctor's visit. They walked across the roof. From below came the whine of a saw. The warehouse was being turned into lofts and Per had some of the work. Per put his hand on Val's shoulder. "Yeah, don't worry about the money...." The doctor owed Per money for a job, and anyway, Val could pay Per back when he could.

The doctor finished his exam, then turned and traced Val's ribs on the x-rays, his cloudy lungs, stress fractures from the force of his coughing. He had walking pneumonia—his lungs were essentially full of water. The doctor prescribed Biaxin and sent him straight to bed, where the doctor's command, or the antibiotics or both released Val into a fitful sleep for days. Sometimes through his sleep Val thought he heard the lope of the cam, slowing, idling, hovering, then its hard acceleration into the distance. Once, as he was turning over in bed, he glanced across the room and saw someone peering through the crack in the curtains, but when he sat up, the eyes were gone, and he wasn't sure anyone had been there, and drifted back to sleep.

Several days later, he showered and cautiously took a deep breath, expecting to be seized by his cough, but nothing happened. In the kitchen, he noticed the wastebasket was filled with empty whiskey bottles, which he took out and dumped with a clatter. As he walked to Per's to join him for work, he noticed a subtle change in the light. He'd been in bed a week. End of August. Almost September. Light softening. The beginning of fall soon. Midmorning, tiling a bathroom in the warehouse, Val looked down at his hands, gray with cement, the nails cracked and dirty. He raised a hand and inspected it closely. It might have been Davis' hand.

Per came in. "I'm breaking for lunch. You coming?" He held up their bag of deli sandwiches.

Val smoothed the cement, turning the toothed edge of his trowel in a semicircle. "I'll just finish this batch, meet you outside." There was a strip of abandoned siding between the warehouse and the river stacked with railroad ties smelling of creosote and overgrown with daisies and Queen Anne's lace where groups of workers clustered to eat their sandwiches, smoke, doze, read the paper, jive…. "Be there in ten minutes. Go ahead."

Val listened to Per's steps fade down the stairs, noticed the absence of saws, hammers, conversations or shouts. The whole warehouse had fallen silent. Still weak on his first day back, he'd been pacing himself. He placed several more tiles, scooped the last of the cement together, flinched. He sensed someone, then looked and recognized the posture, her way of standing in the doorway as if balanced on a stake; she watched him with her struck gaze, her cheeks hollow as if eaten from within. He saw her hand move suddenly by her side and stop, as if to check herself, and then succumb to the impulse to touch her finger to her pursed lips and gnaw the inside of her cheek, her hair longer, but still the same indecipherable swirl.

Val placed a hand on the floor to steady himself, fell back onto his heels, her face angles, pieces that didn't fit, and her gray eyes charged with a fiercely held lie or truth—which, he couldn't tell—and dark circles beneath as if she hadn't slept since he'd last seen her; he stiffly thrust himself up and slid down one kneepad, then the other, and careful to avoid touching her, he pushed past and went down the stairs.

Outside, he paced. He started back inside to tell her that she had the whole rest of the world, that she had to leave. He stopped. No. He didn't have to do anything. He'd ignore her. She could do whatever she wanted. He'd ignore her. That was all; that was all.

Behind the warehouse, Per sat on a stack of railroad ties eating his sandwich and reading the sports page, doubled over on his knee. He inclined his head sideways. "That's your roast beef there. See what the Mets did last night?" Val shook his head no, unwrapped the sandwich, then offered his half to Per. "What's the matter with you?"

"Not hungry." Val swallowed, dry mouthed. "She's here…here in Brooklyn."

"Who?"

As when he'd tried to tell Per about Davis, it was too big, too shapeless. At the same time, part of him wondered why. She was just a woman and, ironically, a hairdresser who never seemed to have a real haircut. "She's..." not knowing what else to say, he shrugged, "a hairdresser—though she never has a decent haircut herself."

Per ate. "Yeah, so what? Old girlfriend?"

"No..."

"Then, so? What? Want her for a girlfriend?"

"No."

"Then, so what? Not an old girlfriend. You don't want her for a new girl-friend. No business with her, then, right? Where do you know her from?"

Val said, "You're right. No business with her. I don't know her from any-where."

"Okay. It's bottom of the ninth, Mets are down by a run, two outs, run-ner on second..."

He'd left so suddenly that he'd forgotten to rinse the cement, which was now set up; he noticed a scrap of cardboard box stuck in it, with the scrawl of an address. He went back to work, laying the next tiles until he finished out that batch, and then found Per, who was bolting some posts in place. Keeping his eyes on his work, Per said, "So what's still the matter with you?"

Val asked him if he knew the address on the cardboard. "Yeah, it's a nar-row side street, old brick houses, a lot of them broken up into apartments, kind of run down like everything here." He gave Val directions. "The hair-dresser, is it?"

He nodded. "Yes. But no, not really."

"You nod yes, but say no."

"I just have to tell her not to come here..."

"Here?"

"To work. Not to come around me."

Crescent wrench poised, Per studied him. Seriously. Curiously. Val thought he saw the beginning of his ironic smile, which didn't quite emerge this time.

He walked up from the East River through the maze of cobblestoned and tarred streets, through his neighborhood and on until he matched the num-ber on the cardboard, where he stood in front of an old brick house, one floor, two doors in front, a duplex, paint worn off the steps and alligatored into a pattern of faded yellow cracks on the porch columns. He moved on, but later found that he had circled back and was again standing in front of the house on the other side of the street. From inside, he heard the muffled sound of a saxophone. He crossed and rang the doorbell. Just as he was about to ring again, the sax suddenly stopped. A man yanked open the door, making it no secret he felt disturbed: rumpled plaid shirt, half-bald, with close-cropped hair and the nub of a ponytail, earring, sax hanging from a strap around his neck, thick glasses.

"Is there a Lee Anne living here?"

"Right, but she isn't in now."

Val looked past him down a long dark hallway. "Mind if I leave her a note?" The sax player went on fingering the keys in quick, impatient patterns. "I'm a friend of hers. You're..."

"I'm Mike, a roommate, is all." The stops made soft percussive sounds. "You can leave the note in her room." He indicated a closed door in the hall.

"How do you know each other?"

"Don't really. She answered our ad in the paper. We needed a third roommate." He reached over to a nicked telephone table and thrust a memo pad at Val, who stepped inside and closed the front door. The sax player disappeared back into his room, played several progressions and then burst into something soaring and beautiful.

Val pushed open her door. Curtains half-drawn, late afternoon light filtering pale through windows streaked with city dust, the house next door too close. An old Deco dresser, blond laminate chipped. He was startled by a ripple of movement in the pool of an old mirror, its silver backing tarnished: himself caught frozen looking at himself. From below it, a jolt of familiarity: crosswords, silver bracelets and earrings. Nail polish. The closet door was ajar, and several of her dresses and a frayed suitcase were visible. A travel iron. There were a few books tumbled in a loose pile on the floor, a reader's pile. She read. He picked up each paperback. Lewis Thomas' *Lives of a Cell.* Auden's essays. And Chaucer's *Canterbury Tales,* into which a yellow legal pad was inserted at *The Pardoner's Tale.* The page was blank, but she had written at the top: Dec. 9, 1980. Was she taking a night class? He remembered she'd been reading Céline in North Carolina. If she was trying to do a paper on *The Pardoner's Tale,* she was stuck: not a word. And why this date almost four years ago?

Confused, he turned to an unfinished game of solitaire spread on a coffee table pulled close to the bed. He picked up the deck, slid out three cards, saw the next play. He carefully replaced the deck on the table, looked around the room. What was it about this space? The shared duplex, the sound of the saxophone coming from across the hall, the dresses half-visible in the closet, the narrow bed…there was no single thing, but taken together they gave him the feeling of a person who, isolated within herself, was being held and pulled by some unknown force. When Davis had left her in Miami, she'd come after him. She was here in Brooklyn now, something still drawing her on. Val looked at the dull reflection of each turned-up card on the table in the window light. There were so few personal items, perhaps almost as if it were her choice to remain anonymous, untraceable, unrecognizable. In North Carolina, she'd come on a bus in the middle of the night, had been living out of a duffle bag on the floor. That was one situation. But here there were still no pictures of a mother or father, no family pictures, brothers, sisters, friends with arms around each other, a dog rolling on a lawn. It seemed to be the room of someone living in a devastated aftermath. But then couldn't someone have walked into his place and said the same thing?

He opened her closet door wider. Before he could check himself, he released the snaps on her suitcase. He had to know something about Miami, Davis, what he'd been running from. And her part in it. If she'd had any part. The suitcase fell slightly open. He looked down, saw some clothes, several envelopes, a folder. He picked up an 8" x 11" envelope and held it up to the light, thought he could decipher the outline of a photograph. He remembered their exchange in the café when he'd caught her cheating at solitaire: *Cheating's part of the game.* As though his thinking otherwise was a lack of courage, a failure of will or imagination. She said: "You think you're not down here in the shit with the rest of us, but you are." He thrust the envelope back into the suitcase. His failing? Maybe…. Without looking further, he closed the suitcase. He sat on the bed and wrote:

*Dear Lee Anne,*

He crossed that out, wrote:

*Lee Anne,*
*I don't know what you're doing here in Brooklyn, but you can't just show up where I'm working…*

He remembered Davis saying, "If you say no to her it comes back funny."
He saw the broken glass, the back door of the bungalow...

He crumpled it, started again:

*Dear Lee Anne, I don't know what you're doing here, but we don't have anything to say to each other and I'd like it if you'd stay away from me.*

Again, he crumpled the pages, stuffed them in his pocket. He noticed a small picture frame on the floor between the bed and wall. He picked it up. A color photo of Davis and Lee Anne on the deck of a glossy muscle boat, obviously somewhere in Florida. Davis with his arm around her.

Carefully inserted into the lower right hand corner of the frame, a cut-out of head and shoulders. Holding it closer, Val felt a hot and cold wave rise through him. It was Val at his college graduation. Davis had called out to him, "Hey, Doofus!" Val turned, and Davis shot—one of Davis' favorite tricks, to get a picture when you least suspected it: here the beginning of a smile as Val realized Davis had caught him again. Val stood suddenly. Where had she found this? In Davis' things in Miami? He straightened her bed and replaced the picture: the three of them in the same frame. He stepped into the soaring sound of the saxophone in the hall. He knocked lightly on the door; the sax suddenly stopped, and the door jerked open. Val put up his hands as if to halt a charge. "Hey, I'm sorry, but I just realized I can't leave her a note. And that it would be much better if you didn't tell her I was here. Please."

"That going to be all?"

"That's it. But it's important not to tell her. Because I just need to see her first. Some things we need to clear up. Face to face."

Perhaps hoping to get rid of Val for good, he said, "She's at work now." He blurted directions: eight or ten blocks this way. Val had no intention of going to where she worked. This was the end of it. He just hoped he could count on this guy not to say anything about his visit to her room. He knew she'd take it wrong.

Onside, on her porch, Val squinted against the late afternoon sun. The picture of himself in her possession fascinated, horrified him, the idea of her having an unknown intention that had fastened onto him, that she had his picture at all...the configuration of Davis and her and now himself in one picture frame. He stepped down, noticed a narrow garage set down a drive with heavy wooden doors, a padlock on the hasp. There was a slight crack where the doors were ajar. He pulled on the handle and the crack widened. He cupped his hands around his eyes, closed one and peered inside. Faint gray light from a small high window in back. Close smell of oil, gas, dust, and afternoon heat. Val cupped his hands tighter to his eyes, found the gleam of the chrome valve covers, made out the low mass of the three-window coupe as his eye adjusted to the dark. For the first time in weeks, he felt what might have been relief, as if he'd just found a small part of himself he thought he'd lost. He stared at Davis' '33 Ford suspended in the darkness. He wasn't crazy.

## *Collaborator*

After returning home, eating, and lying down, he went out and eventually found himself across the street from a bar. A red and blue neon sign flared against the front window's glow. This was a neighborhood, working-class place with drinkers hunched at the bar, in booths and at tables, a baseball game on over the back bar, a couple of waitresses moving back and forth. The light caught on her platinum hair as she walked from a booth. She placed a round tray on the bar top. The man on the closest stool turned and said something and she nodded and smiled, and Val was reminded of the easy flirtation and repartee that Lee Anne always seemed to have with the captains and boat owners, but which excluded him. She drifted toward the front window, glanced up, and Val followed her gaze toward a last thin cloud high overhead just fading from gold into darkness. Hair glowing silvery blue and red in the neon, wrapped in an unreachable silence, she looked directly at Val without seeing him across the narrow street.

After a few days, Val became aware that he couldn't stop thinking about Lee Anne. Perhaps the question wasn't so much when she would show up or where, but what he would do when she did.

When the knock came, he jerked his head, heard his mumbled reply. The book had fallen from his hand. He sat up in bed, glanced at the clock. After ten. Maybe Per. The light over the kitchen counter burned a blur through the plastic sheet. He stood, smoothed his face with his hands, and opened the door.

Though he had perhaps even rehearsed what he would say if she appeared, he'd never really expected her. Or he had. But not really. He couldn't put it into words. And whatever he had or hadn't been expecting, it had not been now. And not this way. Not smelling of cigarette smoke and booze and perhaps too much perfume trying to mask it. She had a look of petulant grief, yet also of determination. He couldn't say a word. When he didn't speak, she said, as if continuing a conversation, "…and, well, sure, that's okay, you don't have to invite me in. I didn't really expect it," the whip of mockery in her Southern accent.

"I shouldn't even be looking at you after North Carolina," he managed. Neither regarded the other directly. He noticed, incidentally, something odd about the way she was dressed.

"Ordinarily I wouldn't be dropping by unannounced at this hour. So consider me sent away even as I speak," she said.

"But—and I'll make this quick—Mike—you remember Mike, as in Mikey the half-bald sax player with the pride-saving ponytail—dropped into where I work a while ago for a beer and even though you told him mum's the word on your visit, I guess bad conscience and even a little loyalty—I am his roommate—got the better of him, not to mention a few beers, as in he finally spilled the beans on your coming into my room while I was out, which I guess I'm saying I don't fucking appreciate!"

The rush of possible replies held him silent: *You follow me here to Brooklyn; you come into where I'm working; you leave your address; it was your roommate who told me to leave a note in your room….* And the big thing that he'd not yet gotten a chance to say—*Whatever you did at that party, if it wasn't for that, Davis would be here….* It was all too much; he just shook his head, could only repeat, "I shouldn't even be looking at you."

"Oh yeah, I know, I guess that's why you came to my place…to not look at me."

"I came to your place to tell you not to barge in where I'm working. And Mike told me to leave the note in your room. And I didn't get into your things." He heard his replies as lame. He realized he'd never seen her in a skirt before.

She said, "Oh, I know, Val, you always keep yourself beyond reproach, you wouldn't go through my things, though I'm sure you had your little moment." If he had imagined anything possibly conciliatory or apologetic about her, he was wrong. It was as if she could only be this person with him.

She seemed to lose interest in what she was saying. "You're seriously not going to invite me in?" Her voice rose just slightly as it had when she'd say Davis' name in North Carolina.

He still had his hand on the doorknob, and for a second he thought of just slamming the door as hard as he could. "How'd you know I was here in Brooklyn—where I was living?"

She didn't answer—of course she wouldn't—and he knew she had to have called his family house, run some stupid little scam on his mother: she was a classmate who wanted to get in touch, she was from Ridgefield, Harvard, Harvard Law, take your pick; she knew enough about him to play it out. It would have been simple.

They still had avoided looking directly at each other, but now they happened to do so, and there it was, exactly what he'd seen in the motel room, almost a sensation that ran through his body; it was as if this moment were an extension of that earlier glance and moment: *together we have him.*

She said, "Well, if you shouldn't even be looking at me, I guess that means you're not going to invite me in. So. A small favor and I'm gone."

Her mocking smile reappeared, as if to say that what they were actually playing out was a necessary lie she'd tolerate a little longer, but that they both knew something else was really happening, had to happen.

He resisted an urge to grab her shirt and shake her hard. "What's that, Lee Anne?"

"I'm just dying of thirst. Could I have a glass of water?"

He returned with the water. She said, "You sleep with the lights on." It wasn't a question. He wished she hadn't noticed his unspoken terror. She drank, handed the empty glass back to him. She surveyed the inside of his place carefully, and, again with a kind of mockery, she extended her hand, said, "Well, if I can't come in, I guess this is really goodbye." He noticed her nails, dark blue, black, didn't take her hand. "Oh, I know, you *have* to send me away…. I'm going to have to be the bad one in this thing so you can save face…I knew that's exactly the way it would be." She turned and was gone. There was a faint trace of fall coming into the air, the warm humidity forming incandescent globes of mist around the streetlights, and the deep smell of the river so close that he might have taken one step and waded into it. He looked up and down the street, but she was gone.

Barefoot, he paced the length of the floor, the sharp edges of the ungrouted tile nibbling at the soles of his feet. Undressing down to his shorts, he lay on the bed, getting up several times to pace, sink back down, pick up a book, only to become aware that he'd been rereading the same sentence. Following the exposed plumbing into the walls with his eyes, he began to drift. He turned on his side, sensed something, a change in air pressure, an ebb and flow of current, perhaps the smell of the river closer.... Tugging the sheet, he drifted, and then he smelled her presence, bar smoke, booze and perfume. He eased onto his side, cracked ribs still tender, the mattress out of balance; he squirmed, trying to get comfortable, something soothing his back. He was suddenly aware that even though he was awake, he knew he was still dreaming, heard her whispering, "...sshh, it's all right, all right, I tried to stay away, but I can't fight it anymore, there's nothing more either of us can do about it now, this is the way it has to be...." He opened his eyes with a sudden intake of breath, was surprised the room was dark. He turned his head. Awake or asleep? The light was out over the kitchen sink, bulb blown? and he felt himself overwhelmed by the rise of an ancient fear, darkness...at the same time, she was there beside him, her hand on his chest...he pushed himself up suddenly on one elbow, a sharp stab of pain in his cracked ribs, her hand still on his chest. He saw her darker shape. Voice thick from sleep, he said, "What're you doing here? How'd you get in?"

She said, so softly he could barely hear her, "Sssh, it's all right...the latch.... I flipped it when you got me the water." She was speaking quickly, softly, her Southern accent hoarse. "Hey, I wouldn't have done it except it was written on your face; it said, 'Help me. Do it.'" She was speaking fast and low, her words running together, her hand caressing his chest, his stomach. "I told you, I'd have to be the one to take the heat, I knew you couldn't..." she slid down full length on the bed next to him, "...it's your stupid honesty I need..." He felt her pulling down the top sheet, still caressing him. He realized now he hadn't been touched in months, and though he wanted to push her away, had to push her away, he was paralyzed. He heard himself groan at the impossibility of it, all of it, her, and Davis right below him each night, the marlin shimmering an iridescent blue, the white shirt in and out of his hands, her words sliding together, "...you're the one who hates lies, this is the truth, I tried to stay away..." She fit herself to his body, worked herself under him, her hair against his face. He could feel that she was still dressed. She squirmed and raised her hips as she worked up her skirt, guided him into her, her sudden heat; he saw her as she'd been with Davis the first night he'd brought her back from the bus station...peeling up her shirt, smoothing her breasts against his chest...she nodded to the rhythm of their lovemaking, and Val, desperate to drive away the image of her and Davis together, still moving in a hard rhythm with her, suddenly tried to find her mouth. She turned her face away from his; still, she held him tighter; he felt her skirt bunched around her waist, the crush of her thighs around his waist. He reached down to loosen her legs, ribs sore. She didn't relax her hold. He was surprised at her strength—her overall bearing suggested otherwise—and, her face turned away, he went on trying to find her mouth...he came suddenly. Still talking quickly, hoarse and unintelligible in her Southern accent, she nodded. Then, slowly, breath by breath, he felt himself coming back to the room, which was:

...the barroom staleness of her hair, the sharp smell of their lovemaking, the sound of their hoarse breath subsiding, a keen awareness that she hadn't let him kiss her, and disbelief that she was actually here—she couldn't be here, but she was—and, too, the trace of a slightly unpleasant smell, perhaps metallic or chemical, deep in her skin, maybe something she used to dye her hair....

He felt her breath catching unevenly, rolled off to one side of her. She lay on her back, and then he felt her suddenly turn away from him with a rustle of sheet and clothing. He still felt her shaking; he groped for her, her shoulder, her face, hot and wet...he realized she was stifling sobs; she pushed his hand away and sat up; he saw her dark against the pale glow of the window, felt her draw into herself, the mattress still trembling with each suppressed gasp. She reached behind her, groped for his face until she found it. She smoothed his cheek, then stood in the dark, tugging her skirt down, straightening herself; he saw her dark shape move, heard her rustling across the room, felt the opening of the front door release a flow of air inside, heard the latch snap back into place, and then she was gone.

He didn't get up, but lay still in the silence and unaccustomed darkness, the windows glowing pale and far away; made no move to turn on the light; the smell of her—of them—still hung in the air. After a while he might not have been able to say that she'd been there at all, but in the first gray light of morning, something coiled on the floor caught his eye, which he made out to be a black thong. When he stood up, wanting neither to get rid of it nor to disturb it, he toed the hard knot out of sight under the tarnished brass bed. He heard her: "...your face said, *Help me. Do it.*" In the pale light of the bathroom mirror, he looked at his face, barely recognizable since

Davis had broken his nose. He couldn't tell what she might have seen in his face...if anything.

She didn't come again that night, nor the next, and he slept badly, starting awake; she had slipped back inside and was standing over him. He'd lie awake listening—was that her breathing?—and then drift into a light sleep through which the sounds of the night and neighborhood burned like a low fire. Awake? Asleep? He smelled her, bar smoke, perfume, the metallic odor in her skin. Wide awake, he would have known for sure she couldn't have come in; after her ruse with the latch on the door, he'd locked it.

At work, surrounded by the racket of construction in the warehouse, he kept feeling her move against him. He had never seen her in a skirt before, but that night he'd noticed her wearing one—and now it came to him why: the obvious reason, that it was easy to pull up; she had thought out whatever she was going to attempt with him.

When Val opened to a sudden knock several nights later, it was, incredibly, almost exactly like the first night; she looked past him; there was no acknowledgment on her part that anything had ever taken place between them—no trace of tenderness, no intimate look, however quick or covert; there was no recognition that they'd made love and that it had shaken each of them. She seemed to have steeled herself, once again, to her singular purpose. He said, "Lee Anne...we have to talk."

Glancing toward him quickly without meeting his eyes, she said, "I know, I know."

He put out a hand to her, to touch her shoulder, concede or offer something. She side-stepped his touch, brushed past him; and in another moment, she had turned out the lights. It seemed so insistently childish that Val surprised himself with a laugh. Was she kidding? Arms extended in the sudden darkness, he groped toward the switches, but before he could find his way, he smelled her close, felt her fingertips graze his face, his chest, and then, speaking quickly, her arms went around him. "...we will talk, we will, but please, not now, not yet, it can all come out, it will, I want it to—it has to! but just let it be this way for a little bit, let what we're doing change things..."

"What *are* we doing?"

"We're fucking...." she said as if patiently making an obvious point to a dull student. She said it without a hint of irony or comic inflection or mockery. It seemed so suddenly ingenuous. "But it's not just that, all by itself…it's…give me a little time, that's all I ask. I don't trust easily. I don't trust at all. Let me try with you—I think maybe I can, part of me—and then maybe I can get back out of this with you a step at a time."

"Out of what?"

She ignored his question. "Some things, once they start, take on their own momentum…. A door slammed shut behind me, a door I didn't even know was there."

"Door to what?"

Again she ignored his question. "If it can be with anyone, then maybe it can be with you. I had no idea it would be so much easier for Lee Anne to keep going this way…. I didn't know it would get to be unstoppable for her." He'd forgotten about her sometime habit of speaking about herself in the third person, had no idea what she was talking about now… "Part of me knows I can't let it go on. If I let it, I have a funny feeling, a bad feeling that there's something terrible waiting. And that no matter what I do, sooner or later I'll get to it. Or it'll get back to me." She was speaking in a halting voice, as if trying to find her way. When he thought she had stopped, she said, "It's like a place, maybe. A bad place. I can't describe it. I think I've been there before. I know it, but I don't." He still didn't understand what she was telling him. Did she?

"What *do* you know?"

He became aware that his arms had remained at his sides as she'd held onto him, that he'd been keeping himself apart to hear her out, but now he raised his arms to calm her, to help her make sense of whatever she was telling him. He thought part of her wanted him to understand, but that most of her didn't; as she'd said, she didn't trust. Did she herself know or understand what she was trying to tell him? When he put his arms around her, she stopped speaking, fit herself to him, her knee between his legs, her hips against his, fingers digging into his back, and in response to her urgency he was so suddenly excited—her excitement or desperation, his the same— that neither of them could stop or pull away.

Afterward, crumpled on the cement floor, half-dressed and entangled in their clothes, he saw himself with her as if from above; they might have been mistaken for lovers in a movie or novel—freedom, abandon, passion, whatever the value was supposed to be. Yet he knew that for them—there was no them—nothing could have been farther from the truth. What were they doing?

He stood unsteadily; groped for her hand in the dark; helped her up from the cold cement floor; felt his way toward the bed. He pulled off the rest of his clothes and stretched out on the mattress, Lee Anne, still half-dressed, beside him. He felt for her, found her arm. She didn't turn to him, but didn't pull away. His hand resting lightly against her skin, the windows glowing far away across the room, he fought off sleep, trying to shape the wording of questions. *A door had slammed shut behind her.* Was it because of something she had done? Or she and Davis? In Miami? And…*something terrible waiting?* Was it the same thing from which Davis had been running? Her only alternative was to go back out—out through the slammed door—with him.

Why couldn't he just ask her about it now? He lay in the dark, his hand resting on her arm. She'd said, "I know it, but don't." It seemed beyond her control. But, he realized, he could at least ask her now about Davis, the gun under the front seat. If he could start her on that, maybe it would lead her back to this other thing she feared.

He turned on his side and placed his hand on her stomach. He could make out her dark shape against the window. He couldn't, he realized, bring himself to say Davis' name to her. He felt panicked at the thought of Lee Anne and Davis together.

When he opened his eyes, he groped for her, but she was gone. He sat up, startled himself by saying her name aloud. In another few moments, the windows silently surfaced grayout of the dark. Davis. Val had been trying to find a way to ask her about Davis. He couldn't do it. Not yet.

She came the next night, and the next, her knock late, sudden, expected, yet unexpected; and each time she appeared it seemed a surprise. Each time was the first time, and each time she left was the last time he'd ever see her. She'd leave before it was light, and some part of him hoped that she wouldn't come back, that he would go up to her place and find her gone, her room empty, gone as suddenly as she'd come, and then he, too, would pack, leave no forwarding address with anyone, break away.

Their lovemaking bore no resemblance to any other he'd known. She seemed to take or provoke what she wanted, allow what she could, which was little to no intimacy or tenderness, kissing or caressing; there was no weaving or building to something. Afterward, she might pull away, remain silent, though still touching some part of him, a hand, his leg, or allowing him to remain touching her. Sometimes he was sure her gasps were sobs, and he'd stop to touch her face or try to comfort her, but she would pull him to her harder, and always she'd turn away when he'd try to kiss her mouth. Always she'd be gone before it was light, before he could clearly make out her face or body.

Once he flipped on the bedside lamp, and she covered her face, turned from the glare of the bulb. "Lee Anne…this is just too strange…. I mean, let's look at each other…"

She lunged across him, turned off the light. "This is all I can do now! Didn't I say, just give me some time…"

He said, "But it doesn't have to be like this…"

He turned on the light again, and she stood suddenly, pulling her skirt down, yanking her blouse straight. She slid into her shoes and was gone, slamming the door behind her.

He woke suddenly to the light off, felt her there. She'd been gone several days. "How did you get in?"

She said matter-of-factly, "I took the key off your ring and had a duplicate made. I let myself in."

He sank down onto the bed. If it weren't so bizarre, it might be funny. She seemed to need to do things like this, if for no other reason than to make a point that she could. She'd said she needed his honesty—was it to offset her dishonesty? He couldn't grasp her contradictions.

He said, "I'd like the key back."

"You'll get it back."

But even as he said it, he knew that pressing her for it was pointless. She would always hold a key in reserve. Or he'd never know. He could change the locks—expensive—and she would just figure out the next thing. He said, "I need to talk."

"So do I. But talk is nothing, anyway."

He said, "I hate this."

He felt her shrug in the dark beside him. "It's just what we've got for now."

Often, it tormented Val; he couldn't imagine how she could be physically attracted to him after Davis, with his hero's body, his blaze of pure beauty; Val secretly felt that she really wasn't; she was with him because she couldn't be with Davis. He was with her because she'd been with Davis. Though he didn't want to be with her, he couldn't push her away.

Val was acutely aware that there were none of the small intimacies or tendernesses he'd known with other women: waking up slowly, stirring, feeling the other person move against you, waken, reach for you. There were no glances, touches of reassurance, looks exchanged of something shared. Nor did he think there ever would be. If anything, he felt more alone and isolated with her, felt a dread, maybe, at times related to the *terrible thing* she felt waiting if she didn't go back *out*. Was there something he was supposed to do or be doing so that she—they?—could go back *out*?

One evening after work he was in the neighborhood supermarket; he leaned on his cart; he watched people shopping together, husbands and wives, couples living together, friends, people who clearly shared something. He thought of all the things people did with each other, how they ate, shopped, cooked—the dailiness of lived life; how they quarreled, made up, made love. They had reasons. They had things they could talk about, name. He and Lee Anne had none of these. He didn't want to be with Lee Anne or think about her, but he thought about her all the time. When she was gone, he felt relieved, yet desperate for her. It was like a low-grade fever. And still it went on. It wasn't a relationship. He didn't know what this was. He didn't know how to get out of it or even where *out* might be.

When she was away from him, he could form few images of her—most of what happened took place, literally, in the dark. He felt blindfolded, that he wasn't himself, that she wasn't herself, that together they were greater than the sum of their unknown parts and being driven by that sum. And.

It occurred to him that each time they came together was a replay of the moment on the dark lawn outside the party, the chaos of it, its suddenness, as though each were stealing something from the other. But then, it turned out she'd really been setting him up with Davis, who had just come outside looking for her—her revenge for his telling Davis she had to go, for something in Val's presence which she took to be a very personal reproach to her, but which she seemed to want or need. That he could actually let himself be with this woman, he had no idea how to think of it, other than that he was a collaborator against himself.

They seemed stuck in that first moment.

The first gray light seeping into the windows. Usually, in her state of half-undress she might button a shirt, pull on clothes, walk to the framed-in door-way, look back at him, abruptly leave. But this morning, she stood out of reach beyond the bed, her face shadowed by the window's pale backlighting.

She said, "I know you'll never believe me, but it wasn't supposed to get this way. Though you're a little to blame, too. Because sometimes I think maybe this is the way you want me to be, the way it has to be for you. Maybe that's your little lie to yourself." Her voice had gotten a little higher, as Val had noticed it did when she felt vulnerable. Barely awake, he raised himself on one elbow. "There's something I have to tell you—you, only you. I mean, I've never really known anyone who could care so much about principles…. I guess you'd call them that. Care about the truth."

She went on. "But before I can say anything, I want you to know…" she suddenly worked her lips, pressed her finger to them, gnawed the inside of her cheek, and Val was careful to hide his reaction to this nervous habit. "I am not crazy. I've got to be sure you're not going to think I am…" She trailed off, then added, "crazy. I can be so much better than what you're looking at—am so much better. As good as you," she added with sudden defiance.

Before Val could say anything, she said, "I'm not as dumb as you think, and I'm not gonna fit in someone's neat little box and make one of those nice *National Enquirer* stories. Victim. It is not that." She spoke carefully. "I know exactly what I've done and why. I know exactly how it started. Most of it. Up to a point."

She struggled with something. "I also see that I have to get out of it. It's just that…this is the part I can't seem to explain to myself…. I can't leave it behind. Maybe *that's* the funny part. Why it won't let me go. And that you—and everyone else—would think it's craziness, or just hate me."

He realized she was appealing to him for reassurance, and he wanted to give it to her, but he was also aware that almost anything he did or said might be exactly wrong. He didn't want to set her off in any way. Maybe *that* was what she wanted: a way not to tell him. So many refracting mirrors within mirrors.

"It's all up to me. Isn't it?" Was he supposed to answer? Was there a right answer? Val knew it all kept leading back to Davis—something they'd done together in Florida, some part she'd played in it, something she wanted to put behind her. He saw the gun resting on the kitchen table between Davis and himself. Start with the gun. Val tried to say his name, *Davis*, but couldn't do it.

She laughed, a short self-deprecating laugh. "I try to tell myself this shouldn't be all that hard. A few words and it could all be over. I know that sooner or later people will have to know, before it's too late—and you're the one, you. I don't want to wake one morning and find myself walled up inside."

He held his breath but felt a sudden exasperation at her endless circling, her finding ways not to tell him. Still propped up on his elbow, his shoulder stiffened, and he winced and sat up. God, she was pissing him off with this.

Her face hardened. She said in a low furious voice, "Just when I think I might take a chance and trust you, you get this look on your face…"

"No, I want you to go ahead with it!"

"No, no you don't. That's what I'm saying. Part of you wants me to be this way. You know, you're so superior. You have no idea what it is, but you're just so, like, hey, fuck you…. I try with you. I try all the time. I know it's fucking weird now, but there's just something about you."

"You've got me coming and going. You're just looking for an excuse not to go ahead! And now you've put it on me. 'Part of you wants me to be this way.' But the real reason is you can't tell me. That's all." When she reached the front door, he called after her, "Go ahead, Lee Anne. Leave. Hey, you know something? I can leave, too!" She came back and stared at him, a look of panic and anger on her face. He said softly, "Just go ahead and tell me, Lee Anne. Nothing can be so bad."

"Nothing can be so bad," she repeated. She looked at him like he was an idiot, turned and walked out.

She stayed away for several days, and he woke with a sense of possibility that he didn't know had been missing, some small expectation still growing in him. If he could talk to his father, hear something in his voice that had once been there for him, something that might signal forgiveness—even though he knew he had done nothing for which he needed to be forgiven—then maybe he'd know what to do next, possibly even find it in himself to leave. Each day he would check the answering machine, hoping to hear his father's voice, slightly formal, a little overly correct, perhaps nonplussed by having to speak to a machine. *Val…this is your father. Are you there? Give me a call. I'm at the office until four, home after five.* But each day that call did not come. Nothing.

## *Held*

He woke to her lying down beside him. She placed her hand on his chest, slid a knee across his thigh, said, "I know you're thinking about leaving. Saw it in your face." She said it the way she'd said *you sleep with the lights on.* Not a question. Then, as if continuing a conversation, in a low voice, she started telling him about Jimmy, and within a moment Val knew without her saying so that he was her high-school boyfriend. *...his Daddy was loaded, but there was always some quarrel, Jimmy wasn't good enough, would never be good enough, and they'd had a huge argument earlier in the day over his cutting classes, and whenever they argued, Jimmy drank too much...*

Days before, Jimmy had set a trap up a river, deep in a swamp, and that night, drunk, he took his boat, a big open johnboat, to check the trap.

Dry-mouthed, almost breathless, Val listened, wondering why she was telling him this story now.

Winding back up into that swamp, spotlight cutting a white tunnel through the black, air so thick you could hardly breathe, she had sat against him on the seat; she was terrified of cottonmouths falling down out of the dark from branches overhead. Drunk or not, night or not, Jimmy knew where he was going. They ran for hours, finally slowing; and there, gleaming in the water, she could see something caught in the trap, see its back and head, its eyes gleaming like electric yellow ice in the spotlight, could see it was an alligator; Jimmy stood, and, swaying so long and unsteady she was afraid he was going to fall in, he raised his twelve-gauge shotgun and fired, and the gator's head just seemed to explode, his body thrashing up out of the water; he fired again, the gator thrashed and was quiet, and then Jimmy just sank down and opened another bottle of booze and lit a cigarette, the smell of gunpowder still hanging in the air. When he finished, he slipped a noose around the gator's tail, released it from the trap and dragged the thing—huge—close behind the boat.

The sky was starting to lighten—trees and growth coming out of the dark—as they found their way out of the swamp and ran into open water where you could see the boat landing, and Jimmy's house with these beautiful big trees on the lawn. By now Lee Anne was wondering what Jimmy would do with the gator, and besides that, it was illegal to hunt gators, there was a big fine if you got caught, but he was just drunk and not saying a word; he brought the boat into the landing, and then, taking off his clothes and carefully folding them, he made a neat pile on the dock. Naked, and not giving a shit, in fact, not even noticing, slipping and stumbling, he wrestled that gator away from the boat. By the time he got it onto the dock, he was covered with blood. He dragged the gator across the lawn to one of those big, beautiful trees.

Lee Anne shifted on the bed beside Val. "I don't know if he had planned this from the get-go or was kinda letting it happen one ruined neuron at a time, but...."

Jimmy threw the line over a lower branch of one of the trees and hauled the gator by its tail until it was hanging upside down, and then came back from the boat with a Marine KA-BAR knife. Just as the sun rose out of the water, he was standing naked and covered with blood skinning the gator. And that's the way his father saw him when he got up that morning and looked out the window.

She stopped speaking, and Val realized he was holding his breath, and when she still didn't say any more, he had to restrain himself from asking her what had happened next, why she was telling him this to begin with, and how it had any connection to what she'd been trying to tell him the other morning. Had he missed the point of the story? Was there a point? It seemed like an image isolated in a lightning flash—beautiful, horrifying, another world completely, inseparable from Lee Anne's thick Southern accent. And then he realized why she had told the story; she was telling him about her life. It was her way of working up to what she had been so desperately trying to confess to him—if she couldn't bring herself to say it directly, she was giving him what he needed to figure it out—part of her, he knew, wanted to tell him and part of her didn't. If he listened carefully, patiently, he could put it together. And, he now understood, she had been doing so since she'd come to him in Brooklyn; he thought of the things in her room—and the things not in her room, what was missing. He heard the echo of her voice other nights in the dark; saw the coffee table with the solitaire game in progress; the picture of Davis and herself and the head shot of Val stuck down in the corner; the yellow pad pushed into *The Canterbury Tales*, blank but for the date, December 9, 1980. What was missing? It was up to him to find the door before it was too late for her—or them.

Val saw the alligator hanging down, the rising sun slanting across the lawn. He waited for her to tell him one more thing, was startled when she began to touch him, and within a few moments, straddled him, but then, almost as if remembering something she was supposed to do, she rolled to one side, pulling him after her. "It's better if you come on top of me."

In the morning, she stood, straightened her clothes, and left without telling him anything more. In the racket of the warehouse at work, Val tried to imagine how much you had to drink—and hate someone—to do what Jimmy had done. What it had been like for Lee Anne to live in that world. He felt something he hadn't quite felt for her; maybe it was tenderness. The atmosphere of the story, inseparable from her Southern accent; the alligator hanging upside down, head half blown off by two shotgun blasts; Jimmy, naked and red in the sunrise.... Something beneath the surface of the story made him uneasy. Something he had to understand. If he'd been thinking about leaving, he now felt held by what she was telling him.

A few nights later, without preface, again in the dark, Lee Anne started telling about her father, that he had been a rocket scientist—a physicist—who'd brought the family—well, it was just her mother—down to Cape Canaveral from—she hesitated and then said very softly, "from Philadelphia." She was quiet for so long that he didn't think she would go on. She said, "It was still called Cape Canaveral then. This was back before Kennedy was shot." She went silent. Her father did some wonderful work for the space program, but then he'd had a nervous breakdown and—again her voice faded, became almost inaudible—he stopped functioning as a scientist; they went to live in a small town in Florida. It was only supposed to be for a short time, but they stayed. Her father was so depressed he stopped speaking. She spoke to him, but he couldn't bring himself to answer. Her mother supported them as the town librarian. She said, "Maybe you wouldn't believe it, but I hung out in that little library as a kid and read everything." Val saw the crosswords perfectly and compulsively filled in, the books by her bed. Yes, he could believe it. He started to ask which town in Florida, but then, afraid he might stop her, he asked as ingenuously as he could, "Do you have a family picture from that time?" He thought that whatever she was trying to tell him might have to do with her family—or perhaps this time in her life—and if he could see a picture, then maybe he'd be able to spot it. Much later, he would remember this moment, this instinct. She reached over and slapped him lightly, as if to reproach him for trying to probe her, thinking she might be so unaware.

He caught her hand and she fit her hand to his and held it for a moment. Suddenly, apart from her grief over Davis, there seemed to be something else in her which was wounded, maybe had been so for a long time, perhaps even destroyed, and which made him feel he had to protect her. His leaving—at least before he could help her—would be devastating to her. Or was he confusing his tenderness with her grief—their grief—over Davis? Everything seemed so entwined. Without knowing where it came from, he fought back an overpowering urge to tell her he loved her.

In the morning, as she was leaving, she said, almost as an afterthought, that she'd gone to see about a job in a neighborhood beauty salon, *Great Lengths*, and that in the next few weeks when the job opened up, it would be hers. She added, "More money than what I'm getting now. Better work. I like cuttin' hair…leastwise that much is real," she drawled. She hesitated, perhaps waiting for his reaction. He turned on his side and said softly, "Well, good, Lee Anne. I'm happy for you."

When she closed the door, he felt her absence; he went naked to the window and watched her striding down the middle of the street, her wild platinum hair bobbing with each step. As she got farther away, he felt more and more desperate; he had to know if she could ever love him. Looking down, he noticed his ribs showing, bruises on his arms and legs, his skin bluish white and goose-bumped against the early morning chill. When he glanced up, she was gone, and he noticed that the very tops of the trees were starting to turn red and yellow, as if they had done so the instant he'd looked away.

Val peered into the front windows of the shop. Several women covered with drapes faced a wall of mirrors; another was having her hair washed. Someone thumbed a magazine under a dryer. Each beautician had her gallery of pictures on the counter—boyfriend, husband, kids, friends, candid photo of friends clowning—plus greeting cards and stuffed animals. He pushed open the door—a chime sounded. A hugely overweight woman behind the middle chair looked up from her work and called, "Yes, sir, we do men's hair. We'll be right with you."

This was exactly the kind of situation that had set Lee Anne off when he'd come up to her place, what she took to be his checking up on her. He never knew how she'd take something. Or how it would get back to her.

"Ah, I thought I was supposed to meet my girlfriend here now."

She gave him a skeptical glance. "I can check." She opened the appointment book lying open on the counter.

"Never mind. I must have gotten it wrong." He thanked her and left.

Outside someone caught his eye. Familiar. Coming out of a long, dark corridor leading to the back of the shop, which he hadn't noticed. He stepped back with an intake of breath—Davis walking toward him!—before he recognized himself reflected in opposing mirrors, jeans and a work shirt and a red headband to keep his hair from falling in his eyes when he worked, which, like Davis, he'd let grow almost shoulder length between haircuts. It hit him that he was working with his hands, which was Davis' life, except that Davis had had a real gift and love for engines. He heard the echo of Lee Anne's drawl from this morning, "I like cuttin' hair."

God, he was suddenly repelled by her. *Cuttin' hair.* That faint metallic smell he sometimes caught in her skin, the smell of that shop—hair dye and permanents, god knew what else. He saw that he had fallen into being a half-assed handyman, a day laborer. He was half-living with a woman he didn't want, someone who'd turned Davis and himself against each other, and who had not just loved but maybe adored Davis, and who Val knew could never love him in that way even if he'd wanted to be with her! She was crazy—this was exactly the word she did not want applied to herself! maybe half-brilliant; she was secretly self-educating; a hairdresser who claimed she was better than he could ever know, as good as he was—as if that were ever a question, and who cared anyway?—and who seemed to admire and resent him in equal proportions because of it, who had made him the rock to which she had fastened and against which she was hammering.

At home, he tried the answering machine to see if there was a call from his father. Still nothing. When he'd left law school, the dean told him that if he were to consider coming back, Val should call him directly. He looked up the dean's number in his address book, wrote it on a pad. Then, impulsively, he dialed his father's office number. If he could just hear his father's voice.... When his secretary answered, Val hung up, again felt a wave of desperation for Lee Anne—*could* she ever love him? He had to know!

When they made love again, he tried urgently to kiss her mouth and she turned her face away, and that, he realized, was his answer, that no, she could never love him as she'd loved Davis. What were they doing? Confused, hating himself, he couldn't keep from asking her, "Could you ever love me?"

She said, "Doesn't matter what I say. We're not there yet." Something she'd said to him before.

Again he asked her, "What's that mean?"

But she didn't answer.

He went on listening for the one detail she would offer or perhaps let slip that would reveal the thing about herself, about Davis, that she wanted him to know, but couldn't tell him. Filled with dread, Val kept seeing Davis' nine-millimeter on the kitchen table.

Together they had Davis.

Then she surprised him, asking him one morning if he could meet her on his midday break up at the bar where she still worked. At lunch hour, he borrowed Per's always-stalling pickup. Just as he was entering the bar, he saw her turn into the street, waited for her. He felt a surge of desperate love for Lee Anne.

When she reached Val, she stopped, but didn't look at him. He wanted to take her hand and at the same time urgently wished they weren't meeting here, where she knew people. He followed her inside, into the stale smell of beer. She led him to a table by a window, and they sat on opposite sides. Avoiding each other's eyes, an almost insurmountable awkwardness between them, they ordered. When the food came, though Val was hungry, he couldn't eat. Nor could she. Instead, she ordered a beer for each of them. He looked for opportunities to take her hand, but she kept her hands below the tabletop, or else fiddled with her silverware, shredded a napkin into small pieces, her nails a dizzying shade of green. He kept sneaking quick glances at her while pretending interest in something down the street. It didn't seem right to ask her why she'd wanted to see him, or note the obvious, the incredible and absurd, that this was actually the first time they were meeting in daylight or even outside his place. He stole quick glances at her, trying to figure out what she wanted now, trying—strangely enough—to see what she actually looked like. If asked, he would have been hard pressed to describe her. Yet once, their eyes did meet, and he was stunned by how beautiful her eyes were—and by a desperate appeal in them—for him to do what? He took a quick gulp of his beer. Finally, he glanced at his watch. He had to get the truck back to Per. Did she need a ride anywhere? She shook her head no, indicated with a nod that she'd be starting her shift here in a while. He reached for her hand just as she pulled it away. Maybe she had just wanted him to see her in daylight.

———

And still they tried. An early fall chill coming into the air as it grew dark, they met outside a Chinese restaurant. Lee Anne pointed at a large drugstore across the street. "I need a couple of things in there." They crossed and he followed her inside.

She picked up a basket and disappeared down an aisle. Val flipped through a magazine by the register, looked around for her, then spotted her in one of the convex surveillance mirrors at the other end of the store. As he turned into her aisle, he saw something in her hand—yellow—that she was dropping into her jacket pocket. Her posture—alert, wary—told him that whatever it was, she was stealing it. He pretended not to see. She placed something in her basket, coolly looked back at him. "Coming?"

Glancing at the shelf as he passed, he noticed a yellow box. Perfume. Fendi. Fifty dollars. In the next aisle, she dropped another item with several others in the basket. When she reached the register, she kept her back to him. She pushed the basket forward on the checkout counter, reached into the pocket, and pulled out her wallet. Yellow. That's what it had been. Her wallet. But that's not what he'd seen in her hand. He watched as the clerk rang up each item and dropped it into a bag: her beloved nail polish, shampoo. Lee Anne handed the cashier several small bills. Val wasn't sure how much. A man in a suit approached the clerk and, leaning toward him, said something in a low voice—Val couldn't hear him—and the cashier nodded, then went on bagging Lee Anne's things, handed her the receipt. Just before they went out, Val glanced back at the suited man, who was talking to the clerk. About Lee Anne?

Outside, they walked toward the corner to cross to the Chinese place. They still hadn't looked at each other. They waited for the light. She looked at him. "Goddamnit, what?"

"Nothing, what."

"Don't give me that shit. You've just got that thing you've always got and then get more of when you think you're right about something."

"Don't, Lee Anne."

The light changed. Val started to cross.

She said, "I'm not crossing." They stared at each other. "God, the way you look at me, you make me fucking crazy! So superior. You pretend to be so good. You're the one who's hiding everything, everything!"

"I'm sick of hearing your 'so superior' routine about me. It covers you when you need to blame me for something. And what am I hiding?"

"You damned well know." Whatever she thought it was, he knew she believed it.

The light changed again. He stepped off the curb. She grabbed his shoulder and yanked his jacket. "Say it now. Just say it."

"Why? What? Why?"

"You're so superior and even when you're so good and not saying something you're just tolerating the shit out of it and that's your way of saying it. So hypocritical."

"Well, you've just got me coming and going, haven't you? Okay, Lee Anne, since you asked me, you stole the fucking perfume. Happy?"

"I knew that's what you thought." She reached into the bag and pulled out the box. He hid his surprise.

He recovered and said, "You moved it. It was in your pocket."

She looked furious. "This is it! This! This is it! I try to talk to you, I want to talk you, I need to talk to you, you're the one I need, but how can I ever do anything with you when you keep believing this kind of shit about me? How can I ever trust you if you won't trust me?"

He knew what he'd seen in the store. But against the force of her will and blaze of anger in her eyes, he started to doubt himself. The light changed again, and people coming out of the crosswalk brushed past, slowed to watch them.

He said, "If you paid, just show me the receipt and that's the end of it."

"If you have to see the receipt for me to prove something to you, it doesn't matter. Don't you get it?" She turned, and though the light was red, she started to step into the path of speeding cars.

He grabbed her arm and pulled her back as a car swept by. She twisted in his grasp. "Christ, Lee Anne! It's not worth killing yourself over." He held her back.

She said in a low voice. "Let me go or I'll start screaming." People were watching them. "I'm counting to three. One! Two! Three!"

He let her go, ready to grab her again if she stepped off the curb.

She straightened her coat, but stayed on the sidewalk. She said, "I'd show you the damned receipt but I threw it out!"

"I don't care what you do. I'm gone." He started walking away.

She held up the box of perfume. "I'm going back into the store. I'm going to show this to the cashier. He'll remember. Come with me. I'll prove to you I paid for it."

He'd seen her take it. But he felt himself waver. What had he actually seen? Suddenly, he couldn't be sure. Maybe she *had* paid for it. Her wallet was yellow. The perfume box was yellow. Maybe he'd really seen the wallet. Maybe he was wrong. He shook his head no, he wouldn't go back with her.

She dropped the perfume into her pocket and took his arm. "Then just fucking let it go," she said in a low voice. "You're the fuckhead, and you know it, and you know exactly why. I want to eat."

The light changed and they crossed. On the other side, he pulled away, but she held on and dragged him toward the restaurant. He let her and they went in and ordered. When the food came, they started to eat. He ate slowly, vacantly, searching her face. She looked back at him, a play of hard defiance and ingenuousness rippling moment to moment like light across her features until she stopped chewing. "Go ahead, look at me. Look just as long as you want." She stared back at him, and then she abruptly stood and walked out.

Per's truck idling at the curb, Val let himself back into his place. It was just after nine in the morning. He was almost never here at this time, but he'd forgotten his tile cutter where he'd left it by the front door. He glanced at the answering machine out of habit, saw the red light flashing. His father? He imagined his voice. "…I know I jumped to hasty conclusions about your part in what happened to Davis, but I realize now there was nothing you could have done…"

He pressed the replay. "Good morning, Val. This is Jim Hollister at Harvard. I'm starting to wonder if this is the right number. I've left three messages already, but haven't heard back from you.

"I've been told that you've had a recent family tragedy. *Even if* you've changed your mind and decided not to return to school, please call me."

Outside, he heard Per's truck stall and die. Val rewound the tape. The dean had left three messages already? There'd been nothing. Had the machine malfunctioned? He replayed the tape, glanced at the front door, which was still open to the street. Lee Anne had a key. And, so…. She had been letting herself in during the day while he was working, checking his messages and erasing them? Did she think once he connected with the dean that would be the end of them, of whatever was happening here?

He stared at the machine. God, there could be no other explanation. Furious at her, furious at himself, he cursed. He had become a collaborator against himself. Maybe he had done it on purpose to find out how she would use the key, if he could trust her. This was his answer. And why, he suddenly realized, she had accused him the other night: *you're the one who's hiding everything, everything.* Though she was erasing his calls from the dean, she still believed it was he who had set something in motion.

God, he hated himself for being with this woman, for being drawn to her, being fascinated by her, unable to break away from her, from the unnamable things that hung over her, for her having loved Davis, Davis having loved her, for her craziness, for her platinum hair with the honey colored roots, and for her eyes, which were always watching for something coming at the end of the street which was never there, and for her weird stories about Jimmy skinning the alligator and for her father who'd had a nervous breakdown and never spoke, and for the unexpected tenderness that he felt at her being buried in a small town library somewhere in Florida, the name of which he hadn't dare ask her, and the thousand crossword puzzles that had to be the weird manifestation of that pain translated into something else, and for his waiting for her to tell him the thing she couldn't bring herself to confess, and for his not being able to say Davis' name to her so he could ask what they had done together—and for his being helplessly reduced to trying to win her trust, and for his not being able to find a way to do it, and for his being taken into her fears that something terrible was waiting for her, still waiting for her, coming for her if she didn't tell him, and tell him before it was too late, and for her talking in cryptic riddles, and for Davis' having been so unbelievably beautiful that she could never love Val, but would always love Davis—that was his own un-acknowledgeable secret torment—and for his waiting now to hear the one thing which would him allow him to figure out what hung in the silence, and for their having Davis together—together they had him—and for, beyond all of this, his still loving her and needing to see her face one more time to know something once and for all...

He groaned out loud into the room.

Had she erased other messages besides the dean's? His father's? He walked to the machine, grabbed it with both hands, raised it over his head.... Just as he brought it down over the edge of the table, he caught himself. If he smashed the machine, she'd know he knew. He set it down carefully. He had no choice now but to erase the dean's fourth message and keep watching her. He felt the sudden clarity of his fury replaced by the familiar return of calculation, of listening into her.

As he picked up the tile cutter and walked out to Per's truck, he stopped. Was he calling the dean or not? Not now. Maybe later. Maybe tomorrow.

## *Where We Were Going*

No part of her touching him, she lay there not saying anything, and he could feel her listening into him in the silence, and his listening into her reminded Val of running slowly on the Hatteras in the inland waterway, keeping bow and stern bearings for sideslip and drift, peering into the shallows for changes in water color, wave motion, surface texture, a sandbar, changes in depth not indicated on charts, or bottom changes that had taken place from unseen currents or storms since the publication of the last chart. Still not touching him, she said, "Tell me what it looked like."

He knew she was asking about the marlin that had taken Davis overboard, and he didn't know if he could say anything, the clear water of the Gulf Stream, looking for the first signs of its shimmer from the depths. When he thought he couldn't take another breath, his voice, dry, barely audible in the dark, startled him from far away. "It was like something swimming out of the sunlight itself…"

She turned onto her side and put her hand on his chest. Always there had been a sense of sexual urgency in her touch, but now he felt something different, that she had gotten where she was going, maybe that they were coming to the end of something. "You asked me if I could ever love you…."

He nodded. "I never asked if you could love me."

"No."

"People can say anything." He heard the whip of contempt and despair in her voice. She sat up. He saw her black as she moved against the glow of the window, her voice close again. "I liked it when you came to the bar that afternoon. How you were just there."

He realized that it was her way of asking him, despite all that was wrong—*everything*—to be there again.

She felt for his face in the dark and then she was gone. He lay quietly. To his asking her if she could ever love him, she never answered. She always said people could say anything, that they weren't there yet. Were they there now?

He took a draft from the bartender and found a table by the window that received afternoon sun. He spread the paper and began to read. Three regulars hunched side by side on stools, smoking and drinking quietly. Some mutual unnamed suspicion and resentment kept them from speaking to Val. Sun warm on his back and face, he sipped his beer, looking around for Lee Anne from time to time. Maybe he'd misunderstood her last night. Maybe she'd changed her mind.

When he checked again, someone had come out of the swinging doors to the kitchen, and he glanced her way—not Lee Anne. But his body seemed to know something before he did; he went light-headed, broke into a nervous sweat. Always Lee Anne seemed to look into a distance, but now he saw in her what he'd felt in her touch last night, something different; the warmth of the room rose to engulf him, the sun just reaching the end of the bar made it blush a deep amber, lit a glass of beer golden. Later, it would feel like the slowed motion of a dream. The kitchen door still swinging behind her, the high, platinum blond bouffant hairdo, every strand teased and sprayed into place, an impossible, perfect confection. He fought the urge to laugh at this incongruous hairdo, laugh or applaud, it was so perfectly bad, so perfectly beautiful, and then, as if the dream were slowing down even more, he noticed one of the men at the bar closest to her take an unlit cigarette from behind his ear, place it between his lips, cock his thumbnail against a wooden kitchen match and in a practiced gesture, snap the nail against the red tip. A spurt of white flame burst above the thumb; a single dart of fire arched and disappeared into Lee Anne's hair; her hair shimmered from platinum into iridescent flame, liquid in the white afternoon sunlight. Could he believe his eyes? As if stabbed, he came fully awake and was across the room in one motion even as the first terrible smell of burning hair reached him; she opened her mouth to scream, he threw his arms around her head, flailing, the flames singeing his shirt; they lost their balance, went down, rolled onto the floor, where he slapped at her hair, and in another moment, someone threw a pitcher of beer on them, quenching the flames.

They seemed to wander, meander, take forever in the fall afternoon sun, the while light slanting through the opening gaps in the tree branches, and across the sidewalks covered with leaves, the brick walls burning scarlet, Lee Anne staring straight ahead, sometimes letting him put his arm around her shoulders, sometimes pulling away and walking apart from him, her arms crossed over her beer-drenched shirt, the sunlight slanting through her ruined hair, people looking after them as, drenched, they walked block after block until they reached his place and he let them in.

And then she sat for a long time on the sofa in one of his T-shirts, her soaked shirt and bra a twisted knot in the middle of the floor where she had let them drop, the sun slanting in the windows, each ungrouted tile casting a thin blade of shadow, every splinter and knot, every grain of the unsheathed two-by-fours etched, the smell of burned hair in the room, and when Lee Anne still hadn't moved, Val led her by the hand to the kitchen sink and turned on the water and gently bent her forward at the waist until her head came under the tepid stream—she let him—and he gently began to work in shampoo, barely touching her, seeing if he was hurting her or if she would protest, but she did not, and then he washed her scorched and gnarled hair, sometimes stopping to rub her back. He rinsed her hair for a long time, patted it dry with a towel, the swim and tangle of burned and blackened ends, different lengths, and offered to take her to a doctor to see if she was okay, but she shook her head no, and, straightening, she looked at him as if trying to identify who he might be, and then, without a change in her expression, she returned to the sofa. He remained standing, unable to cross the room, take her hand, breach her remoteness, her distance; he sat down across from her, and slowly the white faded out of the sunlight slanting through the windows, the room diluted to gray, and then she walked quietly to the kitchen table and pulled out a chair. In a flat distant voice she said, "Can you get me a scissors? Please," she added.

Val went through kitchen drawers and cabinets, returned with several pairs. She weighed each like a blind person trying to imagine how something might look. She took the short pair and placed them on the table with a single clank. As if sleepwalking, she crossed the room and spread a section of newspaper on the floor. She placed the kitchen chair in the middle.

Val said softly, "Lee Anne, we'll have it done. Please. Anywhere you want. I just got paid."

In the chair, feeling for the scissors, she fit her fingers to the holes. She raised her free hand, shaped her head, gently, its shape and contours, the surface of it, the essence of it. She gathered a handful of hair together and, still staring straight ahead, she raised her other hand slowly, fit and refit the scissors to the gathered knot. With the single sound of the scissor closing, a tight, dry sound, Val was surprised to hear a sudden intake of breath, his, as he watched the silent fall of hair onto her shoulders.

She refit her fingers into her hair, gathered it together, again, the dry rasp of the blades. Then the falling of the platinum hair, nearly invisible in the gray light, which was rapidly fading, but still minutes away from darkness. Unable to turn on a lamp, to move, to stop her, to speak, to do anything, Val sank onto his knees on the floor some distance away. She cut her way around her scalp for some time, stopping to gaze out the windows, the smell of scorched hair, chemicals, and shampoo strong in the air. Then, like those of an athlete reaching the limits of endurance, her arms sank back down into her lap and she was motionless. Now it was dark. He heard the metallic clink of the scissors on the Formica table. She stood slowly and brushed herself off. When he tried to stand, his legs were too sore and stiff; he leaned onto all fours, pushed himself upright. Swaying, he took a tentative step, staggering once. He heard the brass bed squeak and settle as she lay down.

He walked to the edge of the newspaper, a faint glow on the floor, cement where the tiles had stopped, the kitchen chair still squarely in the middle. Kneeling, he felt around until, fingers brushing the hair, he gathered a handful of cuttings, and slowly, fearfully, he brought the burned hair to his nose. He looked at it lying in his palm, turned his hand over and let the hair sift back down onto the paper, then brushed his palms against each other.

Beside the bed, he thought to ask her if she'd like something to eat, or anything else, but then changed his mind, or rather couldn't break the silence, couldn't speak, and returned with a glass of water, which he placed on the floor next to her. Then he lay down on the bed and encircled her within his arms—she was curled up, her back to him—and he gathered her close against his chest and held her, the scorch of her hair in his nostrils, and he felt himself begin to slide down into sleep.

He awoke to find Lee Anne gone, a fine shedding of chopped hair on the pillow. In the kitchen, without stepping onto the paper, he carefully raised the chair and set it aside. He slid the newspapers toward each other and when they were rigid enough to lift, he carried them slightly bowed into the bathroom as if on a table top, cautiously pushed them into a V and tipped the hair into the toilet, tapped the paper several times, then carefully folded it to hold any stray hair. Val raised his hand to flush the toilet, but, unable to do so, he stared down at the clumps of hair floating on the surface of the water. The dry rasp of the scissors in the fading light, until they had finally stopped and there'd been silence. This silence now. Like the watery, silver undulations above a flame, something still remained in the air. It was, he realized, the pure essence of her relentless will to go on no matter what, and Val knew he loved her for it.

That night rain, rain rattling window panes in gusts, rain gurgling in gutters, and then slow, steady, pouring rain, and Val coming out of a thick sleep to open the front door and look out, watching and listening to the rain, breathing in the cold wet smell, startled by the rhythmic appearance and disappearance of his breath, which became…

Midmorning. The small café a couple of blocks from the warehouse. Val coming out with a coffee-to-go and Danish. He set the Danish on a low stucco wall, was just peeling the lid off the cup. "Val." He jumped, scalding his fingers. He hadn't actually seen her hair after she'd cut it in the dark, and she'd been gone before he'd awakened in the morning. Now he saw it was still platinum, but cropped short, tousled, swirled. Her face was no longer hidden and her features emerged, the high thick cheekbones, the beautiful eyes. It was the face of a fighter, someone who had been hit, who had a ferocious will to hit back. A bulky, green army surplus field jacket swallowed her.

He offered her the coffee and Danish. She worked the saliva in her mouth before she seemed to recover, shook her head no.

"Take it, I'll go back in and get another for myself."

"Goddamnit, will you stop! I don't want the fucking coffee and Danish. Just eat! You eat! I won't!"

He put them down on the wall and crossed his arms. "Your hair came out… I mean, it looks nice, in a different sort of way…"

"God, you can be such an idiot."

He watched unhappily as his coffee steamed.

She said, "I'm okay." Softened. "Thanks for what you did the other day. The way you were with me."

He thought to ask her what she'd put on her hair to make it so flammable, but they had fallen into silence and everything he said was always wrong and what difference did it make now anyway?

"Val…." She took a deep breath. "I'm pregnant." She looked away. "Maybe you just gathered that now with the food…." She glanced quickly at his face. "No, of course not." He watched her breath in the chill damp air. He was back in the bow of the Amazing Grace, her purse spilling onto the bunk. A packet of birth control pills, half of them missing. He started to say, "...but you can't be pregnant..." He stopped himself.

She said, "It's yours, no one else's.... Just want to take care of that little item. You're so suspicious of me, though I can hardly blame you. I know you never believe me about anything. But this gives us the chance to change everything. It's not too late. This can be our starting point." She dug into her pocket, handed him an envelope. "Here. Read it." He didn't take the letter. "No, take it. You're the one who always needs proof..." He knew she was alluding to their argument over the perfume. "Or I could just puke for you. I'm sick every morning. Will you say something? Jesus, I'm pregnant."

But he was seeing her as they had rolled on the floor in front of the bar and then, when they'd come to a stop, her hands had been over her stomach instead of where, he realized now, he'd expected them to be, beating at the flames in her hair. He was back in the motel room in North Carolina looking at her, a promise between them, and her purpose, her relentless sense of purpose, that she was going somewhere; this, he suddenly understood, was where.

She seemed to read his confusion. "Don't act so surprised. Did you do anything about birth control?" She shook her head no, in an exaggerated way, a mockery of his anticipated response. "Nooo. Did you ever ask me what I was doing about it?" Again she shook her head no. "Hey, chick's supposed to carry the ball, right? Take the consequences, right? You didn't even think of it."

"What do you want, Lee Anne?"

She said, "I want you to marry me."

"For two months you wouldn't even be in the same room with me unless the lights were off. I get it now, 'Talk is lies. We're not there yet.' This is what you had in mind."

"I wasn't thinking about anything. I just knew I wasn't having any more lies."

"Than the ones already there."

"I told you it's not too late to turn it around."

"I've been waiting."

She shook her head. "It's never been in your eyes that I could tell you more. Never."

"That's always been your out."

She shrugged. "We did this together and now it's here." She smoothed the lab report in the envelope, pushed her hands into her pockets. "Marry me and we'll figure it out. If you don't, I'm getting rid of it."

"Face it, it doesn't work between us. You won't even tell me..." he shrugged, "I don't even know what it is you won't tell me. We're only together because...." He stopped.

A stubborn look came over her. "All of that could change. You're the only person I can do anything with."

"You don't take off your clothes when we make love."

"I told you I was doing the best I could."

"You won't even kiss me."

"I know everything, Val. I did what I could. Saying these things won't change anything now. Except. This already changes it. This is a new beginning." She placed the flat of her hand over her stomach. Said matter-of-factly. "You can't love anyone else. I can't either. Neither of us will. We'll always be there."

Val looked up. It was misting. It scared him, what she'd just said, that it might be true. He glanced up at the rain lightly drifting down sideways out of a white sky. As with everything else they did, Davis was silently present. Val groaned out loud. Could he even be entertaining thoughts of marrying her?

She watched his face. "Marry me. If you don't, I'm getting rid of it."

"Just like that. How can it be one or the other?"

"Because there's no such thing as being a little pregnant."

"We can figure something else out."

She faced him. "There is nothing else to figure out and it *is* one or the other. Don't look blank. Whether we talked about it or not, it was always there."

He didn't answer. Always there. Something had been there from that moment in the motel room. "Okay, the hard facts of the case, counselor," he looked at her sharply, that word conjuring Davis and North Carolina. She went on, "You didn't do anything and I didn't do anything because no one wanted to do it—give me another explanation."

He didn't answer.

"Yeah, that's what I thought. You can't. Now like it or not, that's all, Val. And I'm not getting left again. And definitely not with a kid. So, okay, here it is. If you're marrying me, then you're at my place before next Thursday at 1:30. That's one week from today. And if you're not there, I'll know that's my answer. I don't want to hear the why's and wherefores and maybes and kind-ofs and all the rest of it."

"Right, because talk is lies. Isn't that your theory and modus operandi?"

"Be sarcastic if you want. If you don't show up by 1:30, I'm in a cab and on my way to a doctor. Don't doubt me. I've already made the appointment."

"Just like that, boom."

"Yeah, just like that. I'm not going to go back and forth with you on this and nothing you can say will make me change my mind about it. Don't call me, I'll hang up. Don't try to meet me at work. If you do, I'll make such a fucking scene they'll take you away in handcuffs. I'm not kidding. It isn't negotiable. So you think about it, Val, and either you're there or you're not."

She turned to go. He grabbed her sleeve. "Hey, it's not that easy."

She jerked her arm out of his grasp. "You're right. It's not. It's complicated. But that's what I'm doing." She walked down the street without looking back.

Val became aware he was still holding the steaming coffee, then flung the cup end over end into the street.

## *She Does What She Must*

Even if he wanted to marry Lee Anne, things would be impossible with her. Val knew that. He saw her flattening her hand over her stomach. Maybe, as she had said, this would change everything. He heard her saying it. *Not too late*. Other times she'd said …*get out before it was too late*. Out of what? He knew they had to be connected: her fears, the thing she was trying to get out of, doing something before it was too late. *This can be our starting point.*

*Marry me and we'll have it….* Maybe they could try to be together for a short time, slowly get used to the idea; why couldn't she give it a little more time? Why did it have to be by Thursday?

Though he knew she'd stolen the perfume, he'd let the moment get by him when he could have called her bluff. Now, he realized, he was in the same situation. Though she'd said things were a certain way, though she'd said *stay away and don't call*, he saw he should come after her, that maybe she even wanted him to stop her. Whatever else happened between them, he couldn't let her kill it. He knew she didn't want to; that, in fact, she was desperate for him to stop her, to call her bluff.

He dialed her number. Someone answered, and there was confusion. Several voices. Someone calling her in the background. She answered.

"I knew you'd do this. I said *don't call*. Just make up your mind, Val. It's not negotiable for me."

"It would never work for us. It doesn't. But I'll take the boy. You won't be stuck."

"One-thirty, Thursday, Val. That's three days from now. Be there or that's it." She hung up.

Cold snap. Early morning frost. Val looked at white-frosted footprints in the tree strip by the curb. A while later, down by the East River, water brilliant, blue-black, lower Manhattan shimmering in the distance, cold and clear and far away. Uncrossable, freezing water. He had until tomorrow. But he knew that she'd do exactly what she had said. Tomorrow was Thursday. He'd wake up and know.

In the morning, he arranged for Per to let him take the truck at 12:30 to go up to Lee Anne's. It was a fifteen-minute drive at most; that would leave plenty of time, make him early. He didn't think he'd be able to stop her or talk her out of anything. Maybe some small part of him was hoping that if he showed up willing to marry her, then she, reassured by his willing-ness, would back off, not insist upon it, not follow through on her threat. If that didn't work, he wasn't sure, but maybe he'd marry her—the important thing was that they keep the boy no matter what. If things didn't work out between them, they'd still always have the child. All of it was wrong, but he could see no other way....

At 12:20, he walked downstairs to get the keys from Per, but he was gone; someone said he'd just stepped out to the hardware store, he'd be right back. Val quelled a wave of panic. At one Per drove up.

"Oh, my god, man, I completely forgot. And hey, the engine is stalling and dying. Keep revving it."

Per slid over, still revving the engine, indicated that Val should take the driver's seat; he eased out the other side, and Val took off. He drove several blocks; a car ran a yellow light at an intersection, Val hit the brakes, and the truck stalled. He tried to restart it, but it wouldn't catch, and, finally, the engine reeking of gas, he pushed the pickup over to the curb, locked it, and started walking. He broke into a jog, waved at a passing cab; the driver pointed at his OFF DUTY light. Val walked a few steps, again broke into a jog, and finally reached her street. It was almost 1:40. He thought he saw a cab turning at the far end of the street. He broke into a run, shouted in a hoarse voice, waved his arms. Gone.

Hands on knees, he gasped for breath. He walked toward her place, pressed the buzzer. A roommate he didn't know opened the door.

"Lee Anne?"

"She just left."

"In a cab?"

"Right. Couldn't have been three minutes ago." He pointed to the end of the street where Val had seen the cab turning.

"Did she say where she was headed—the address?" He could still get there in time to stop her!

The roommate shook his head no. Val felt something go out of him. "Want to come in and wait?"

"I don't think so." He sank onto the porch railing. "Maybe I'll just sit out here for a while."

The roommate said, "Could be some time." Then: "Okay, suit yourself, ring if you want to come in."

He closed the front door of the duplex. Val crossed his arms over his chest and perched on the railing. Slowly, silently, the afternoon clouded over into a mute white sky, the neighborhood noises of Brooklyn—cars, dogs barking—receded far away, and Val felt a damp chill rise through the soles of his boots and through his clothes. He rang the bell and the roommate opened the door and went back down the hall to what he was doing. Val heard a sitcom laugh track as a door opened and closed.

He stood outside Lee Anne's room in the dark hallway, and then he pushed open the door and stepped inside, closed it behind him. The room much as it had been several months ago, the few personal things on her dresser, pile of books on the floor by the bed, bigger. He looked between the bed and the wall for the picture of Davis and herself on the deck of the boat, the head shot of himself at his graduation tucked into the corner, but it wasn't there. He glanced at the dresser. The bottle of perfume they'd fought over, the box on its side. He lifted the lid and smelled it. Lovely in itself. Stolen.

He noticed the light outside was fading, spotted the yellow pad still stuck into a book, *The Canterbury Tales*. Except for the date written in her handwriting, *Dec. 9, 1980*, the page was still blank. Not a word. He picked up another book. Florida. He riffled the pages. Swamps. Alligators. Seminole Indians. Early land development. He snapped it shut. Another with a picture of a rocket rising on the cover. She was a reader, though he couldn't see any pattern to her interests. Well, okay, her father had worked at Cape Canaveral. He glanced around the room. Still the sense of it as uninhabited, perhaps anonymous, as if by design or compulsion.

He sat down in a sprung armchair to wait, looked out the window. Almost dark. Though it was impossible, he'd been ready to marry her. Maybe she'd changed her mind at the doctor's office, was on her way back now. He felt hopeful. If that were so, then what? He'd marry her now. A light in the house next door went on, a dull glow in the room.

It was dark when she silently pushed open the door—sudden burst of TV news from another room. In the hall light, her cropped hair platinum, skin white, bloodless. Holding a brown paper bag awkwardly in the crook of her arm, she stepped into the room, saw him, but made no sign or acknowledgment; moving stiffly, she placed the bag beside the bed. Val glimpsed a box, read: *feminine protection*.

She remained standing and looking out the window, her eyes far away. Putting out a hand like someone falling awkwardly in slow motion, she guided herself gingerly down to the mattress, kneeling, unfolding herself—Val pushed away an urge to help her, knew she wouldn't allow him to touch her—and she eased onto her back, her hands, not quite meeting just below her breasts, a child playing dead.

He sat on the bed beside her. He reached for her hands, now lying one atop the other. She pulled them away.

Val said, "Why didn't you wait for me? I came."

"You weren't coming."

"I came! Per's truck broke down. I got here a few minutes late."

She shook her head no. "I told you. 1:30."

"I was here at 1:35."

She shook her head no. "You had a week—enough time to be here if you really meant to be here."

He said, "Lee Anne…. Why couldn't you have let us work it out?" But even if she'd known the answer, she wouldn't have given it to him. She turned her head and looked out the window into the night sky between the two houses.

She moved a leg, perhaps to rise; her face tightened and she lay still, and then said in a toneless voice, "There's a suitcase in the closet. Pull it out." Val did so. "Inside..." He opened it to a tangle of clothes, a hair dryer. She said, "...there's an envelope."

Val found it, maybe the one he'd discovered some months ago, but left closed. She said, "Go ahead. Open it."

She snapped on a light beside the bed and Val squinted against the glare. He looked down at an 8" x 10" black-and-white photo.

"Davis." As she said his name, Val realized that neither of them had ever said his name aloud to the other, their collaboration, carefully avoiding it all this time, an almost impossible feat. The picture had been taken at night; he was caught and isolated in the burst of a flash. He was crouched behind the windshield of a boat, his hands on the wheel, the boat hot and full of muscle, a Fountain or an Aronow, maybe a Cigarette. A wall of spray exploded at his elbow, a white wake boiling behind into the dark. At the edges of the flash, the ocean, huge, black. Davis' long blond hair was blown back in the wind, his eyes slit by the rush of high speed. He had the aura of speed and beauty that Val had seen about him so many times—on a motorcycle, in the roadster, on the football field. He was looking at the camera and laughing with a look of joy and triumph, perhaps contempt.

"Davis," she repeated, again breaking their taboo not to speak about or acknowledge him. She said it as though she were summing him up, offering Val an essence or secret. Val looked at the photograph, a dozen questions tangling together: where was he, where was he going, whose boat...

"Keep it."

"...when was this taken, who took it?"

As if reading his thoughts, she said, "I could feel it the whole time.... You wanted to know about Davis." She stared at the ceiling. "You've always known, anyway. You know, but don't know."

He saw her face tighten in a web of pain as she switched off the light, plunging them into darkness. It echoed: *know, but don't know.* Something Per had once said about waking up in a hospital in Japan. "I just know what they told me, but I don't remember the thing itself." What she herself had said... when? The same phrase. Momentarily, he was confused. "Lee Anne..."

"Don't ask me. Not a word. You already know."

He hesitated, "Lee Anne...if you had just waited for me."

She said, "You weren't gonna make it. Or were gonna dick with me if you did." He didn't answer. Maybe it was true. "I was ready to marry you."

She shook her head no. "Nothing you say or do can make it different now. Just go." He didn't move. "When you think I'm no longer there, I'll still be there." Her voice was tight with pain.

He said, "I'll come by tomorrow, Lee Anne."

He reached for her hand, but she turned away from him onto her side and didn't answer.

Outside, Val looked back at the duplex, the loom of Brooklyn flushing the low clouds red. He realized that her giving him the picture of Davis was meant to be a revenge for his not being there in time this afternoon, a test she had known he'd fail; and for the abortion, itself; for the knife edge they'd been walking, which had gone over to hatred today on her part; for neither of them having been able to stop his getting her pregnant; for everything that had gone bad between her and Davis; and for something that, he suddenly knew, had been grievously wrong before he or Davis had ever appeared in her life. He started walking in the cold.

In the morning, Val came back to see Lee Anne, but her roommates—Michael, the sax player, and the other one, whose name he never got—wouldn't let Val in. With sullen, proprietary hostility, they kept him on the porch and shook their heads no. Should he try to explain himself, or push past them? He'd felt a kind of hope when she'd said she was pregnant—he'd seen himself holding a boy—but now he felt a keen sense of grief and desperation.

He studied the picture of Davis, and all of the questions that had rushed up the other night returned: where had he been going and... What might he find out? He had to forget the picture; there was something wrong and poisonous about it, and about Lee Anne's having given it to him the way she had; now that something was over or no longer possible, instead of their having a child, she was giving him Davis, or half of Davis, some part of him, but withholding the rest. As they weren't going to be together, it was a last desperate attempt on her part to get to him. He slid the photograph back into the envelope.

He called to let his mother know he'd be leaving his place in Brooklyn. Oh, and where was he going? Cambridge. He didn't say *back to law school*. As if by saying that, he'd be admitting he'd been wrong about everything—his leaving, his dream of doing something with boats, with Davis, just everything. He didn't know if his return was acquiescence, defeat or an abject attempt to please his father...or just that he'd run out of choices for the time being. His mother asked him what he was doing about tuition. Val said, "I can get my student loans back." His mother lowered her voice. "I'll cosign them for you."

"Thanks, Mom." And as if he were now fully present by his not being mentioned, Val asked, "How's Dad?"

"He's very tired." His father, relentless, had never shown signs of exhaustion until word of Davis overboard. "He's spent the last couple of days undergoing a series of tests in the hospital."

"What kind?"

"Blood work. X-rays."

"But, I mean, for what, exactly?"

"Well, that's just it. We're trying to find out."

For Val, it would be some indefinite time in the future—months, perhaps even years, he couldn't be sure—before the word *cancer* would emerge, reluctantly, mutedly, into conversation, slowly begin to trail them. But later, he would remember this conversation as the beginning of something.

Each night, Val held off sleep as long as possible, reading before he would start to slip beneath the surface of the room, the sky vast and infinite overhead, the motion of the boat, the stop-start whine of the reel, something moving below....

If she wouldn't let him see her, he would try writing Lee Anne. He sat down with a pad at the kitchen table. Davis had said, "You don't just leave Lee Anne. You do anything else, but you never say no to her. Say no and it comes back funny." He had to write her something that would make it better for both of them:

> Dear Lee Anne,
> You tell me nothing I can say or do can make a difference, but...

He couldn't find the thing he wanted to write. He sprawled across the brass bed to figure it out. With the lights on, he stared up at the ceiling; the lights shimmered, dimmed, he drifted...

... felt something coming closer. Now it was moving back and forth in the air. Fierce rage. Hovering over him. He couldn't move. He thrashed awake. The place was dark. He held his breath. He'd left the lights on, he was sure. The windows glowed across the room. He felt for Lee Anne beside him on the bed, but she wasn't there. He flicked on the reading light. No one. But his skin was still tingling, warning him, and the air itself held a charge of fury, hatred. Turning on the lights, he walked back and forth through the place. He looked down at the kitchen table. The pad exactly where he'd left it:

*Dear Lee Anne…*

Val turned away, then back. Something askew.

The pad had been cut in half. Shears and her front door key lay between the two halves. Val felt for the chair and sat down.

Then he was up and moving. He placed the last of his clothes in his duffle, gathered together the tools he'd acquired in a box. He cleaned out the refrigerator and placed everything worth saving into a cardboard box along with some canned goods, and walked the boxes over to Per's front steps in a couple of trips. Turning off the lights, he picked up his duffle and crossed to Per's. Knocked. Rumpled from sleep, Per came to the door.

Val said, "Per. I'm sorry to wake you, but I've gotta get going." He slid the boxes one after another inside the front door, handed him the keys to Keith's. Val started to thank him for everything, but Per put out a long arm and pulled him inside. "Hey, you don't get away from here so fast now. You fuck up and wake me at two o'clock, even with all these gifts," he indicated the tools and food, "then you come in."

In the kitchen, Per turned on the gas oven and poured each of them a shot of bourbon and sat down. "Okay, this first!"

They drank. Per refilled the glasses. "You leave in the middle of the night… Can't wait until morning. So, hey, now you talk to me a little."

Val told him what had just happened. Per nodded, "I try to tell you I see it in her all the time she comes and goes, this thing she just did." They drank. "Now tell me more. The rest." Val related some version of the last few months, but couldn't bring himself to tell Per about Lee Anne and Davis, how they were together before. None of it. When he finished, Per said, "Hey, I know you leave out maybe half of something…but that's okay. I tell you about the guy in our group who goes into the Porta-Potty, he smells the shit, now thirteen years are erased, he's back in a rice paddy in Vietnam, the cops take him away two days later, he's still trying to hold down the street with an assault rifle…. I tell you I see this same look in her eyes, something in her waiting."

Per poured one more shot, but Val shook his head no.

Per said, "She'll keep after you, I think. She wants something." He drank the shot. He said. "She can't help it, either. She does what she must."

Val uncovered his shot glass and Per poured. Val drank, then stood. Per followed him down the hall. Val noticed that Per was limping badly—recalled his way of saying it, that the government paid him for the steel inside his body. They stepped around the boxes of tools and groceries, shook hands, and Val put on his heavy coat and picked up his duffle.

Air clear and cold, Val started walking down the deserted maze of streets, the cobblestones and curbs white with frost, the bridge lights—Manhattan Bridge, Brooklyn Bridge—brilliant in the dark. As he reached the station, he realized it might be an hour before the train came at this time of night; shifting the duffle to his other shoulder, he turned toward the Brooklyn Bridge. Face freezing, eased by Per's bourbon, he navigated the walkway, the lights swooping up toward the stars, the air freezing, lower Manhattan lit up before him, Brooklyn behind, the water of the East River black far below. When he set down the duffle to rest, he could feel the fury to which he'd awakened in the stillness. He walked all the way up to Penn Station, dozed against his duffle for a couple of hours, and first thing in the morning caught the train to Boston.

## An Ocean Bottom

Val looked up a former classmate, slept on his sofa for a week while he found an apartment, saw the dean and was formally readmitted to the law school. He retrieved a few of his things that he had stored in someone's attic. He was aware that every moment distanced him from Lee Anne, from the instant he'd come awake to her palpable rage hanging in the darkened room, almost as if it were living and breathing, to the pad cut in two. Val remembered the way Lee Anne had appeared in Brooklyn, silently standing in the doorway when he looked up from his work in the warehouse.

Though everything seemed to take him twice as long to read and reread, and he'd forgotten a lot of the legal vocabulary, he was glad to be buried under so much numbingly routine work. He couldn't imagine what kind of lawyer he'd be, or if he'd be one at all, just that he could do this much now. Still, he found himself thinking about Lee Anne, what she kept trying to confess—was that even the word?—and how, if she could have told him, it would have made a difference to her—or to them.

Once, he thought he saw her—he'd been walking out of a bookstore off Harvard Square, had glanced into a coffee shop across the street. She'd just raised a cup and looked away quickly, but not before their eyes met—her cropped hair was now black, but her eyes unmistakable. A truck passed between them, and when it was gone, the table was empty, just a cup there. A second time—it was weeks later—he saw her at a bus stop half a block ahead in a crowd; she turned her back to him just as the bus came, and she got on. Could it really be Lee Anne?

His fear jolted him into a moment of clarity. He had betrayed her. *Together, they had Davis.* They'd been going somewhere together. Gotten there. Then—unintentionally?—he hadn't made it in time that Thursday afternoon. In so doing, he'd given her the biggest no a man can give to a woman. Perhaps his secret reason was that he knew she could never love him as she had Davis. Maybe none of it was true. Endless, endless...

In early spring Val met Kazz, who was getting a Master's in art history. Every day he spent with her, he felt a growing sense of relief, as if he were putting a small, saving distance between himself and Lee Anne. Kazz was beautiful. She was direct; there was not the sense of something terrible hanging over her. She was not isolated, but had knowable friends. She didn't look at him with contempt. She didn't make him feel that he had to save her from something—or was it something in herself?—or make up for a wrong in her life. Her face seemed whole, not broken into fragments. He did not feel a terror—a place she'd been? an imagined state of mind?—emanating from her skin, nor did she, incidentally, have a faintly metallic smell. She didn't believe she had to get out of something or someplace before it was too late—or that something terrible was coming toward her. She didn't speak in broken sentences, insist everything spoken was lies, or refuse to answer him; nor did he feel something in her waiting to be discovered. She had a simple belief and pleasure in herself and other people without being naive or vain or self-centered; an easy laugh; a thick sweet smell—hair and skin and the sharpness of sexual heat when she was excited; she didn't keep her clothes on when they made love; she wasn't angry at him for something he didn't understand, or find it contemptible that he had been stunned by just a little bit of garden-variety prosecutorial misconduct that had sent some asshole who'd deserved it anyway to the slammer for life; she could look him in the eye; she didn't mind that he had to sleep with a low light on because of something he could only allude to, a recent boating accident; nor did she treat him as a head case, nor dramatize things by being overly solicitous and pitying him…. She had never known Davis.

Her plan was to finish her Master's and return to the West, to Arizona, where she had applied for a job at the Arizona Museum in Tucson. She was from a large, old Arizona ranching family, and one afternoon she showed him a box of snapshots taken of relatives at a reunion on a cattle ranch in Kingman in the early fifties. High desert range. Mountains. Clouds etched silver-white receding into the distance. A spring-fed swimming pool by a ranch house. A windmill and water tower. In the black-and-white pictures, cactus, dogs, even people seemed to have a silvery outline. It was far away from tides and from the sunlight slanting down and disappearing into the ocean water, far away from Lee Anne and from his father's silent disapproval and lack of forgiveness for something he was sure he hadn't done. Though Val knew how someone else might see it—that this was too pat a solution— he was sure he really did love her.

When Kazz was offered a curatorship in Tucson, it became a foregone conclusion that they would go together when Val finished law school. They'd married in a simple ceremony in a small town in Arizona—the idea hadn't been to exclude their parents, but just that it was urgent for them to be married then and there. Afterward, Val had written to tell his parents, and sometime later, a box arrived parcel post, a plated silver service with the simple note, *Congratulations*, signed by his mother and father in his mother's handwriting, icy in its correctness and wordless reproach. Then Kazz became pregnant. With each step taken, Val felt as if he were putting up a protective barrier between himself and something he couldn't name. He passed the Arizona bar exam and went to work for the public defender's office.

His parents came out after Michael was born. Val ceremoniously placed Michael on his father's lap, and his father held the baby in his lap with a gentle, glad smile that momentarily emerged from out of an enormous distance. His father appeared much older than before the accident, had circles under his eyes, looked as if something were hollowing him out from within; the spring had gone out of his step, and the power and certainty out of the set of his shoulders and speech. In brief telephone conversations between Val and his mother, the words *cancer* and *remission* had guardedly emerged in a hushed voice, appeared and reappeared, as if they were always ahead of Val, or behind, he wasn't sure which. His mother pronounced the word *cancer* in a hushed voice—perhaps believing that by doing so she could lessen it or not draw its attention. He and his father spoke little during his visit, and Val had been both pained and relieved when he'd left.

When the first of the unsigned postcards arrived, Val felt a dread at the sight of Lee Anne's handwriting. How had she found him? But then that wasn't really a question. When Kazz asked him about the cards and sender, Val dismissed the whole thing. *Nothing, nobody, just an old friend.... Forget it.* And Kazz had. But more cards came. Stopped. Then started again. Kazz had been curious, then jealous and angry, and finally, as they had persisted, alarmed. She said, "Look how long this has gone on." She said, "This is just not normal." She said, "This is stalking." At times Kazz talked about getting a restraining order. Val thought this was wild-eyed. For what? Postcards? The cards would leave a bad feeling in the air between them.

From time to time, Val pulled out the saved cards—in which something cryptic, elliptical always seemed hidden and alluded to—and reread them. At times Lee Anne seemed to be writing almost out of a place, a physical place or room, or a moment stopped in time, or both. What could she still want? Sometimes he thought it was just to spite or torment him. Other times, he had the sense that she wanted what she had wanted in Brooklyn—for him to take her out of something—and that she thought or believed that only he could do it. It was too crazy. She was stuck somewhere. It couldn't be just from what had happened between them, could it? Should he write? It was endless. He wanted to ask her about everything that had gone unspoken between them. Surely now she could answer. At least about the picture of Davis—where had he been going? But, unable to look at it, Val had put the photo away. And even if he did write, and she answered, he knew he couldn't—or wouldn't—believe her. Mainly, something warned him not to acknowledge her in any way.

Mostly Val tried to forget everything. He went on working for the public defender's office and quickly advanced from defending felony DUIs and simple possession cases to vehicular manslaughter, sexual assaults, armed robbery, and homicides. Val liked the esprit de corps of the PD's office and most of the other lawyers, and perhaps perversely, liked the altruism of the low salary even while resenting it; still, it was a version of law practiced with idealism; he liked meeting down at a noisy, working-class bar beside the Southern Pacific tracks on Friday afternoons for beer and the inflated rhetoric of the other lawyers as they discussed cases, jived about their victories and defeats, railed against prosecutors and judges, played pool, stayed too late and missed dinner. Though some of the more senior PDs prepared to go to trial by only reading the police reports and getting their shoes shined, it was not a nine-to-five job for Val and some of the other more energetic lawyers. They liked to joke that each year in the PD's office was a dog year—seven years anywhere else.

Val gained a reputation for being smart and resourceful, for being charismatic and having a sense of humor; he was a good cross-examiner; juries liked him. Perhaps the downside for Val was that he identified too much with a defendant's being frightened and finding himself caught in the wheels of the criminal justice system. He could take nothing at face value. He identified with the family and friends, the wives and lovers of the defendants, and would do everything he could for his defendant.

Most judges liked Val because he tried his cases well, understood the legal issues thoroughly, and made his defense exciting. They knew he'd fight. He found it moving and redeeming to be able to stand up and say good things about his defendants before sentencing—that so-and-so was a good father, a good husband; that his employer had always trusted him, and except for this one mistake, this single moment of human weakness.... Often Val's impassioned presentation of these mitigating factors made a big difference in the sentencing.

When he argued before a jury, it became crucial to him to win over the judge and jury; it was his way of putting his world view to the test; if the jury gave him the verdict, it was confirmation, vindication; if they did not, it would send him reeling back into himself wondering what was wanting in himself and leaving him with a gnawing feeling of doubt—that perhaps he had missed something, one small detail that would have made a difference—and that maybe the world wasn't as he had thought. This, in combination with his relentless suspicion of police and prosecutors, often drove him to make extreme and wild motions on behalf of his defendants.

Six years into serving as a PD, he made such a motion in the Dewey Holland case. Dewey was the twenty-year-old son of a former basketball star who had played at the University of Arizona. He had crashed a party and ended up brandishing a gun when the students had threatened to kick him out. Two university cops had been called; they pushed their way into the crowd. One grabbed Dewey. When he struggled to get away, the second cop drew his gun and fired a shot, accidentally killing his partner. Under the felony murder statute, Dewey had been indicted for murder, which had enraged the black community. It had been Val's case. Well-known for his right-wing views, Bill Lynch as presiding judge of the superior court, oversaw the lottery system of assigning cases to judges. When the choice of judge for the Holland case was made public, it turned out to be Bill Lynch, himself, with whom Dewey's chances would be the worst. The black community and press claimed that the system had been rigged. While perhaps it might be technically correct that Dewey be indicted for felony murder, Val hated that the situation and indictment made it a capital case. He hated it more that he would have to try it in Lynch's courtroom.

It wasn't that Lynch was such a terrible guy. He had good instincts about people under his tough exterior. In general, Val and he had liked each other in the past; Val knew that he could be very sympathetic to a defendant who was just an ordinary guy who'd gotten caught up in something stupid. He also knew that when he felt a defendant was a hard case or a danger to the community, he didn't follow the law—he just did what he wanted...like Craig Benoit in San Francisco. Val was sure it wouldn't work to try Dewey Holland before Lynch. He'd have to find some way to get a different judge.

Lynch had once been a fullback on the football team, but had since become a chain smoker, and, in fact, he smoked on his bench even though NO SMOKING signs were posted throughout the courthouse and in each courtroom. On the strength of that, Val had made a pretrial motion for a change of judge—that Judge Lynch recuse himself from the case as he was violating the law. This divided the legal community. Some were delighted at Val's chutzpah and resourcefulness. Others thought it was the kind of thing that gave lawyers a bad name. An editorial had appeared in the *Arizona Star* entitled "Playing Fast and Loose with the Law." It took Val to task for this cynical motion. Val didn't care in the least what the paper and legal community thought. It seemed an appropriate response to the inappropriate charges, which to Val were even more reckless and cynical—and racist.

Ordinarily, another judge would preside over a hearing to recuse an assigned judge from a case, but within a few days Lynch reconvened and in front of a packed courtroom—press, and members of the black, legal and law enforcement communities—Judge Lynch had said that as he didn't want there to be any doubts about the outcome of this case, he would recuse himself without a hearing. But he took the opportunity to make a long speech, vilifying Val and all practitioners of what he called *gutter law*.

Val was absolutely indifferent to the speech. He'd gotten what he wanted: the case was reassigned. Period. No longer able to try the case under Lynch, the prosecutor reassessed his situation, and Val quickly struck a plea bargain wherein Dewey Holland pled guilty to aggravated assault—a six-year term—and in return the prosecutor dropped the homicide allegations. At two-thirds time, Holland would be out in four years. It was a big victory.

This was the way it went for several more years, Val identifying with his defendants, highly suspicious of the prosecution, doing whatever he had to do to win on their defendants' behalf. Occasionally, a close friend would confide to Val after a few drinks that he really respected Val, but that it would be good for Val to step back and protect his feelings a little more....

Then Val made a mistake. It was a brilliantly conceived strategy in a hopeless case, bred out of its very hopelessness. And it might have worked, but for the defendant himself. A drifter in his mid-twenties from Texas, Tom Jackson, had been staying in a cheap motel in town and had run out of money. Aware that there were two businessmen in the next room, he went to them on the pretense of asking for directions; he threatened them with a gun, tied them up, stuffed rags in their mouths to gag them, and stole their car and money. The maid found both of them suffocated the next morning, and Jackson was picked up driving their car.

The evidence against Jackson was overwhelming. He had their car, money and credit cards. His fingerprints were found all over their room. Two other motel guests had seen him leaving the room. As if all of this weren't enough, he'd confessed to the police and he'd done so in a way that wasn't especially remorseful. The cops had released one inflammatory part of the confession in which he'd referred to stuffing rags into their mouths: "I knew they'd die, but I did it so I wouldn't have to listen to their pathetic whining." That in itself tried and convicted Tom Jackson in the newspapers. He'd been indicted for murder; the prosecutor would be seeking the death penalty.

Val had taken a liking to Jackson. He was brash and charming, funny, impulsive; he claimed he had not meant to kill the men, and the fact that he had bound and gagged them bore this out. Why would he have tied them up if he'd meant to kill them? He'd just wanted enough time to get away; he knew the maid would find them. A stupid mistake. These more reasonable aspects came out when Val got to know Jackson. In fact, Val knew the first time he read Jackson's confession what he would find behind the belligerent tone and stupid remarks, because he'd seen it before in other defendants: a horrible background of family abuse in which one grew up as either a victim or as the bully in charge; there was nothing in between. To survive you never allowed yourself to look weak or show vulnerability. Caught by the police and terrified, Tom Jackson would naturally say the opposite of what he felt. No way he could show what he would see as weakness, that he'd only meant to gag the men, not kill them. He had to take the offensive. Though there had been no abuse in their family, Val instinctively understood all of this from the rage between Davis and his father, from Val's experience with Davis. He was moved to find a way to try to save Jackson and became even more motivated when the case was assigned to Judge Mead, who was death-penalty oriented. But what to do?

Then Val came up with a strategy, the only one that he thought could work. He advised Jackson to say when they came to trial that he wished to represent himself because of an irreconcilable difference with his defense attorney—Val. If he represented himself, he would know nothing about the rules of evidence, what motions he might make, and so on, and would leave such a tangled trail in the trial record that the case would be tied up for years in appeals. Appellate courts would be reluctant to allow someone to be executed under these circumstances. The case might ultimately end up being retried, the more time gone by, the better. His client would stay alive. Witnesses' memories faded. Witnesses died. The inflammatory emotions of the community subsided. It opened a window for another chance. It seemed the only possibility.

At the beginning of the trail, Jackson did exactly as Val had advised him. He stood up next to Val and told the judge that he wished to represent himself. When defendants asked to represent themselves, judges would then hold an exchange in which they would make it clear to the defendants that they understood the ramifications of their actions. The judge asked Jackson why he wished to represent himself. As instructed, Jackson said that he and his attorney had an irreconcilable conflict. Judge Mead asked him what that conflict might be. Val reached over to grab Jackson's sleeve to stop him from answering, but before he could, Jackson said, "Actually, I like Mr. Martin a lot. He's the only one who's cared about my case. I think he's a great guy. He told me to do this."

Jackson then went on to represent himself in the most inept of ways. The jury found him guilty. The trial was not without its moments of grim humor. When Jackson was asked if there was anything he wished to say before sentencing, he said, "Yes, your honor, I think you're a dog-faced fucker."

Judge Mead was hard of hearing. He turned to the court reporter. "I'm sorry. I didn't hear him. Could you read that back?"

The court reporter, who couldn't stand this particular testy and difficult judge, read in a loud voice, "The defendant says, 'I think you're a dog-faced fucker.'" The judge nodded. He then sentenced the defendant to death, which, in Arizona, was the gas chamber.

As expected, the case was then appealed. Because the trial court had made an inadequate record as to the basis for the judge's choosing the death penalty—he'd failed to adequately articulate his reasons—the case was returned to the judge for a new sentencing. But the victory was short-lived. The case went back to the Arizona Supreme Court, and the sentence was upheld. The court wrote that when Jackson had spoken in open court, he claimed that his attorney had advised him that they had irreconcilable differences; but in fact there were none; Jackson said he thought his lawyer was a *great guy;* it had been his attorney's tactical decision to have Jackson represent himself; therefore, Jackson's inadequate representation of himself could not be a basis for legal complaint. Jackson, not the legal system, would be held responsible for his inadequate representation. The Sixth Amendment claim of ineffective assistance of counsel would not hold up. Jackson was again sentenced to death. Just before sentencing, when asked if he had anything to say, he again said to the judge, "I still think you are a dog-faced fucker." The judge again nodded and again sentenced Jackson to die in the gas chamber.

The strategy might have worked brilliantly if Val had just been able to stop Jackson from answering the judge in time.

The whole case had then gone to Caroline Lowery, a talented habeas corpus attorney, skilled at convincing federal courts to reverse death sentences. She said to Val, "I understand why you did what you did, but the federal courts have been reversing a lot of these cases when a good trial attorney does it right. You could have taken that route." She berated Val for his extreme cynicism in constructing such a defense and leaving her so little to work with once the case had collapsed and been reversed. Although she did everything she could, there were few grounds upon which to appeal, and Jackson's case started moving toward an execution date far more swiftly than many other death penalty cases that had been delayed for years.

Val had been disbarred for a year for telling a lie in open court.

A lie. Was it? Maybe very technically, but Val couldn't see it that way. It had been an attempt to save a man's life in a hopeless case. Or had it been his tunnel vision, each step leading to the next, culminating in what they called a lie? Was that strategy really the only way left? Had he, without knowing it, been trying to circumvent the pain of a trial? He'd known what would be coming; the prosecution holding all of the cards; the grieving, bewildered and furious families of the businessmen, the wives and parents, the friends all right there in court; the jury most likely very unsympathetic. He'd known the case was unwinnable, and that he was going to lose someone he understood, and whom he wasn't supposed to like—for years, his friends had been telling him he had to distance himself from his defendants—and who would appear to be a monster.

In a way, whether it was Tom Jackson or another defendant, that was something he'd never gotten used to; most of these guys were fairly ordinary people, often likable, who somehow, after a lifetime of abuse, or a night of drinking or doping, made a stupid mistake. What could he conclude? Fairly ordinary people could do monstrous things...? A lie in open court? Val had just been trying to save Jackson.

Disbarred, Val went to work for a friend, a carpenter, a former defendant who'd since been paroled and who said, "Hey, *vato*, even if I had no job for you, I'd still pay you ten dollars an hour.... You got work as long as I'm breathing." Val liked working in the desert heat, having nothing more to think about than simple labor—framing, whatever it might be, speaking Spanish with the other carpenters and laborers, dozing in the heat after lunch in the broken shade of a *palo verde* or mesquite tree. The more physically exhausting, the better.

After a while, following his earlier interests in photography, drawing and design—he'd once hoped it would be applied to boats—he answered an ad in the paper. There was an acute shortage of teachers. He'd be a good fit. Learning as he went, he started working at a large arts-magnet middle school, all the time thinking that he would eventually go back to being a lawyer. Part of him was sure he would, was watching himself and waiting. But he didn't. His friends had no idea what to make of him. Here was this guy with a Harvard law degree, ten years in the PD's office, a guy who'd been a good defense attorney, combative and resourceful, and, yeah, things had taken a weird turn on the Jackson case, and his being disbarred like that was kind of iffy.... But teaching art to kids? What was that?

But now Val found himself fascinated by the students—sixth, seventh and eighth graders—their bright energy, their goodness, their anger, the awakening of their sexuality, the way he could sense by their behavior what was right or wrong about their families, which they brought with them into the school— father not at home, or drunk and verbally abusive; or the child living with an aunt, the mother in jail.... He was trying to understand something about who he was or had become. Some days he looked around his classroom and found it almost unbelievable that he was actually here with these kids.

One afternoon there was a sudden fight in the room—two big eighth graders—and as Val stepped in to break it up, his shirt popping a couple of buttons, fingernails scratching the backs of his hands, the hot breath and fury of the boys close on his face and body just before the monitor came and helped him, he felt an ancient familiarity, and after the boys had been taken to the principal's office and written up, a peculiar blankness and absence that he couldn't shake.

As the classroom emptied out and he was straightening the room and turning off his computer, he suddenly realized what he'd been doing today—this hadn't been the first time he'd broken up fights. It was what he'd done for years with his father and Davis, which was to step in between two furious males and try to keep them from killing each other. He sat down at his desk, the afternoon sun slanting white in the windows, the mountains purple in the distance. Maybe, in a way Val couldn't bring into focus, he'd been doing that, some version or variation of that, in the PD's office, trying over and over to save someone from a kind of fury he had unwittingly set in motion—Tom Jackson, so many others, Val stepping between two opposing forces: society and someone who wouldn't or couldn't play the game.

He glanced around the classroom. Several weeks before he'd given the kids a project: make a collage of your dream bedroom using pictures from magazines, fabric and colored paper. It could have anything in it, any size, any scale, anything, never mind *reality*: rockets, waterfalls, a horse, the moon, a snow-covered mountain, redwood trees, a new Camaro, all of them together.... Now he eyed the collages. He was amazed at what emerged from which kids—the most silent, sullen, often the most furious or disruptive kids would make these blazingly beautiful things.

The sun slanted deep into the room. Maybe by coming into this school, he'd taken that part of himself that had wanted to build and design boats, and translated it into this—teaching art. Maybe he'd been trying to go back to the time and place where Davis had been in his life when the dyslexia had first appeared—seventh and eighth grade—and Davis and everyone around him, not knowing what was happening, had started to go crazy...

He watched the screen-saver spiraling endlessly in on itself, glanced back at the collages as if they might be a code he could read; he sensed he had just caught a glimpse of an intention in himself—placing himself in this school—that went beyond his will or awareness, and that was slowly and inevitably drawing him toward something he couldn't see or understand, and that no matter what he did or how he did it, the intention kept reinventing itself in new guises, was still pulling him toward some conclusion.

He hadn't let himself think of Lee Anne for a time, but now he felt her presence, as earlier he'd felt the fight envelop him with his father and Davis; he felt her as she would come into his place in Brooklyn in the dark, lie down next to him, half her clothes kept on because she still loved Davis.... He heard the custodians in the hall emptying wastebaskets. He walked to the window and looked at the mountains; sometimes when hiking in the desert, he stared at the horizon, distant in the clear desert air, recently, in geological time, an ocean bottom, and it would remind him of being at sea; even now he could still feel something pulling him, a charge in the empty space, something here in the dry air...

He saw Lee Anne's hair suddenly burning in the white sunlight. Heard the dry rasp of the scissors in the darkening room. He looked around at the collages. He had been on his way to marry Lee Anne that Thursday. He turned off the computer. As the screen-saver faded into blackness, he felt a quick lurch in his stomach, the marlin and Davis getting smaller beneath him where the blue met the black....

Gathering together his folder and grade book, he pushed open the side door, smelled the dust and creosote. He walked toward the car thinking about Kazz and Michael, and, his steps quickening with fear, how much he wanted to get home and see them. As he slid behind the wheel he felt himself again enveloped by her presence—Lee Anne's. He heard her saying, "You can't love anyone else...I can't either. We'll always be there." Starting the car, he pushed away a knowing that together they'd once had Davis in Brooklyn.... And that together, after all this time, they still had Davis.

# THE MARLIN TAPE

## *The Grady-White*

Val took a sudden step away from the water, snail shells crunching under his shoes. Through some trick of time and place, water surface and sunlight, the white bluffs of Long Island, twenty miles off, hovered above the horizon with the blood-flushed scarlet of a heart or lung in the shimmer of air. Val, skidding on seaweed and rocks, started up the beach with an urgent need to hear Kazz's voice.

Inside, he raised the black receiver, dialed before he became aware of its silence, remembered the phone was disconnected. His eyes slid across the pink Formica table, stopped on the video cassette labeled in Regina's handwriting, June 11, 1984.... He felt something clench in him. He knew. He was going to watch the marlin tape before the day was over.

He pushed out the screen door of the cottage and walked quickly across the overgrown back lawn to a stone wharf several blocks away. Val dialed the pay phone, his house in Tucson. No answer. He tried Kazz at her office. A busy signal. He noticed an outboard on a trailer in a driveway, a For Sale sign taped to its hull; he drifted across the street to look it over. A Grady-White. He called her office again. This time she answered, and Val felt a flood of relief at the sound of her voice.

"Kazzie…"

"Oh, god, there you are. I just left a message at your mother's hoping you'd be calling her. This is a bad time for you not to have a phone."

"What's the matter?"

"Things are reaching an unbelievable pitch around here with Michael. He came home after school yesterday and.... He was just so weird."

"How?"

"Everything, just everything..." Kazz went on. In the house, he pulled a huge sewing needle out of his pack, said he was going to pierce his tongue; he put the needle on to boil, grabbed a big, dirty paw full of ice from the freezer and jammed it against his tongue to numb it. He played his music so loud the pictures were shaking on the walls and when she asked him to turn it down, he stormed out. She found two failed exams in his backpack. He didn't come home until five this morning, smelling of booze and dope, and when she asked him where he'd been he slammed her against the wall. She thought things had started getting out of hand when Celestino sold his boat a few days ago. That day he went up on the roof and wouldn't come down and when she tried to talk to him, he spat at her. "He said you never come through for him when he needs it. And that's absolutely not true. You've always been there in every way. And I told him so."

"Did he tell you how I didn't come through for him?" But of course Val knew Michael meant Celestino's Mako; he had said, "Davis would have gotten the boat."

"He spat at me. Val? What are you thinking?"

"Wondering what to do for him now. The right thing."

"I don't think he knows, himself, but I do know that you have to be here now to give it. He wants you to be decisive. In fact, I think he's waiting for you to do something."

Val said, "Part of it is, I don't see how I can leave my mother yet."

"What's that mean? Are you coming or not?"

"It means I just need a little time to think what to do."

She said, "Okay, call me." Her voice softened. "It doesn't help that I can't reach you. I'll be here at my office a while more. I'm either here or home. Just stay in touch. I have a meeting, I've got to go."

After she'd hung up, Val realized he had forgotten to ask her how the opening of the show had gone at the museum. When he called her back, there was no answer. Val walked across the massive uneven stones to the end of the wharf. Michael somehow kept slipping beyond his grasp. Part of it, he sensed, came out of something he wasn't doing. Val was aware he didn't act because he was afraid to repeat what his father had done with

Davis—push him farther and farther away, drive him into more extreme positions until he was finally out of reach. Feeling Michael getting away from him, Val suddenly knew what his father must have felt as they'd stood in the front hall in the fading November light and he told his father he'd just left law school, no reason given, and that he was taking a boat south by himself, and couldn't be talked out of it.

Val started down the wharf toward the phone. He picked up the receiver, dialed Kazz's office once more, abruptly hung up. He walked toward Stan Miller's beach house, stopped in the middle of the street, circled back to the Grady-White on the trailer. He climbed into the boat. Center console. Instruments. Radio. GPS. Compass. Running and navigation light switches. He rotated the stainless wheel and the Johnson 150 turned behind him. He noticed a list of features neatly itemized and placed in a plastic sleeve on the console. A price. The boat looked well maintained and in good condition. He hopped down, peered under the hull, and then started back to Stan's.

Suddenly Val knew in a way he'd never known that before he could go any farther with Michael, he had to be able to answer his questions about Davis. Yes, there was something to tell him. No, there wasn't. Get rid of the thing Michael claimed he saw in Val's face. Doubt. Guilt. His father had always held him responsible for Davis' death, and though Val had fought it, he had succumbed to his father's view of himself. Whatever was there, Michael assumed the worst, had even said, "When you're straight with me, I'll be straight with you."

In the beach house, he picked up Lee Anne's postcards. Flipped through them. Were they part of it? Fragments of something, which he didn't think Lee Anne herself completely understood, but which seemed to take her over, almost of its own will. She knew something. Part of something. About Davis. Or maybe it was something else. The cards had an atmosphere. Like a place, a room that terrified her. An actual place? He read through the cards. A place with Davis? Here was one from some time back about a piano coming into the house. She'd had nightmares for weeks after. Why nightmares about a piano? Kazz had said, "She wants something from you. I don't think she herself knows what it is." Like a child. Like Michael now. Wants something, but doesn't know what.

Val saw the woman in Walgreens ten days ago. The way she'd bolted when he spotted her at the end of the aisle before he'd caught a good look at her…had to be Lee Anne. Why would she have run if she hadn't recognized him and wanted to avoid him? But then why was she there, eight blocks from his house, if she hadn't wanted to see him? Coincidence? Impossible. Yet Kazz had been sure someone was in the house that same night. If it were so, could it have been Lee Anne? Sometimes it almost felt as if even though she'd hated him since Brooklyn, she still wanted to trust him with something in her—or wanted him to know about or play a part in it. She'd said that she saw herself telling him—only him—something. Why else would she keep writing him? It kept coming out in pieces. As if she didn't quite know it. As if it were leaking out of her. Which was the way it had been in Brooklyn. Pieces. She couldn't seem to go past a certain place or moment in time in herself.

Whatever her situation, he now understood he had to know once and for all what that thing was. Yet, he realized, he'd been afraid to contact her in any way. What could that set in motion? After Brooklyn it would not be good. And even if she could or would tell him about Davis, how could he know if she were telling him the truth? He couldn't. It seemed impossible; he wasn't even sure exactly what it was he was trying to understand.

The sun was sliding down behind the beach houses, evening coolness rising into the air when Val tried Kazz again. She wasn't at her office, but when he tried her at home, she answered. Her voice sounded thick, slightly choked, almost as if she'd been crying. "Kazzie?"

"Uh huh."

"What's the matter?"

He heard her take a deep breath. She said that she had to keep reminding herself that she believed Michael was basically a good kid…. He didn't go to school today. "When I got home, your son had pierced his tongue."

"Why's he always 'my son' when you don't like something he did?"

She didn't answer that. "I come in from work, there's a trail of blood splashed across the kitchen tiles. His mouth was so swollen he could barely speak. Of course I'm wondering about such stupid, irrelevant things, like, did he damage the nerves, will he get an infection; and when I try to ask him, he just leaves the house. Val, I need you here. Are you coming?"

"Yes."

"Which flight?"

"I'll call you back."

"Will you stop saying that?!"

"The phone at the house is disconnected. I'm at a pay phone."

"I need you here now."

"I'm coming. I have to make a plane reservation. I have something to take care of here."

"What thing?"

He couldn't answer. He didn't know.

"You have a son. He needs you."

"That's exactly my point!"

"I don't get your point!" She hung up.

He started for the beach house, planning to pack and leave as soon as possible. He slowed, then came to a stop. He walked back to the Grady-White. He placed his hand on the hull. Now he understood everything. Everything. It was coming to him so fast, he had to remain silent and still to make sure he was getting all of it. Or that it wasn't coming to him distorted by.... Kazz had said, "He's waiting for you to do something." Could anything be clearer? Still trailing his hand as if afraid to sever his connection to the hull, Val took several more steps around the boat. His opportunity was right here. His solution. Everything in one stroke. *Wuss.* By buying this boat, he could show Michael he had no fear. Isn't that what Michael had loved about the picture of Davis? "The Bomb! Dude!" No fear.

Val remained with his hand on the gunwale. The details clarified in a moment. Michael had already failed or missed three finals. He'd have to make them up. Summer school. So make something good come of it. Ask Kazz to send him here now. They'd have the boat together for several weeks at the beach house. It would be just him and Michael. He would give Michael what he wanted—was he really asking so much? It was perfect. Val stood up and walked toward the house. He rang the doorbell.

A man answered, maybe ten years older than Val. Val told him he was interested in the Grady-White, and the man invited him in. Val was startled by the sound of his own voice, at his coming into this brightly lit, cheerful living room, the smell of dinner cooking in the kitchen, someone else's domestic life. The man glanced out the window. "Almost dark. Not much we can do tonight, but I can go over a few things with you." He extended his hand. Introduced himself. Ryan. He went on to tell Val that it was a one-owner boat; it was seven years old and had been perfectly maintained. An all-purpose craft. Eighteen feet. He returned with a folder documenting the maintenance—every receipt—and went over the boat's various features and extras. Fish finder and depth gauge. Good GPS. Marine radio. He was including a set of three-year-old charts. An anchor and two hundred feet of line. Life jackets. Eighteen-gallon fuel tank. Even had a new stainless-steel propeller. They agreed to meet first thing in the morning—nine o'clock—and check it over in daylight.

Outside, Val let his eyes get used to the dark, and then looked up at the stars and the Milky Way overhead, the boat massive and silent on its trailer. At Stan's he turned on lights, put on a jacket, and silently made some dinner, cheered by the blue glow of the gas flame, the smell of food, and the familiar ritual of cooking. He ate quietly, the tea-colored wood of the front room glowing in the lamplight. The beach house itself had the narrow beam of a boat. He tried to imagine Michael here with him, couldn't quite do it, but felt hopeful. On some level he knew it would be a beginning. The boat would make something right between them, and afterward other things could begin to flow from that. As he ate, he fought back waves of rising nervousness, remembering he was going to watch the marlin tape before the day was over.

He placed the tape in the slot of the VCR. When it didn't engage, he didn't push it in. His head went heavy, and, too tired to sit, he slumped onto the banquette, pulled his sleeping bag tight around him, and curled up. From far away, Val heard the rhythmic slap of waves on the shore.

He awakened with a start. Grabbing a flashlight off the table, throwing on a jacket, he walked outside. Chilly. The stars, brilliant, reached to the horizon, the Milky Way burning phosphorescent overhead. Now that it was late, the constellations—Boötes with her bright navigation star, Arcturus; the Big and Little Dippers; Cygnus and Cassiopeia, Virgo and Scorpio farther to the south—had swung to the west. He walked across the cracked deck, switched on the flashlight. Dark and still, the water reached the top step, and where the deck had crumbled on one side, the water had flooded. Aiming the light, Val followed a single, thin streak to a puddle the size of a hand. He flicked off the beam and looked up at the stars. No moon. Spring tide, but above normal. He searched for some configuration of moon or planets that might explain the flood, but saw nothing. Behind him, the front room glowed blue with the light from the TV screen.

————

Water moving…. Val groaned and turned on his side, pulled the sleeping bag up to his chin. Where was he? The cockpit of his father's boat, Davis sleeping on the other seat; he stirred. The funeral today…. Val saw the coffin sliding into the hearse. The plainest coffin. *What your father wanted…nothing better than Davis himself had*. No, that was over. He opened his eyes to the TV screen pale blue in the morning light, the marlin tape still resting in the slot of the VCR. He glanced at his watch: 8:30. He was supposed to see Ryan about buying the boat at nine. He lay there quietly. The Grady-White. For Michael…. He sat up. The tape. He hadn't been able to watch it.

Ryan pointed out the boat's various features. When he finished, he looked up at Val. Val glanced across the lawn, gleaming with morning dew in the sunlight. This, he could see, would look crazy to anyone: buying a boat almost two thousand miles from home to use for a couple of weeks. It would be hard to explain or justify. He couldn't even begin to think of the conversation with Kazz. And yet, given what was happening with Michael, he thought it was exactly right. The only thing to do. He could at least take the next step.

"She looks good. Can we put her in?"

Ryan slipped the old station wagon into reverse, hitched it to the trailer, and they pulled the Grady-White to a boat ramp a few blocks away and backed her down. Val held the long bowline as she floated free of the cradle, then waited while Ryan parked the car. As he came walking down the ramp, he said, "She trailers nicely. You can do sixty-five, seventy on an Interstate and hardly know she's back there."

He took the bowline and drew the boat in close. Taking off their shoes and socks, they waded calf-deep into the water. "Still a bit chilly." Val held the bow steady for Ryan as he struggled to hoist himself over the gunwale. Val pushed the boat out and hopped in. Breathing hard, Ryan stepped back to the center console, lowered the engine into the water. It caught on the first try. Backing slowly, Ryan put it in forward, swung the boat around, and then, slowly increasing speed, he shouted, "Ready?" Val was already holding the stainless-steel grab rail. Ryan pushed the throttle forward, and the bow rose out of the water. Then, as the boat came up onto plane, the water blurred and the boat solidified under their feet. They ran without speaking for some distance. Ryan stamped a foot and shouted, "She has a solid platform." Val glanced at the speedometer. She was doing thirty-four knots. His eyes watered in the wind. He could feel warm and cold air currents, smell pockets of cut grass, rank ocean bottom, an indefinable but distinct boat smell—oil, slight mildew, bilge.

Ryan brought her into a slow turn, shouted, "Tracks well." Behind him, Val could see the curve of beach houses, thought he could make out Stan's place, the size of a matchbox turned on its side. They traded places. Val brought the Grady-White into a series of slow turns, each time holding on with one hand as he braced himself. They slowed, and Ryan switched on the depth gauge: thirty-five feet. He turned on the GPS. He shouted that he'd programmed in waypoints from New York to Cape Anne and over to Long Island. He punched up a local red bell buoy marking a reef three miles away and pointed at the display. Val watched the thin line of their course on the screen. He swung her ninety degrees and the line veered, then straightened as he returned her to course. Val had always loved navigation, and even though he was living in a desert, when they'd brought out hand-held GPS systems, Val hadn't been able to resist. He'd take long hikes in the mountains and desert, watching the thread spin out with a child's pleasure and satisfaction. Now he watched their course unspooling on the screen. They tried the marine radio, which was okay, and in fact Val knew that everything on this boat was in good shape. As they ran toward shore, he felt something coming back to life in him, a kind of certainty, an old knowing beyond words. And, too, that he could be okay again on a boat. He watched the beach coming into focus and detail. He had only one thing left to do: make a decision. He saw Michael's face breaking into a grin. For once, he wanted to be a hero to Michael. Give him his dream. Just give it outright. He had no idea how he could begin to explain himself to Kazz.

Hanging over the bow, Val looped the line through the ring on Stan's mooring, ran it through the chock, and cleated it. He walked aft and turned off the engine, heard a gull crying in the silence. He was startled by a sound, looked to see the boat's wake uncoiling in serpentine waves down the shore. He raised the motor, climbed into the old, cracked dinghy that had rested on Stan's deck, pushed off and lowered the oars.

Without taking a stroke, he drifted. Ryan had brought down the price on the Grady-White a bit; though still more than Val could afford, he'd had to buy it. Val decided to leave the boat in the water for the time being, keep it on the mooring in front of Stan's house. School would officially be over in a week or ten days and Michael could be here soon after. Ryan was on his way to Boston that afternoon on business, would be gone for a week; he'd left the trailer in Stan Miller's driveway. If for any reason Val had to get the boat out before Ryan got back from Boston, he could borrow the station wagon from his wife. Val only wished Michael were here now.

He drifted, looking over several other boats on nearby moorings— a Boston Whaler, a Bullseye, a large catboat. He noticed how the boats were silently swung in the same direction, bow to the current on the falling tide. He pulled a couple of times on his right oar, turned the dinghy's bow toward the rocky beach in front of Stan's, and began to row.

Head bowed by the short cord, Val had been talking to Kazz for some time. He was relieved to hear that Michael had come home last night. He'd awakened this morning with his tongue less swollen, blood crusted on the pillow. He'd refused go to school. Another final missed. Now, as Kazz finished, Val said, "I've got something I want to tell you. Just hear me out before you say anything…"

He'd been doing a lot of thinking in the last few days—did she remember telling him how she thought Michael was picking up on his negativity? Did she remember saying that to him, using that word? Negativity? Yes, kind of. Well, he'd thought it over and she was right; he was fearful in his relationship with Michael, his approach to things. He hadn't come through for Michael on some basic emotional level. He'd come to see this clearly.

He turned around the telephone, bent his knees, straightened. With nothing more left to preface it, he told her he'd bought a boat. Before she could say a word, he said, "Wait. Just let me finish." He went on quickly to tell her about the Grady-White—how carefully he'd checked it out, how good it was. And his plans for renting a car with a hitch and trailering it back to Arizona. How this was what was needed between himself and Michael, all of them, how this was the leap of faith, the change in direction.

"Kazz? You there?"

"You asked me to hear you out. Are you finished?"

"Actually…" he realized he wasn't. He'd come to a harder place yet. "No." He went on to say that Michael would have to go to summer school to make up his courses, but now they could bring something good out of it first. They could have the boat together for a few weeks if she'd send Michael…. He stopped.

Kazz was silent. "Are you finished now?"

"Yes."

"You're telling me you've just bought a boat—we own it—and that you want me to send Michael back there to you now? Do I understand you correctly?"

"Yes. Kazz, I have this beach house for as long as I want."

There was a silence. Kazz said, "Val, everything else aside, does this make sense—to reward Michael when he's just been as bad as he can be?"

"That's just the point. We have to look beyond that kind of tit-for-tat thinking. Let's break out. Go to another level."

"How much was the boat?"

"Are you getting what I'm saying about going to another level?"

"Yes. How much was the boat?" He told her. "Val. Val…. You know, we almost never argue about money. If we disagree on anything, it's about Michael. But money…no. Still, that *is* our money. And we were saving it for the mundane and thrilling purpose of putting on a new roof."

"I can go up with a bucket of tar and some patching material and get us through another year. Don't you see how important this is?"

"I see how you see it's important. I hear you."

"Can I make you understand that we just have to go beyond?"

"Yes, I understand. But I think what I'm saying is that there is no beyond for me. I just can't see it, Val." She paused, then said softly, "Listen to me. Come home. Please. Just go back to the guy who sold you the boat and tell him you've made a mistake. And come home."

Val looked across the street at the house. "Kazz, I can't."

They hung up at the same time.

In the last light of day, he looked out from the deck. The boats had silently swung on their moorings as the tide had turned, darkness rising in the water beneath its silvery stillness, the Grady-White etched against the horizon as night came on. Swallows, twisting and turning, fed on invisible insects overhead. Inside, fighting back a sharply rising uneasiness, he made dinner. When he glanced up from the stove, he noticed the TV screen glowing blue into the room, the marlin tape still resting in the VCR slot from last night.

## Fuck You

The VCR clicked as the cassette disappeared down into the slot, whirred into play. Out of habit, Val half-expected to hear theme music, the narration of previews. The screen went gray and flickered, the display silently counting. He heard something. A soft laugh? Someone saying, "Press this?" He thought he recognized Regina's voice. And someone else: Magnus? He couldn't make it out. Then: the underside of a tree's branches. The camera swung, stopped. Sky. A lawn. A dog trotting across the grass and Magnus walking toward the camera with his arm outstretched. Val thought it might be their backyard, a place he'd never been.

And then a guy walking down the dock carrying two boxes of groceries. The person was strange, but familiar. Himself. Seventeen years ago. As he spotted the camera, he waved. "New toy, Regina?" He looked like someone else, his gaze and smile still open, his nose unbroken.

The camera, stop and go, picked up some of the guys on the dock. Captains and owners. Snatches of conversation. A few laughs. Waves. Some shots of feet and car doors. Regina was still getting the hang of the camera. There was Benny Greenberg, one of Magnus' pals, stepping out into the cockpit of the *Nauti-Gal*; he caught sight of Regina and blew a kiss.

Val and Davis. They were laughing in front of the roadster, arms around each other's shoulders, and Val made a show of bowing and presenting… He swept his arm over the engine; the camera closed in on the blinding glare of chromed-out parts. Davis' sudden whinnying laugh.

Val felt himself pierced by a pain and yearning at the sight of them together, of Davis still alive and actually moving in the world, Davis with a boy's sudden grin, yet with his hero's body—narrow waist, wide shoulders, powerful arms and forearms, and his blond hair reaching to his shoulders. He suddenly pulled a golf club out from behind his back and raised it as if to hit Val, and when Val pretended to cower, he laughed his laugh. If there had ever been any doubts about it, Val had none now. Michael was Davis. Davis was Michael. Built the same, shaped the same, moved the same. And Michael even had the high-pitched laugh, mocking, delighted.

But, enough! Val reached to turn off the machine, yet watched as Davis and he split apart, Davis dropping the club behind the seat, and Val saw something he'd never noticed, that Davis and he had the same way of moving, of holding themselves. Davis opened the driver's side door, back to front, suicide door, and, still laughing, he abruptly stopped. He swept the hair off his face; his eyes narrowing with fear and suspicion, he took a long careful look around the parking lot and marina; it was the same expression Val had seen within minutes of his arriving on the first day, Davis flinching as a Corvette pulled in with a squealing of tires. He'd seen it later when two big guys had come into the bar where they'd been playing pool, and for days after. If he had thought the nightmare of what had come out of those days had distorted his perception—at times he had come to doubt his memories to the point that he even wondered if he'd actually seen Davis with a gun—if he'd ever had any doubts, Val clearly saw Davis' fearful expression now. With one last look around, Davis ducked into the roadster. He grinned for the camera, started the car, and there was the roar and lope of that big cam as he swung it around. He heard Regina say, "Fade out. Whew!" And Magnus, in his Southern accent, "Idn't that something?" Regina said, "Which? Davis or the car?" And Magnus: "Both." The camera followed the roadster, sound fading in the distance.

Then Lee Anne: the camera drifting up behind her as, half-crouched, she fingertip comb-fluffed her hair in the side-view mirror of a parked car. A crescent slice of her face moved in and out of the silvery reflection, her upper lip slightly pulled back from her teeth. Sensing movement, she suddenly turned and, startled, she threw her hand toward the lens. "Jesus, don't sneak up on me like that!" She bolted from the camera, which tracked her as she walked quickly away without looking back.

And which found her again: slumped in the fighting chair. Another day. In moody preoccupied silence, she gnawed the inside of her cheek, kept her eyes on Davis, never letting him out of her sight now that she'd caught up with him. Val came into the frame as he and Davis talked with their backs to the lens, Val pointing at something, Davis nodding. Lee Anne's eyes moved back and forth between the brothers as if working on a problem, calculating something. She pinched several hairs down over her eyes, smoothed them, looking for split ends. She glanced at the camera, tried to stare it down for a second, then, features whitened by sunlight, she threw a hand in front of her face.

There were several more days of stop-start shots: Davis, Val, Lee Anne, their comings and goings; there was one of the three of them drunk and getting into the roadster, Lee Anne suddenly losing her balance; she grabbed at both brothers to steady herself, got a handful of Val's shirt. Val reflexively reached out to steady her as Davis pushed Val away so hard he stumbled, fell to one knee. He looked down to straighten his torn shirt, Lee Anne laughing at something Davis said.

Val reached to turn off the tape, but the tape played on. He'd thought that his way of remembering had distorted this time beyond all possible understanding. But he noticed now that there really was something—he could see it—that Lee Anne and Davis kept watching for beyond the camera frame. And that somehow their interaction wove him into it. When it was just Lee Anne and Davis alone, their heads would come together, and he could almost sense the thing concealed between them, a fear, the same fear, shared, or perhaps a separate fear that seamlessly fit the other's. It had remained with her in Brooklyn in her gaze, her posture. Per, too, had seen it in her eyes. Called it *something in there waiting*. But if Val had doubted that it was there, he could see it now as the tape played. He remembered the furtive way Lee Anne had of eating, her face close to the table, her starved and hunted look. He saw that when the three of them were together—that shot of them drunk—something in or about Lee Anne seemed to pit Davis and Val against each other....

The next shot: late in the afternoon. Slightly out of focus, something massive overhead, black, outlined by a corona of flaring sunlight. The camera focused. Several marlin, huge, hung up at the weigh station....

There was a long sequence of Magnus' triumphant taking of his big marlin the next day, Davis safely handling the wire in the same way he always did, the three of them landing the huge fish.

Breathless, Val remained frozen before the screen, the tape playing on. He backed across the narrow room until he bumped into the banquette. He slumped and then tipped onto his side as the screen filled with water, and again the horizon had the easy swing and rhythm of the boat. Now almost unrecognizable, Val moved in front of the camera, his nose broken, his face and eyes swollen, Davis on the other side of the cockpit, his back to Val, arms crossed, wireman's gloves tucked into his back pocket. Val heard the sound of the line stripping off the reel, the fight with the marlin already in progress, the small marlin which had been foul-hooked in its back and which would never jump, not once, just pull and thrash, and which would come to the stern in a short time, and now rise through the water, wire leader glinting in the sun as Davis' gloved hands brought it in hand over hand, the fish on its side, tail working slowly, and then suddenly rolling back onto its stomach, Val's voice loud, "Watch it, Davis, she's going to run!" Davis' gloved hands releasing the wire as the marlin thrashed and dove, the reel screaming, Regina backing up to include the three of them in one shot, Magnus in the chair, and then again Davis methodically taking up the wire and pushing it clear with his foot, Val standing on the other side of the chair; he could hear shouting above the engines, not quite able to make out what was being said.

Now Val had the tagging pole in his hand as Davis worked the fish back to the stern, and Val forced himself to sit up and watch…. He saw himself lean overboard and push the pole toward the fish, which was out of sight below the transom; Val remembered how the marlin had darted forward and suddenly turned and that he had shouted a warning to Davis, "Let him go!" He thought he could almost make out the warning now, distorted through the sound of the reel and engines, the jostling of the camera. Val leaned toward the screen; he could see his mouth moving as he shouted, "Let him go, Davis!"

And Davis, who had his eyes on the fish, now turned to look at Val, maybe for the first time that day, and yell something back, which Val, through the noise, had not been able to hear, and which he still could not quite make out, but Val could read his lips, and the second time, he heard the intonation through the scream of the reel and rev of the engines, "…fuck you!" He saw himself drop the tagging pole on the deck as Davis continued to hang on with his knees braced against the gunwale. Val saw himself reaching for his wire cutters. "Let him go!" Again saw Davis mouthing, "Fuck you!"

Val extended the wire cutters toward the leader—in a second it would be over. Then, as Val had heard every day since, heard in his dreams, there was the sudden squeal of deck shoes, the crack of Davis' body slammed against the transom covering board; and Davis disappeared from the cockpit.

Val sank back onto the banquette. Eyes closed, again and again he replayed Davis' gloved hands wrapping and unwrapping the wire leader, but he could not see anything snag on the wire—his gloves, his clothes, nothing. Again and again he heard himself shouting, "Let him go!" And saw Davis holding on and then that one moment when he'd taken his eyes from the fish, something you never did, his last words to Val or anyone else: *fuck you.*

*Fuck you.* It had been in his walk, in his laugh, in everything he'd ever done from the time he'd been twelve. *Fuck you.* It had been the source of his power and charm. Defiance had saved him when his classmates had laughed at him: *dumb shit*. Defiance had made him quick and street-smart, always ready with a put-down, the wisecrack that broke up the class when the teacher turned to the board. Defiance had made him a last-second hero in football games. Defiance had made him swing when he was supposed to be taking, and get the game-winning triple. Defiance had gotten him kicked out of Clemson for assault and ended his football career. Defiance had made him the only one you wanted to have around and on your side and yet impossible to be with. It had gotten him into something that was following him up from Miami. Defiance. Fuck you. In what would be the last second of his life—with Lee Anne's sudden kiss between the three of them—defiance had killed him.

In the middle of night, he awoke, blue light glowing into the room. He stumbled to the table, and groping among Michael's pills and Lee Anne's postcards, he found a stack of paper, a pen, and wrote:

> *I have to know where Davis was going in the picture you gave me that night in Brooklyn.*

He thought about it. What if she still wouldn't tell him? He would plead his case. He started to write:

> *I have a son. He's in trouble. I have to save him....*

But he stopped. He put his head down on his hands and dozed, and then pushed back from the table and eased onto the banquette, and once again unable to rise or move, sleep or wake up, he kept seeing Davis and himself coming and going in the roadster, Davis still alive and moving in the sunlight, Davis so unbelievably beautiful, throwing back his head to laugh. And then Val was in a time and place he'd never been before with Davis. Davis had lived, been picked up out of the water, as Val had secretly always known. And Val had been visiting and taking care of him all these years. Now his beauty was gone. He was paunchy, balding. He slumped in a chair across the room. He'd been complaining bitterly, accusing someone of something—a judge, their father, someone—perhaps Val. He'd just gotten into trouble, again, and had a long rap sheet of DUIs, assaults, probations, and last chances; he'd been married three times, had a million women in between; he'd started his own business, had gone Chapter 11, had worked for other people—as mechanic, deck hand, captain. Davis was still angry at Val, and Val was still trying to make things okay for Davis. They'd just argued. All the time Val had been aware that there was a fear coming off Davis and that both of them were watching for someone coming up from Miami looking for Davis....

He woke with a jerk, a spasm of fright, body damp with sweat, became aware of dust spinning in the window light. Lunging for the TV, he fell to his knees and ejected the cassette. Stood. He glanced through the screened porch and saw the Grady-White silently hanging on its mooring against the horizon. He'd take the boat back to Ryan, maybe stop payment on the check if it came to that.

He looked down at the table and noticed something scrawled on a sheet of Stan Miller's legal stationery, a single streaming sentence or question:

*I have to know where Davis was going in the picture you gave me that night in Brooklyn.*

It was, he realized, a letter. To Lee Anne. One that he, himself, had written, though he had no memory of doing so. He folded and placed it in an envelope, which he addressed to the PO box always on the front of her cards. He walked down to Ryan's and rang the bell several times, but there was no answer. He saw the station wagon with its trailer hitch pulled under a tree and looked inside to see if there were keys, checked under the mat and in the glove compartment, searched for a hide-a-key behind the bumpers and in the wheel wells. Nothing. He walked around to the side of the house, but the curtains were drawn.

He crossed to the pay phone—glanced at his watch. Three hours earlier out in Arizona. Michael, with his swollen tongue. Would he be going to school? He couldn't quite see Michael, kept feeling Davis moving beside him. He picked up the receiver, became aware he was unable to remember the voice in himself that he used when he talked to Kazz, and hung up. He started walking quickly, found himself some time later in front of a mailbox; he looked down, was surprised to see the envelope addressed to Lee Anne—a letter, it turned out to be, wasn't it? A letter to Lee Anne with, he vaguely recalled, Stan's office address on his letterhead stationery. Unable to think things through completely, he watched himself mail it; he walked faster against the rise of a growing conviction that he had just given in to something. No matter what she'd written, he'd never acknowledged or communicated with Lee Anne after Brooklyn. That had been the end between them. A wrench. Now he realized that his silence had been an extension of their prolonged battle of wills, which had started in the first moments they'd seen each other, and though there had been time and distance, everything that had ever been between them—North Carolina, Brooklyn—was still there: standing in front of the drugstore holding the yellow perfume box; the morning after she'd cut her hair, the empty room, the gleam of her will incandescent in the air; Davis. It was as if no time had passed. As if they had, in fact, remained connected by his silence. Now he had somehow given in. He returned to the beach house, but couldn't stay inside, and continued through the front door and onto the deck, where he looked out and saw the Grady-White hanging on the mooring.

He returned to the house one afternoon; it had been how long? two? three? days since he'd written the letter. Something fluttered between the screen door and molding. He caught the pages as they fell, read the first one.

> Val,
> Missed you. Envy your not having a phone out here. This fax came for you to my office earlier today. Thought it might be important. Apologies for poor condition of P. 2, a bad transmission.
> Stay as long as you want. I'm away for four days but will look in on you when I get back. Best, Stan

Val flipped to the fax. Across the top she had written in the same block caps she had once used to do her crossword puzzles: VAL MARTIN. He recognized her handwriting:

> In the dream you came by boat. You were standing in my house. It was night. You stood in front of the window and even though it was dark, I could see the water behind you.

He turned to the next page, also a fax. Lined and streaked and fogged. Hard to make out. It seemed to be…a diagram? A design? A sketch? No; something copied from a book? There were small numbers scattered here and there. Where were his glasses? Also a smaller inset, hand-drawn. It was familiar, the style of it. He knew it from somewhere. At the bottom, in small letters, it said simply: *Friday. May 24. p.m.*

That, he thought, was the day after tomorrow, wasn't it? Inside, he stared at the fax. How had she come to send this to Stan? He shuffled through the things on the table. Stan's business stationery. With his address and fax on the letterhead. What Val had written her on.

He reread the fax: *In the dream you came...*

He sorted through her postcards and picked up her last one. Noted the postmark. Three weeks ago. He reread it:

> *Dreamed of you again, you were coming to visit me, you came by boat, then you were standing in my house. It was night. You stood in front of the window and even though it was dark, I could see the water behind you.*

He looked at the fax. Except for what was written at the bottom of the card—*I forgive you nothing*—their wording was almost identical. Turning it this way and that, he looked at the second page. Outside, he folded the diagram and tucked it into his shirt pocket, and then he dragged the dinghy across the deck, eased it down onto the beach and flipped her over. He dropped the oars inside and pulled her across the beach, bottom grinding on the rocks. He eased it into the water and rowed out to the Grady-White, secured the dinghy to the midship cleat and climbed into the boat. He opened the locker under the center console seat and dug out several orange life jackets, the packet of charts. Kneeling on the floor of the boat, he took out the faxed diagram, rotating it this way and that and flipping through the charts, stopping to compare it to enlarged segments. Within moments, he came to the tip of Long Island. Gardiners Bay. Shelter Island. North Cove. He turned her diagram around and aligned it next to a section of the chart. It was identical. She'd photocopied the section. He looked at her smaller inset, which started with a red bell. She'd straight-edged a line in. Next to the line she'd written a number. He read the detail. A dock. A white flagpole. A large house set back on a lawn. It was that simple. *In the dream, you come by water...I can see the ocean behind you....*

She lived in a house on the water. It seemed unbelievable, impossible, yet at the same time it made perfect sense, inevitable, that she'd be living by water.

He sat back on the floor. He noted the number she'd written next to the line from the red bell to the dock and, tracing the same angle through the magnetic compass rose, realized it was the course heading from the red bell to the dock. Checking the chart, he saw that it was thirty-eight miles by water. Realistically, maybe two or three hours away by boat. He replaced the chart in the locker, rowed in, and dragged the dinghy across the rocky beach and up onto the deck. He sat down on the crumbling concrete, and, looking up at the sound of a gull, he watched the Grady-White swing around into the tide.

# LEE ANNE

## *A Movie Run Backward*

...I look across the lawn toward the dock and the water and then back down at the letter, reading and rereading it, his handwriting, sixteen years, did I believe he'd ever answer? earlier I was on my way from the downtown office to show a house, and then I had an urge to drive all the way back here, I cancelled on the house, went straight to the mailbox, but already knew it was there, still I felt surprised, and yet it was like that moment when I got on the plane for Arizona, like seeing Val and Michael, knowing he had a son and then actually seeing him, each thing leading to the next, opening Val's back gate, finding the key under the flowerpot, and letting myself into the house—I can still feel myself walking from room to room as if I'm outside of myself—and then, too, there was the picture of Davis on the dresser, which confirmed something, and now with this letter, it's the same feeling, inevitable, another step taken...

...I reread the letter, one sentence, like the fragment of a broken con-versation coming from a long way off on gusts of wind, a phrase, and then nothing, and then another word or phrase, I take several deep breaths, I am enveloped by North Carolina, Davis' last day, and the days leading up to it, Val writes about the picture of Davis, nothing more, but that is everything, that he writes me now tells me for sure something has been happening in his life, a big change, I woke that night a few weeks ago already, dreamed of him in the house and felt something moving, then I left for Arizona, and now I know that wherever he has been hiding in his silence, in the desert, behind his brick walls, and within himself, perhaps his last hope or illusion has slipped away....

I look out at Brent's boat at the dock, his forty-six-foot Bertram, Brent loves that boat, and now, letter in hand, I know what happens next and how to do it, in a way I have the feeling that it's like everything's already happened, like I'm watching a movie I saw once and forgot being run backward to some beginning point though I don't know where that is—will I know it when I get there?—and I feel like I reawaken and can only see each step just as I am taking it... I turn to go to the telephone and think, funny, the way I've stayed in touch with him, Morgan, as if I always knew that a part of my life would come back, that it was just a matter of time, or that I'd never really left it, the way North Carolina and Brooklyn are still there in Val's letter, that it's maybe who I really am, most, or became most, can't say for sure...

I pick up the receiver and then decide why take the chance? hang up and get in my car.... As I drive to the pay phone, I look for Brent, he has followed at different times, and though he's supposed to be at work in New York today, who knows where he really is? or if it's not him, then maybe he has someone else watching me, and it's an old habit, anyway, to look in my rearview mirror, to watch what's happening around me, not to be found....

Where he actually is mentally, Brent, at this moment, is like he remains on hold, he is paralyzed, in check, a moment of pure inspiration on my part, I flew back from Arizona on the offensive, came in the door and told him I wasn't going to talk about where I'd been, what I'd done, apologize about anything, explain anything, told him that I'd stopped off to see a lawyer before coming home, almost told him that his pre-nup would never hold up, but stopped just short of that in the last second, thought that would be taking it too far, I did tell him I didn't care what I'd signed, that it wouldn't stop me from doing what I wanted, which now, more than ever, is one of the few things I do care about, I told him if he so much as laid a hand on me that I was moving my ass out once and for all, and that if he thought that was a problem, I'd get a restraining order, said a lot more, which I can't remember.... And none of which was true, but all of which has set him back on his heels, but only just for the moment, and all of which makes him crazier, dangerous, he always has to feel in control, but it is all now just a matter of time, and if I can get what I want and get myself out of here in one piece...

Timing is everything. If it happens right, Brent has it in him to set the rest in motion, though exactly how is still not yet quite clear.... This reminds me of a time Brent got completely out of hand and I said to myself this isn't who I am, I moved into an apartment, and when I was alone, I thought I'm not going back, and then I started thinking hard about what I'd signed, and about his house, his boat, his money, and that it was a joke, the pre-nup, that I had let him railroad me, that I'd get absolutely nothing if I filed for divorce, I went to see a lawyer and we went over it, and he said that I never should have signed the agreement, what had I been thinking? I couldn't answer him, that it was a kind of marital suicide, that was his phrase, that this thing made me powerless, a non-participant in the marriage, that marriages weren't just about love, but children—Val has the child—property, and that this arrangement kept me from holding Brent accountable for his actions, or even in check, a lot of lawyer language, but the bottom line here was that there was nothing I could do, but stick it out, and upon his death, I'd become his beneficiary, and receive everything, *if I stuck it out,* that was exactly the way he said it, *stuck it out,* and I was thinking if I lived long enough, if it didn't kill me first...

And then I went back to my apartment and bolted the door and I thought I'm not going to take this, and I'm not going to go out empty-handed, either, and I wondered how I had delivered myself into the hands of this man, couldn't help but wonder at myself for having done so, heard the lawyer say, *what were you thinking? you signed everything away right from the beginning,* his own sister, Moira, said *don't marry him,* I knew not to marry him, kept hearing the lawyer's phrase, *marital suicide,* and then I started thinking that somehow or other, there had to be a way, and that I wasn't going to let Brent do whatever he wanted and then just walk away when he was ready, I still hadn't decided to move back in, but I could feel it in me, maybe I would go out, but now Brent came with flowers, the demeaning promise of a new car, promises, I wasn't fooled, and still knowing that this wasn't who I really was, I decided, what the fuck, I'd take the car, consider it a down payment on something long owed, take all I could, and find ways to get more, that Brent deserved everything I could dish out, and I deserved everything I could get hold of, and I delivered myself back into his hands, the hostage returned herself to the marriage, but after that, things were different, I knew it was going to be him or me, and if it's him or me, it's going to be him.... And so I came back and we've gone along a while more....

Was I trying to have a kid or was it just *la-di-da* about birth control? And if so, perhaps trying to have a kid was the last lie or illusion, but now that it's gone, there will be no more self-deceptions about that or about the changes that might have taken place, courtesy of the doctor...

Now I think about beating Brent at his own game and how it's just a matter of tossing him up and catching him again and staying well back out of the way, it is like juggling a chain saw until the moment is right.... The way it is, Brent knows something is coming, he is canny and can feel these things, in that way he is a little like me—sometimes I think more so than I want to admit—and I sense him turning within himself, searching, asking himself, where is it coming from? which way.... He knows that since I've come back I don't care, have nothing more to lose, that it is just a matter of time....

After I came back from Arizona, I knew he'd go through my things looking for some clue, so I left everything there for him to find, the travel brochures, the airline ticket, make of it what you will, Brent, and then I realized, too, that now I had the pictures, and I hid them where he could find them, Val and Michael, he's always said he knew someone was there, and now that he's discovered them, the dice are bouncing, the ball is dancing on the blur of numbers, and I am watching him closely, he has looked at those pictures of Val and Michael walking under palm trees in the park at sunset and has been and is obsessing, who are they? and who are they to her? and why did I go see them when I did? and how long have they been in my life, and was he my lover? or could he still be my lover? and worse, still, is this a son I never told him about? and are they the ones he has always felt were there, and in a way, he would be right on all counts, and again, it will lead him in a circle, why did she go to visit them now? I know how Brent's mind works and I know what it is to obsess, feel the ground sliding beneath your feet and frantically try to construct something that will hold, and so, day by day, I stay in this house, Brent momentarily in check, obsessing, and step by step, there is that unmistakable feeling in the air of walking in the dark and wondering how much weight to put down before you are already falling, and it is funny, but only in the last few days have I realized that I felt that way all the time with Davis, though with Davis it was a turn on. I knew Davis wouldn't come after me, that I was safe, though in a funny way that turned out not to be true, either, with Brent, it's the same, yet more so, it can be terrifying, and yet this feels both right, the way things should be, and I don't know why that is, and all wrong, always has, exactly the way I don't want things to be, and either way, I still don't know why I am with him, have never known…

At some point, I won't and he won't, we won't, be able to go any farther like this and I only hope I'm safely out of it first.… Now each day is like winding something tighter and tighter, hoping it will keep going, can I make one more turn before it snaps? and so I am holding my breath and winding him tighter.… I am, as the expression goes, living on borrowed time.

As I drive toward the pay phone, Val's letter lying on the seat beside me, I know Brent is supposed to be working in New York, but I watch the rearview mirror anyway, maybe he's in New York and maybe he's not, safer to assume he's not, no way to live, but that's my life, at least for now…

…at the payphone, I dial Morgan in Baltimore, a voice message comes on and, what? I'm going to leave a message, say what? like call me at home? no way, he would know better anyway, still, I'm about to say, hi, me, Lee Anne, how're they hanging, back in touch later and then I check myself, realize this is not the time to start leaving my voice in someone's mailbox, who knows where and when or how that trail comes back, never leave a trail, except, I guess, the one I want to leave now for Brent, and then I realize that though I can't even begin to think it, this call is the next step, that it's starting to happen for real, and from now on, each of these steps are unlike any I've ever taken, leave a message after the tone, I hang up without speaking.… Part of me wants to stop now, I think…

But later in the day I try him again and this time he answers the phone himself and we arrange to meet—I tell him what to wear and where to go and when and to bring someone, a woman, preferably nondescript, I give him a few more instructions—I haven't seen him in years and am not sure what he will look like now, but he did tell me some time ago that he'd come north to get out of the sun, he has one of these butterscotch, freckled skins, Irish or something, melanoma in that Florida sunshine, one of the first guys I met back in Miami when I started working in that bar, but he caught it, the melanoma, just in time—and then I think some more and realize that even if Brent is watching me or having someone watch me, and he sees, or someone sees us meet, that nothing will happen, not yet, and I don't think he'd go after Morgan because it's me he wants and because he will want to know where it's leading before he does anything—I think. I hope. Still, handling Brent is like juggling a chain saw, Brent's suddenness, another time I was meeting someone, Brent kicked in a door, I was, well, not in another man's arms, but showing a listing to a woman who was wondering out loud if she could live with a pink kitchen and I was wondering if I'd yet reached the moment with her where I could suggest that the kitchen might be painted, and, like, how had my life come to this, I mean, tell the truth, I could have gone on cutting hair, when I first started there was more than a little desperation in it, and it was kind of a goof, like, what? a hairdresser? well, it was something I had to do, and better than being a waitress, and I'd kind of grown to like it and was good at it, not, I guess, who I was supposed to be, it was me, Lee Anne, but Brent and Brent's mother didn't care for a wife, daughter-in-law cutting hair or owning a beauty salon right here in town or anywhere else, really, it didn't look right, it didn't smell right, oh, please, dear, it just wasn't right, in fact, she couldn't figure it out, or me, his mother, as she had said, me with my innate carriage, she used that exact phrase, *innate carriage,* and then, this thing I did, fingers in people's wet hair, no, like she just couldn't put it together, Lee Anne cutting hair, the *Allure College of Beauty* was my Harvard, met Davis there, if I hadn't met Davis, then my life would have been, what?…well, with my Southern accent I guess she thought I'd start going barefoot, she just didn't get it, that's a whole other thing, no matter, anyway, for the time being I wasn't cutting hair, I was selling real estate, just a side hustle, but at least respectable enough in their eyes, so I'm showing this house and Brent kicks in the door—the bolt tears through the jamb, the door splits—and he sees me with this woman who just about shits as Brent explodes through the wood, he looks at me and this woman, can't believe his eyes, looks past us, looks at me, like, wow, I've got my clothes on, it was hysterical, the woman screams, I'm kind of startled myself, I say, *oh, don't worry, it's just my husband, I think there's been some misunderstanding, hasn't there, dear?* Brent, have you met Mrs. Wilson? am I the one or is it he who says *suffering succotash*, it was wonderful, like is it Tweety and Sylvester, or one of those mice, a cat or bulldog throws himself at a door, the mouse opens it, or is Tweety Bird, the bulldog, no, the cat, flies off into space, suffering succotash, later I laughed, though at the time it wasn't so funny, I saw something in his face, too, that Brent was startled, actually disappointed, that I wasn't being fucked by some guy, that he couldn't tear us both to shreds, confirm his worst fears, too, that women are scum, Brent goes back and forth between being needy—I keep seeing something in his gaze that I know from somewhere—and thinking of women as bitches or sluts, I don't even know what word he'd use, or I am, slut, but actually it was that exact moment when he kicked in the door, the damage that told me where this could go, as if the movie were already running backward, had been for some time and I had just looked up and noticed and realized it, and maybe Brent is going to get his chance, soon enough, I hope.... Of course, he had to pay for the door and it was fun watching him stammer out his apologies to Mrs. Wilson. For weeks after he was just baffled, he knew he was going to find me with someone, who? Mrs. Wilson, and Mrs. Wilson did buy that house, new door frame, by the time the carpenter got done quite expensive, really. Brent paid for it....

After I make the call, I get back in the car, and then suddenly calm—resigned?—for the first time all day, I take Val's letter out of my purse just to look at it again, unbelievable after all this time, I knew he'd have to come back, and I say to myself, if and when it comes to it, with the right lawyer, it could hold up, I'll put this away in a safe place, and this, too, is more of it. I start thinking about the right moment to respond to Val and for the first time notice there is a fax number on the legal letterhead of the paper he used.

...and, like, the next morning I come back from leaving Brent off at the station, his four days in New York, walk out onto the porch with my coffee, sit in a chair, and I think about Morgan down in Baltimore actually getting ready to come up here, or maybe he's left, already en route, probably in a rental car, it would be too stupid of him to use his own, Morgan out there and moving toward me, and part of me thinks, this can't really be starting to happen, I can't have set it in motion, and right then and there I think, stop it, it's gone far enough, when he gets up here, I'll meet him, pay him off, we'll agree on something fair for his time and trouble, maybe he'll take twenty percent, a decent kill rate, and that will be that, and yes, once I make this decision, I'm, like, relieved, but a while later, another part of me says, no, it has to happen, get out of the way, and I give myself over to the inevitable, go into the house and get the Polaroid camera, I cross the lawn and walk out onto the long narrow dock, my footsteps knock hollow on the planking, it's high tide and the Bertram rides above the dock, and I survey the boat, the sweep of her beautiful lines, $490,000, glass and chrome, and then I turn and look out and find the red bell, the channel in to the dock, turn again to see what he'll see, the house and lawn, and I remember leaving Vermont locked in the snow and ice and think that I could just be gone tomorrow, gone as far as I can get, maybe just clean out whatever I can take and go now, get away, how did I get here? I've asked myself that every day, part of me wants to disappear completely and start over, I did it before I met Davis, and I did it when I went to find Val in Brooklyn, though that was really, in a way, the life I'd started with Davis, I'm not sure, just that I know Val and I are still together, and then I was starting over again when I married Brent, it got wrong, though part of me still thinks when I met Brent that something in me knew exactly what it was doing, recognized him, I don't know what it was that I or it was recognizing, still now I think I could be gone tomorrow, just disappear completely and start over, though someone like Brent would come after you, would never stop until he found you, in that way, we are alike, relentless, and part of me—stubborn? thinks of Brent and that agreement and how he is sure he has me in a corner, I hear the lawyer, all you can do legally is stick it out, I wonder, how many times can you do that? start over, and start over empty, anyway, I look out at the buoy, and I think of Val, hear the doctor's voice, *damage*, coming through the painkiller, the thing that keeps winding me tighter is that Val knew what we were doing, he understood, we were there together, Davis between us, and then when the time came, he just turned and walked away, left me bleeding, Val and Michael in the park, I close my hand around a spring line and feel the rhythmic pulse of the water loosening and tightening the Bertram, wind and water like a heartbeat through the line, I look in at the massive bulkhead, and I think it's like watching a movie run backward to its beginning, all I can do is watch, myself, too, and see what happens next, I smooth the dock line through my palm, feel the twist of its heavy strands, and then, releasing it, I walk to the end of the dock and take a picture of the boat's name on the stern, the camera whirs and spits out a blank, I go to the bow, shoot again, the registration numbers, I look down and watch the images rising like smoke, I take pictures of the flying bridge, tuna tower, cockpit, the camera clicks and whirs until I finish the pack, and then, pictures stacked in hand, I walk to the end of the dock and look out at the buoy, hold up a fingernail and measure the distance across the water, the bell buoy half the height of my nail, underneath it all, a little part of me knows that I haven't set anything in motion, that it has set me in motion and from far off I can feel someone or something trying to form or take shape, maybe a word, maybe a name, I turn from the boat and look out at the buoy, I'll just have to wait until I connect with Morgan to see what happens next...

———

I look up from my desk and see a woman walk into the office and realize that it's her, she's perfect, five-six, a little overweight, in a brown dress, she has to be the one. You'd never notice or remember her. Perfect. She asks the receptionist for me, and I get up, she approaches, introduces herself as Mrs. Carlson, Jane Carlson, she offers me her hand, and I make a big production of getting my bag and keys and the listing together, I pick up a large accordion-style file folder, and say in a loud voice, I'm on my way out to show the house on Maple Avenue to the Carlsons...

Outside in the parking lot, he's sitting behind the wheel of a green Ford Explorer, there's the rental sticker on the back bumper, and he's looking straight ahead, and when I see him through the window in a blue suit, a fedora on his head, I almost burst out laughing, but the hat is good, makes it harder to pick a man out of a line-up, and the suit, nothing could be more unlike the Morgan I knew than this, I'd never seen him in anything other than jeans or shorts and bright-colored sports shirts...

I say to her in a loud voice, *you'll just follow me?* and she nods and walks over to the Explorer and gets in, I walk to my Mercedes, the car Brent bought me when I moved back into the house, and as I get in, an uncertain feeling, someone watching? I glance around, cars passing, I pull out, they fall in behind me and we start driving toward the listing, and even if Brent has someone reporting on me, it will never read as anything other than Lee Anne showed a house to some couple at two o'clock in the afternoon....

We pull into a circular gravel drive in front of a two-story, weathered-shingle affair several blocks from the water, For Sale sign in front, and we get out and I make a show of leading them around the property, front and backyards, the garden, and then I fit the key to the front door, push it open, and we're in. As I close it, a sudden rise of something, terror, in my throat and chest as I hear the deadbolt snap into place, I sense a kind of darkness, a moment's panic, and, hiding this from Morgan and the woman, I walk to the mantel, place my card among twenty others, turn, Morgan reads some-thing in my face, but doesn't speak, I walk to the front window, a car drifts down the street, I don't get a good look at the driver, I walk through several first-floor rooms until I know the house is empty, of course it's empty....

Hat still on, Morgan says in a soft, too-close voice, *you're looking great, kid, how ya been doin?* his Florida Southern accent a reminder of another world, and I come over and give him a quick hug. Back then Morgan seemed like a grown-up, and now he's pushing fifty or so and just looks worn, another version of grown-up, time's gone by, but of course, if he'd stayed, he probably wouldn't have lasted this long, and still, I thought I could count on him, I lie now and say, *you're looking great yourself,* pluck the sleeve of the suit and smile, *very nice.*

*Like that?*

Deep smile lines, clear hardness in his gaze, eyes the color of ordinary stone whose beauty was brought out by cutting and polishing, blue shot through with shards of brown, and something else too, his eyes, the unnerving stare of something that exists in nature, is of nature—the gaze of a gull or fish...

I'm still looking for the hit that tells me, go ahead with it, or else tell him it was all a mistake, pay him off, send him away, and go back to...to what? His gaze tells me nothing. I feel both encouraged, and also the hard jolt of knowing that after this meeting there's no more second-guessing myself and it will go out of my hands.

Seeing him standing in front of the mantel in his banker's suit, you could light a fire on the andirons, place a snifter of Courvoisier in his hand, and there he'd be on the back cover of the New Yorker, weathered businessman.... Brent, ironically enough, wears a pinstripe like this to work when he goes into New York, and I think, if you saw Brent dressed like this could you tell that he's a guy who could, in a pumped-up heartbeat, yank you out of your car, kick in your ribs, kick the shit out of you, leave you half-dead and bleeding by the side of the road, that he's a guy who can without warning hammer his wife, then cry with remorse, panic like a child at the thought of her leaving him.... This suddenness, this un-readability of people has always fascinated and repelled me, drawn me against my will...and now I'm waiting to see what it will be in myself....

I turn and look back at the woman Morgan's brought with him—*Maggie, would you please excuse us for just a moment.* He calls after her as she's walking out, *have a look around, we shouldn't be too long,* and I hear her footsteps fade as she starts through the house. He turns his feral gaze back on me, takes off the hat, and I see his hair has thinned and is no longer the shock of reddish gold, but is a blend of premature white, again, not what I'd remembered or expected.

I circle the room, the strange house and closed windows no comfort to me, and, waiting to hear what I'll say, I become aware that I still have my folder under my arm, I walk into the dining room to put it on the table, and then I release the elastic, I gaze out the windows at the back garden, open the folder and pull out the Polaroids.

When I hear my voice, it is all business.

*I want you to take this boat.*

I hand him the snapshots and he goes through them. Shot of the name on the stern. The registration numbers on the bow. Several angles of the boat.

*It's a forty-six-foot Bertram.*

I pull out a series of charts and spread them on the table, flip to a chart showing North Cove. I've placed an arrow where Brent's house and dock would be, and I've drawn a course heading in from the buoy, if that's how he decides to come. I have another hand-drawn map to our house by land and a small city map. I orient him and show him several possible approaches. By water. By land. It's up to him. I show him, but don't tell him. You don't tell Morgan how to do it. That I leave to him.

I go over it in detail: where it is, the dock, the boat, and obviously that it should be at night; I give him duplicate keys to the Bertram. Cabin. Engine. He listens carefully. I tell him that it's up to him, everything, how he does it, but if he's caught, I'm counting on him not to…

Morgan is looking at me with those eyes, and I say, *okay, don't take it personally, maybe it goes without saying, but I'm a little keyed up. I don't want you to strip it, try to hide it, sell it, or take a single thing off her. I want you to run her out to where it's deep enough…*

We turn our attention back to the chart and I circle an area several miles off shore with my hand.

*…deep, I repeat, and I want you to open her up and send her to the bottom. I don't want there to be a trace of her—life rings, cushions, bumpers,* nada. *Open her in deep water. Like, obviously, I want you to be able to get back safely and disappear. The Bertram has a ten-foot inflatable with an eighteen-horse Johnson, but you'll have to find something else to get away in. Sink the inflatable out where you sink the boat.*

He nods again.

I push the charts and maps over to him and he studies them and then folds them up. He puts the Polaroids in his pocket.

*The owner is a maniac. If he comes after you, there will be nothing easy about it. He has guns. He's a good shot. He's relentless and in good shape. And he's very paranoid. He's supposed to be in New York, but back by tomorrow night. Riskier, I know, but this is what I was saying when I told you that I wanted you to take it when he's actually home. I don't want to know any of the details, Morgan...how you do it, when you actually do it...*

He drops the keys into his pocket, nods, like, imperturbable.

Overhead, I hear his friend Maggie, her footsteps fading in and out of the rooms.

I say, *when you do take her, I don't want you to uncleat the lines...*

He looks at me, a question. *I want you to cut the dock lines. They're new, the lines. When the owner comes down and finds the boat gone, I want him to look down and see the new dock lines lying at his feet and I want him to feel your presence, that someone was there. I want him to feel like he's completely lost control. That someone with a sharp knife cut his lines while he was sleeping.*

He looks at me with interest, which he masks, but I see he wants to ask me whose boat, but he's too cool for that, knows it's not what I'm putting on the table.

Suddenly, I decide that this is the moment to make him my, like, spiritual partner. And I know he can find out whose boat it is from the registration papers on board. I say, *the owner is my husband, Morgan, it's his boat. It's his baby. It's what he's got instead of a kid. I want him to wake up in the morning and look out the window and see his five-hundred-thousand-dollar Bertram gone, I want him to see the lines cut, and I want him to know that some fucker came in the middle of the night while he was sleeping, slipped on board his boat without making a sound, a mere two hundred yards from where his head lay on a pillow, and took his boat without his ever hearing a thing. I want him to feel terror deep down in his bones in a way he's never felt anything before, I want it to flood him like falling in love, I want him to know that he's been done, rolled, I want him sleepless and scared and talking to himself. I want to push him as far as he'll go. Not to mention I want the boat turned into the insurance money. Would it push you a little bit, Morgan, if someone did that to you?*

He just looks at me with those eyes. I see the smile line deepen in his cheek.

Then I think, that last might have been a mistake, flat out connecting it for Morgan, that the owner is my husband. Has his attention sharpened? Refracted. Or am I just imagining it? Too late now. I push ahead.

*Last but not least,* I say, reaching into my purse. I pull out a wad of hundred-dollar bills in an envelope and hand them over. I kiss him on the cheek and he replaces his fedora and we walk to the front door. Taking a deep breath, I open it, and, looking up and down the street, I follow them out, locking the door behind me.

I turn between the glass coffee table and the piano, measuring the space for something, looking for a balance point. Beyond the window where Val stood in my dream, I can see the Bertram tied up at the dock, the flying bridge, the sleek hull white and beautiful in the afternoon sun. Across the room, the weight and silence of the Steinway, its lid closed, strings taut in the dark wooden interior. I catch a glimpse of the neighbor's house and porch and lawn through the trees, wonder at its distance, and know that I will answer Val's letter sometime, but when? Closing my eyes, I extend my right arm and fingertips, and, one step at a time, I walk forward, feeling the empty air for the swoop of polished white marble rising from the table, waiting for it to come to my fingers, have I missed it? it's a word coming from a long way off; eyes closed, I take another step, hand sweeping back and forth, and here it is, smooth fit to my palm, it is as familiar as a hidden caress, my hand taking pleasure at the curve of my ass, my breast, familiar, reassuring, yet completely strange, this is me, but who is that? I close my hands around the white marble, abstract sculpture. I open my eyes and look down and find I'm standing with the polished curve of the thick glass table pressing just below my knees, and without lifting it, I release the mute marble, I close my eyes and continue walking into the next room, and when I open them again, I am standing in front of a desk looking down at the fax machine, but I think, not yet.... The movie runs backward and I watch for where I next come in.

## *The Bertram*

Brent calls from the apartment in New York. These evening calls are my bed check. Am I here? Am I out? Am I in the arms of another man—he always says he feels someone there. And even if I am here, what if I go out again? Often he'll call again, two or three times, odd, irregular times, thinks nothing of calling me at four in the morning to say he was thinking about me, worried about me. I don't argue anymore. Tonight he is casual, far too relaxed for Brent. Something about it doesn't seem real. *What did I do today? I showed a house. Which house? Would you know if I told you? Try me.* I tell him. *Maple Avenue,* he repeats, as if he knows. He's not interested in me. These are little details for arming himself so he can check up on me later, or just ask me again when he thinks I'm not paying attention. Will I slip up? Can he catch me in a lie? We still have not, amazingly enough, talked about my disappearance to Arizona, but I know that can't stay as it is much longer, that from the airline ticket, the various receipts, and most of all, those pictures of Val and Michael, he has his own ideas, but he is biding his time, trying to make sense of what I am doing now. I know him. Right now it is so big that he can't begin to see around it. Suddenly, I think, is he really in New York and I decide, why not? go ahead, I ask him, *where are you?* He says, *what do you mean, where am I?* I say, *are you calling from the apartment? Of course I'm in the apartment, why? Oh, it's just this connection, you seemed, I don't know, almost around the corner. What about the connection? Oh, Christ, Brent.... No, what did you mean by that?*

After he hangs up, I reconsider, I call him right back, but there is no answer, and suddenly, I'm sure he is not really in New York or at least in the apartment, but if that's not so, where is he? Not too far away, I think... close by... too close by.... I am suddenly, like, very uneasy, and though I suppose it is pointless since Brent obviously has keys, I lock every door in the house, go upstairs and get in bed and try to read for a while, and then I turn off the light and lie here in the dark, thinking about Morgan moving around out there in the dark, I have set him in motion, I am trying not to listen, but I listen hard for the taut burst of an engine kicking over...or, perhaps Morgan will just cut her loose on the tide's turn and let her drift silently off the dock some distance before starting her up, who knows what he will do, still, I keep listening, then shift my attention to sounds in the house, I'm listening hard, movement on the stairs, I just don't think Brent was in New York, that phone connection...

...after a while I can't help it, I get up and walk to the window, look out across the front porch roof, but the boat is still there, a white shape out at the dock. Hands on the windowsill, I listen into the house. Something is wrong. I look to the edges of the lawn and across to the house next door, but see nothing moving and feel all but certain that the boat will be here for the night, I did tell Morgan to take it while Brent was home, which is tomorrow night, I get back in bed and try to settle down, but I can't stop listening into the house, and then it hits me, it's been years since I've actually seen Morgan, how could I have ever made that connection for him, that Brent was the owner of the boat, he would have found the name on the registration if he'd cared to look, looked her up in Lloyd's, but just to hand that to him, that Brent was my husband, a mistake, never connect two people that can be kept apart in something like this, why would I make a mistake like that? that is not Lee Anne, Lee Anne always knows better.... I turn toward the door to the hall, so easy for Morgan to go back to Brent and sell me out; it's just money to someone like Morgan, and if you fuck up, you get what you deserve.... *That* was always the bottom line. Davis *knew* that. If I can make a mistake like that, then who am I if not Lee Anne?

I sit up suddenly and turn on the light, look toward the door to the hall, which is ajar, but there is no one there, and, breath subsiding, I wonder when I became such a coward. Lying here now with the light on, I hear someone moving out there, closer now, Morgan in a banker's suit and fedora, I hear the creak of footsteps, when he removes his hat, his hair is white, and with another step closer I realize he is covered with scales and I know this is cancer, and I jerk awake and gaze across the room at the dark windows, for just a second, I'm sure that I'm in Arizona, in Val's house looking out at the pool and trampoline, drifting up the hall, Michael's room...

I sit up and put my bare feet on the wooden floor just to feel it hard under my feet, now I'm in Val's bedroom, I pick up the folders in the dusky light, open them, all of this beautiful color rises like perfume into the room, a bouquet of children's paintings, Val an art teacher in a middle school of all things, not so different, maybe, than my being a hairdresser, or selling real estate, or even being married to someone like Brent, does that mean Val has become more himself or less? I don't know, and how does he see it? and is this pity or contempt I feel for him? he wanted to do something with boats, design or build, and do it with Davis, and Davis built that roadster, the Chevy small block covered with chrome, I go back there every night, I hear Davis talking...

Davis would go on how he had this brother, how great, how smart, Harvard in three years, and now he was in Harvard Law School, even before I ever met him I started calling him the Great Val, don't think I liked it, him, something, didn't like what Davis didn't know he was saying about himself, that he was fucked up, not good enough, a mechanic—I'd look at his beautiful hands, all cut up—that he couldn't be at Harvard, and if that was so, and he wasn't, like, okay, and he was with me, which he was, then what did that make me? some bitch hairdresser, make us? Davis had these newspaper clippings, his father's big cases, which, like, always made the paper—"...Settles for Five Million Dollars"—Davis called them his father's home run balls and there were a lot of them, he would never call or talk to his father, loved him too much, but didn't talk to him, and kept these clippings, the father was there, but not there, the clippings, I always hated to open a newspaper, some kind of queasy blankness, and in myself, too, that black news type, those pictures, up close they were tiny dots, faces hidden in them, I just shook my head at the clippings and told Davis to fuck himself, I didn't want to see his father's clippings, I didn't care about the Great Val, either, or Harvard Law School, though I was a little curious, the father, the brother, it was, like, there they were, up there, and you know, like, Davis flipped numbers, telephone numbers, addresses, everything, not dumb, but wired funny, and, like, stubborn, with all that upside-down-inside-outness he goes ahead and takes a symbolic logic course in college I guess just to prove something to himself, be what you can't be, defiance, kept the textbook, the failed tests still folded up inside, like, it was in his stuff, the textbook, did he think that one day he'd do these problems and then and only then would he be okay? that's what I know he secretly thought, why else would he keep it? when I came across that book, found all those failed exams, he grabbed it from me, I yanked it back, I tore the binding in half, flung the halves on the floor, shouted:

> "When that Aprill, with his shoures soote
> The droghte of Marche hath perced to the roote,
> And bathed every veyne in swich licour..."

...I went on like that and Davis kind of reeled back and said, *like, what the fuck is that?* It had just popped into my head from a long way off and for a second it was like panic for me, *what had I said?* and then I realized, *Chaucer, it's Chaucer, asshole,* and he said, *like, who?* and I said, *like, it doesn't matter, he can kiss my ass, I love you, that's what matters, you can send half the book to your father and half to your brother and they can stick it up their asses and speak, like, Chinese to each other,* I opened the door and threw the halves out onto our little porch, he laughed, and then it was like something let go we fucked our heads off, I wanted him to know he was okay as he was, could be okay with me, his life with me, the halves of the book were out there for days, pages fluttering around, Greek, we kept stepping over them....

A while later Val wrote Davis, said he was taking a leave of absence, couldn't stand law school anymore, said his father was furious, but he was doing it anyway, the letter was full of all this stuff about how he'd been in a prosecutor's office all summer, and this big case where they'd hidden the evidence that would have let the defendant off the hook, silenced a witness....

I mean, I think we were both kind of pissed at Val for reasons we couldn't exactly explain—our lives, Davis killing himself on these big engines, hands cut up, and without really knowing anything about Harvard, I knew it was a ride above the shit world, and it pissed me off that he didn't know that, couldn't see that, or thought he was too good, or just what? I didn't know, it just pissed me off, though of course, by then Lee Anne had shown Davis the way out, and he was taking it. It was funny to be so pissed off for reasons you didn't really understand at someone you didn't know. I don't guess that Davis cared to question it. I think part of him was kind of glad in a way because sooner or later maybe he was going to get to see his brother, but then, nervous, because there were some things Val couldn't find out about. He knew Val couldn't come to Miami. Or he'd have to find a way to keep Val from coming to Miami. That part we both knew...

And some small part of me, like I said, was kind of curious, too, to meet the Great Val, he was already on such a pedestal, I think even before I met him I was gunning for him... I can't say for sure, curious and impressed and gunning.... Is that possible?

But it, or he, Val, didn't really matter one way or the other because he was still only a letter on a table, and Davis and I got onto other things and forgot all about Val and the letter until the thing started with the grand jury, and then Davis left me in the middle of the night, panicked, or his excuse, anyway, disappeared into thin air, until I realized the answer to where he'd gone was written on a paper bag he'd tossed in the garbage, and, like, I was right, a phone number, and I followed him and woke up in North Carolina and there he was, the Great Val himself, and Davis, and me, the three of us together, just there, all of a sudden, all at once, nothing I'd ever given much thought to, the three of us together.

And right from the first moment there was something funny, weird, a bad vibe, I couldn't tell what it was, whether it was coming from me—I was so pissed at Davis the way he'd just left me like that—or from Val, or the way we all were together, I just didn't know, but there was something there with us. It felt awful and got worse by the minute...

I see Val, taller than Davis, rangy like a cross-country runner, something quiet and sure about him, everything held inside, he carried himself like nothing could really touch or get to him, thought before he spoke, it was like he was choosing his words the way most people pause before they pick a favorite color, and he had, like, good manners, but it was like they were to keep you at a distance, I think it was like he'd never had his balls broken, it wasn't so much the world could kiss his ass, exactly, but just hey, I don't know, he'd had something like Harvard Law School in the palm of his hand and couldn't see it, which pissed me off, and was maybe even a little too much like me.

But I've gotta say, too, it was funny, at the same time, part of me really liked that something in him, his quiet, his confidence, it made me curious, drew me to him, like he had some secret about himself, a good secret, maybe, that he believed in himself, he wasn't like most of the men I'd known, noisy, full of threats and intimidation, and honestly, even though I loved Davis, part of me thought, if I could be safe anywhere with anyone, *if,* then maybe it could be with him, Val; still I hated it that he thought he wasn't ever going to have to get into the shit with everyone else, or wasn't that really Lee Anne? her hating it? maybe it was I liked him for the things I couldn't stand in him, is there a word for that? Is it envy or something else? and all the time I was with him I never knew what I was going to do or say next, I was scared about what had happened back there in Miami, and the way Davis had left me, and freaked that first chance he got he was going to do something like that again, that it was all slipping away…

And what I noticed right off, was that Val couldn't keep his eyes off me— was he onto me? I'd catch him staring at me with this quizzical look on his face, as if he could see or hear something other people weren't getting, but he just didn't know what it was, hey, it was, like, the whole Lee Anne thing, I had no doubt in my mind, Davis didn't see it, had no clue, but Val got it, in San Francisco he'd found that exculpatory evidence concealed, one name written on a scrap of paper, and that scared me, but turned me on, even made me feel, like, I don't know, it's hard to say now, but that like someday I could go out of it, that maybe something more real could happen between him and me, maybe, I don't know, that part is confusing now and may not in fact even be true because I loved Davis…

But one thing I saw right away, for sure, was that Val was trying to get Davis to ditch me, and I thought that was like he dug me, himself, and he couldn't face it—scared, turned on—so he wanted to push me out, no matter what, I wasn't going to let Val get between Davis and me, when that happened, then it got all funny for real, well, no, it was already strange, because when Davis got up to North Carolina with Val I saw Davis was no longer quite making him out to be the Great Val, but something else had taken over, took over, Davis started pushing, I could feel his edge...and that made me think it's funny how you can never really love the people you think you love or say you love once they're actually right there in front of you, other things are there, it was that way for me with my mother when she came home from rehab, I loved her so much, but couldn't stand to be seen with her in public, her funny walk and slurred speech, I'd walk behind or in front of her, ignore her, pretend I wasn't with her until I had to translate for her, couldn't stand it that I'd do that, I loved her too much, something funny like that was happening to Davis with Val, I could see it, something started pushing them, pushing me, pushing all of us, and I knew we were coming to a moment where...

Funny, now, I remember two or three days before the party, we were just going down the road in Davis' roadster and we passed one of these North Carolina Public Power trucks pulled onto the shoulder, a bolt of lightning on the door, the lineman was in one of these gondola cherry pickers rising to work on the lines, and I turned and watched him silhouetted against the sky rising into the air until we were out of sight and then I felt like completely weird, couldn't speak, something terrible happening, didn't know what or where, I couldn't shake the feeling, and a while later it hits me, like how could I have forgotten? three years before I pulled into a gas station, there's a guy lying on the ground working under a car in a vacant lot next door, his legs are sticking out, there are these puddles everywhere from a downpour the day before, the guy is just bending his knees to start working his way out when a forklift backs up with this big load and severs an overhead power line, next thing, everyone's running to this guy under the car, I didn't know what was going on, later someone said the juice shot through the wet ground and electrocuted him, they were trying to give him CPR, the whole thing happened like in between the time I got out of the car, unscrewed the gas cap and reached for the nozzle at the pump, twenty seconds at the most, the guy was gone...

...so we pass this guy floating up toward those power lines in the gondola and then I look at us in the front seat of the roadster, Davis driving, me in the middle, and Val on the door, and we're all touching shoulder to shoulder, and it hits me, like we're always where we're touching, the three of us, in a car, a boat, a booth in a bar or restaurant, like I could feel a current going through us, like what was happening to one of us was happening to the others, but I didn't know anything more yet....

I try not to, but I can't help myself. I get out of bed and walk to the windows and, pressing my face to the glass, I cup my hands around my eyes and look into the dark, but the Bertram is still out there at the dock and though it's ridiculous I fight off spiraling panic that Morgan will sell me out, that I've made a deadly mistake by cluing him in that I'm married to Brent, I just know better.... In Florida with Davis I was cool. Is this me, the same person? Or maybe that's just the way I remember it, that I was cool, who knows what's true, maybe I was in a panic, then, too, it's all dreams and memories and they keep changing and something I don't know is pushing to surface, still pushing...

I stand at the windows and listen into the house.

...just that I could always feel a current passing through us, and I knew I had to do something to save myself, it was like there was someone or something there pushing us out of shape, the three of us a bad chemical combination, and oh, that's right, then Davis grabbing that guy when he poured champagne on that huge blue marlin at the weigh station, that blind look in his eyes, walking him backward to the edge of the dock, he would have been smashed in the cockpit of that boat below, but everyone grabbed Davis in time, Davis was just outraged at the sight of champagne being poured over that fish, you'd have to know Davis to understand it, Davis had a heart like boy, like, a reverence for things, I can just hear Davis' sudden laugh if he could hear me say something like this, he liked to push everything away with that laugh, me, too, his reverence was, like, for the beauty of things, like simple things, like those marlin, even Davis probably couldn't have said what it was, I can hear his sudden laugh, I mean, that's what it was he felt, champagne on that blue marlin, it was just too ugly, too wrong for him, it went against Davis' sense of how things should be, what I did later, too, the kiss the same thing, even me, it just happened...

...so it was like that whole day was weird, that man floating up in the air, but things had been going wrong before, like, I knew when I saw that chick walk by Davis and I got a look at his face—her face, too—that he'd screwed her, and I hit him, I wasn't going to take it....

Suddenly there was Val in front of me at this party, the Great Val, it was just us, and something had been going on from even before I met him, and I saw Davis coming up behind him, and I saw this distance in Val, distance and hunger, and there it was, I just pulled him to me and kissed him and for a second I felt this heat go through him, this passion he couldn't control, even as he was kissing me he was fighting it, I did it, I think now, to teach them both a lesson, Val, that he couldn't just walk over everything, that he was down there with everyone else, he wasn't safe, I wanted to get to him, make him know that he was like everyone else, and that he was hot for me, and that if he was hot for me, well, that was just tough shit, and that he couldn't get Davis to push me out, and I wanted it, like, for Davis, that he couldn't be in my bed and then run out on me in the middle of the night—the moment I woke I knew he was gone—and be out fucking some bitch a few days later, I wanted to make Davis jealous and realize that he loved me, but I didn't really know any of that, I just grabbed Val and kissed him and there was this quick heat, and then so quick there was Davis standing over Val, Val knocked out and bleeding, Davis turned and looked at me and for a second I was sure he was going to hit me—maybe that's what I really wanted, I don't know, I can't remember, and all the time there was this funny sense that I knew this moment, had always known it, was always going away from it, always coming back to it…. But Davis didn't hit me, he just grabbed me by the shirt and then had me by the arm and dragged me across the lawn….

In the car, I can't be sure, I might have said something like, we have to go back and see if he's okay, but Davis just looked at me with contempt and started the engine, and then was driving, not saying a word, like a stone, that '33 Ford a rocket down those roads, needle pinned up there at the top of the speedometer, I was beyond caring, we were headed back toward Florida, I wanted to say something, but it was like I was in another time or space, couldn't come out of it, but it was also dawning on me as we drove that maybe I'd won, that Davis and I were together, it was just him and me, or it would be if he wouldn't be too mad later, and then after a few hours he started to slow down and then he pulled over, we were someplace in Georgia, and we sat by the side of the road, that cam idling, which always reminded me of the gait of a hobbled, four-legged animal, a horse, Davis looked at me from his side of the car a long time—what did he see? what was he thinking? I have asked myself that so many times, what did he see when he looked at me? Was it even about me? Whatever it was, he came to some kind of decision, put the car in gear and started to turn around. I grabbed his arm and said, *no, let's not go back, let's keep going.* He pushed me away. I grabbed the steering wheel. He yanked my hand off the wheel. Looking straight ahead, he started driving back the way we had come, and I have thought, too, of that moment so many times, like, why did he turn around, was it to go back and work it out with Val? Or to prove something to the Great Val? Or to me? Or had he just realized that he couldn't go back to Florida and didn't know what next? For a while I thought he was going to dump me at a bus station in the next small town, but he didn't do that, either. If only we could have kept on going that night, even another five or ten minutes, that would have made all the difference, and over and over, I kept wanting to say, *no, let's not go back*—was he waiting for me to say it again? Even if I'd have argued with him or snatched the wheel, five minutes would have made a difference. But I couldn't speak and at some point on the way back I think I could feel him start to slip away from me, and the sun came up and we were still driving and then we got back to the marina and pulled into the parking lot and I could see a lot of the boats had already gone out, I saw the Hatteras wasn't at the float, and for a second I was relieved, she's gone, they're gone, all of them, and Davis won't wait around, we'll have breakfast, rest, be gone before Val gets back, and then I looked again and I recognized its flying bridge and tuna tower and outriggers in the channel, I saw that open expanse of water, and without looking at me, Davis jumped out of the car, motor still running, and started walking down the dock, that fast walk, his hipster walk, tough, nothing could touch him, he went down the dock and I saw the boat slow and then go into reverse and that space of water close up between the hull and the float and Davis hop on board into the cockpit and that was the last time I ever saw him....

So many times I have felt that moment, that sudden heat running through Val and myself, Davis joining it.... Most of the time I tell myself it was just a kiss, one kiss, and nothing more, and so many other people have done so much worse, I had a girlfriend who used to fuck her boyfriend in the afternoon on the way home from work, be there at dinner with her husband a while later, I mean, come on, I'm not saying it's right, but like compared to something like that it or even other things I'd done or even am doing—I mean, look at my whole Lee Anne thing—it was like nothing, really, it was a kiss, one kiss, and like what was I supposed to do, anyway, I wasn't going to take it.... Brooklyn, though, was something else. Brooklyn was different. Brooklyn was itself. And the rest of it, too, I guess...

I stand looking out the window into the dark at the Bertram and see Val and Michael walking side by side in that slanting light beneath palm trees. I watch them. They walk toward me. They walk away. In sunglasses and straw hat, I am unrecognizable to Val. Michael, of course, doesn't know me... never knew me.... Wouldn't recognize me. He is not mine. I am not his.

I remember that last day in Brooklyn, waiting for Val to come, watching myself, and when I knew he wasn't coming, I felt a stillness in myself, and it began to spread into a cold certainty, and even when I wanted it to stop, I couldn't stop it, and then I got up and I went down the porch stairs and the cab was waiting at the curb, and I took hold of the handle and even then I looked up and down the street one last time for Val, when I didn't see him I got in and the cabbie said, *where to, miss?* and I searched again through the back window at the street and then turned and gave him the doctor's address....

When I got back Val was waiting in my room, but it didn't matter any-more because he wasn't there when I needed him, it was either he could or he couldn't, and when he couldn't, I just had no choice and I did what I did, if I'd had a gun, I would have shot Val and stepped over him on the way out, but I lay down on the bed and then I suddenly remembered the picture of Davis, all the time we were together, Davis was there between us in our silence, Davis was what we had.... I sent him away with the picture of Davis. Davis is what we have.

I stand at the window looking out at the Bertram, which remains silent beyond the lawn at the dock. I go on listening into the house.

When the sun comes up, the boat is still there, hull golden and electric with veins of water-light, and all I can think as my panic spirals is, *God, Morgan, I handed it to you, but please don't sell me out.*

In the evening I pick up Brent at the station coming out on the train from New York, or, at least he appears walking off a train and strolls toward the car. He is carrying two squash racquets, a briefcase, and the *Wall Street Journal*. He appears to be too relaxed, which tells me something is not right, and when he gets in the car, he never quite looks at me, never gives me his searching look. It's as if he has made up his mind about something and doesn't need to check me out. Has he really been in New York? He'd never answered his phone that night when I called him back.... Where was he? If I asked, he'd say, *what? I was in the shower.* As if I were crazy. I think of

Morgan stopping in front of the mantel in that closed house, turning, his unblinking stare, his removing his fedora, and the surprise, the shock of his reddish gold hair now gone white and thin: Brent's money is as good as mine and he has much more of it. I have no idea what's been happening out there and I cannot read Brent, but trying to hide my shallow breathing, I feel my skin humid and electric with fear....

Small talk in the car and at home, pauses, stops, starts, each of us walking in and out of rooms, glancing at each other and avoiding each other and looking away, but Brent never challenges me, which isn't Brent....

The night is endless, my listening for Morgan, for the start of engines, for Brent beside me to do something. I expect to wake with his hands on my throat.... Toward morning I doze off and then I am wide awake and it all comes into focus quickly, it is as I had imagined, and hoped, but so much more, more everything, more frightening, more real, not just something imagined, I can't decide if it is the real or the imagined that scares me most, it is Brent suddenly in the bedroom doorway with this look on his face, terror, rage, it is his presence which jerks me awake, and it is like the beginning of something I know too well, like Brent's kicking in the door of that house, like when I walked in from Arizona and rather than waiting for him to start I was suddenly talking, I was telling him how it would and wouldn't be, I was bluffing, and we are still living in the rapidly collapsing space of that bluff, now it is collapsing faster, I sit up, *what?* I'd forgotten how bad it could be with Brent once he goes into this state, just the feeling coming off him, I don't have to act now as I'd thought I would, *what?* I repeat, alarmed....

*See for yourself,* he says in that low voice, and I get up and pull on a robe and again say, *what is it?* And maybe even a part of me wishes it wasn't, but I follow him downstairs and outside. I take a step and then stop and take another step, Brent is just ahead of me, I look across the lawn at the empty dock, and it is so weird, I knew it was coming, and this is what I wanted, but it *is* terrible, he stops and turns and looks at me, the boat, I say, *where's the boat?* He doesn't answer, but is walking again and I am following him across the lawn and out onto the dock, our steps suddenly hollow on the wood as if each of us echoes the other, and we stop and stand apart looking down at the water, into the water.... I don't dare say another word, and Brent just picks up a dock line and I look at it, and it is exactly as I had requested of Morgan, the dock lines are cut clean, Brent holds the severed line, and he has this look on his face, it is the look I've seen so many times when he's said,

*I can always feel someone there,* and also, too, the look I'd seen on Val's face, that things weren't as he'd thought when he'd come back without Davis, and perhaps now, too, oddly, on Brent's face there is a triumphant expression, as though this confirms his worst fears about everyone and everything.

*My god,* I gasp, and don't know if I am genuinely surprised or amazed or what, and if so, why, because I knew—I hoped I knew—this was coming; *my god,* I repeat, kneeling to pick up a severed dock line and caress the slashed tufts of nylon.

Brent turns and faces out to open water as if by looking at it long enough he would actually be able to find the boat, and suddenly a little part of me wants to laugh, but I'm afraid if I start I might never stop, actually, I'm afraid to do anything.

Still holding the dock lines, he takes several steps toward the end of the dock and then he stops once more and turns slowly, looking in all directions, like a man who knows something is coming, but he doesn't know from which direction, just that he hears it approaching…. His eyes remain focused in the distance, trying to take it all in, the water, the house, the lawn, the dock, his place—or what he'd thought was his place in it—but that it's been fractured; as yet he doesn't know how or why or what it means. He suddenly looks at me and then into me…. It's personal, but impersonal, as if I'm an object, part of what he's weighing against everything else, my disappearance and return from Arizona, the snapshots, the plane ticket, all of it has remained in suspension and unexplained and now along with them there is this, and for a second I think of words—say something, anything, comfort him, *it's insured, Brent;* or, *they'll find it;* or, what? But I don't dare say a word, if I get one word wrong, or glance, or expression, he'll know something…. I just stand there holding the severed line as Brent brushes by me and goes up the dock and back to the house to call the cops and Coast Guard…

A while later, there are police and Coast Guard officials all over, men in uniforms; it is somehow familiar, I think I remember men in uniforms; there are pictures of the boat handed over, there are interviews—and of course a couple of these cops have been here before for our little domestic disputes, and, though nothing is said, that is embarrassing, and also just the fact that they are cops, and cops coming into the house, and so many questions: *did either of you hear anything at all during the night? did we see or notice anyone unusual around the house, the grounds, the dock?* and et cetera. There is an inspection of the property, the beach, the dock, which makes me want to laugh, *what, the guys dropped their car keys, their wallets, they trailered a forty-six-foot boat across the lawn, shall we look for tire tracks?* and pushing a laugh down in me, I realize I'm much more nervous than I thought—how much can show? and then everyone is gone and abruptly Brent decides to get out of here and play squash and is off to his club. It will help him to smash that hard black little ball.

I find myself staring out at the water and thinking of the Bertram, of Morgan opening her up miles off shore out there in the dark, of the first wallow and lurch as the water rushed into the engine room, of Morgan stepping off into a runabout, of the sound of things crashing in the salon—TV, glasses, dishes, of seawater rising fast in the dark, hissing over the hot engines, flooding up out of the bilge and across the floorboards, the bunks, rushing in through the open portholes, of her listing, of water pouring over the stern into the cockpit, then one end, most likely the bow, swinging upright, and of her sliding down into the black water, her long silent descent to the bottom, where she sends up a cloud of silt and settles, of her lying down there now in the dark where she can't be found...and of the insurance money.

Most of me stops worrying about Morgan selling me out to Brent. But a little part of me, still uneasy, whispers, *you never know how it can come back...*

Because, like, I'm thinking about Davis and our last days in Florida before he ran.

Then I look out at the empty dock and it hits me how final and irreversible it is all becoming, how each step is taking me farther and farther, and again, a little part of me says, stop now, just go, disappear, I almost plead, *let it stop here,* and I watch myself to see what I will do...

But I don't stop.

While Brent is out trying to calm himself by smashing a small dense ball against a hardwood wall with a racquet, I stand in the living room and see Val exactly as I saw him in my dream weeks ago before I got on a plane to Arizona and know that the dream, itself—I sent it to him once—is the only answer to his letter, and I write how I saw him come ashore by boat and stand here by the window, and looking out at the end of the dock and buoy, I realize that there is no other way he can come, except by water, and I send my answer to the fax number on the legal letterhead, the paper he used, where is this? A lawyer, yes, but *who* is this? I send him my dream, details of the chart and know that I need to say nothing more.

I leave them in the fax machine here at the house—my letter, the charts—as if I'd forgotten them: they are for Brent to find. This scares the life out of me, but it is the next thing in the movie running backward.

Brent does find them—they are impossible not to find…. He doesn't touch his dinner, gets up abruptly and leaves the room. I can feel him, sleepless, obsessing, trying to restrain himself. We leave them lying there in the fax machine, what I supposedly forgot, what he found, our shared lie. He used to slap me, shake me, I can't even think about it, but now he has matured or we have matured together, and we are doing this instead. Now he is waiting and trying to figure it out. There are so many things for Brent to sort and try to put together. There is my trip to Arizona and there are pictures of a man and a teenage boy, neither of whom he has seen before, and there is my threat that I'll leave him for good and he knows I will, I've done it before though I came back…. And there is his beloved boat suddenly disappeared and now there is my letter addressed to Val and left in the fax, a real name at last for Brent, and a date and a time…. Are any of them connected, he wants to know. Is the man under the palms the same man I've faxed, and if so, what of it? And is he the same one Brent's always known was there? I can feel him obsessing, trying to put them together. And I am trying to hang on just a little longer….

After I leave Brent off at the station, I drive back to the house. Brent goes wherever he goes. Though he was dressed in his blue suit and had his *Wall Street Journal* and is supposed to be in the city for the next three days, I know he will not go to New York. He will go somewhere to wait and come back to watch the house. What Brent and I know separately and together is that some time tonight a man whom Brent has never met will come to the house by boat. If Val doesn't come, then I am wrong about everything. I waited for him once before in Brooklyn and he didn't come—or come in time. This time he will come. If he doesn't come now, then I will lie to Brent one more time about the fax and escape with nothing more than my life. One way or the other, my life as Lee Anne with Brent is almost over….

# NIGHT CROSSING

## *The Dock Lines*

Too late…. Val raised his oars, watched drops stream thickly down the blades into the darkening water. Overhead, the sky was a startling blue-black—night seeping down already—and in the east he was surprised to see the first faint star. Too late, too late to be starting. He felt the dinghy slowing and measured the distance back to the rocky beach, to the house, which he had cleaned this afternoon, washing and drying the dishes, sweeping the floor. As he took out the trash, he looked across the lawn and made out someone, motionless, watching his every move from behind the silvery windshield of a parked car: his father. Hands shaking, breath fluttering quickly, Val sat down on the back steps.

Clearing the Formica kitchen table, he'd swept the disarray into a plastic shopping bag: the marlin tape; Lee Anne's postcards; her letter, which had been sent to his parent's house in May of 1984 just before she'd gotten on the Greyhound and come north to find Davis; the Polaroid of her half-naked; also, the game of Tangoes; the picture of Davis; Michael's pills; Lee Anne's three-page fax. All of it into a baggy pack, along with a new waterproof flashlight, four extra batteries, two liters of drinking water, a sandwich, several candy bars, a flare gun and fresh set of flares, and a foul weather jacket, as well as an extra sweatshirt and a cheap pair of 10 x 23 binoculars. The knife Kazz and Michael had given him was clipped into his pocket. With the certainty that he wouldn't be coming back here until late tonight, he closed and locked the windows.

He'd meant to leave much earlier to have enough daylight to find all his buoys along the Connecticut shore, to be able to see the lobster pots and anything else floating, and then to find his way over to Long Island, but, last minute, he'd made some rough calculations on gas usage, and thinking it unlikely that he'd find a gas dock open after five on the Long Island side, he had driven down to West Marine to get two plastic, five-gallon jerry cans and a funnel for extra fuel. He'd finished gassing and loading them an hour ago. He took another few strokes now. Too late....

He rowed slowly toward the Grady-White until he bumped lightly against the hull; reached up and grabbed the gunwale, automatically shipping the inboard oar as he pulled the dinghy alongside. He dropped the pack in the boat and climbed aboard. The gunwale and decks were already chilly and slick with dew; a light, variable wind earlier in the afternoon had died off as the sun had started slanting down, and now just the faintest opaque silvery sea mist was starting to rise and hover like smoke above the surface of the water. He nudged the bag under the center console seat with his foot, and, leading the dinghy up to the bow, he secured her to the mooring buoy.

Radio and TV towers strobed low on the horizon—Long Island. On this side, lights in the houses had come on, their reflections bleeding into the water. Though they couldn't have been more than fifty to seventy-five yards away, they too, seemed vastly distant. Gripping the cold stainless-steel bow pulpit, Val plunged his hand into the water. Cold. His hair, his face, his skin were damp.

Behind the center console, he placed his key in the ignition, switched on the control panel, the bow and stern, and the red and green running lights. He lowered the outboard, the hydraulic motor humming as the propeller and shaft disappeared into the water. Checking to see that the engine was in neutral, he pulled out the choke, turned the key, and the motor caught instantly with a cloud of oily exhaust; he let it idle and then pushed in the choke, and the motor eased and ran evenly. He switched on the GPS and watched it download, brought up the packet of charts, and punched in the first waypoint. The depth gauge displayed seventeen feet, and tiny icons of fish appeared on the screen.

At the center console, he snapped the lanyard holding the ignition key to his belt loop—if for any reason he went overboard, the lanyard would tighten and pull the key from the console, killing the power so the boat wouldn't run on without him. He eased the engine into forward and swung the bow around, heading slowly straight off shore for several hundred yards, turning to watch his wake uncoiling silver in the calm water and setting the moored boats into a wild, rocking-horse motion; a line of lobster buoys slid by on his starboard side as he brought the boat around in open water, heading for what would be the first buoy, a red nun several miles to the east. He wished Michael were with him. This was what Michael wanted.... Val was doing this for him, wasn't he?

He watched the silvery shore lights streaming by a couple of miles off to his left and punched up the first waypoint on the GPS, studied the course threading itself out in slow motion on the glowing screen, listened to the drone of the motor, the sound of spray sluicing from the stern chines with each rise and fall of the boat in the smooth water. He zipped his jacket against the cold wind, wishing he'd thought to bring gloves, and wiped his eyes, which were tearing from the boat's speed. Checking his watch, he knew he should be coming up on the first buoy; he reached for the flashlight, slowed, and switched on the beam, pointed it to where he thought he'd find the red nun. The beam slid this way and that across the water, but he saw nothing, and, slowing more, he shined the light to the other side, and then to midships and off the stern—maybe he'd already passed it. Or maybe he wasn't there yet. He held his course, swinging the beam back to where he'd originally thought the buoy should be off the port bow, checked his track on the GPS. A glint? He eyed the compass for the bearing, swung the bow around and followed the white tunnel; the cat's eye glow of numbers jumped liquid into the light. He made out the nun, mute, caught in a swirl of dark current, matched the numbers to the ones on the chart: the right buoy.

With a rise of relief, he studied the chart, brought up the next waypoint on the GPS, and switched off the light. Blinded, he kept his eyes closed, opened them, and slowly the sky filled in with stars: the Dipper, Cassiopeia, Scorpio low on the southern horizon, the swirl of the Milky Way across the celestial equator. He gave the engine gas, found the next buoy after a search, and noticed his fuel was lower than he'd anticipated—maybe a trick of the way this gauge registered, maybe his uncertainty about the tank's capacity. He decided to keep a close eye on it and run on to the next buoy, and then the next, each requiring the same back and forth, time-consuming search until he came to his last buoy on the Connecticut shore at Saybrook, the green bell coming huge and ghostly up out of the dark in the flashlight beam, the clang of her bells drifting across the water, her numbers and superstructure stained white with gull droppings, her light strobing in even intervals. The buoy rose and fell slowly in the ground swell, a deep line of current silently carving around her, and Val kept his light on the buoy, reluctant to have it disappear.

He ran for some time in and out of warm and chilly pockets of air, suddenly smelling the thick oiliness of fish, the pungent iodine reek of seaweed, of ocean bottom; the lights of Connecticut fell farther behind as he headed south, and those of Long Island, sparse, grew brighter, and then he slowed the boat and turned off the engine. Running lights glowing red and green on the bow pulpit, he drifted, listening in the silence to the faint lap of water against the hull. He felt his pack beneath the seat, reached inside. Something hard and compact: Tangoes, the puzzle of geometric shapes. Val tossed the game into the dark, heard a splash. He felt the packet of Lee Anne's postcards. These, too, he dropped overboard. Now something else. An envelope. Her letter to Davis after she'd awakened to find herself abandoned, along with her Polaroid self-portrait. He tossed them overboard. A plastic baggie: Michael's pills. He tossed them. One last thing: The video cassette. The marlin tape. This, too, he suddenly flung as far as he could into the dark. He saved the picture of Davis that Lee Anne had given him. He drifted on, looking up at the stars, brilliant and close overhead. The area due east on his left was completely black where the Sound opened out into Block Island Sound and the Atlantic.

As if waking up, he restarted the engine, brought the Grady-White around onto its course. Watching for running lights and looking back over his stern for the ferry, he glanced at his log—twenty-six knots. He pushed the throttle forward, and the boat climbed up to thirty. He thought he could make out, just faintly, the light on Orient Point in the distance; at the same moment, there was an enormous thud; he was thrown back hard; he staggered; the bow shot up, and the boat heeled so steeply he was almost tossed out; he heard the engine race, whine, make a choking gargle as the impeller came out of the water, and then there was silence as the boat went dark.

Dry-mouthed with adrenaline, hands shaking, Val groped his way to an upright position, felt the floor of the boat for water. Nothing. Confused, his hand brushed the key hanging on its coil, and he realized that when he'd been thrown backward, the lanyard had tightened and jerked the key from the console as it was supposed to do, killing the engine. He groped for the flashlight, here, there, crawling in the bottom until he found it rolled back to the well; he turned it on, swung the beam around the boat; on first inspection, things seemed to be intact. The jerry cans were askew, but their lines had held them in place where they'd been secured, and they hadn't leaked any gasoline. The anchor compartment was thrown open, the anchor and a pile of line flung on the deck. He unsnapped the lanyard, reinserted and turned the key, and the lights came on. He studied each instrument: GPS, VHF, oil pressure and fuel, compass. All were lit and seemed to be okay. Even if he were miles off course, which he wasn't, what could be out here to hit in the middle of the Sound? He knew there were no reefs or shoals; the depth gauge showed 112 feet. He leaned overboard and inspected his way around the boat. At the bow, just below the waterline, there was a deep gouge, but it didn't seem to have broken through the hull, though he couldn't be sure. Maybe it had cracked the fiberglass. He replaced the anchor and coils of line in their compartment, and, swinging the beam around, he made a minute inspection of the interior, but still could find nothing. He raised the motor and saw with relief that the prop had not been bent or the blades broken. That, considering the sound and force of what he'd just felt, seemed lucky.

He swung the light around on the water, bow, midship; off the stern he thought he could make something out. He lowered the engine, started it—it ran—and, holding his breath, he put it in gear. The boat moved forward. He circled, followed the beam, slowed. Looking down, he made out a waterlogged telephone pole wallowing just beneath the surface, complete with broken wooden crosstrees and protruding steel rungs encrusted with barnacles and sea grass. He watched the long sea grass undulating silently in the current. He'd hit it full force at thirty-five knots. He carefully explored his way around the inside of the boat looking for water seepage. Kneeling, he shined the light in the bilge, feeling with his fingers; he didn't detect any pressure or increase in water. As a precaution, he took out two flares and jammed them into the center console near the flare gun where he could grab them in a hurry.

At a cautious twenty knots, he ran toward Orient Point, picked up the light on the breakwater, and when he felt the slosh and crosscurrent yanking of Plum Gut, he knew he was skirting the big tide rip. He picked up the next buoy, ran farther south into Gardiners Bay, all the time watching for boats;

he'd seen few, and those had been far off; the drift of a distant light, a wake rolling silently out of the darkness and suddenly rocking the boat. Still on the lookout for the ferry, he ran south into the huge bay, sparse shore lights enveloping him in the distance on all sides—Greenport, Sag Harbor—shining where he estimated them to be, though he couldn't be sure which were which; distance and directions played tricks on the water in the dark and he hadn't been out here in years.

He started looking for the red bell that Lee Anne had indicated in her fax, checking the GPS and the charts and then shining the flashlight across the water, periodically inspecting the sole of the boat in the white beam for any signs of seepage. The bilge glistened with dampness under the engine well, but it was most likely dew and had been that way all night. If it turned out water was seeping in, and worse came to worst, he could run the bilge pump a few times or open the drain plug in the stern, or both, to run the water out. The gauge again showed fuel lower than he'd calculated, and vindicated his decision to delay and bring the extra gas in the jerry cans. He debated putting the gas in the tank now, but then thought he'd hold off and at least find the dock. He glanced at his watch and again had the urgent feeling that he had to finish this up and get back quickly before it was discovered he'd been gone. He directed the beam across the water looking for the bell buoy, the last one on his course.

Moving slowly forward, checking his compass heading and the GPS, he ran on behind the beam and suddenly the buoy towered over the bow. Val threw the boat into reverse and just missed it…. He shined the light up on the numbers. This was the one. He checked the compass for his bearing to the dock, maybe a little over a mile, and then, switching off the light, he eased forward. There could be anything between the bell and the dock: anchored boats, moorings, lobster pots, oyster stakes. He saw several spaced concentrations of lights ahead—houses, he thought—and smelled land, warm after a day of sun, and, keeping his heading, he ran slowly toward the lights.

Now he thought he made out a denser darkness, uneven, across the reflection from the shore, and he killed his running lights and ran ahead quietly. He shifted into neutral, cupped his hands around his eyes to screen out all other light. Something off to his left? He felt his way ahead, turned the wheel suddenly, glanced lightly off the hull of a boat on her mooring, looked up and made out a mast against the stars. Ran ahead. Another hull.

Maybe a powerboat, also on a mooring. He eased toward the dark inshore shape he'd detected, and, much sooner than he'd anticipated, he bumped something hard enough to stagger him back a step. He put the boat in neutral, then into forward. Groped in the dark. Felt rough wood. A piling? The hollow echo of space, wood over water.... A dock. The right one? He held onto the piling. It seemed to be a long dock that went up toward a lawn. And there was a good-sized house, a porch light throwing white light down onto the lawn, a window lit behind it. Still holding on, he made his way forward, drew a length of anchor line from the bow compartment, doubled and secured it on a cleat, looped it around a piling and fastened it on the same cleat, swore at the mess of the anchor line. He looked up at the dock, listened, then took off his jacket. Reaching down into his bag, he pulled out the carefully wrapped picture of Davis. If this was actually her house, he would be incredibly lucky to find it in the dark on a first try.

He felt a ladder, climbed several rungs, something brushing across his face as he did so. On the dock, he bent down to see what had touched him, found a line glowing faintly in the loom thrown down from the house. When he pulled, the line came up without resistance. Half of it was wet. He examined it closely—it seemed to be a dock line. Cut. Not frayed, but cut cleanly. He looked around, saw another line. This one, too, had been cut. He put down the picture of Davis, walked back and forth pulling up lines, each cut, each either left lying on the dock or hanging in the water. From their placement, he could see that they had secured a good-sized boat, forty feet or more. He glanced up at the house, some distance above the water, its faint glow thrown onto a walk leading to the dock. Again, he ran his hands along the line. Wet. Smooth. Clean. There was no growth or slime on it. Whoever had cut the lines had done so very recently. What was going on? He vividly recalled Lee Anne telling him about her high-school boyfriend, his rich father. House on the water in a bay in Florida. She'd sought and found the same situation—someone with money? He recalled the rest of the story, the boyfriend naked and covered with blood and skinning the alligator with a KA-BAR knife at sunrise. He smoothed the dock line in his hands. He couldn't make sense of any of it, nor find a connection. Coincidence? He had just the vaguest sense that he'd been here before, if, in no other way, in her telling him the Florida story that night in Brooklyn. Suddenly uneasy, he dropped the dock line.

He remained motionless, and, checking an urge to bolt, picture of Davis in hand, he walked back down the dock to his boat. Something was wrong. And what was he doing, anyway? If it wasn't already too late, he had to get out of here quick. But, Michael.... A huge sewing needle through his tongue. Slammed Kazz against a wall. *When you're straight with me, I'll be straight with you. No one ever wants to talk about Davis.* Davis: Spook. Head-hunter. Val climbed down the dock ladder, felt for the Grady-White with his foot. He clung to the ladder without moving. If he left now, he would never have answers for Michael. He saw no other way of stopping whatever was driving Michael. If nothing else, to remove the look of perpetual doubt Michael saw—and detested—in Val's face, which was, really, the view Val's father had of Val. Heart pounding, Val climbed back up the ladder.

He started quietly up the dock. Across generous, luxuriant lawns, there were houses not too far away on either side. Another private dock some distance off. He could make out several powerboats tied up, a flagpole at the end. Rich people. It was strange to think of Lee Anne among them. In Brooklyn, she'd been desperate. Poor. Crazy. Cut off. He, the same. Her room in the house she shared. The sense that the person who lived there wished to remain anonymous: some cheap jewelry and clothes that might have belonged to anyone: library and secondhand books in a stack by her bed; a game of solitaire in progress; crossword puzzles; and the battered suitcase. But no traces of anything personal except for the small framed picture of Davis and herself—and himself, a head shot, stuck into the bottom. As for the rest, he knew nothing more than the familiar, palpable hush of something secretive, of an aftermath, anonymity. Given that, he couldn't imagine her married to anyone—nor that she could have changed much even if she were; she would still have kept that part of herself sealed off, that room vacant and intact as it had been. Why—or how—else would she have continued to write him? He started up the slightly rising walk toward the house. Warm here. Almost balmy. Smell of water and flowers and tide.

He studied the first-floor windows throwing light out into the darkness; the second floor was unlit. He reached the wide stairs, aware that he was trying to move quietly, though he didn't know why; he wasn't doing anything wrong. It was the cut dock lines.... Not right. He climbed the three steps, paused to listen, looked along the porch: wicker chairs, a white wrought-iron table, a glider hanging from chains. A newspaper. "George Bush pledges to leave no child behind even as he touts his tax cuts..." May 28, 2001.... Ordinary enough. Something in him felt momentarily reassured.

*Town & Country. Better Homes and Gardens.* Things were okay. Look, she was married. Her weird postcards over the years were what? He didn't know. A collection of passing moods, longings, resentments. Everyone had them. But those dock lines…. In all the time he'd been on boats, he'd never seen that. And her empty room in Brooklyn—the hush of an aftermath. A hiding place.

## Piracy

The front door was open. He looked through the screen, stepped back and peered in the lit window, tried to catch a glimpse inside. She obviously didn't live alone in this house. Strangely, he'd given little thought to the man she might have married. Now he tried, and couldn't begin to imagine him. For the first time he wondered: where was he? And what if he came to the door? How would he explain who he was and what he was doing here? He was startled by his own blind spot or inattention, which in turn gave way to massive doubt and confusion within himself. Why hadn't he even considered all of this? He realized to what extent he remained stopped in time with her: Brooklyn. What else wasn't he seeing now?

Face to the screen, he looked inside. A curved glass coffee table in front of a large sofa in the middle of the room, a phone lying on its side. Beside the phone, a squash racquet. A sleek marble sculpture stood alone on a square base in the middle of the table, like an animal's horn, slender, graceful. A floor lamp stood at one end of the table. Behind it was a fireplace with a broad mantel. The living room opened into another large space behind it that was dark—he could just make out a dining-room table and chairs in the shadows.

He rapped lightly on the screen door. Waited. Listened. He rapped again. He called quietly, "Hello…" startled by the sound of his voice in the stillness, then added, "Lee Anne." That, too, startled him: her name out loud. He opened the door, hesitated, and stepped inside. Wrong house? He saw a barometer and wind gauge mounted on the wall, the red digital numbers silently flickering with the rise and fall of air currents. He crossed to a large window and looked down onto the lawn to see what might have been observed of his coming up from the dock. Lee Anne…where was she? The last time he'd actually seen her, he realized, had been late November, years ago, the afternoon having slowly grown dark as he waited, her door opening and her stepping inside with the paper bag, a box visible: *feminine protection;* the way she had stiffly unfolded herself onto the bed, her face webbed with pain. Now he connected the words at the bottom of her last postcard: *I forgive you nothing.* Was *that* it? After all this time?

Uneasy at being in someone's house—whose?—and sensing something at his back, he turned and looked into the unlit part of the room; he saw a massive—how had he not noticed it?—black Steinway grand piano, a putter gleaming across its closed lid, floating in the shadows. His first reaction: no. Nothing more. No. Then: this is completely wrong. He walked across the wide room and touched the piano. He remembered a night in North Carolina. Davis. Lee Anne. They'd walked into a bar. A guy playing a piano through the noise and talk. He and Davis walking ahead, but Lee Anne frozen by the door. She put her hand up to find the wall, almost as if groping, blind; they found her alone inside the car a while later; she was staring through the windshield.

Smoothing his hand along the curve of the piano, Val remembered that Lee Anne had written him—how could he have forgotten?—that some time ago a piano had come into the house. She'd started having nightmares. Nightmares for weeks. From her cards, he'd come to see a space, a room from which she wrote him, or perhaps a place in another time, one she'd left years before, or one she'd imagined, in which there might be a piano, and now he ran his hand along the curved hull of the Steinway and had the uneasy sense that he'd come to be in that room and time. He took a step toward the window.

"In my dream, that's exactly where you stood."

He jumped at the sound of her voice, embarrassed that she might have seen him start. Her Southern accent was exactly the same. Hardwood floor creaking under her, she walked out of the darkened dining room and stopped.

He said, "That's what you wrote in your card. 'In the dream, you stand by the window.'"

The hoarseness of his voice, he knew, betrayed his nervousness at being here...

"That window."

...and at the jolt of sexual disquiet, which she had always brought with her—and which was still there, exactly as it had been the first time she'd come in with Davis at four in the morning. And there was something else familiar about her that he couldn't quite bring into focus.

He'd expected to see her hair as it had been in Brooklyn, bottle blond, spectacular, platinum, hiding half her face, but it was now some dark shade—still not her natural color, he knew—and Val again felt a spasm of dislocation, confusion, perhaps even longing for the way he'd remembered her.

It seemed completely strange, yet natural, that they could be talking to each other after all this time without preface, the way her postcards never bothered to address him, just continued what couldn't seem to stop, break, resolve....

He glanced again at the squash racquet on the coffee table. "You're married."

She smiled ironically, and this, too, he remembered. "I couldn't live alone and play squash—or more like I couldn't afford a house like this if I weren't married?"

Which was, he realized, what he'd been thinking. "I didn't say that."

Yet she had him back where she'd had him from the first moments—off balance. Maybe this, too, was why he'd come. He'd never understood his reaction to her. He noticed her eyes, her pupils—hugely dilated. Stoned? He didn't think so. The dim light? Then he recognized the familiar aspect of her presence, still there, knew why her pupils were dilated—it was fear. Fear was what he'd always felt from her, fear and the sense that something terrible was coming, moment to moment, and though when he was with her, her fear had been inseparable from his own terrors—sleeping with the lights on, suddenly jerking awake—he could now clearly identify it again, feel himself being drawn back into its distorting field; he felt sharply afraid.

He became aware he was holding the picture of Davis, knew that she was remembering giving it to him that night she'd come back from the abortion. He hadn't anticipated this, the obvious, that the picture and the night she'd given it to him would be inseparable. He surprised himself by saying something stupid, incongruous. "I tied up at the dock." Added, "The dock lines are cut."

"I'm aware of that, thank you."

"What happened?"

"Someone stole my husband's boat." He waited. "A few days ago. That's all I know—all anyone knows." He watched her.

He stumbled on. "Big boat to hide."

"Acute observation." She shrugged, then said, "You've always looked at me the same way."

"How's that, Lee Anne?"

"With a question."

He didn't know exactly what was happening here, but thought he'd better put a quick end to it. "My question is this and then I'm going." He turned the picture of Davis toward her.

"I got your letter. I know what your question is, Val. I knew anyway. You're not saying any of the things people say who haven't seen each other in years. 'Where are you working? What did you do after we last saw each other? Who did you marry? Any kids?' I know, for instance, you went back to law school."

He decided not to ask her how she knew, was fairly sure she'd followed him to Cambridge. Still, he carefully thought out his possible answers. Went back to law school. Got married. Moved West. Have a son. Sensed she knew everything about him anyway, though wasn't sure how. But he surprised himself by saying, "My father just died, Lee Anne." He suddenly hated mentioning his father's death in her presence. "Ten days ago."

She seemed to recede; there had been something starved-looking about her at times and now he thought he saw it in her face. When he didn't think she'd react, she said, "Brooklyn."

As if it were an answer: that she understood his feelings about his father; that she knew he'd ended up in Brooklyn because he'd had to leave his family house, literally, and for good; that it was the end of something between him and his father, and that Brooklyn had been the first place he could find to go when they couldn't be near each other after Davis; perhaps, too, *Brooklyn* was her way of saying that Davis was what we had. He held up the picture.

"I just want to know what this meant, Lee Anne. That's all. Why you gave it to me. Where he was going. Why you said to me that night, 'You know, but don't know.'"

She leaned slightly forward in the way a person does to hear better. She seemed to listen into the house. She came back into herself, took several steps toward him. He caught her smell: hair, skin. She looked as if she were trying to recognize him—see into him. She said, "I kept talking to you all this time even though you weren't there. Why is that?" She added, almost as a perplexed afterthought, "I think I could have loved you. You, of all people."

"Why me 'of all people'?" He was surprised at the petty way he felt irked. He loved his wife. He had no idea why he was really here. Davis. Something else, more...

"Oh, just how you could never leave anything alone, nothing, no one ever good enough, true enough, I was always trying to justify myself to you...." She picked up the picture, veered. "Or maybe it was just Davis we loved and..." She shrugged, veered again, "And how can you know if anything I'd tell you about this," she indicated the picture, "is the truth, anyway?"

"I'll know."

She smirked at him. "You will, counselor?"

She took a step sideways, glanced past him, as if she were waiting for something. She picked up the picture, said as a distracted afterthought, "I shot the picture...you had to have figured out that much."

"No, how would I?"

He felt the pull of something in the house, outside the house, he wasn't sure....

She said, "Davis had beautiful hands."

"He did. But you could miss it. They were often cut up and greasy."

"Mechanic's hands," she said simply. "He could do anything with his hands. Maybe he just didn't see it as a gift most people valued..."

"A lot of people did."

She drifted. "I did." He heard her tone change, the ironic whip coming back into her voice. "And there were others..." she added vaguely in a way that made him sure that she had someone specific in mind.

She walked to the other side of the table and glanced toward the stairs and into the darkened area, looking for something, perhaps relieved not to find it. What—or who—was she looking for? She took a nervous breath. "You really never got it, Val? The way Davis just came up to see you like that in the middle of the night? You couldn't put it together with this?" She tapped the picture. "You disappoint me. Really." She sounded as if she meant it.

"I failed your test?"

"No test. But then, I've always thought you've known anyway."

"You just wanted to leave me with something, Lee Anne?"

She shrugged. "I'd been working in a neighborhood bar, partying, kind of here and there with some people," she hesitated, "and had some ideas about what they did though no one talked about anything. I saw a lot of cash at times.

"After I started living with Davis, I saw that my pals liked him; they knew he worked with boats and engines, and one of them took me aside and asked if he'd be okay to do a job. They needed someone to run offshore one night to meet and refuel a boat—they were running bales in Cigarettes, Aronows, blowing past the Coast Guard; I said he could do anything on boats, and even if he didn't want the job, he'd never spread the word around. So they talked to Davis and he said he'd do it. Davis was a good navigator."

"My father taught him to navigate."

Lee Anne said softly, "Oh, Jesus, Val…"

"My father taught him. Taught both of us."

"Okay. Your father taught him. Well, what he did with it was, he took this boat; it was a lighter filled with fuel; he ran ten, fifteen miles off shore, pitch black, lights off, but all kinds of players swarming around out there, radar search planes, the Coast Guard, coastal traffic, freighters, who knew what else; he met these guys out there in the dark—really, I don't know how he did it, a needle in a haystack, and he refueled them and they got their dope ashore.

"Davis came back in the morning and he was lit up, laughing and digging it. He loved it. He pulled out this waterproof bag of cash, opened it, it was just reeking of resin, twenty-five grand for a night's work, there was even a little sand in the money, it was…" she laughed softly, her face came alive and she snapped her fingers and did a little cha-cha step, "La Carmen Miranda touch, the sand in the money. Also, a kilo of knockout shit for us to sell or use for our own amusement…. I tell you, I've never smelled money like that…perfume, yes, spilled booze, yes, but this stuff, no…. Anyway, we had to wash the dough before we could spend any of it."

"Launder it?"

She smirked. "No, you've been watching too many movies. I mean, like, wash it with Pine-Sol and water to kill the smell. We washed it and hung hundred-dollar bills all over the bathroom on twine…" She zigzagged her hand over her head to show him. "Back and forth… I mean, you couldn't spend money smelling like this. Everyone would know. You'd walk in the bathroom and there were bills hanging from wooden clothespins. We'd wash a little each night. Needless to say, we weren't entertaining." She pressed her finger to hers lips, gnawed the inside of her cheek.

"You got him into smuggling."

"It wasn't like that, in neon. It was more someone needed something done and asked me about Davis and," she shrugged, "I connected him to some people…and little bundles of tax-free cash appeared. Davis wasn't out to hurt people—some of these guys were scary, but for Davis, it wasn't really even the money, it was the game, the action…"

Val looked down at the picture. "And so that's what's happening here? Davis was running dope for the people you hooked him up with?"

She gave him a look. "See, this is the thing about you, Val, this, like, tone in your voice. Made me wonder why I kept talking to you all this time. I always felt accused by you. Well, it doesn't matter. Were you listening to me just now?

"I told you he wasn't doing things he didn't already have in him…"

Val remembered Davis coming out of the darkness of George's garage, a bare bulb burning over an engine. A teenager. Wiping his oily hands on a rag. Something in his face already. Secrets. Contempt.

"Okay, I introduced him to some people. But he did what he did because he wanted to. It lit him up. He loved it. I didn't make him. No one did. You couldn't make Davis do anything. You do know that. Maybe it was more like we made each other possible."

"As in he wouldn't have done it if he hadn't met you?"

"Who's to know? But have it your way." She looked down at the picture. "Davis was not running dope here. He never ran the stuff. See in this pic-ture…. Look, Davis would take a legal boat and he'd cruise the waterways—the canal, the marinas, the Intracoastal—and he'd spot good boats and get their registration numbers. Or he'd take pictures. Or I'd write them down and note their locations. Sometimes he'd go with Billy, a guy he worked with. We'd look for the best boats or the newest and biggest outboards, twin-engines, or just whatever. Picking a boat depended on where it was going. If it was just going to be stripped and chopped…"

"Chopped, Lee Anne? Chopped?"

She shrugged. "You knew."

Val didn't understand why she kept making this point, but didn't say anything more.

"Stripped or chopped, that was one thing. If the boat was going over to the Bahamas," and now Lee Anne tapped the picture, "then he'd look for a name-brand boat, thirty feet with, say, twin outboards, you could make from a third to half the street price on them. Crappy boat was the same felony as a great boat so might as well be selective. With a phony bill of sale, the boats could be registered in the Bahamas. Or they could end up in the

Caymans, Belize, Honduras, the Virgin Islands.... Gee, respectable people getting these good deals and never wondering why...like they really didn't know? Don't talk to me about what people do and don't know.

"Anyway, we'd check things out pretty good. Before he'd make a move, we'd get the registration numbers. I knew someone who could run those registrations and find out about the owners. We'd get the guy's home phone—and then you could find out when they were at work or on vacation. You could look up the lien holder..."

He noticed there seemed to be a pleasure in her as she talked; she was brightening, coming to life, filling up with something, more of a personality in the telling, itself.

"Now, with boats already in the water, Davis liked to perform at night."

Val couldn't help but note the word *perform*. Her word. But actually right for Davis. Everything a contest, odds stacked against you: the bigger, the better.

"He'd climb on a boat, pump the fuel ball, pop the engine cowling, open the ignition harness and jump the connections. He'd use either a starter button or a screwdriver." She snapped her fingers. "It would take him just a couple of minutes and he'd be gone."

"And things like battery switch locks?"

"He'd crank them hard and they'd break. If the boat was up on davits, he started the hoist, and while the boat was riding down, he had the engine going before it hit the water. He was a wizard.

"If he wanted to cash in fast, he stripped the boat right away; you could drop out the four bolts on a big outboard and that was four or five grand right there. One boat, I remember, had eight grand worth of instruments, fishing gear.... There was a big black market and all of this stuff was untraceable.

"Hey, no one was getting hurt on this. Insurance companies paid off owners and they'd shut up and go away happy. If you had false papers, you could run a boat over to the Bahamas and sell it...like this one." She pressed her finger to the picture. "That's where we were going. We stole that boat out of one of the Miami waterways, ran it across the Gulf Stream that night, sold it in Nassau, took a few days of fun in the sun, and flew back."

Val suddenly became aware that he was tired of standing. No, just tired. Exhausted. "You said you'd find out about the owners before Davis stole a boat—if there were lien holders..." She nodded. "Why?"

"Because once you knew that, you could go to rip the boat with a phony repo order already made out, which was just killer for trailer boats. Trailer boats were for broad daylight if you had the nerve. Florida. A million boats. Trailer boats on every corner. You'd just drive up during the nine-to-five."

"You'd just drive up and haul someone's boat away?"

"Exactly. One day, just after noon, Davis went for a trailer boat. We called the guy's workplace first and found out that the owner was supposed to be away on vacation so we went out to his house. Davis was just lowering the trailer onto the hitch of the pickup. He's bent over the crank. And this guy appears out of nowhere and jams a cocked .45 to Davis' head. The guy said, 'Move and you're dead.'

"Davis says, 'I'm not moving. Can I talk?'

"The guy says, 'You can talk, but you're going to the slammer.'

"Davis never missed a beat. He said, 'I want you to call the cops right now.' Which completely threw the guy. Davis said, 'You're interfering with an agent of the bank.' He said, 'I'm not moving, but reach into my chest pocket.' The guy's holding the gun to Davis' head. He reaches over and pulls out the phony repo order. The guy starts reading. It was letter perfect. The guy's boat. Registration. Lien. The guy's name. The guy sticks the gun in his pants. 'Gotta be a mistake. I'm paid up.' Oh, Davis was beautiful. He was perfect. Davis said, 'Hey, buddy, I don't blame you for being pissed.' You know, he could rap with people. 'Call and check it out for yourself.' Davis sat down on the trailer tongue. 'I'll wait here.'

"The guy looks at Davis, who sits down on the trailer, and goes into the house to call the bank. Now anyone else I knew would have hopped in the truck and run for it. Davis jumps up, waves me in the rest of the way, cranks the boat trailer down onto the ball—this is right in the guy's driveway—and we were gone in less than, like, thirty seconds." She shook her head.

"*We? We* were gone."

"We were gone. I was driving the truck. How'd you think I knew all this?"

"He could have told you."

"We were gone. The phony repo order was Lee Anne's idea." A jolt as Val remembered how she used to talk about herself in the third person. *Lee Anne.* Val heard the pride in her voice. "I mean, like, that day, he would have been busted if he hadn't had it." She shrugged. "See what I mean? It was both of us. But Davis, I mean, what other guy could bluff with someone holding a gun to his head? He was unbelievable."

At that, she suddenly seemed to deflate, go a long way off into a kind of blankness. And for a moment, Val drifted into the blinding white light of Florida, the suffocating humidity, the glare of a cement driveway, the metallic grind and pop of the crank as the tongue lowered and Lee Anne inched the pickup back to meet it. The gun suddenly pressed to Davis' head. And Davis, so cool, actually able to speak, no, not just speak, but challenge when most people would be paralyzed. Val knew this side of Davis so well, the side that had learned to bluff with his back to the wall, that, failing and humiliated, had learned to cover, to be charming and nimble. Defiance. His last words: *fuck you.*

But now Val was surprised to find himself confused by, what? Oddly, he thought it was envy, that Davis had it in him to do these things; and repulsion for the same reasons. The waste of it. And, something else. Another surprise. Jealousy that he had something so intense with Lee Anne, and that, whatever it was, however damned it might be, it was so completely of their own making, that, right or wrong, they were following it to…he couldn't imagine exactly what the conclusion might have been. But, he realized, he did. Davis had run from her. And from something else. And he'd had the gun with him.

He noticed Lee Anne was gauging his reaction, and he remembered that time in Brooklyn when she'd stolen the perfume. He'd confronted her on the sidewalk, and she suddenly became furious and adamant; she'd paid, she'd thrown away the receipt, dropped it on the floor in there; did he want to go back inside? She'd prove everything to him! She had bluffed so convincingly that even though he'd seen her steal it, he wavered. Now she glanced at him with this same calculating look. And suddenly, he knew that there was something about this story that was too rehearsed, too perfect.

He tapped the table. "Someone took this picture of Davis…and maybe it was even you. *But…*" he shook his head. "I don't believe you, Lee Anne. The false papers, selling the boat over in Nassau, the cash smelling of dope, the repo order, the .45 to Davis' head. None of it. Sounds wonderful. *But…*" he shook his head no.

She looked at him with contempt, with perhaps pity and even disappointment. Then she said with mock consternation and contrition, "Well, counselor…"

"Will you fucking stop that!"

"Looks like you've got me. I almost forgot, Val, there's no fooling you.

You're just too smart. The Great Val." Her old mocking name for him. She walked into the dining room, disappeared into the dark and returned with a metal box in her hands; she froze in mid-step and, without turning her head, she listened for something behind her.

When she reached the table, she placed the enamel box in front of him. It had a red tartan enamel pattern on it and the words *Walkers Shortbread*. "Here," she said. "I knew you wouldn't believe me. And you didn't. Thanks for not disappointing me. And so: here's some proof."

But her voice lost its contempt and thickened with nervousness, and he caught the sharp edge of panic in her. "Open it." And then she added. "Might be good to hurry up, as in, let's move this along." He looked around, didn't know what she was talking about: *hurry up*. She read the look on his face, glanced toward the front door, behind her. "Just, please, open it." She wavered. "Look, you really have to go. Please."

"I will," he said. "In one second."

"Not in one second. Now." She looked desperate and yet resigned.

Val pried up the lid. Inside, a jumble. Some official-looking papers. He picked one up. A repossession order filled in with registration numbers, dated 1984 and signed...there were several of these; and a snapshot of an outboard, maybe twenty-five feet, on a trailer. Val recognized the identifying black stripe: a Grady-White, inside what appeared to be a warehouse. The huge Johnson outboard, unbolted, was being hoisted above the transom by a forklift. Davis stood midships and had both of his arms raised in mock victory. Val glanced down at the box filled with snapshots. These phony repo orders had obviously never been used. Not needed. But one had. And one had been enough to save the day for Davis. He sorted through pictures. Boats, dozens, in various stages of being stripped. One being sunk, the bow sticking up out of the water.

"Chop shop." He was surprised to find that he could barely speak. He again glanced at the first picture: Davis grinning with his arms raised. The lawyer, barely still there in him, thought, so stupid of Davis to have had his picture taken. Evidence. Registration numbers visible. Evidence. Each one a count. Stupid for Lee Anne to have kept all of this stuff. Why? Something she couldn't let go of. To show him one day. Years later. This day. Evidence. Stupid of her to have kept them, too. But no case. Felonies committed years ago. Evidence. When she'd realized they weren't going to be together, she saved all this stuff to show him...what? The worst in Davis. To get to Val.

She was making her case. Val was her case. A feeling of sickness rose in him.

"Your revenge on me, Lee Anne? At last?"

"You're the one who came back." Lee Anne suddenly took his hand and said in a stricken voice, "Christ, Val." She pulled the open box to her. "You wanted to know. And I always thought this was what I wanted to see. Your face when you found out about Davis. I did. It was. I was pregnant. I wanted something with you. I wanted to keep it."

"And there I was walking around and thinking—hoping—that Davis and I could get together and do something with boats, buy, build, deliver, sell, something…" He paused. "God, you and Davis must have just been laughing at me every second we were down there—do something with boats. No wonder you were looking at me that way." He hesitated. "One more thing, Lee Anne."

"Go, I'm telling you. Please." She looked terrified.

"What happened to make Davis run out of Miami with a gun under the front seat of his car?"

"Does it matter? Isn't this enough?" She pushed the box on the table. "No? Okay, Val, suit yourself. We'll see it through to the end. Maybe we'll finish. Maybe not. Maybe I've been wrong about everything." But she didn't look convinced. "Davis had a friend he'd met working in the boatyard. Billy. He brought him into it to help him on some jobs. They trusted each other. If they'd seen trouble, they would have warned each other."

"How so?"

"Sometimes they stole boats for a guy, people just called him Mr. Smith." Val shook his head in disgust: Mr. Smith. "Someone would get in touch with Davis and tell him, Mr. Smith needs such and such a boat for a run, and Davis and Billy would steal it for him. Cigarettes…Fountains. Muscle boats.

"One morning, Billy doesn't come to work in the boatyard. He doesn't call in. No one hears from him." She licked her lips nervously. "But on the second day when Billy still doesn't come to work, Davis knows something is wrong. He calls me and then he suddenly leaves work at the boatyard."

"And that's when he starts calling me in North Carolina…"

"He goes over to Billy's place, finds the key, goes in. Everything's just sitting there. Nothing missing. No one's fed his dog. His truck's there. His clothes. Everything. It's eerie. And Davis gets out of there as quick as he can.

"Next day I wake up and something hits me. It's one word: *piracy*, kind of a quaint, weird word… first thing I think of is that word. I remember coming across it in the *Miami Herald*." Val recalled her doing crosswords. If anyone would notice an odd word or context, it would be Lee Anne. *Piracy.* "I dig into a pile of old papers and there's an article about a grand jury having been convened some time back and the guy being investigated, Hector Cruz. Ongoing investigation.

"They're looking at all kinds of charges, smuggling, conspiracy, receiving stolen property, murder. And there's that word: *piracy.* Hector Cruz. The whole thing gives me a funny feeling, like I know what this is, but I don't know why. And then a while later I'm giving someone a haircut and it just hits me, that Mr. Cruz is Mr. Smith who Davis and Billy have been stealing muscle boats for. *Piracy.* Someone somewhere has been talking and giving names to the cops and grand jury."

"Right. They get someone small and squeeze him until he rolls over and gives them the next guy and the next until they can put it all together. So Billy was doing the talking."

"No, not Billy. Never Billy. But I get that they've got someone, and he's been giving people up, guys who can be witnesses before the grand jury. It's Cruz they want. And the Feds are working their way toward him, pulling their witnesses in one by one, the small ones first. Billy and Davis got him his boats. Mr. Smith. Hector Cruz. Don't you see?

"I see. They're getting called in front of a grand jury. But if Billy and Davis were going to be hauled in, they'd have been subpoenaed. They'd have been served. They'd have subpoenas, Lee Anne."

She suddenly looked exasperated. "I fucking know that! That's my point. If Billy had been subpoenaed, he would have had the fucking subpoena. There hadn't been any subpoena."

"Well, that's what I'm saying, too. But how can you know that there wasn't?"

"Because the second Billy was served, he would have warned Davis."

"Okay. Billy didn't get a subpoena, but he still took off and left everything behind and went…where?" Val was confused. "I don't get you."

"Billy. Had. No. Subpoena! It hadn't been issued yet!" What was Val not understanding here? "There was no subpoena of Billy because Mr. Smith— Mr. Cruz—had someone inside the prosecutor's office who was tipping him off whenever a witness was going to get dragged in before the grand jury."

"How could you possibly know something like that? Even begin to think it?" Lee Anne just stared at him. Her courage, her resolve, had returned, her face was hard, defiant. She was either the most paranoid or the most brilliant person he'd ever known. Maybe for her they were inseparable. "What you're telling me is that Billy doesn't come to work, leaves all his stuff, disappears, and so Davis somehow connects Cruz's coming under scrutiny before a grand jury to Billy's disappearing, and what? he figures he's next...?"

"No! Davis *knows* something is wrong, but he doesn't know how or why or what. He never has a clue about Cruz's being Mr. Smith or about the grand jury. Lee Anne figures it out." Lee Anne. That third person thing of hers again. Still doing it after all this time. He'd forgotten how strange it was, though in Brooklyn it had just seemed to be part of the way everything was.

"It's impossible. It's just too nebulous, too much of a leap. And federal grand juries—that would be federal stuff—are extremely hard to interfere with. And even if it all were true, it's not provable."

She cut him off. "Is that right? Billy's body turns up floating in Biscayne Bay a few days later. He'd been cut to pieces. It's on the evening news. It's in the paper. How's that for proof?

"The next morning there are cops all over the boatyard trying to find out everything they can about Billy...and Davis. And asking questions about everyone else. And looking at every boat in there. So don't tell me how it was, counselor. I got it right!"

"Why didn't they just arrest Davis right then?"

"Because Lee Anne had figured out that everyone would be after him *before* they could get to him. The cops. And Cruz's guys who did Billy. Lee Anne figured it out and warned Davis. But that was when Davis took off— when they found Billy. There was just one other little problem. Davis left me sleeping in the middle of the night without a word. Oh, and I think there's one more thing you should know. It shades the picture a little. Weights things. Just a little. Davis and I were married five weeks before he ran out on me. I wasn't quite the little wayward slut you thought I was. I was his wife."

Val felt his mouth go dry. Speechless, he turned toward the front door. He came back to himself. Really, what was he doing here? To find out about Davis so Michael wouldn't become whoever Davis was in this picture that he loved so much: *The Bomb!* As if to disown this last, *his wife,* in fact, disown all of it, put it right once and escape once and for all, Val said, "I'm here, Lee Anne, because of my son. I'm here for my son. That's all." Even as he said this, he realized it was a huge mistake to be talking to her about him. She had never let Brooklyn go, and something seemed to have happened or to be happening now in her life that had pushed it deeper into her. In his own way, he'd been so stuck in the past, the fragments of her postcards, that he had given little thought to her present, to whom she had become now. As if to will it so, he said, "I'm going back to him now."

## *Three*

He turned to leave. He glanced over at her one last time, but the look of spite was gone from her eyes. In fact, she no longer seemed aware of his presence. Terror and fascination on her face, she appeared young, almost like a child; she seemed frozen.

At the same moment, Val felt the back of his body, his skin, every nerve ending, coming awake as though detaching itself from his spine; it was as if his back had taken on a life of its own. Without moving, he felt his eyesight widen and deepen, and sensed something at the edge of his field of vision. He turned his head slightly and saw just within the darkness of the dining room a form, someone standing motionless.

The man took several steps, quick and silent, and Val, still turning, braced himself, aware of his inventorying the objects in the room for something he could pick up: the putter on the piano, too far.... He heard Lee Anne, far away, "Brent!" desperation in her voice. "Just stop and he'll go and I'll explain everything and then I'll go, too."

And still turning his body and bracing for the impact, Val saw Brent stop. Balanced so that he might move either way, Brent looked from Lee Anne to Val. Val took him in: his cropped black hair; his eyes, bloodshot, bright and unnaturally chemical blue, like a gas flame; coked, Val thought, he's on something: his face red, the veins standing up in his swollen neck, and his skin reeking of nervous sweat and alcohol, which repelled Val; and it repelled him, too, that Lee Anne could be with such a man, and realized, almost irrelevantly, that this was, of course, the man who owned the squash racquet—that's why he moved the way he did; he was practiced at quickly covering the enclosed space of a squash court. He had the powerful, mus-cled build of an athlete who played games of explosive speed.

He heard her say again, "Brent..."

He said, "I've been listening to you going on and I still don't get it. I want to know now. Now! Who the fuck is this guy, Lee Anne? Who *is* he?" His voice was thick and hoarse with rage. He turned on Val. "Who the fuck are you and what are you doing here in my house talking to my wife at ten o'clock at night? Am I supposed to be a fucking idiot? Do I look like an idiot, Lee Anne?"

Val was surprised to hear his voice, toneless, far away. His voice might have been mistaken for calm. "I don't want anything here and I have no relationship to Lee Anne. There's nothing to worry about." And how utterly lame and unconvincing he sounded.

He looked at Val and a quickening of recognition—almost cunning—came into his eyes. "This is the guy you went to see in Arizona!"

"I didn't see him."

"Am I an idiot? This is the same guy in the pictures you took down there. There are pictures! I found the pictures, Lee Anne."

"You were supposed to find them, but we never saw each other." As if it were winding down to the absolute end of something final and impossible, her voice sounded tired.

Val said, "I didn't see her. Had no idea she was there."

Brent said, "Shut the fuck up! I'm not talking to you! I'm talking to my wife! This is the guy, Lee Anne. This is the same guy! What do you mean, I was supposed to find them?"

Now Val remembered, that night after the movie, Kazz's insisting that someone had been in the house.... He'd dismissed it. He looked at Lee Anne with sudden knowing. He saw something in her face that now confirmed it, suddenly felt a deepening dread, that whatever was happening here had a much larger dimension which he did not begin to understand. He said simply, "Lee Anne."

Brent was nodding, "This is the guy, Lee Anne, and now he's here. How much am I supposed to take? What the fuck is he doing here and what are you doing with him?" He turned toward Val. "What the fuck are you doing here?"

Brent snatched the box and dumped everything out on the table, flung the box with a clatter. He picked up several snapshots, studied each and tossed them onto the floor. "Boats!" was all he said. He looked closely. "Stolen boats! I heard it all!" He picked up the picture of Davis' running the boat over to Nassau, several more snapshots. "Stolen fucking boats!"

He pulled another set of pictures out of his chest pocket and compared them to Lee Anne's boat pictures.

"And this is the same guy who was with our friend here in those pictures..." Brent pointed at a picture of Michael walking beside Val in the park near his house. Though he had no idea where the picture had come from, Val suddenly understood Brent had mistaken Michael for Davis. Lee Anne shook her head, no.

Brent spun and snatched a handful of her hair and tried to slap her, her hair covering her face as she twisted away. She pushed him, trying to pull out of his grasp.

"This is the guy who stole my fucking boat! I'm supposed to be in New York tonight, while you fuckers set up... What?" He pushed her away from him and turned on Val. "She goes down to see you. You come back here. You steal my boat. What else? While I'm in New York, the two of you..." He went speechless with rage.

Terrified and seeing how ludicrous this had become, how incomprehensible and impossible to explain—Brent's confusion, his own—Val did the last thing he anticipated he'd do. He laughed. He was about to say, "Would I be here if I'd stolen your boat? This is a complete mistake. Let's just stop, back up and..."

He sensed a blur of movement, felt the room suddenly slide out of focus, became aware of himself staggering backward; still trying to recover his balance, he staggered again, fought to get his breath, keep the room in focus before him; Brent hit him once more; Val felt his mouth fill with blood, managed to raise his hands enough to partially block the next punches. Brent's face was close; he seemed to be panting or snarling or talking to himself, perhaps all three—Val couldn't tell. Brent hit him again with the exponential strength of craziness, and Val went down, felt a thudding snap at the base of his skull as he hit the glass coffee table, Brent on top of him. Their faces were almost touching as he reached for Val's throat, and Val, arms lost somewhere and immobilized, turned his head and bit Brent's hand as hard as he could; Brent screamed, hit Val with his free fist, his ring tearing at Val's face; now Val found his hands, pushed Brent back. Brent still on top of him, his face suddenly close, and Val, still unable to move, bit his cheek. He felt a surge of pain go through Brent; Brent jerked back, grabbed his face, caught a handful of Val's hair and banged his head against the floor. For Val, the room was fading; from far off he heard something, a howl. He heard a thud, like a bat hitting a melon, felt Brent tremble. Brent slumped onto Val. There was another thud, another; Val convulsively heaved against Brent, met no resistance; his face and hands covered with blood, he pushed again, and Brent rolled off him onto his side.

Heartbeat by heartbeat Val became aware of himself. Brent was motion-less, and…there was something about the way his shadow darkened the floor; he glanced up and saw Lee Anne standing close to him, panting, an object in her hand; he saw it was the white marble sculpture that had been on the table, noticed a thick tuft of black hair on a corner of the base. She seemed almost unrecognizable, someone he'd never seen before. She was panting and looking down at Brent, and Val thought she was going to hit him, too. He threw up his hand to ward off the blow, saw snapshots scat-tered about the floor; long glistening shards of broken glass—once the cof-fee table; the telephone had skidded across the room.

When Lee Anne made no move toward him, he looked back at Brent; something strange about his shadow, the way it kept silently moving even though Brent remained motionless: smooth, dark and shiny, the shadow slid toward Val. Then it came into focus, so red it was black, and he saw the blood spreading out from under Brent's head. He pushed himself complete-ly upright. His vision seemed to be obscured. He reached up and felt blood thickening his scalp, his hair, found the ragged edge of a gash; he felt his face, looked at his hands; he was covered with blood, he wasn't sure whose, his or Brent's, again he looked up at Lee Anne, but she seemed to have gone out of herself. He thought he could hear her whispering something, "…please, please, please…"; he glanced back and saw the blood still silently advancing toward him; he jerked back out of its way, and then, gingerly pushing away long, broken shards of the coffee table, he crawled over to Brent and felt his neck for a pulse, found none, thought of mouth-to-mouth resuscitation, but, staring down at a raw place in Brent's cheek, recoiled at the raw teeth marks. His.

Still on his knees, Val reached up tentatively toward Lee Anne, and when she made no movement to hit him or resist, and, in fact, remained motion-less, he fit his hand to the white bone of marble where it met her hand, and tugged it gently. As if waking up, she looked down at her hand, and then at him, almost as if she'd forgotten he was there. He pulled harder and took the sudden weight of the sculpture. Seeing the dark shadow, smooth and perfect, still spreading across the hardwood floor and now almost reaching her feet, Val found her knee and pushed her, and, startled, she took a wob-bly step back. He raised the sculpture close to his face and examined the square base, where he thought he'd seen a tuft of black hair, and where, in fact, he did now see the hair embedded in what looked like a thick chunk of bloody bread dough; entranced with the silent movement of the blood as it advanced across the honey-colored hardwood, he crabbed back out of its way, and absently reached out to replace the sculpture on the glass coffee table. When it met nothing, he glanced over and saw the gleaming shards angled across the chrome frame; he set the marble piece on the floor beyond the blood. As he pulled back his hand, he stared at the perfect red print each of his fingers and palm had made on the polished white marble. He opened his hand.

Once more, he leaned across the still-widening puddle, placed his fingers across Brent's carotid artery, but felt nothing; a moment ago his veins and neck had been bulging as he'd been screaming at Val; Val had stolen his boat, he was the man in Lee Anne's pictures, in Arizona. He peered up at Lee Anne, who was still staring straight ahead. Whatever else had happened, he knew that Brent had almost killed him and that Lee Anne had just saved his life.

He felt the warm thickening in his scalp and glanced across the floor at the massive Steinway, its ribs and sounding board white and secret as the fluted, sunless underside of a mushroom, the three bronze pedals gleaming. Still unable to stand, he started crawling across the room to the telephone, glanced back over to see Lee Anne empty-handed, still looking down, still whispering; he noticed his bloody handprints following him across the hard-wood. He suddenly knew that this moment had been coming to Lee Anne for years, and that it wasn't just about Davis, or him, or his leaving her in Brooklyn, or her sending him fragmented postcards since, or her com-ing back to Tucson to see, but not see him; that it was much bigger. For Lee Anne this was the culmination of a dynamic she didn't understand. He stared at the bloody handprints. Yes, she'd just saved his life, but she had also set the situation in motion. He suddenly heard Per's phrase that last night in Brooklyn: *something in her waiting.* Tonight. This was the thing. She'd even tried to warn him several times. In the end, against her will, it had happened. None of this came to him in words, but more in quantum leaps, flashes of knowing.

He picked up the telephone and fumbled with the buttons before getting a dial tone. Fingers trembling, he dialed 911, and then, as it rang, he was suddenly confused. Was he calling the police? Emergency paramedics? Were they the same number? Which did he want? If he asked for the paramed-ics and they couldn't revive Brent, the cops would come. Or they'd come anyway. He turned off the phone, put it down and started crawling toward Brent. He had to revive him. Now! But how long had he been lying there? Seconds? A minute? Several minutes? Halfway back to Brent, Val noticed the white marble sculpture resting in the middle of the floor, individual strands of black hair catching the light. He stopped, stared at Brent. To revive him, he'd have to open his mouth, hold it open, bring his mouth down to Brent's to blow into his lungs. He couldn't bear the thought of touching him.

He studied the white chunk of flesh on the base of the sculpture and then became aware of himself crouched on the floor. What was he doing? Crawling? He steadied himself on all fours, pushed up onto one knee, remained there, and then, both hands on the floor like a sprinter in a starting position, he pushed as hard as he could, and swaying, he stood. He took a step, staggered slightly, took another, steadied himself. Weaving toward the phone, he leaned down, lost his balance, recovered, and managed to reach it. Taking several more steps, phone in hand, panting, he slumped heavily into the embracing curve of the piano.

Fingers thick and sticky with clotting blood, still trembling, he stabbed at several buttons on the phone until he heard the dial tone. As he pressed the *nine*, he looked across the room. Lee Anne was now at the far end of the curved sofa, where she sat, shoulders slumped, feet placed neatly side by side, her hands in her lap like a prim, very tired schoolgirl. She stared through the open front door onto the porch. He'd never seen her inhabit her body that way. Brent lay motionless, broken glass and blood gleaming around him; the blood seemed to have slowed or stopped its movement altogether. On the other side of the room, the snapshots of Davis and the phony repo orders were scattered everywhere.

Val pressed the next number, *one*. Suddenly saw the room as one in a series of crime scene photos, dozens of cases worked as a public defender, inseparable, the same case. This case. Now he became aware of the entire room, himself included standing on one side of it, and more, a bird's eye view of the house, the lawn with its dock in front and its cut dock lines, and the Grady-White tied up in the dark at the end of the dock...

...and he was here now covered with blood and leaning against a piano and pressing the last number, *one* of 911, and Lee Anne, Lee Anne's husband, Brent, dead, a few moments dead, bite marks on his face and hand, Val's teeth—how to explain that to paramedics? Brent's skull smashed. Val saw his handprint on the white marble.

And....

Brent had recognized Val. From pictures that Lee Anne had taken. Recent snapshots Val hadn't known existed. *The guy you visited in Arizona.* He heard Brent's voice rising in sudden comprehension: *this is the same guy! He stole my boat!*

He completed dialing 911, and the phone started to ring, and as Val heard Brent's accusations still rising in his ears, he suddenly knew that the cops would see it exactly as Brent had.

But, he realized, he had Lee Anne, who could tell the cops what had really happened. That he'd just come to find out about his brother, Davis. And he'd come into this scene, a stolen boat, which he knew nothing about. But all night there'd been something weird going on with Lee Anne; she was afraid, waiting for something, wanting Val to get out of there, as if she knew something was about to happen, and yet waiting for it, and then he was fighting for his life.... And Lee Anne had smashed Brent to stop him from killing Val. Saved Val. Almost as if she knew she would have to....

"This is 911. Is this an emergency?"

...but if there were pictures of Val taken in Arizona, recent pictures, and Lee Anne had visited—it seemed she had—there would be evidence of it—plane tickets, hotel receipts; and if Brent's boat was missing, then cops could make a case that Val and Lee Anne were lovers—they'd once been—and that they'd conspired to kill her husband, Brent; ridiculous, he didn't even know him! But then, he didn't have to know him to kill him. Here he was, dead—and what? They'd conspired to kill him, stolen his boat, for what? insurance money? and what else? Val could see this guy had money. This house, more. Could hear it coming at him. They'd killed him for the money and to be together.

The cops show up, take them into custody, into separate rooms. Val tells his story, his truth, the truth, which is unbelievable—the single fact that he's alone in another man's house with his wife at ten at night and the guy ends up dead is insurmountable; but he tells his story. Once it's on the table, it's infinitely malleable. Given the evidence in front of him right now, just the evidence in this room alone, he knows the cops won't believe him. They will take him apart. The evidence is overwhelming.

Lee Anne tells her story, probably with a detective and maybe even a prosecutor already leading her. *Okay, what happened tonight, this guy, an old boyfriend, you'd visited him just a few weeks earlier in Arizona, his wife knows nothing about you and him getting together, right, now he comes to see you....* He had no idea what Lee Anne would tell them.

But Val did know: in all the time he'd ever been with Lee Anne, he'd seen huge changes come and go in her. Tonight alone she'd gone from being vacant to terrified, and then again to defiant and smug, her face animating with spiteful pride as she'd run down some of her scams. Then, wounded, as she'd seen the pain in his face. *I wanted something with you.* Even now, sitting motionless on the sofa, staring through the screen, she looked like someone he'd never seen before. But he knew that she'd come to life again, reverse herself once more when she saw that it would be either her or him. She'd always been a survivor, a fighter. It would be her word against his. And he knew she could pull it off. He could hear her thick Southern accent, her fearsome, unpredictable brilliance at work. She would be able to make the details of this night work for her. He slumped against the piano and surveyed the room; if it came down to her word against his, which it would, since there were no witnesses, he'd never be able to convince the cops that he had just come over here to find out something about his brother and then go home, go back to his wife and son. Cops. Evidence. Information. Indictment. Trial. Jury.

Head swimming, he heard the voice repeat from 911. "Is this an emergency? Hello?" He didn't say anything. "Are you there? Can you hear me? Are you able to speak?"

He thought to call out to her, *Lee Anne,* to ask her what had happened, what was happening, and he again looked in her direction and even might have tried to say her name, but couldn't speak. And, still sitting on the sofa, she didn't look like herself.

The voice came out of the phone. "Is this a fire, medical, or police emergency? Can you hear me?"

He raised the phone to speak, opened his mouth. Now he saw them, Kazz turning toward him with a look of tenderness in her eyes, and Michael, too, his boy's face just beneath his recently evolved, adolescent's mask; he saw Kazz and Michael falling away—and he realized how much he loved them, and felt as though they were being physically torn out of him, couldn't understand how he hadn't been able to see them clearly before. Why hadn't he just gone home with them after his father's funeral? It would have been so simple. He'd be with them now. Val heard himself moan.

The 911 operator said, "Are you there?"

As though he had been traveling through the air at great speed and now had suddenly slammed to a stop, Val felt panic impale him. He'd never see Kazz and Michael again.

"Can you hear me?"

Val fumbled with the button, hung up and remained slumped against the piano. Still staring out through the front door, Lee Anne slowly turned her head toward him as if fighting her way through the force field of an enormous distraction. She found him and he looked at her and felt himself lost in how they had remained connected to each other. And now there was this.

The phone rang beside him, and he jumped, reached for it, but then drew back his hand. Who? He realized that it had to be 911, that they had, of course, received this telephone number; they were calling back to check on the caller. Lee Anne looked at the telephone and then at him. Once more the phone rang and he made no move, just became aware of his hand poised, and he and Lee Anne watching each other, and then the room accelerated again, his head swimming as another stab of panic went through him and he realized that if he didn't answer, they would be able to use the telephone number to find the address, perhaps already had, would send a cop to check it out, and...

He, or Lee Anne, should answer the phone and tell them the call was a mistake, that everything was all right; he tried to pronounce her name again, but couldn't—did she know what he was thinking? Would she answer it? She made no move.

He picked up the phone as it rang again and placed his thumb to the answer key, but didn't press down yet. It was simple, he'd answer and tell them everything was all right, it was just a mistake, a misdial, no need to send anyone out...

And they would....

Would what?

They'd ask who had called, confirmation of the number and address, and who were they speaking with now...

And he'd say, he'd have to say, the name of the owner of the house, Brent...

Brent who?

He blanked. Brent who?

He looked over at Lee Anne...

He had no idea.

And if he spoke they'd have a recording of his voice; and they kept a taped log of their telephone calls. Each voice had a distinct identifying print, no two the same—and if and when they investigated, they'd know the caller wasn't Brent; that whoever he was, he had lied, tried to conceal his identity; Val felt it suddenly spiraling, another piece of evidence falling into place against him; he glanced over at Lee Anne.

But, simple. If she would just pick up the phone, she could answer their questions; she lived here, and no one would have to know he was in the house, had ever been there...

She remained sitting, made no move to rise, just watched him with a far-away look as the phone went on ringing.... Should he signal her to answer? Would she? And if she did, what would she say? He realized he had no idea. She might say it was a mistake, as he hoped, and get rid of them; or that there'd been an accident, or that...was he thinking about this right? He knew he couldn't be, but what was the right way?

He tried to take a deep breath. He had a call in to 911, but he hadn't spoken. So? So they had no recording of his voice. But they had the number here. And they had called back. No one had answered. Where did that put him?

They would send a cop or sheriff out to the address to check on the caller.

He looked at his watch. The cop would be here...when? Depending on how many calls the cop had before he could get to this one, it would be soon. Maybe a few minutes. He pushed himself off the piano and reran the situation. It all still pointed in the same direction. Once cops were on the scene and once he and Lee Anne were questioned about what had happened, it would be impossible to make himself appear innocent. Lee Anne's snapshots of him in Arizona, any receipts Lee Anne had from a trip out there, the cut dock lines... The details were too overpowering. And finally, he just couldn't imagine Lee Anne under pressure from the cops admitting she'd killed Brent, that it was all a big mistake, and she was very sorry and... and maybe it wasn't a mistake.

He looked at Brent lying between the sofa and the shattered glass table. He became aware of a boat's wake, each wave hitting the shore in the still-ness. He'd forgotten the water. With Brent's body, it was a crime scene. Without his body.... Val turned his head and looked out the window toward the dock. His boat. The water.

And he saw the only thing left. If there was any hope at all of his ever seeing Kazz and Michael again, he had to get Brent out of here. If Brent was gone, there could be suspicions, but without a body, they couldn't make a case…. He had to get Brent out and clean up the room and disappear. And then, maybe, he had a chance. No one here had seen him come to the house. No one had any idea he was here. He hadn't left any word. He looked at his watch.

He had at least a few minutes, maybe longer, before a cop came to check. What was there to lose? If he didn't do something, he knew what was going to happen to him. He was dead. So, what? Was he actually going to move Brent's body? Impossible! Beyond stupid! He saw Michael and Kazz looking at him. If he was ever going to be with them, he had to do it.

## His Only Chance

He surveyed the room, reached up and explored the gash in his scalp. The blood was clotting. He felt his way through the rest of his bloody, tangled hair. His swollen face. Bruised, gashed, his head shot through with pain, but the gaping cut in his scalp seemed to be the worst damage…. He touched an eye, which he noticed was beginning to swell shut.

He thought he heard someone say something…*help me*? Was that him? He couldn't be sure, but he found himself walking unsteadily…. In a large kitchen, blinking against the light, he washed his hands, wiped them on his pants. Pushing open a succession of doors, he found a bathroom; he threw open a cabinet and grabbed a stack of towels, ran back into the living room. Lee Anne was standing now.

He stared down at Brent. This was impossible! Better to take his chances with the cops. He stood panting, heart pounding, then bolted out the side door. Froze. Silvery liquid eyes. Two raccoons held themselves rigid, dropped down from plastic garbage cans, each with cinderblocks holding down their lids; he returned with two half-empty cans. Grabbing a towel and wrapping his hand in it, he picked up shards of glass, dropping them into the cans until the area around Brent was cleared of the largest pieces, and then, on his knees, he spread a towel over the puddle and watched it instantly darken. And the next towel. And the next. Splinters of glass grinding. He mopped the floor, pushing towel after saturated towel into one garbage bag, then a second, and finally, cautiously, he pulled Brent toward him....to...where...the front door? He realized that the only way to get him to the door without leaving a trail was...He looked back and saw Lee Anne standing vacantly, neither encouraging or discouraging him. She indicated nothing, her face unreadable.

Still on his knees, he sagged, placed his hands on the floor, his head in his hands. This couldn't be happening. This was impossible. He looked up. He had to stop. Had he gone crazy? Anything would be better than this. He would explain the situation to the cops; he'd panicked, he'd made a mistake; yes, he'd acted as though he were guilty because he knew they'd think he was guilty; he'd done nothing; this guy, Brent, whoever he was, who he'd never seen before in his life, drunk, enraged, had burst into the room, accusing him, him and Lee Anne of...of everything! and next thing, the guy'd been hitting him. He'd knocked Val onto the floor. He was fighting for his life, and Lee Anne had hit Brent, Val had nothing to do with that, in fact, the guy was going to kill Val, he was sure that if Lee Anne hadn't done something, he would have killed Val....

Head still in his hands, he moaned; he pushed himself up onto all fours. He'd have to get Brent out the door, and the only way to do that without leaving a trail of blood would be to...

Val glanced at his watch, knelt beside Brent and lifted his head, slid a garbage bag down over his head and shoulders, worked it all the way down to his waist, and cinched the plastic tie. Panting and moaning, he suddenly, with a burst of terrified energy, rolled Brent onto his side, fit his shoulder to Brent's waist, and fumbling for something to grab hold of beside the plastic garbage bag, gathered the seat of Brent's pants into his fist. He worked Brent's dense weight across his shoulder, and, legs trembling, he slowly stood with Brent in a fireman's carry; he turned, and, staggering slightly with each step, he walked him to the front door, where he flicked off the outside light and stepped onto the porch.

Staggering faster, he went down the stairs, footsteps grinding on the gravel walk, silent as he stepped onto the lawn. And as he heard his steps knock under him on the dock, Val suddenly thought, yes! this could work! it's the wrong thing to do, but it's the only thing left! With the faint glow thrown from inside the house, he saw the darkness of the boat where it was tied up, and, catching his breath, legs burning, he found the ladder. Pivoting, Brent still across his shoulders, he gripped the ladder, and, feeling for each rung with his foot, he descended—the tide had dropped several feet—until he found the boat. Hanging onto the ladder, he felt for the gunwale with his foot. He hit something solid, and, feeling beyond, he tried to lower himself onto what he hoped was the sole of the boat. He lost his balance, but, keeping his hold on Brent, he fell heavily into the bow, lay on the sole in pain. He freed his arms from under Brent, his thighs and back burning from the effort. He looked back up toward the house and listened, but didn't hear anything. He stood and felt for the ladder.

Again, the startling grind of his footsteps on the walk froze him, and he became aware of the distant sound of voices and music woven together. A woman's laugh, sudden and shrill, followed by a chorus of drunken laughter and her louder laugh, triumphant. He quickly climbed the porch stairs, the outside light still off, and burst into the living room, looking this way and that. Brent was gone. In the boat. That was good, wasn't it? Lee Anne stood watching him. In a minute, he'd talk to her. He'd have to try to understand something. But now, what next? The garbage cans, with blades of shattered glass sticking straight up…

Stiff-legged under their weight, he carried one, then the other back outside, shards of blood-stained glass beneath his chin, more evidence…but, maybe, okay, the table had broken, there'd been a nasty cut…they'd never believe it. But still, without a body, they could have suspicions, they could have accusations, but they had nothing concrete…nothing. If it came to it, they'd have Lee Anne's story, but that was all. She could say anything, but no one had seen Val here…so far. In fact, by getting rid of Brent, wasn't he guaranteeing that she'd have to remain silent? And they'd have nothing on her either. Or…who knew, who knew.

He felt his thoughts speed ahead until they were an indecipherable blur. He just had to get out of here. He noticed the two cinderblocks where he'd flung them on the ground, grabbed one in each hand and walked them back into the living room, set them down just inside the front door. He glanced at his watch. How long had it been since he'd called 911? How much time could he possibly have left? This was taking forever! He had to get out of here now! Better just to leave things undone—what things!?—than be found here, with Brent lying in the boat.

He looked around the living room, grabbed the three garbage bags stuffed with blood-soaked towels, and, pushing open the screen door, he stumbled back down to the dock, dropped them into the boat. Another trip: he placed both cinderblocks carefully beside the garbage bags. Hands on knees, doubled over with a sharp stitch in his side, Val fought to catch his breath, stumbled back up toward the house.

Again, the terrible room. Another garbage bag. He gathered up the snapshots of Davis scattered across the floor, the repo orders and....where were the Arizona pictures of him that Brent had mentioned? He turned and looked at Lee Anne. There was so much to ask her! This! All of this! There was no time! She had to give him the rest of those Arizona pictures! Or maybe she'd say there weren't any, that he was confused. Or maybe there really weren't any! There was no time to find out. That was the thing, there was no time.

He looked at Lee Anne, became aware that he was so thirsty that he could hardly swallow...and was it him, or was the room...something wrong, different. He noticed he had to turn his head back and forth so that he could see. He stumbled into the kitchen and gulped water from the tap, more water, gasped, went on drinking, mouth rimming the cold metal faucet, he had to finish this thing up, he was taking forever, he went on drinking, gasped, glanced at his watch, soaked another towel and wrung it out.

In the living room, he grabbed the phone on the piano—clotted dark with blood—and started to wipe it, tossed it into the garbage bag with the pictures of Davis; he fell to his knees, swabbing the floor and his tracks to the door, gave it up and tossed the towel into the garbage bag. He had to get out of here now. With his one eye swollen, he turned his head and body to find Lee Anne standing on the far side of the room. Cocking his head like a bird or horse, he saw himself, grotesque, covered with blood, a black plastic garbage bag trailing beside him; in the short time of his coming to this house, he'd been turned into something terrible, unrecognizable, even to himself—himself most of all!—a beast.

He dropped the bag and crossed the room until he stood in front of Lee Anne. He realized he'd been talking to her the whole time, arguing with her, reasoning with her, talking to himself, and now he looked into her face and wanted to say, *They'll be here any second. Any second. What will you tell them?* But he didn't. She took several steps back, and he realized that she had been slowly but steadily backing away from the center of the room while he'd been on his knees, in and out of the house, and now, almost in the dark dining room, back to the wall, she stood, shaking her head, no. No to what? To everything that had just happened?

He turned from her and snatched the garbage bag, pushed open the screen door, and once more surveyed the room, turning his head in his grotesque, one-eyed way—the piano, the chrome coffee table base; a blade of glass gleaming under the sofa, he'd missed it!—and what else!? And Lee Anne, watching him, one hand at her side, fingertips spread and touching the wall, and the beautiful hardwood floor, smeared and clouded and beaded in places with water. The sculpture was right in the middle of the floor where he'd left it when he'd taken it from Lee Anne, his blood-stained handprint wrapped around the white marble. If he hadn't noticed it…isn't this exactly what was wrong with everything now? So much he was looking at and not seeing, or seeing wrong. He knew that! Was it too late to stop? He stared at the black hairs gleaming, then lunged back into the room and grabbed the sculpture.

The tide and boat were much lower. Val climbed down the ladder and set the sculpture and last garbage bag somewhere in the dark boat. Groping overhead, he released the anchor line from around the piling; he dropped it in a tangled heap in the bow, and, switching on only the instrument lights, he started the motor, pushed off the dock. As he pulled away, he saw a blue light silently strobing into the trees near the house; it disappeared, reappeared brighter as it came up the drive.

Running lights off, Val gave the boat more gas, and, watching for boats moored in the dark, he ran slowly away from shore, garbage bags snapping in the wind as he gained speed. They were blowing overboard! He slowed, shifted into neutral, and, stumbling over tangles of anchor line, skidding on the plastic bags, he felt for the cinderblocks and sculpture, stumbled over Brent's legs. He heard himself mumbling, as if overhearing someone else, *don't…don't…go back…go back…* And yet he continued groping frantically through the slippery tangle in the dark of the boat until he'd weighed down the garbage bags.

At the center console, he put the boat back into forward, gave it more gas. Again, he looked toward the house and saw the blue light still flashing, now smaller, and knew that enough time had gone by so that the cop had come to the door—front door, back door? Could he see in? Had Lee Anne gone out to meet him? No matter, the cop was talking to Lee Anne, had to know from her face that something was wrong. Had he come into the house? What was she telling him? *Thank god you're here!* Maybe she was showing him the broken glass, telling him about the intruder… *He's just left. By boat. Out there!* Maybe she had just collapsed into his arms. No, not Lee Anne. Whatever had happened, was happening, the cop, before doing anything more, had put a call through to the Coast Guard. Val glanced back toward shore, the blue light still flashing as he ran into the vast darkness of Gardiners Bay.

Now he realized that he had no idea where he was going, knew that he might be headed toward Plum Gut, which he wanted to avoid, but other than that, where? He had only the waypoints entered into the GPS across the Sound and to the last bell, and he realized that course wouldn't work for him. He'd have to head out of the Sound—past Montauk—and into the open Atlantic if he were going to find enough water to drop Brent. He couldn't drop him in a hundred feet.... And not in this bay. But he had no waypoints beyond his course. Watching for running lights, for the sudden overhead flashing of Search and Rescue, he heard himself mumbling, "Go back! Go back!" He was shaking all over. He switched the compass and GPS lights on, glanced at the fuel gauge with the needle just touching the "E" of empty. He felt under the instrument panel for the flashlight, and, pulling out the chart series, he turned it on. Gardiners Bay. Cupping bloody fingers around the barrel, he slid the white light over the chart. Buoys. Waypoints. Depth sounding sprinkled everywhere. The faces of land masses peering up at him. Light blue for shallow water. Where *was* he on this? If he could find some buoys off Montauk, enter the waypoints into the GPS, he could set up a course.... He stared at the numbers, but could understand nothing. Enter waypoints into the GPS? He was completely blank; couldn't remember how to do it. He realized he was holding the chart upside down, heard himself moan.... If he could just head out through the eastern opening of Gardiners Bay, he'd run due east off shore until the depth finder showed at least two hundred feet. He looked at the fuel gauge, remembered the jerry cans of gas. Twelve gallons. Not enough, but better than nothing. He'd fuel the tank. Not enough to get home, but maybe enough to reach New London. Later. Better to get out first. He switched off the beam. Blinded, he found the numbers as they slowly resurfaced on the compass. He was headed north-northeast. That would put him right into Plum Gut. Turning 360 degrees to survey the shore lights, he saw a long, dark stretch to the east where he knew Gardiners Island, Montauk and the open Atlantic should be. He turned the wheel until the compass needle rested on due east. As the bow came around, he noticed the steering felt thick and sluggish, the boat heavy and somehow wrong in the water. He checked his speed. Seventeen knots. The hull would be heavy at this speed. Remembering the submerged telephone pole, and unsure of what else was out here—reefs, buoys, boats— he dared not run faster. Heavy…it was the additional weight. He tried not to think of Brent and the cinderblocks and what he was going to have to do. Had to do. It was his only hope. He heard himself moaning.

Watching his fuel gauge, he ran on for some time, checking the night sky for the sudden appearance of flashing lights swooping across the water, waiting for the searchlight to burst over him. He was surprised his depth finder still showed only eighty to ninety feet and considered a look at the chart again…. Now he thought he could probably just open the garbage bags and dump the bloody towels overboard, that they would saturate and sink, but no, he'd do it all at once, Brent, the cinderblocks, all of it.

He ran on through what he hoped was the dark eastern opening of Gardiners Bay—it had to be—and on out into the Atlantic. He noticed the water getting slightly deeper, but the needle of his fuel gauge had now dropped halfway through the letter E. He watched the numbers on the depth gauge…120…175…123…196…. Val realized he couldn't go any farther or wait longer.

Shifting into neutral, stumbling over tangles of anchor line and the cinderblocks, Val felt the garbage bags in the dark, and tearing open one after the other, he dumped the bloody towels overboard, dropped the bags in after them. Switching on the flashlight, he surveyed the floor of the boat. Brent's top was halfway in the black garbage bag, his bloody and water-splashed pant legs sticking out. Trailing from the bow locker, haphazard coils of anchor line had spilled on top of him. Val opened the compartment, took out the small Navy anchor and pulled out the rest of the line in clumps and snarls. Cut the line into sections? He wasn't sure. Not yet. Maybe. He placed a cinderblock next to each of Brent's legs, teased out and doubled a section of line, ran it through the block, and, fumbling with large, uncertain granny knots, he tied a length around one of Brent's ankles. Kneeling in the midst of the tangle, pushing back coils of line, he reached for the anchor, picked it up, hesitated. Loop the anchor and several lengths of line around Brent's waist? And the second cinderblock to his other ankle? Then how would he get him out of the boat? Crouched on the floor, Val couldn't think. He doubled several lengths of line, again threaded the loop through the second cinderblock. Moving slowly, almost as if he were drunk or countering the effects of anesthesia, he knotted the cinderblock to Brent's other ankle. Now, the anchor line and anchor around his waist? Not needed, was it? Val studied the tangle of line. Cut the anchor line free of the boat? No, not yet. He'd keep Brent and the line attached to the boat until he was absolutely sure he knew what next. He stared at Brent's blood-soaked pants, the black garbage bag cinched around his head and chest, the cinderblocks. He saw that Brent had lost a shoe—a Nike cross-trainer—and wondered where it was—the house, the lawn, the dock? Felt a kind of detached interest. Was it bloody? Would it be easy to find by cops? He felt too exhausted to register the panic—or else, he couldn't feel any more panic than he already did. He crouched in the bottom of the boat, listening to the idling outboard, and then, without standing, he slid a cinderblock closer to the gunwale. Now he would, what? He would stand. Place each block on the same side of the boat. Pull Brent over to that side. He looked at the open compartment, the anchor line shackled to a ring. He ran through the steps. Cut the line at the ring. He remembered Michael's knife clipped to the inside of his pocket. Okay. Move both cinderblocks to the same side of the boat. Move Brent next. Then push Brent overboard first. Then push all the line overboard before the blocks. Make sure there were no tangled coils near any part of Val. Watch where he placed his feet. Push Brent's body overboard first. Then stand clear and drop both cinderblocks at the same time. The flashlight beam slid from the anchor compartment to Brent's body to the blocks. Val saw flashes of crime scene photos. He heard the water lapping against the hull, the outboard idling.

Through his numbness and exhaustion, he felt something rising in him. At first he wasn't sure what. Perhaps the beginnings of quiet. Calm. Or maybe something returning. The first knowing that he couldn't do this, didn't have to do this. Didn't want to do this. It wasn't who he was. He sank down and slumped with his back against the center console, knew he wouldn't do it. How had he come so close? This, Val realized, was the worst of what had happened to Davis in Miami; he'd lost who he was.

He sat exhausted, terrified, but back inside himself, perhaps completely himself for the first time since word had come that his father was going into the hospice. He remained motionless, too exhausted to move, gathering strength to stand. He'd go back. He'd have to take his chances. He'd find a lawyer, someone who would be able to convince a jury he wasn't guilty...of...what charges? Murder one? Two? Manslaughter? He couldn't think farther, just that he'd go back. Maybe his turning himself in might help. Whatever else he did, he wasn't dropping Brent overboard. He pulled himself upright, slumped on the console, thought of Kazz and Michael. However it worked out, there'd be nothing he'd have to keep secret from them. Holding Lee Anne apart from Kazz all this time had eaten a hole in Val without his having realized it until now.

He looked at the compass, then off to the west, where he thought he could make out the flash of Montauk's light on the horizon. He remembered the fuel gauge on empty and realized that this was the time to empty the jerry cans into the tank. He'd need the funnel. Where had he put it? Maybe under the seat? He pointed the light down. His pack. Nothing more. Probably knocked back into the stern in the confusion. Toeing aside tangles of anchor line, he started aft, and, swinging the flashlight beam ahead of him, saw, in a single instant, a silvery movement, what? water rising out of the bilge and silently advancing toward the center console! Instinctively shifting his weight back, Val reached for the bilge pump switch just as the water rose over the battery; the lights went out, the engine silent, and he felt the boat go soft under him, water sluicing in the flashlight beam in a solid black wall over the stern and quarter, the softness underfoot deepening into a wallow; he felt the starboard side of the boat rise, the suction of the hull as it gathered speed and kept on rolling, and, grabbing blindly, still clutching the flashlight, Val felt the boat roll completely over onto him.

Groping for a gunwale handrail, things dropping and snagging—charts, jacket, coils of line, the funnel, his bag—Val felt the encircling whip and cinch of line snaking and tightening around his chest and legs. Hanging on as hard as he could in the air pocket, the beam careening in the white interior of the hull, Val saw the black garbage bag around Brent's body caught in snarls of line, and then it disappeared underwater, and Val felt the body and cinderblocks jerk him down; he dropped the flashlight, and, trying to work free an arm, he slid his hand sideways, groped toward his pocket, the knife, located it, the flashlight sank below him, getting smaller, he inched the knife into his hand, fit his thumb to the hole in the blade, snapped it open, dug at one of the lines around his leg. The flashlight, a tiny point of light far beneath him, disappeared completely into the black. Val felt the boat shifting as it continued to roll, heard something snap and release, felt himself jerked under, his head suddenly yanked below the black water, now a vise of pressure closing on him. Twisting and turning, flailing blindly at the lines entangling him, he plummeted down, felt a burning stab of pain in his head and chest, his lungs, fought not to gasp, went on cutting at the line in the freezing black water, suddenly felt something release him. He kicked his legs, his arms, and, letting go of the knife, lungs searing, fighting not to breathe, he swam—which way was he going? up? down?—he drove his arms and legs in the icy black water; throat bursting, he fought not to breathe; his head grew lighter, far away. The fire in his chest pushed up into his head; he gasped, inhaled a chest full of water, choked as he burst the surface. He gasped for air, nothing came in; he flailed, gasped, still nothing; he choked, suddenly puked up saltwater, and gasped again; puked more water, took in air, went on coughing and gasping, slowly caught his breath.

He became aware of tangles of anchor line still trailing from his waist and legs, reached down and stripped them away. He reached tentatively for the boat, felt nothing, splashed in the water. Lunging this way and that, he still felt nothing, and then, caught in a new rise of panic, he flailed in several directions for some time before he could check himself. The boat—if he could hold out through the night, maybe, when the sun rose, he'd be able to spot the overturned hull, get to it, hang on.

How far away could the boat be? Panicking once more, he flailed for the boat before he could make himself stop and tread water slowly. He saw the blackboard in the bait shop, water temperature, large chalked numbers, fifty-eight degrees, and thought *it won't kill me if I can just make it through the night.* He knew that out of the Sound and ten miles off Montauk the water was colder, but still thought, stubbornly, it won't kill me if I can just hold out until morning and find the overturned boat. But, realistically, head-high in water looking for an overturned boat, six inches, a foot, two feet out of the water, and—wasn't the underside painted blue? Find that? He saw the undulating swarm of eels and shiners in the tanks in the bait shop, was aware that he'd been gashed and cut in several places, knew of the big sharks out here. He felt his chest and legs and arms hanging below him in the freezing black water and realized that there no longer was a boat, that the hull had cracked when he'd hit the telephone pole; it didn't take much—sometimes only a screw knocked out from a swim ladder below the waterline; in two or three hours a bilge could fill, and that, he realized, was exactly what had happened; or else there'd been a small crack below the waterline, or a fitting for the depth gauge transponder knocked askew, one or all three or something else; and while he'd been in the house, water had slowly been seeping into the boat, flooding the bilge; he'd felt its heaviness when he'd slowed and then changed directions. And the boat, seven years old, had poor or deteriorated flotation and it had gone down.

He looked up at Virgo and the Big and Little Dippers and Scorpio and the Milky Way blazing down into the water, and, moving his arms and legs, he thought of Kazz and Michael, that their lives would go on without him.... After a while, he could feel his body drawing numb into a center that was getting smaller, and he apologized to his mother for the pain his death would cause her. His death, not far off now, had started just minutes ago with his sensing a man standing motionless before he saw him, Brent, yet Val recognized that moment, had always known it, was always coming back to it, Davis on the dark lawn, Val himself lying on the ground a moment later; he'd known it ever since, someone just at the edge of darkness.... Sometimes it was his father; sometimes Lee Anne; sometimes Davis; they had been there for seventeen years, each trying to kill him; Davis for his wanting Lee Anne; Lee Anne for his losing Davis overboard, and for his not stopping her from killing their kid, and for his not marrying her; his father for his losing Davis overboard when his father had already lost Davis years before; and maybe it was himself most of all waiting there at the edge of darkness because even though he knew none of it was his fault, he couldn't find a way out. Tonight was supposed to have been his way out, his way back to Michael and Kazz.

Now as he went on treading water, he heard Lee Anne's Southern accent slow and hypnotic in the dark in Brooklyn, her breath in his ear, her boyfriend Jimmy drunk and naked and covered with blood skinning the crocodile on his father's lawn as the sun came up, and Val understood that was exactly the way his father saw him, that he had skinned Davis—meant to do it—because his father had loved Davis more, put Val second. And yet, staring up at the stars and starting to freeze, Val thought, hadn't it in reality been Val hanging upside down from that branch at sunrise, his father, then Davis, and again Lee Anne covered with blood, each one peeling him?

He realized that no one would ever know exactly what had happened to him. If and when she had to, Lee Anne would use the evidence—there was enough—to finish the story her way, shift the blame to him. She had his letter, the pictures she'd taken of him in Arizona, her husband's stolen boat.... She would have any number of possibilities. Everything pointed at him. She would put it together and she would have the last word. He felt himself getting colder and farther from himself, and he hoped he would be able to pass out and that it would be like drifting off to sleep. He hoped that when he did nod off that he wouldn't wake and struggle as he slid beneath the surface, that he could not know the rest, and that it would happen before the sharks got him.

He moved an arm slowly and felt something bump him and came awake with a stab of adrenaline and knew that his passing out wasn't going to happen soon enough, and that the sharks had already found him. Drawing up his legs, stretching out on his side to make himself as small a vertical target as possible, he felt the bump again. Throwing out an arm in terror, he knocked something hard and smelled gas!

Feeling his way along the side of the boat, he groped until he found what he thought was the transom. Here was the engine, leaking gasoline. He clawed at the oil-slicked underside of the hull, feebly kicking his legs until he'd worked himself partway out of the water. Legs still trailing below, teeth chattering, he hung on, dozing, slipping into the water, coming fully awake, clawing his way back up. Overhead, the constellations swung, Scorpio sliding down to the southwest, Pegasus and Cygnus rising overhead.

In a trance, he decided he'd have to take a desperate chance if he wasn't going to freeze to death; he let go and dove under the boat, surfaced inside. There was an overpowering reek of gasoline still leaking from the jerry cans in the air pocket. Feeling his way to the center console, he groped until he found the flares by the flare gun where he'd stuck them earlier, miraculously still wedged in place; he dove again, came back up gasping, clawed himself higher up out of the water, and, freezing, hands shaking, he fired the first flare. He watched it arc up to the stars, explode, and, hanging in the air, light up the sky and water.

Val started awake, still hanging onto the outside of the hull. He realized he'd been dreaming or hallucinating, but now he thought of trying just what he had dreamed, diving under the hull, seeing if the flares and gun might still be jammed in the console; in another moment, he realized that if he broke the air pocket, and if that was the only thing holding up the boat, it would sink, and he held on.

Then he felt something. The hull jerked and trembled violently. A while later, he felt it again, almost as if something were yanking on it, but he couldn't imagine what it might be; he clawed up as high as he could reach onto the capsized hull as he felt the shocks and tremors coming from below.

Then the constellations started to fade in the east, and, one by one, the stars; the eastern sky lightened; and the sun, huge, came up directly beneath Val, and he rose out of the water on it, and then, just before the sun emerged completely, he slid back down onto the underside of the boat, and the sun detached itself from the water and rose out of reach. Val could see the sunlight slanting long and flat through the water, the blue tension of the surface, the shaft and propeller against the sky.

He looked in every direction and saw nothing but horizon—no buoys, no boats, no wakes, no land, nothing but water and horizon. Thirsty, shaking with cold, he held on as the sun rose higher. He swallowed and felt his tongue thicken in his mouth. The sun rose higher still in the glare. Again, he thought of diving down under the boat to see if his bag was jammed under the seat; he saw the bottles of water inside, each one clear and sweet. And if the water was still in there, the flares would be there, too. But if the boat sank…. He just couldn't risk it.

The air filled with high-pitched voices, and, as they swooped closer, he realized that each was howling furiously: why wasn't he home with Michael, how could he have done this to his son? And another, his father: where was Davis? you were supposed to take care of Davis! And Lee Anne: the Great Val, we had something, I wanted something with you, a charge in the air around her; he flinched as Brent came at him reeking…. Val jerked awake, fingers slippery with engine oil, arms wrinkled and rainbowed with leaked gasoline. He tipped his head back and saw a thin white vapor trail, caught a flash of silver as the jet went soundlessly on its course out of sight. Flinched as he looked back down and saw faces moving inside the wet hull, heard them talking.

The sun rose higher and the voices went away and returned; Lee Anne, more furious than ever, louder; birds, he saw their wings backlit silvery by sunlight, the hard curve of their beaks, the stab of light in their eyes; he heard more voices, felt hands, and when he turned his head, he saw a rusty hull towering overhead, inhaled the ocean-bottom stench of fish, of diesel. He felt hands taking him up, heard the drone of an outboard, and then again felt himself being lifted, this time from the inflatable onto the deck, where he was surrounded by winches and mountainous nets swinging from booms and gulls crying and screeching and circling overhead…

He was carried to a cabin, stripped of his wet clothes, dried and dressed in warm clothes, given water and hot tea; he was wrapped in blankets and then stretched out in a bunk, a heater set beside him, crewmen moving in and out and murmuring. Someone said from far away, "We hoisted your boat up on deck...." The man leaned in so close he could have kissed Val. He hovered above as if peering down into Val, and Val thought he saw a glimmer of something—horror?—and then Val couldn't hold on anymore and let himself go and slid down beneath the surface of wherever he was going—water? sleep? He no longer knew.

Val felt his delirium rippled by sudden noises, voices, lights flashing, engines starting. He felt spaces opening and closing and changing around him, hands lifting him, lowering him. Several times he felt himself trying to rise from sleep. Below him, the immense freezing darkness, and he struggled to climb higher. He surfaced in a room with curtains drawn, fluorescent lights, an IV hanging, a needle in his arm. He closed his eyes and felt himself sliding down again.

After several days he was awake and eating, and doctors had examined and talked to him; though he was in a hospital room, he was still floating alone under stars in the black ocean, gone away from Earth.

# ASHORE

## *The State of New York*

Val was still drifting…Michael's child hand in his as they walked in the park together, Kazz laughing once in her sleep, then, still smiling, now sitting up in a chair and gazing out the window…when a man came into the room. He was Val's age, maybe a couple of years older, a bit of a gut, burly; yet with pale white skin, blond hair going gray, a receding hairline and light blue eyes, he seemed delicate, almost translucent. He was carrying a folder and a shopping bag. Val knew he wasn't a doctor. Without having to think about it, Val recognized him as a cop. He introduced himself, Bill Dickerson, showed his identification. He was a sheriff's department detective. He mentioned Val's amazing ordeal and how lucky he was to have been picked up—a chance in a million. In fact, if one of the crew hadn't just happened to look up from his work and see a flash…it was the sun hitting the stainless steel prop of the overturned Grady-White…Dickerson shrugged and didn't finish the sentence. How grateful Val must feel to the fishermen, which, of course, was true, though Val had not met or had a chance to thank them. Dickerson said, "I'm a sports fisherman, myself. Stripers and blues. You just never know. Things can go wrong out there fast." Dickerson paused. He was still standing. He indicated a chair beside Val as if to say, "May I?" Val nodded, wary of the formality. He set the shopping bag on the floor beside him. As he sat down, his jacket slid back and Val saw his gun. Dickerson said simply, "I'll get to the point."

He reached into a folder and placed a stack of glossy, 8" x 10", black-and-white photos on the table beside Val. Val picked them up. They seemed to be of a fishing boat. A trawler. The one that had rescued him. The deck. Mountains of netting. He looked more closely. He saw a boat. His boat. The Grady-White. On the deck. Line trailing from the boat. Val lifted the picture and held it up close. Something in the line. Several more pictures. A huge snarl, some of it slashed, but the rest drawn tight into an enormous knot, and within that tangle, a body. Close-ups. Val could see the teeth marks, the missing chunks of flesh, and the cinderblocks cinched tightly around the flesh of the ankles. Val suddenly remembered the violent yanking tremors going through the hull, felt himself go cold and breathless. He heard the crewman's voice before he passed out in the cabin. "We just brought your boat up on deck..." The look on his face as he peered down at Val. Surprise. Horror.

He glanced up to see the detective looking at him. He said, "Is there anything you want to tell me?"

Val pushed the pictures away and made an enormous effort to bring himself back. He realized the pictures were an attempt to shock him into a sudden explanation, a confession, or at least to get him to say enough to trip him up, confuse him, start the process of later trying to reverse himself.... He remembered when he'd been a defense attorney how crucial it was to keep pictures like these out of evidence when possible. Once a jury saw them, the case was all but lost. He was surprised to hear the marked coolness in his voice. "Are you arresting me?"

The cop said, "That maybe depends on what you tell me. You're picked up on a boat. There's a body weighted with cinderblocks still attached to it. It looks like murder, doesn't it? Do you have something you want to tell me that can help you?"

Val drifted again and then came back from a long way off and repeated himself. "Are you arresting me?"

The cop shrugged. "I'm willing to listen."

Val recognized the moment. The start of a game. An old game he'd once come to know well, but hadn't played in a long time. One he'd finally been relieved to stop. Now he thought Dickerson was pretty good. Willing to listen. Empathetic. Low key. He knew that Dickerson would already have a warrant for his arrest. That Dickerson probably knew little or nothing about him yet. From police reports, he would know that something had gone wrong in Lee Anne's house several nights ago—how many was it now? It seemed like years ago. He probably also had Lee Anne's statement. Val didn't know what Lee Anne had said, but he suspected she had come out of her trance, pulled herself together—how many times had he seen her face go from vacancy to hard defiance—and said whatever she'd had to say to save herself. In fact, Lee Anne had saved his life the other night by killing Brent. He still wasn't sure why she had chosen to do that, but he did know now that if it were to be one or the other of them, she'd choose herself; and that he was up against a fearsome brilliance in Lee Anne. He glanced at Dickerson, who was watching him. He was back in an old game. Val realized he was behind in the game. Way behind.

He surprised himself, "If you're arresting me, then why would you interview me before you Mirandize me?" Val felt something change in the room between them. They'd had their two minutes. Val felt Dickerson hold his affable mask. Val said, "I mean, you might get a confession but without the Miranda it's coerced, it'd be thrown out. Of course, it's your word against mine, and mine, under these circumstances, should be easy to discredit. You go for the conviction first. If you get it, I'm the one who's got maybe five to ten years of appeals, always an uphill battle, and then it's still my tough luck...."

"You seem familiar with the law."

"And you were counting on my not knowing it. I've been in the water fifteen hours, and as you said, I'm lucky to be alive, but I'm still not an idiot."

The cop pushed the pictures back toward him on the table. "I didn't say you were an idiot. I only asked you if you wanted to talk to me about these pictures."

"And I asked, 'Are you arresting me?'"

As if to suggest, have it your way, Dickerson shrugged. "Yes, I'm arresting you." He arrested him for first-degree murder and Mirandized him, and Val came back from a long way off when the detective said *you have the right to remain silent.*

Val said, "May I make my phone call?"

"Make the call and then I'm taking you in." He pulled the warrant out of his jacket, placed it on the table beside the pictures. "Your doctors say you're well enough to leave the hospital. I'm booking you into the county jail." He indicated the shopping bag beside the chair. "I brought you some clothes, courtesy the State of New York."

"Thanks."

"Figured you for large, extra large, pants: 36, 34."

"That's about right, but you're going to turn out to be wrong about everything else."

"We'll get to see, won't we?"

Val said, "I'd like to make the call in private, please. If you don't mind." Val looked around. "I promise I'm not going out the window."

"You can try, but we're on the fifth floor."

"Could you give me the name and phone number of the jail? It's for my attorney."

Dickerson wrote it on the back of his card, slid it across the table. "I'll be right outside the door."

After he'd gone out, Val placed a collect call to Stan Miller and reached him at his office. When Stan picked up, Val gave his name and Stan accepted the charges.

"Val. God, where'd you disappear to?"

Val said, "It'll take too long to tell you now, but I'm in a hospital. I'm okay. As soon as I hang up, I'm being checked out of here and I'm on my way to the county jail." Val gave him the location and said, "There's too much to explain, but it's for murder. I didn't do it. I think I was led into something. Revenge, maybe, but that doesn't seem right. Or maybe that's not all of it. Or enough. It's something else. Something more." He thought of Per's saying, "Something in her waiting…. She does what she must." None of it would make sense to Stan. It didn't make sense to him. "I'm just babbling, but the main thing is I didn't do it, Stan, which probably won't matter. I panicked and ran, and that made it worse. Probably hopeless. Could you find me a good criminal lawyer? One who can deal with the State of New York."

"I know someone."

"And could you call Kazz and my mother and tell them… I guess tell them what I told you, that I'm getting taken in for murder. And that it looks like I did it. But that no matter what, I didn't kill anyone. I just don't know if I'll be able to make anyone believe me."

"I'll come over there."

"I'll tell you everything when you get here." Val hesitated. Jails. Surveillance. "Stan! Listen. When you get here, say you're one of the attorneys representing me and they should give you a private room for an attorney-client meeting. Anything they overheard us saying and recorded would be inadmissible anyway, but just to be on the safe side...."

"Got it. See you soon."

Val took the clothes out of the shopping bag, khakis and a plaid shirt. He stripped off his hospital pajamas and dressed, and then sat back down. His thoughts were speeding, but he couldn't focus on anything. He went to his room door, and, hesitating—what was the best thing to do here?—he knocked on the door, and Dickerson immediately pushed it open, and looking him up and down, he nodded, a kind of approval; he waved at someone Val couldn't see and a uniformed deputy walked over, and Val stood back to let them into the hospital room. The deputy took a pair of handcuffs off his belt and told Val to turn around and place his hands behind his back. Val felt the cuffs snap around his wrists. Dickerson Mirandized him again, perhaps for the deputy's benefit—now he had a witness—and then, one on each side, they walked him out into the hall, the deputy with his hand tight around Val's biceps, doctors and nurses, orderlies and patients stopping to watch them as they made their way to the elevator, then rode down to the street. As they walked out of the hospital, there were cameramen from a couple of local TV stations who followed them the short distance from the front door to a sheriff's marked car. The deputy opened the back door and guided Val into the back and then Dickerson and the deputy got in the front, on the other side of a steel grating, and started driving, all the time saying little, occasionally making small talk about a recent Yankees-Red Sox game, about one of their kids, seeming to forget Val was there. As they drove, people gawked at Val from passing cars, and Val watched them, free to go anywhere, do anything, watched them turn off and disappear from sight. In another few minutes, Dickerson pointed at a complex of low brown buildings surrounded by chain-link fence, gleaming razor wire on top. Without looking at him, Dickerson announced, "County jail."

They passed through a checkpoint in the fence, an armed guard's station, and as they reached the complex, they drove down a ramp, which took them underground to a loading dock, where they stopped. Dickerson opened the back door and helped Val out. He stood unsteadily and squinted against bright floodlights, noticed video cameras. As a public defender, he'd come into places like this many times, had felt their foreboding authority. They walked across the loading-ramp stairs. When an outer door was buzzed open, the three of them entered. Dickerson and the deputy slid their guns to a prison guard on the other side of a window, and then the deputy removed the cuffs from Val's wrists and placed them back on his belt. Val was buzzed through a door into a room where he was strip- and body-cavity searched by a corrections officer and then, given his clothes back, taken down a hallway to another room; here he was ordered to surrender everything personal. Val realized he had no idea where his wallet and watch had disappeared to. He looked at his wedding ring. The trustee indicated to Val that he couldn't keep it. Val slid the ring over to the clerk, who placed it in a manila envelope and labeled it with a marker. He fingerprinted Val and then pointed down at the tennis shoes Dickerson had brought him. "Shoelaces." Val pulled out the laces, which went into the envelope, and he exchanged his clothes for a red jumpsuit that had black letters stenciled on the back: PRISONER, COUNTY JAIL. The clerk gave him something that Val recognized as a thin blanket.

Now a corrections officer escorted him into a white corridor and said into a walkie-talkie that he was bringing a prisoner in from booking to C wing. They walked up a ramp, and Val realized he could no longer see windows. They faced a guard in a Plexiglas enclosure who sat at a console of black-and-white TV monitors. The guard buzzed open a door and they walked into C wing, where they walked down a straight corridor, which, Val knew, had been constructed that way so that there was no place to hide from view of the guard station. On the way, he noticed a room that he would later come to know as the day room, where prisoners watched TV and smoked; a cafeteria, where every tray, plate and plastic fork was counted out and counted back; and a bathroom and shower facility. Now he was led to a solid steel door with an 8" x 4" view window. The corrections officer opened the door with a huge, grooved key, and swung it open. He waited for Val. Val walked in. He saw a bed platform with a thin mattress bolted to the wall, a stainless steel sink and toilet without a toilet seat bolted to the wall, and a narrow steel shelf, also bolted to the wall. The guard closed the door behind him and locked it. Val looked back through the viewing space, saw the corridor. Though the long hall was air-conditioned, the room was not. It was hot and close. He walked to a small, high Plexiglas window covered by a heavy steel grating. Beyond, he could see what looked like an enclosed exercise area, and beyond that, the outer perimeter: the chain-link fence, trash blown against it for as far as he could see. From somewhere far off came the faint smell of low tide—or maybe it was the stench of the toilet.

Some time later the guard would come, and he would be escorted to the day room, where the prisoners looked up as he came in. They were sitting at fixed tables with Formica tops and steel legs bolted to the floor, which reminded Val of elementary school. The room was thick with cigarette smoke. As Val sat down, one prisoner leaned forward and looked at Val closely. "Hey, man, I just saw you on the news. That was you, they got you from the hospital. You greased some rich North Cove guy and fucked up out there when you tried to dump him from a boat.... The boat, all that shit. That's you. Yeah, man, you in the big time now."

He took a drag on his cigarette and looked at Val. Everyone in the room looked at him. Someone else echoed, "Yeah, man."

And someone behind Val said, "We just your basic burglars and car thieves and petty dope dealers 'n shit, but you up there, dude."

Val stared at the TV. Someone laughed. Someone else said *just, like, shut the fuck up*. Val stared at the TV without seeing or hearing it. *Greased some guy. Dumped him from a boat. Yeah, man.*

There was nothing in the private visiting room but a table bolted to the cement floor and several chairs. The deputy pointed to one. Val sat down and placed his cuffed hands on top and waited. He saw Stan's head appear in the small window in the door, and then the door was opened and Stan was let into the room. When the door closed behind him, Val saw the deputy watching them through the glass.

Val stood, blurted, "Stan, you got here fast."

Stan couldn't seem to do anything more than stare at Val's red prison jumpsuit and handcuffs. He finally managed, "We flew over. There's a small airport just a few miles from here." Val couldn't read Stan's eyes.

The prospect of explaining suddenly seemed so exhausting. And everything was so connected to everything else. Where to begin? How much to say? Val said, "I was in a boat that overturned and spent fifteen hours in the water off Montauk. The Atlantic side."

"Jesus. Fifteen hours! The water's freezing. You're lucky to be alive!"

"I want to tell you everything, but I'm too tired."

Stan put up his hand. "It's okay. I understand. I've brought you a criminal lawyer. He was a classmate of mine. Practices in New York State. He's terrific. Barry Shapiro. He's waiting outside. I just thought I'd come in first, talk to you alone for a few minutes. He's expensive, but don't worry about that right now… I can help you if you need money. Let's just not sweat that for the time being. The main thing is Barry is good. He's very smart. And juries believe him. In fact, juries love him."

"I didn't kill anyone, Stan," Val blurted, suddenly shaken by his loss of control.

Nonplussed, Stan started to bite a fingernail, then thrust his hand into his pocket. He said uncertainly, "No, no, of course not." Stan had been standing just inside the door; now he took a step toward Val, closing the distance, and put his hand on Val's shoulder.

Val said, "I had to find out something about Davis…that's what it was about. I made the trip for Michael's sake. Things had gotten so bad with him. And the way he's been looking at me. Doubtful. Suspicious. He thought—thinks—I did something to Davis…." He stopped. Where was he going? "Stan, it was so weird in that house the whole time I was there, and Lee Anne…" He trailed off.

"Who's Lee Anne?"

"Lee Anne." He sighed. It was so big, so complicated, so ongoing with Lee Anne. He tried it different ways. Lee Anne was Davis' girlfriend—his wife, or so she claimed. She was my…. He couldn't find the word. "We were once involved. She had been with Davis. We were involved after Davis," he added quickly. "Lee Anne gave me a picture of Davis the last time I saw her and…."

"When was that?"

"Sixteen, seventeen years ago." Stan gave him an odd look. Uncomprehending. "I can't explain it. I just had to find out about the picture. For Michael. That's why I was there that night."

Stan nodded, but Val thought he was starting to lose him. Had. He wasn't telling it right. He slowed down. "It was just nightmarish in her house—something was going on in there that I still don't get, which I think Lee Anne was making happen. But then she saved my life. She must have had a reason. Afterward, I saw how it looked—blood all over the floor, Brent—she was married to him—he was just a maniac. He thought I stole his boat. And the room itself, weird, this huge grand piano…I knew she couldn't be in the same room with a piano. And then something she wrote in a postcard, too, about seeing me there in her dream…" He suddenly heard himself gathering momentum as he babbled further into incoherence. He forced himself to stop and then start again speaking slowly. "I knew I'd never be able to make anyone believe what had really happened. I panicked and ran. With Brent. His body. That's how I ended up in the boat, which was really for Michael in the first place. Look, man, she's going to try to save herself. If anyone can put it together and make people believe her, Lee Anne can do it."

Val stopped, exhausted and overwhelmed. There was so much to explain. It suddenly seemed inexplicable. And he saw that he hadn't been able to make himself understood to Stan.

Stan said, "Okay, Val…okay, you know you don't have to figure it all out now. I'm going to get Barry." Stan turned toward the door. "I can wait outside so you can talk in private."

Val shook his head. "Actually, I'd feel better if you stayed in here. I have nothing to hide. I just don't know if I'll be able to make anyone believe me. A jury. If I were my lawyer, I'd look at this as an unwinnable case."

"Well, the good thing is that you're not your own lawyer." Stan turned toward the door.

Val said, "Stan, did you call my mother and Kazz?" Stan nodded. "What'd my mother say?"

"There was just a long silence. Then she said that she was afraid for you when your father died—there had just been too much wrong for too long."

Val felt himself register confusion. That his mother had anticipated… exactly what? "Nothing else?"

"She seemed too stunned to say more."

Val realized he'd been expecting her to say that there had to be some mistake, that he was innocent. "Nothing else at all?"

Stan shook his head no.

"And Kazz?"

"She just kind of groaned. Then she asked what happened and I said I didn't know the details yet. Said she'd come as soon as she could make arrangements. I told her what I told your mother, that I'd get back to her when I knew more."

Val had no idea how long he'd been talking, just that he seemed to be traveling through the events of his whole life and then coming back to the gaze of Barry Shapiro, who sat across from him. Shapiro had huge, pale blue eyes and sat with his chair pushed back, but he leaned so far forward that his head hovered just above his hand, which rested on the table. Sometimes he took notes or asked questions, but mostly he just listened to Val; he never seemed to blink or look away, so that at times Val found himself caught to the point of distraction by the patterns in the blue-gray irises around his pupils. As he went on, Val kept thinking he could or would pull it all together and come to a conclusion, a definitive statement, which would distill exactly how it was, something irrefutable, irreducible, but somehow he kept on skidding, unable to gather the pieces; he looked up to see a thin bar of sunlight in the top of the window and knew that he had to finish before the light was gone, but when he next looked and saw it had disappeared, he was still talking; he thought of that same sunlight falling across the vast surface of the ocean and reaching into the darkness below even as he spoke, and fought back a wave of terror rising in him. He gripped the table, looked into the irises of Shapiro and then back to Stan, whose thick glasses showed nothing more of his eyes than a silvery glint.

It was strange to tell about Lee Anne. He realized that everything that related to her had been isolated inside him for years. He couldn't explain how pervasive her presence had been. He went back to North Carolina seventeen years ago. He went forward to buying the Grady-White for Michael a few weeks ago. Back to Lee Anne's postcards. He went to Davis' last day on the Hatteras. To Brooklyn. He talked about the picture of Davis. What Lee Anne had told him the other night about the repo orders, stealing boats in Florida, Davis' having to run when Billy had been murdered. He kept coming back to Lee Anne. He told about everything that had happened in the house with Brent. He heard himself falter to a stop, and he remained looking at the links of his handcuffs.

Shapiro remained silent for a while, and then he said quietly, "Okay, Val, you've given me a lot to work on. Stan told me you were in the PD's office, and I know you know, but I'll remind you, anyway, that you don't want to talk to anyone in here—or let anyone provoke you into it. Dickerson will come back and try to make you feel it's all hopeless; he'll try to make you believe there are things he knows that you don't, and that he's your only way out. Don't talk to him no matter what he says or offers. If he persists, contact me. You'll be making an initial appearance, probably tomorrow…. I'll find out what time. It'll be a million on the bond. Someone from pre-trial services will be in to see you. I'll check on that. I'll find out when your charges will be on the grand jury's calendar. I'll find out when and where the arraignment is, and we'll enter a plea of not guilty. In the meantime I'll get police reports. Just don't talk to anyone now, no matter what. If there's anyone in your cell, don't talk to him."

He stood and came around to Val's side of the table, took both of Val's hands in his and squeezed them, then stepped back and, gathering his notes into a folder, waited a moment for Stan, who also stood.

Val suddenly asked, "Have you seen the pictures?"

"What pictures?"

"The ones I mentioned that Dickerson brought to the hospital this morning. Brent's body on the deck of the trawler. It was brought up with my boat. No, of course you haven't."

"I came right here, but I'll get them. I'll get everything."

Val stared down at the table. "His body is tangled in the anchor line. The cinderblocks are still tied on his ankles. There are huge chunks torn out of his body. Sharks. You can see the teeth marks. When I was hanging onto the boat, I could feel the hull trembling. The whole boat shook."

Shapiro put his hand on Val's shoulder. "That's over now." He appraised Val. "They may try to put an informer in with you. Someone seemingly sympathetic who'll get you to talk about the case. Don't let yourself talk, Val. Keep yourself under control."

"The pictures…they were like tabloid photos." He heard himself going on. Was he under control or not? "How can I make people believe what was really happening? That I was turning the boat around and coming back? I don't think it's possible." Shapiro kept his hand on Val's shoulder.

"We'll take it one step at a time. We'll find a way."

Val looked at Shapiro. "I was an attorney. I know how this works. You're a juror and you'll look at those pictures and you won't be able to believe the defendant isn't a monster!"

"You've been through a lot, Val. You need to rest now. That's all. I'll be back tomorrow."

He heard himself going on. "And Lee Anne…you don't know her. When she appears as a witness before a jury, she's got a way…she'll be convincing. Something about her. You hear her and believe her. She stole something once. Right in front of me. I saw it. But when she got through with me, I didn't believe my own eyes. The only way I could get away from her was to just leave her. Once she gets inside your head, you can't forget her. She stays in there and just keeps talking." Val saw Stan and Shapiro exchange looks. "I know what I'm saying."

Speaking quietly and patiently, like a parent extricating himself from a child's frightened grip at bedtime, Shapiro said, "I'll be right there every step of the way. Just try to rest." Shapiro turned to Stan. "I'll be outside in the waiting area."

After he'd gone, Val said, "He thinks I'm losing it. I know what I'm saying about those pictures. About Lee Anne, too." But Val heard the odd tone of his voice and suddenly knew that he couldn't make himself understood and that he'd better stop. He said to Stan, "I can't thank you enough for coming."

"We'll be here for a few days now. We're with you."

"I didn't kill him. You do believe me, don't you?"

Val looked for Stan's eyes but caught only the silvery glint off his thick glasses as Stan made his habitual slight gesture of adjusting his frames—was it a nod? Impossible to tell.

As Stan repeated what Shapiro had said, "Just rest for now," Val felt a sudden rise of desperation.

The next afternoon, Val was led into a room in the county jail and placed in front of a TV camera, where he made his initial appearance. He knew how these things appeared from a TV screen, the prisoner's look of displacement as he sat, his head and shoulders visible in a chair, the video usually appearing later on TV news, the stark lighting, the newscaster's narration, however it would go: …Martin made his initial appearance. Charges. Bail set at… The whole thing took ten minutes and then Val was led back to the day room. Later, someone from pretrial services came in to interview him.

## Dickerson

Nights, Val woke thrashing. He was floating alone in freezing black water, something coming up from below, someone or something just rising out of the dark at the edge of his vision. He mopped a floor thick with blood, which kept silently spreading across the room. If he didn't wake during the night to the sound of his moaning in terror, he woke in the morning exhausted, and the days and nights seemed to run into each other as he drifted away from Earth.

Barry Shapiro opened a folder filled with newspaper clippings that went back several days, including the time Val had been in the ICU. He slid one toward Val.

"Man Rescued at Sea"

Val skimmed the article:

Local fishermen.... Man found drifting in the Atlantic ten miles northeast of Montauk hanging onto an overturned boat. ...one chance in a million. A deck hand noticed a flash of light...reflection off the stainless-steel propeller...suffering from sunburn, severe dehydration, hypothermia...semi-conscious.... They made a grisly discovery....

Another article:

"Man in Guarded Condition"

...authorities waiting to question unidentified man who remains in intensive care...anyone with information about the incident is request-ed to come forward.

Val froze and looked at a grainy black-and-white photograph of the trawler's deck. It seemed to be the one that the detective had shown him. The body in the snarl of anchor line. The cinderblocks. He glanced up at Barry Shapiro. "This is the photograph I was telling you about the other day. It tries and convicts me."

Shapiro said, "After the grand jury meets, we're making a pretrial motion for a change of venue."

Val shook his head. "Once any jury anywhere sees these pictures, it won't matter."

Val picked up another article.

"Night of Terror"

A local woman described a night of terror...It started with a 911 call, which aroused suspicion when no one spoke to the operator.... This led local authorities to an area woman's home... It now appears she was in such a state of shock she could not address the 911 operator.... In fact, she did not speak of the incident to the investigating officer. He found nothing out of the ordinary.... It was more than 48 hours before she could bring herself to come forward after her first call to 911.

Val read that she said that she had been married to the alleged assailant's brother, a former football star at Clemson, who had died in a freak fishing accident almost seventeen years before and that since then the brother had remained obsessed with her. He'd sent her postcards for over sixteen years, none of which she could bear to keep and had thrown out. He'd cast a shadow over her life, created strife and jealousy in her marriage, emotional turmoil that had resulted in several miscarriages. He couldn't and wouldn't leave her alone. And she'd become terrified of him.

She had saved his last letter, which had been sent as recently as ten days ago, and which revealed his obsessive nature. Unsigned, and with no salutation, he had written:

> I have to know where Davis was going in the picture you gave me that night in Brooklyn.

According to Mrs. Connor, Mr. Martin, perhaps believing he could persuade her to leave with him, came for a late-night visit and confronted and threatened her husband. An exchange of words escalated into violence and Mr. Martin, enraged, struck several quick blows, killing Mr. Connor, which propelled Mr. Martin into a frantic attempt to hide the body.

Authorities are also investigating the connection of this incident to the theft of Mr. Connor's boat, which had been reported stolen just ten days before.

An unnamed police source suggested that Mr. Martin might have had a partner who knows something about the boat's disappearance. Mrs. Connor was a beneficiary of the insurance policy, and she has suggested that Mr. Martin thought an insurance payoff might induce her to come away with him. Authorities are not sure of the connection of the theft of the boat to Mr. Connor's death, and continue to explore this bizarre story.

A police spokesperson said, "We're exploring this from all angles, pursuing all leads. We're looking for information on the whereabouts of Mr. Connor's boat, which was a forty-six-foot Bertram, and any witnesses who saw or heard anything that night." The 88-CRIME number was listed, which would protect the identity of the caller; there was also a reward being offered for information.

Val said to Barry, "See, what she's done? She's reversed everything. She was the one who wrote me all this time. I never answered. She always sent unsigned postcards. I saved them and kept trying to figure out what they were saying. I always had the feeling that she was trying to tell me something that she herself didn't understand; they almost made a kind of sense." Val laughed sardonically, raised the cuffs, "But now I get it." Barry looked at him, perhaps with an underlying skepticism and patience, and Val felt what he'd started to feel the other day, that he was talking too much. He had to stop talking, stop for good. Stop talking to everyone. He would. But he went on now. "I mean she just wrote these things and I wondered what she wanted. My wife said she wanted something from me, but didn't know what it was. Each time a card came, it disrupted my marriage—that's what she wanted, I guess…. I don't know.

"Ironic, because I saved the cards, every single one, right up until the night I came over here and then I threw them overboard…I just wanted to get rid of them once and for all, just all of this. That's what I was trying to do. My father had just died…." He tried to draw the connection, couldn't. "The cards would have contradicted her. Now they're gone."

Barry glanced from the article to Val, tolerantly, patiently. Perhaps dismissively. Did he believe Val?

Lee Anne. She'd done exactly as he'd feared, turned everything around. Yet something else, he was sure, had been going on that night. In fact, it seemed that she had tried to warn him several times to leave. She'd known something was about to happen and seemed to be struggling with it—or changing her mind—trying to hurry him out of there. Something she herself had set in motion, yet was trying to stop. Could that be so? He still felt the sensation come and go on his skin, the charge in the room around her just moments before Brent appeared.

He remembered the look on her face after she'd killed Brent—her face itself, a child's, a schoolgirl's, unrecognizable, and the sound of her voice, far away, almost inaudible, *please, please, please*…. He remembered the powerful sense of dislocation of time and place, that when he'd come into the room, he had entered the world of her postcards.

None of it mattered now.

He stared down at the clippings on the table. Barry Shapiro had started speaking in soothing tones, tones Val himself had used with defendants, and Val was trying to focus on what he was saying, but really, it didn't matter. He knew things about Lee Anne that Shapiro couldn't know, which no else could know. He understood nothing. One thing, though, he knew for sure. It was too late for anything to be done.

———

Each day, the same routine. Lights out at nine p.m. Up at six. A guard opened your cell door and took you to the day room, where the prisoners watched TV. It was always and indisputably the same, an aerobics program in which three pretty and supple women in tights went through an exercise routine. The prisoners watched it in silence. Eyes fixed to the screen, no one said a single word. Val could see it was their painkiller, their Novocain. The black prisoners smoked Kools and Newports; the white prisoners, Pall Malls, Camels, and Marlboros. It embarrassed Val to turn either left or right, to see their eyes. Afterward, the guards came in—it was as if they were breaking a spell—and let them outside for an hour of exercise. For that hour, Val could walk in an endless circle in the enclosed area. Then, the cafeteria, where plastic forks and plates were counted out, food was distributed and eaten, and then everything was counted back. At eight they were taken back to the cells and then again returned to the day room by a new guard who had just come on with the change of shift.

The days were endless. Sometimes the prisoner who had spotted Val as the guy on the news would lean close as he passed behind Val in the day room, his voice a low, challenging taunt, "Yeah, man, you in the big time now...oh, hey, yeah man, and Harvard educated...." The first time Val had been startled; how had he known that? TV. "Whoa. The big time! They teach you that shit in Harvard? Couldn't quite get that dude out of the boat 'n shit and get away.... Almost made it, dude, almost...."

Endless days, and then the airless cell where you couldn't hear anyone else, except when one of the other prisoners went berserk. One night, the screamer was Val awakened by his own nightmares, Val catapulted into the smell of the toilet in the closed room.

Dickerson himself came in to see Val and tell him that the grand jury had just finished meeting, and to have him sign the indictment to show he'd received it, perhaps for dramatic effect, which was not needed. Val's hands were shaking; they had indicted him for first-degree murder, obstruction of justice, criminal trespass, etc. As Shapiro had said he would, Dickerson tried to make Val feel that his case was hopeless; he implied that he'd developed a lot more than Val or his lawyer or anyone else could know. He suggested that certain new evidence had been turning up and that if Val would consider talking with Dickerson that they might be able to get around some kind of corner. What corner? That would depend on what Val had to say.

Though he was aware of the game Dickerson was playing, he had to restrain himself from opening up. Perhaps he just didn't want Dickerson to think that he was the monster who had tied the cinderblocks to Brent's ankles. Still, he kept himself in check, said nothing, and Dickerson nodded when he finished the interview, handed him his card as he stood, and said, "No? Okay, well, keep thinking about it. One thing…you were once a lawyer, so you know your guy isn't going to be able to get you anywhere against this…" He opened the folder and again showed the picture of Brent's torn body spread on the deck of the trawler. "You know it and I know it. And he knows it. He'll take his big fee, but he knows it." Dickerson handed him his card.

"You've given me one already."

"Talk to me and maybe we can do something. I have my own ideas about how things are, but you have to talk to me first. You can call me anytime. Day or night. I have a beeper. People who are innocent usually can't wait to make a statement. You've said nothing. That seems to be telling me everything. The grand jury didn't need much convincing."

Val laughed. "Un-cross-examined testimony." He had told himself he wasn't going to get drawn into anything.

Dickerson reached into his pocket and slid a couple of quarters across the table. "You can call me from the pay phone."

Val didn't take them. Dickerson said, "My offer won't stand much longer. When it's gone, it's gone."

"If you're offering me a plea, talk to my attorney. The system rewards people for copping a plea when they're innocent."

"I'm saying I may know some things, but I need to hear from you before I can put my cards on the table."

"I'm insulted that you think I'm so fucking stupid."

"Think it over. You have nothing to lose. Murder's a capital offense in New York State. You're dead where you're sitting now." The coins remained on the table between them. Dickerson dropped them back into his pocket. "You know something? I'll bet Lee Anne would have taken those quarters."

In his cell, Val started thinking about Lee Anne. She was going to remain free. And he was going to be tried and convicted. Without knowing the details of her personal life, he thought, from the little he'd seen—house, property—that she stood to inherit a lot of money. Well, that was it, wasn't it? The money. She'd needed someone to take the heat. It was so obvious. Nothing had ever been resolved between them. Or she, he suddenly understood, had resolved exactly what she had wanted. Looking around his cell, he laughed out loud. She had, in fact, resolved everything.

He stretched out on his bunk. Lee Anne had connected Davis to certain people, pulled him into something a step at a time; it had been part of their love affair, the way they'd loved; and Davis gloried in it, probably hadn't seen himself as a criminal, but perhaps as someone just playing a game, a new game, another game, and winning right up until it had started closing in on him. Val had been drawn to Lee Anne. He knew there was something wrong about her. Reversing every conscious step he'd hoped to take against her, pushing her away, leaving her, not answering her, he'd come back to her once more. And that once had been enough. Here he was, in jail, charged with murder. And yet, he knew he had to see her again. Again, it was *just once more*. He looked at the yellow legal pad and pen that Stan had brought him and knew he didn't dare write her; at the same time he was already trying to figure out what to say.

He just kept staring at Kazz. How long had it been since he'd seen her? A month? Longer? He had no idea. He hadn't spoken to her since they'd argued over buying the boat for Michael. That had been, maybe, two weeks ago. Another life, Another person. How incredible that she was actually here in front of him. How beautiful her eyes. And beautiful, too, the sense that she brought with her of being outside and moving through the world, which also quickened his despair—that he couldn't be with her. The burnish of separate dailiness had already begun to render her face minutely unfamiliar.

When she'd come into the room, he hadn't been able to keep from looking down at himself in red jail-issue, wrists handcuffed. He'd asked, perhaps through his embarrassment, where Michael was; she'd seemed startled that he'd ask such a question. She said that she'd left him with friends in Tucson, that she didn't want him to see Val here. *Did you want that?* He'd said, no, no, of course not under these circumstances.

Periodically, he would drop his voice to a near whisper and warned her to do the same; in these visitation areas you never knew who was listening.

They'd talked awkwardly, her flight, how was the motel where she was staying? And the situation with Michael in school? Failing? She said she was taking care of it, that he wasn't to worry or think about it at all. There was so much he had to tell her, and tell her now, urgently, and then he was talking and all the time he kept thinking how beautiful she was and how lucky he had been to be with her and how had he lost sight of it?

He talked much as he had that first day with Stan and Barry, things he never could have imagined telling anyone, now he was telling them all to Kazz, why hadn't he done it sooner...?

Like Barry, she, too, returned his gaze unblinking, her eyes fixed on his. When he touched on Lee Anne, he'd falter, sometimes look away or down, then force himself to raise his eyes and continue. Like a play of light continually unfolding in a window, he saw hurt, patience, curiosity, sadness, tenderness, anger, exasperation passing silently across Kazz's face and through her eyes as he talked on. When he saw doubt, that, more than anything else, frightened him.

He told her that the boat had been for Michael and Michael only, that he'd never intended to see Lee Anne...she had given him the picture of Davis. Remember the picture in the bedroom he'd brought out? The one of Davis driving the boat? She'd given it to him. And this was, well, this was after, they'd had a love affair—at the end—not really a love affair, it was something, he didn't know what to call it, and she'd gotten pregnant.... He'd gazed out the window a long time and then come back to Kazz's face, which tightened; she'd gotten pregnant, she'd wanted him to marry her, it was just impossible, and she'd been with Davis—had he already mentioned that? And he just couldn't be with her, he was with her, but didn't want to be; she'd come looking for him, found him in Brooklyn; he couldn't seem to stop it, seeing her, and, pregnant, she'd give him an ultimatum, marry her or she'd have the abortion; she wasn't going to be left again; and she'd come back from that, the abortion, and then she'd given him the picture of Davis that night, and it had never left him, none of it, but... "What could I say to you, or anyone, Kazz?" She didn't answer. "Kazz? What could I have said?" She still didn't answer.

Kazz said, "I could always feel her there. Those cards. That she wanted you to do something. I just don't know why you couldn't or wouldn't talk to me—well, in a way I think I do now. That she was Davis'...." Val looked at her sharply. "I don't mean it that way. That she was—had been—with Davis. And you didn't feel right about that, any of it, but that it was a way of hanging on...." He stared past her. She stopped altogether, shook her head. "I can't seem to say any of this in a way that you can accept. I'll just speak for myself. That you couldn't go beyond it, that's the part that hurts most—that I could feel it all there—and that you denied it to yourself, wouldn't talk to me." She sighed. "I guess that's just part of the tangle of this."

Val made a determined effort to go on. He told her how he'd already turned around to come back when the boat had capsized. He couldn't read Kazz's face as he spoke. "You believe me, don't you, Kazz?"

Pain on her face, she kept looking into his eyes. "What did she tell you about your brother? You left that out."

"That he was a thief." He started to tell her the details, but just said, "He was a boat thief."

She nodded. "What difference could any of it have made now?"

"I had to know once and for all. Michael thought Davis was some kind of hero...and that I had something to hide. Lee Anne kept saying 'You know, but don't know.' It was always there." He shook his head. "Even when I told myself it wasn't there, it was there. She stayed inside my head. I just was never sure, finally, what *had* happened to Davis." She didn't say anything. "Do you believe me, Kazz?"

She said simply, "You're still in love with her."

He looked up at her in surprise, said quickly and emphatically, "I was never in love with her." Val searched her face. Kazz knew him better than anyone. It was almost as if he were hearing undeniably bad news. "Kazz. I was never in love with her." She didn't answer.

In his cell, he saw Kazz's final look of doubt, which she couldn't hide, the way she hadn't been able to answer him, wouldn't answer him.... Maybe he had been coming back for Lee Anne in some way. Had he ever understood his motives? He heard Kazz say, "You're still in love with her." He wasn't sure anymore. He felt his hold on the truth slipping.

The Fourth of July came and went with the muted sound of fireworks, sudden, close and distant, the top of a sustained display flowering liquid silver, blue and red, which Val could make out through the grating in the top of his cell window, making him think of families and buddies and lovers watching, each explosion rolling toward him with a delay after the flash. A trial date was set and Barry Shapiro made a pretrial motion for a change of venue, which was denied. Barry could not conceal his indignation and disappointment and perhaps discouragement that the trail would be here in the county. Shortly after, Val was arraigned and formally entered a plea of not guilty.

So many of the details had already been sensationalized in the local papers. The lurid elements seemed to be irresistible to the press. Brent had money and good looks, and his family was well known. His boat had disappeared just days before the murder, and the papers hinted at the killer's having an unnamed accomplice and unrealistic designs on both Lee Anne and the insurance money he thought she would collect. No one had seen any traces of Brent's boat. The Coast Guard continued searching for it. Lee Anne had stated to the police that Val had been obsessed with her, and there was endless speculation on their shared past: a brother, a love triangle, a freak fishing accident. Finally, and irreducibly, there was the picture of Brent's body taken on the deck of the trawler. It was the answer to an equation that, no matter how cleverly worked, could only come out one way. Val knew that when Lee Anne got up on the witness stand and started telling her story, she would make a devastating witness. He realized that perhaps she had been waiting her whole life—or at least since he'd left her in Brooklyn—to get up before a roomful of people and tell her side of things. And hadn't she, in fact, detested him before she'd even met him? Wasn't he already *The Great Val* in Davis' letters? Davis had written that she'd laughed at him, said derisively, "I could almost love him." Yet she'd tried to have a baby with him. How or why had it gone on so long? It didn't matter now. He just knew that it was all going to be used against him.

He tried and retried his own case based on the evidence, and realized there was no way he could win. He realized that no matter what he said or how he said it, Shapiro wasn't getting it, couldn't get it—Lee Anne and himself, seventeen years. It was just outside his experience. It was outside of everyone's experience, including his own—his idea of himself. Stan? Kazz? He looked in their eyes and saw that they didn't believe him. But Val realized that Dickerson seemed to know or understand something. Could it help him? Hurt him? He didn't know, but he was going to have to do something now, no matter how risky, or possibly stupid, to get Dickerson to act on his behalf if there was something to be done. He picked up Dickerson's card, requested a deputy take him to the pay phone in his wing, and punched in the numbers to his pager.

Dickerson came into the room, badge on his belt, holster empty—he always wore the holster on his hip, but inside his pants, and Val now wondered abstractly if it was a special holster, and if he had to buy his pants large in the waist to accommodate it, and if so, what that did to their overall fit.... Dickerson looked different, and Val realized he had what appeared to be a painful sunburn; he noted his thinning blond-gray hair and couldn't help but run his handcuffed hands through his own thick hair as if to reassure himself that it was actually still there.

Dickerson smoothed his fingertips against his cheek and said, "I was out fishing when I got your call."

Val wondered if that was an implied threat—a way of saying, this had better be worth my making a trip over here.

Dickerson touched his flushed forehead. "Forgot the hat, and sunblock doesn't do it."

Val thought, Jesus, had he really thought he was going to talk to this guy? He was so obvious, the small talk, the buddy-up act, as if to say, hey, if it weren't that you're in here, we'd be hanging out together. Val looked away as he caught the scent of aloe vera, and his heart started racing. What was he doing? He had a lawyer, a good one, who had an investigator checking out some things. He'd said from day one, no matter what, don't talk. Val had known it. Don't talk. It was simple. Don't. Talk.

Dickerson pulled up a chair and sat down across from Val. Val stared at his folded hands. Dry-mouthed and hoarse, he asked, "Any luck?"

Dickerson shook his head no.

Val said, "I hear that stripers have been making a comeback in the last few years."

"Maybe, but it's only a rumor as far as I'm concerned."

"Hearsay."

"Yeah, hearsay."

Val smiled, but he still couldn't raise his eyes. They sat in silence. Dickerson said, "You wanted to see me, maybe talk about striper fishing."

His presence didn't feel unkindly. That, along with everything else, was perhaps what worried Val. He said, "I..." but his throat was too dry to continue. He cleared his throat. Dickerson left the room, returned with a cup of water, and Val nodded his thanks and drank. Dickerson sat back down.

Val said, "I want to tell you what happened." Dickerson nodded. "I don't want to be tape-recorded." Dickerson raised his hands to show he had nothing. "Are you wearing a wire?"

"No."

Val shrugged. "I can't search you anyway."

"I'm telling you I'm not."

"People lie."

Dickerson half-rose from his chair and held out his arms to simulate a searchable posture. "I'm not recording. And you're right. People lie. If you want to talk to me, you'll have to take a chance. But I'm telling you now, Val, there is no recording device anywhere on me or in the room."

Val said, "I want to speak to you off the record. A free talk. I'll tell you everything—the truth—but only on the condition you won't use any of it in evidence against me."

Dickerson said, "I work for the State of New York."

"I want to talk off the record."

Dickerson got up and walked to the window. He looked out, then said, "Okay, Val. I'll agree. But how do you know I won't lie about using it against you?"

Val said, "I don't. If it comes to it, all I'll be able to do is deny I ever said it, which won't matter anymore...."

"What do you want from our 'free talk'?"

"You said maybe we could turn a corner. That you were looking into some things. If you really are, I want to give you what I can give you."

Dickerson nodded.

Val fell silent. He thought of Shapiro's warning, his own better sense, Kazz's look of doubt—that his own wife didn't seem to believe him: *You're still in love with her.* He intuited that Dickerson, under the cynical cop exterior, was a guy who needed to find the truth of something. And Val still somehow, naively or not, believed that the truth, once found, would be on his side; he would take a chance and try to use Dickerson for his own ends. If Dickerson couldn't find anything, well, he couldn't be any worse off than he was now, which was fucked. Free talk. He started talking.

As Val talked, Dickerson brought out a small notebook. He held it up as if to say, okay? and Val fought off panic and shrugged his indifference and Dickerson rapidly started taking notes.

Val told Dickerson everything that had gone on in the house that night, everything, until he lapsed into silence. Dickerson went on writing, clicked his ballpoint pen; he looked back over his notes. His face showed fatigue.

Val said, "I know how it must sound. That it wasn't me, that it was Lee Anne who killed Brent. I knew it would be my word against hers. I know how it sounds when I say that I was going to turn around and come back with his body, that I wasn't going to throw him overboard!" Dickerson looked past him. "Don't you see how she's reversed everything?"

Dickerson flipped through his notes, but didn't answer. "The postcards she sent you....you don't have any of them?"

"I told you, I threw them overboard. I had them for years and now they're gone."

"Just so happens," Dickerson said in a neutral tone. "Don't things always seem to work out that way?" It wasn't a question. Was he mocking him?

"And you don't have any of those stolen boat pictures or repo orders, know where I could get hold of them?"

Val shook his head no.

"Or the pictures Lee Anne took of you in Tucson?"

"I never actually saw the pictures. They were just something Brent was ranting about."

Dickerson flipped through his notes again.

"When did you think you saw Lee Anne in the drugstore in Tucson? Approximately?"

Val gave him a rough date and Dickerson wrote it down.

"And Miami, was it? About seventeen years ago? Davis? The stolen boats? Davis and Lee Anne? And this guy, Hector Cruz?"

Val nodded. "Seventeen years now."

Dickerson lapsed into silence. Val studied him closely. God, he couldn't read his face. He knew all of these guys shaded testimony, lied as witnesses. Sandpapered witnesses, they called them. Had he just given more to use against him in trial. Had he given him something that he could use to get him out of here? Because, he knew, if Dickerson couldn't do it, it wasn't going to happen. As Dickerson popped his ballpoint pen in the silence, he could see from his face that it hadn't happened. Dickerson tentatively touched his sunburn, winced as the momentary pressure left a bloodless white absence under the flush.

"You said that if I talked to you that we might turn some kind of corner."

Dickerson glanced at his watch, slipped his notebook and pen back into his chest pocket. "I'll be getting back to you."

Afterward, Val felt doubt and regret welling up in him. What had he done? Against his best impulses, could he trust himself to help himself? Since North Carolina, it often had seemed not. If Dickerson used the information against him, Val could always deny it. That now seemed to be all that was left to him, anyway.

When, after several days, a week, ten days, Dickerson still didn't get back in touch with him, Val couldn't eat and started breaking into nervous sweats, sitting down, standing up and pacing. Then he impulsively scrawled a letter to Lee Anne. He wrote that as she was no doubt well aware, he had been indicted by the grand jury and was going to trial. He wanted to see her once more. He didn't expect an answer. He didn't care anymore. It was just something he wanted. Maybe if he could see her face one more time he'd begin to understand…what?

He was surprised when she replied. It was like all the other postcards she'd ever sent—as though she were talking into a void, no salutation, no signature. On this one she had simply scrawled a date and a time. He was even more surprised by the nervous leap in his chest at the sight of her handwriting.

Dickerson wasn't exactly apologetic at not getting back to Val, but he did offer that he'd been out of town working on something. Now Val noticed more about him—his flat New York accent, his fastidiousness, which seemed to be at war with his belly. Val said, "I have something to show you."

Val pushed the postcard across the table. "This is the way she would write me. They were all like this…no 'Dear Val'. And she never signed them."

Dickerson examined the card, but seemed unimpressed. "What's your point?"

Val tried to hide his desperation. "We'd talked about turning a corner… I'd talk to you first, and then we'd see…"

"You talked off the record. Have you now thought about writing a statement?"

"No," Val said. "Did you believe me last time?"

Dickerson studied Val. "I hear a lot of things from a lot of people when they're in trouble. They tell me something, it's one way. A while later, they tell me something else…"

"I told you the truth."

Dickerson shrugged, *the truth.*

Val heard Kazz saying, "You're still in love with her."

Dickerson stood.

Forcing himself to sound more neutral, Val tried again. "You said you would be checking on a few things."

Dickerson turned toward the door. "Right. To be honest with you, I wouldn't get my hopes up, Val." As an afterthought, he picked up Lee Anne's postcard and reexamined it, placed it back on the table. For the first time, Val thought he saw traces of pity, perhaps even contempt, come into his expression.

"Do you think she'll show up?" Before he could stop, Val heard himself start to laugh softly. Dickerson let go of the doorknob. "Something funny?"

Val nodded. "Not really. But…" It was hard to explain. "From Lee Anne, realize, there was always a kind of implied threat…and even though it took her seventeen years, she finally made good on it. I think if she says she'll be here, she'll be here." He laughed again. "I mean, that's the very least of it for her now, isn't it?"

Dickerson searched his face once more, couldn't seem to come to a conclusion, and went out.

Val was hot—his forehead clammy—but at the same time he could feel the almost cellular iciness of the ocean still within him. He stretched out the links of the handcuffs. Maybe this was the worst part of it, that he was giving away whatever he had left of himself by letting her see him—in jail, in a red jumpsuit, in handcuffs.

There was some movement outside in the hall and then the door was opened and the deputy let her into the room. She remained just inside, the deputy's face frozen in the window behind. She took a step, stopped, stood as she had the first night after Davis had gone overboard, as if balancing on a sharpened stake. Val sat at the table. A surprising calm came over him. He looked for her eyes. The very last time he had seen her, she'd gone completely out of herself—or his own distorted perception made it seem that way; her posture appeared to be of someone he hadn't seen before; he'd had a feeling that he'd been looking at a young girl. But now, he realized, all of those impressions had been symptoms of his panic. Now she again seemed to be the woman he'd known in North Carolina and Brooklyn.

At the sight of Lee Anne, he felt the terror of her living room that night, the way Brent had pinned him and the way she'd swung the white marble sculpture as a club, blood silently advancing toward him on the floor moments later. Here within the block walls and linoleum floors, she seemed incapable of such an act. Finally, he said formally, almost as if reading from a script, "Thank you for coming."

She looked at him, but a little past him, too.

As his words didn't seem connected to anything inside him, he reminded himself to be careful. He stretched the links on his handcuffs. "They're real."

He could find no small talk, thought it pointless to attempt, and said, "No one believes me, Lee Anne. You're home free. All I want to know is what was really happening that night?" She didn't say anything. "If you can tell me that, I think I could finally just let everything go. Is this what you were looking for?" He again held up the cuffs. "Did it play out right? Was there a plan?"

She pressed her lips together, as if to speak, but then he saw a look of calculation in her face. And fear.

He said, "I requested a private room—I've been meeting my attorney here. There's no way anyone can overhear or record us." She took in the room, looked back at him with perhaps the trace of an ironic smile.

"All I asked was, is this what you wanted? Or am I kind of a throw-in? An afterthought. You can tell me that much." When she still didn't answer, he said, "I guess it must have been. Was it all those years of thinking about Brooklyn and how I failed you?"

He saw her start to say something, but again change her mind.

"You know, Lee Anne, I just have to tell you, you were right about me—you, and now that I think about it, my father. You were both right. You and my father, the last two people I'd ever put together, have a lot in common." He laughed, surprised, distressed. "I should have been in law school the whole time. My freaking out after my experience in San Francisco wasn't really about justice and ideals. It was probably more about me. Just ego. Maybe that's what your contempt for me was about, your *Great Val* routine. I was a sore loser. I'd have been contemptuous, too, if I were you. I mean, letting a little personal sensibility get in the way of opportunity. I panicked once and ran.... So did you figure I'd panic and run again that night with Brent?"

She shook her head. "I don't think I knew there'd really be a night with Brent. Not really. I didn't know what you'd do."

"But you wanted me to come."

"I knew you'd come."

"Because I had to find out about Davis."

"I just knew you'd come back and talk to me again."

She said it so simply—like a child—that Val was thrown for a moment. He recovered and forced himself to push ahead. "Still, you wanted me there. Needed me there to start whatever it was. Brent and I together."

"I can't say it was like that."

"But he just happened to be there. In a jealous rage. You knew he was a jealous guy. And his boat was gone. Someone took it. And you did know you would get the insurance money. And the newspapers said you'd get everything else, too. He had money."

"It's not how the papers say."

"He didn't have money?"

"He did. Does. Did."

"And you will get it."

"One way or the other, I was going out. I had to get out. It was time. I didn't want to go out empty handed, to just be forced out one more time without anything."

"God, Lee Anne, why me? Why didn't you just divorce him and get your settlement and...." She shook her head no. "Why not?'

"Because if I filed for divorce, I'd get nothing. We had a prenuptial agreement. I signed it. I guess," she said with tart irony. "I didn't have a smart lawyer like you to represent me, Val."

He shrugged. "So what? You couldn't file so you needed to make him go away, and I was still somewhere out there and you knew I'd come back sooner or later and...."

"And because I could, Val."

She smiled with slight contempt. That she had a kind of power. That she could. Yet at that moment, Val had an eerie sense of unreality, as if everything she had said, was saying, was from a script, real, yet somehow unreal to her—not what really mattered. That something else mattered. He pushed ahead.

"And the cards you sent all those years, Lee Anne. Was that because you could, too?"

She gazed past him.

"And your coming down to sneak around and watch me and take pictures of me and my son, because you could?"

She didn't answer.

"My wife was right. You were stalking me."

Val saw the look of calculation come into her face.

"It wasn't exactly like that, Val."

"Like what? None of that happened?"

"It happened. It just didn't happen in such a calculated way. The way you're making it sound."

"How did it happen?"

"It just took me forward a step at a time."

"What took you forward a step at a time?"

She gave him a quizzical look.

"What do you mean 'it'?"

"I just knew what to do next."

Val hesitated. "Okay, call it what you want. You took steps to make something happen or push something until it happened and now you're saying it just kind of happened by itself. You knew Brent would be somewhere around that night I came. You made sure he'd be around. You kept looking for him. You were scared. You knew he was coming sooner or later, knew how he'd react. And he did. He went crazy. I'm losing my wife and son so you could get rid of Brent and collect and have me take the rap. You know, Davis said to me, 'You don't just leave, Lee Anne...' I've thought of that so many times since."

She started to go and then turned back to him. She'd almost reached the table when she stopped. "You're forgetting one important thing."

"What am I forgetting?"

"I killed him, but I saved your life." She said it with a sudden tenderness and anguish unlike anything he'd ever heard from her before, that this is what mattered.

"You saved my life. I do know that."

"Brent was going to kill you. He would have killed you. You were dead."

She looked at him, but Val still had the feeling she was watching something coming out of a distance. "You were dead. I killed him, but I saved your life." Once again she looked emptied out of herself, almost bewildered. She turned, studied him with an anguished, confounded tenderness, and walked quickly out of the room.

Val slumped in the chair, gazed at the closed door, his wrists and hands hanging loose in the cuffs. He touched the red shirt—damp with sweat—squinted into the silvery glare of the lights, looked over when the deputy pushed into the room. Val walked in front of him down the corridor. This time, instead of taking him back into his wing, the corrections officer opened an office door and let Val inside, closed it behind him.

Dickerson indicated a chair beside the desk, and Val sat down. Dickerson returned with a Coke, opened it for him. Val held the cold can between both hands for some time and then took a swallow, pressed the chill aluminum to his forehead, set it on the desk.

He raised his arms as Dickerson pulled up Val's shirt and released the harness; he placed the wire on the desk. Dickerson sat down and pushed the tape recorder to one side, seemed contemplative. "You never know. Sometimes they talk, but the thing doesn't transmit or record. Be surprised how often these things don't work. Sometimes it transmits, but you can't get them to talk. Sometimes you only get that one chance and nothing happens and you never get another."

Val took another swallow of the Coke. "I'm amazed she talked at all. Didn't really think she would. She's always been so canny. It's almost as if she's let go of everything that's gone before and moved on to another agenda."

Dickerson said, "Sorry I had to squeeze you for so long, but I thought if I could push you into a corner, you'd dance for me. I knew that sooner or later, it would be you. Her thing just didn't feel right from the beginning. The deputy who went out there to answer the original 911 could tell from looking at her there was something wrong; she didn't say two words, just nodded her head to his questions. She couldn't talk. And she declined his offer to come in and look around. There'd been domestic violence calls from Brent and Lee Anne before."

Dickerson went on. "She didn't actually come forward with her story about you until you were found and brought in on the trawler, and that was a day later, and with your being in the ICU, another day before it was in the paper. So what was that?"

Dickerson shrugged. "Maybe she's waiting to see when and where you turned up...or if you turned up at all. If there's no sign of Brent, maybe that's the end of it and that might work for her, too. Maybe. At least, for the time being. He's gone. There's no trace of him. His boat's gone. She knows nothing. No one knows nothing. Maybe that'll work. So she just watches and waits.

"But…" Dickerson smiled sardonically. "You were either more incompe-tent or more conscience-bound than she'd thought. Or both. Let's say the whole thing went exactly the way you claimed. You panicked in the house. You go to dump Brent from the boat. But you find you can't. You come to your senses and turn around, but then the boat goes over. Just like you said. Ordinarily that still would have been the end of you—ten miles off shore. Freezing water. Very unlucky.

"But then you get very lucky, too. You get picked up by the trawler and come back in on the tide. Lucky.

"But then very unlucky. Because there's Brent snarled in cinderblocks and the anchor line. And it all goes into the paper: the picture, the story. Only now does Lee Anne decide to come forward—this is three days after that 911 call. Now she suddenly brings us her story about you killing Brent."

Dickerson shrugged again. "Why didn't she tell the deputy you'd been there the second he showed up? Fall into his arms sobbing. No, I'd never seen anything like that. Waiting for three days when the sheriff had been there fifteen minutes after you'd supposedly terrorized her and killed Brent. No. I just couldn't find any reason she'd do that. Still, who knows exactly what's going on here? Something had terrified her. Something was wrong." Dickerson felt his forehead, gingerly worked his peeling sunburn, resolutely placed his hands on the desk, went back to peeling.

Val was stunned to hear Dickerson now. He'd used Dickerson; there'd been something in him he'd read, maybe a skepticism, and Val had taken a chance and been right.

"But these two had been fighting some kind of battle, Brent and Lee Anne…it looked like they'd been trying to kill each other for years. Rashes of domestic violence calls. There'd been a restraining order. Brent had a trail of DUIs, reckless endangerments, and was known to be a drunk. I pulled his record."

Dickerson looked at the tape recorder. "I knew something was funny, but the evidence played out upside down—right for her, wrong for you: Brent's body tied to your boat. Your fingerprints all over their house, your blood, his blood…. It was her word against yours and everything was lining up for her."

Dickerson shrugged and went back to working his sunburn.

"I ran you and you came up clean. Not even any parking tickets. Course I made some calls and found out you'd been disbarred for a year. But I thought about you and you just didn't look like the type to come in and kill a guy. But then again, who ever knows? Anybody can be anybody. After I talked to you, I talked to your wife, and she confirmed a few things that you'd told me. She said there'd been cards from Lee Anne. Exactly like the last card you showed me. No 'Dear Val.' No signature. They'd come the whole time you'd been married. Didn't make that much sense. Your wife said there'd been a videotape. She'd never seen it. Said you'd never watched it, either, but she knew it had the fishing accident on it. Again, it was like you said. Some other things checked out. Little things. She said there'd been a picture of your brother running a boat somewhere…that you came east for your father's funeral…. None of this would have done anything for you in trial, nothing exculpatory, but I just kept looking at little things you'd told me and every single one checked out…."

Val picked up the Coke, turned the hole toward himself, but put it back down without drinking.

"I ran Lee Anne's credit card records, and they confirmed that she had made a trip out to Tucson at the time you thought you'd seen her. Whether or not she was stalking you, she was visiting Tucson."

Dickerson shook his head. "So, what did I have? Her story didn't make sense for her, but the evidence did. Your little details matched your story, but here you are with Brent's body. But where'd it take me? Would you kill Brent? To run off with Lee Anne? What was it in for you? I couldn't see it. Obsessed and in love with her as she claimed." Val averted his eyes. "You just didn't look crazy to me. Or crazy enough to kill." Dickerson laughed, short, sardonic. "No, there was nothing really in it for you. But there was a lot in it for her. The boat, a way of getting to him, making him crazy—or should I say crazier—the insurance, a cash bonus; property, his estate. And, like I said, everyone knew Brent had been in scrapes, knew him as a danger-ous, unpredictable drunk: one moment, he's charming as hell, the next, he'll knock your teeth out.

"She had no way of divorcing him and getting anything…. She was stuck. This way she could get out and come into money and property at the same time. There was nothing in it for you and a lot in it for her. So I looked harder."

Val thought about it. Dickerson was right. Of course, he was right. The details bore out and filled in parts Val hadn't known. But he was distracted. There was something else. He remembered the sense of the house, of feeling dislocated when he'd come into the living room, as if he'd gone back in time to some place she'd written about, or he'd imagined, or sensed in her, a room, a piano, something that had given her nightmares; he saw her sleeping half-dressed in Brooklyn, always half-dressed, still in love with, maybe even married to Davis; he remembered, too, what Davis had told him, that something seemed to escape from her and hang over the bed when she slept. He'd felt it, too. Awake. Asleep. He lost the thought. "Why did you hang me out?"

"You weren't exactly cooperative, Val."

Who had played whom? Val wasn't sure. "I was within my rights not to make a statement."

"Absolutely. I was within my rights, too. I was within my rights to make you feel hopeless and desperate."

"If you hadn't been able to get Lee Anne on tape today, would you have gone ahead and prosecuted me even though you'd doubted I'd killed him?"

"Val, I'm paid by the state of New York."

"Just as long you get someone?"

Dickerson didn't answer. He stood, came out from behind the desk, and unlocked Val's cuffs. "I shouldn't do this—against county jail regulations—but I'm trusting you." He placed the cuffs on the desk.

Val wrapped one hand around the opposite wrist, smoothed his skin.

Dickerson held up the tape cassette. "I'll take the new information to the county attorney today and we'll see about dropping the murder charges. Probably come back to you, the lesser charges, as obstruction of justice—concealing a crime, trying to dump Brent's body. That will reduce your bail and get you out of here. Then you can have your attorney deal with the new charges. Nothing on your record, maybe you'll end up with five years probation, a few hundred hours of community service. You're here a while longer until I can run all this through." Dickerson reached into his pocket and handed Val several quarters. "Might want to call your wife and high-priced attorney." Dickerson dropped the tape into his pocket. "You helped yourself by taking a chance and trusting a cop. It broke the jam." He stood. "I'm still following up some things you touched on."

"Which ones?"

"Florida. Miami." Val was blank. "Lee Anne. We've been researching her down there through the courts and computers in the early eighties. The years she said she was there with your brother."

"And?"

"We found a Lee Anne Wilder in Miami. But when we ran our Lee Anne's fingerprints through the computer, it spat them out—no match."

"What does that mean?"

"It means it found another Lee Anne Wilder living there with the same social security number, same date of birth."

Val looked at the handcuffs lying on the desk, but didn't touch them.

"We checked on that Lee Anne Wilder. She's a thirty-nine-year-old woman who used to live in Miami, but is now living in Fort Lauderdale; she has a verifiable birth certificate and social security number. The Lauderdale cops sent up pictures of her. She looks almost exactly like our Lee Anne."

Val ran and reran Dickerson's words, confused, a kind of terror pushing up from inside. "So what are you saying?"

"I'm saying the woman now in Fort Lauderdale is the real, verifiable Lee Anne Wilder."

"But there could be two women named Lee Anne Wilder."

"Yes, but there can't be two with the same social security number."

"So what, who.... Lee Anne is not really Lee Anne Wilder?"

"No."

"But somehow she ended up with her name—you said she looked like this woman?"

"The Lauderdale woman has a couple of kids—but the two women look almost exactly alike. It's a case of identity theft."

"Then who is Lee Anne?" His voice sounded faraway and strange. "This Lee Anne." He tapped the desk. Here.

"We don't know. And she isn't telling us anything."

"What's she doing?"

"She just stares past anyone who talks to her. Sometimes she gives this little kind of crooked smile. Kind of like everything here is unreal or a very wry joke."

Val knew that smile too well. He picked up the handcuffs, turned them in his hands. He looked at Dickerson. Dickerson met his eye and just nodded.

## An Educated Girl from Philadelphia

A day later, Lee Anne Wilder was arrested. Once more the papers picked up the story:

"Local Woman Charged with Husband's Murder"

There was a picture of Lee Anne in handcuffs being taken into custody, long dark hair obscuring her face as she ducked her head to enter a sheriff's car.

And the subhead:

"Boyfriend released on bail. Charges reduced to obstruction."

Another picture showed Val. It was a telephoto shot taken from across the street just as he was coming out of the county jail and about to get into a parked car. He had tipped his head back and was looking up at the sky.

Within a few days, a local paper ran this headline:

"Bizarre Story Takes Even Stranger Turn"

The article began:

If she's not really Lee Anne Wilder, then who is she?...

Another headline:

"Mystery Woman Not Talking"

"Police continue inquiries"

And under her booking photo, there was a caption:

"Who is she?"

The article asked that anyone having any knowledge of the woman or her case get in touch with the police directly or call 88-CRIME.

Now the story was picked up by the wire services, but still no one came forward.

In the meantime, a local man stopped in at the sheriff's office. He was just getting back from a cruise up to Nova Scotia and had been out of touch for weeks. He had been catching up with his local papers and read about a boat, a Bertram, which was stolen back in mid-May. Having left before dawn at the start of his trip, and just as it was getting light, he had noticed something and veered off course to investigate. At first he'd thought it was a reef, but knew there was nothing in that location. Then he speculated that maybe it was a whale. As he came closer, he saw it was the bow of a powerboat sticking up out of the water. He tried to punch in the coordinates on his GPS, which wouldn't take them. He'd had some electrical work done just before leaving and apparently a power surge had shorted it out after he'd gotten under way. Still, he'd gotten the coordinates with a handheld, battery-powered GPS. He wrote down the registration numbers visible on the bow. He stayed with the boat, looking for survivors, found no evidence of anyone in the water, no life rings or rafts or life jackets or bodies; the boat continued to float for some time—maybe fifteen more minutes as the sky got light—and then suddenly gave a lurch and went down within thirty seconds. When he tried to call the Coast Guard, he discovered that his VHF was also dead. He waited until he reached Boston later in the day to report his finding to the local Coast Guard group. In fact, a search through the Boston Coast Guard log revealed that there had been such a report and that a helicopter had been dispatched to search the area; they had filed a report of finding nothing, but no connection had been made to the stolen Bertram—an oversight, a misplaced piece of paperwork, a misfiled report.

Now, with this new information, and the GPS coordinates, the insurance company sent a boat out to see if they could find the Bertram. The salvage team tracked the area with a video sounder, and within hours, a spike of more than twenty feet appeared on the screen. After another day of search-ing with a side-scan sonar and GPS, the crew was confident they had located something in two hundred feet of water. They were going to send divers down to confirm it was a boat—and, if so, to see if the registration numbers matched up with those of the Bertram. If it was Brent's boat, they were going to investigate the cause of its sinking and see if the boat could be raised.

Val would later learn from Dickerson in the afternoon of the day that he was released from the county jail—it had been over two months since his arrest and was now late August—that an attractive woman in her late fifties had arrived in town before noon and had gone directly to the police. She had a faint hesitation and a slur in her speech—it sounded like the echo of a foreign accent; she had just the slightest hitch in her walk, barely detectable. She had beautiful gray eyes that seemed to be trying to burst out of her face and escape when she talked. She carried a brown manila envelope and a scrapbook. When she mentioned the woman known as Lee Anne Wilder, she was referred to Dickerson, who took her into his office. She said she had seen the booking photo of the woman known as Lee Anne Wilder in her hometown paper, the *Philadelphia Inquirer*—this had been the day before— and she had driven up. She introduced herself as Margaret Desjardins. She opened the manila envelope and spread a number of items on the desk: a birth certificate for Christine Margaret Desjardins. Tiny footprints taken at the time of her birth. A pile of family photographs, which she placed to one side. And several newspaper clippings. She slid the clippings in front of

Dickerson. They sat down side by side behind his desk. The first:

"Prominent Local Psychiatrist Murdered."

There was a picture of the doctor. Still young. Maybe in his late thirties. Serious. Beside him, a second picture: his murderer. The eyes too intense, focused on something else, and with perhaps a plea in them.

Dickerson read how Dr. Desjardins' patient, Paul Freivogel, had been mistakenly released from a psychiatric facility where he'd been confined for two years. He had stopped home—he lived with his mother—gone into his room for a short time, and then continued on to the doctor's house. It was late afternoon. He rang the bell. The doctor's eight-year-old daughter answered the door. He asked for her father, and she went to get him. When Dr. Desjardins came to the front door, Freivogel pulled out a gun. A struggle ensued in which several shots were fired. Desjardins died almost immediately. His wife, several steps behind him, was hit once, was in intensive care. This was the daughter's account. The daughter is staying with an aunt. Police continued to search for the man the daughter had identified as Paul Freivogel.

Accompanying the article, there was a family picture taken several weeks before the incident. A young girl sat between her parents on a sofa in a posed portrait, a girl with beautiful eyes that matched her mother's.

There were several more articles. A profile of the murderer, Paul Freivogel, whom Dr. Desjardins had treated for several years. When Freivogel had become delusional and suicidal, Dr. Desjardins placed him in the facility. He'd remained there on and off for almost two years until his mistaken release. Authorities were investigating.

Dickerson studied the follow-up articles.

One headline read simply, "Police Search for Killer."

And another article, dated a week later, in which the police found Freivogel in a hotel room in downtown Philadelphia. Before he could be taken into custody, he killed himself with the same gun he'd used to kill Dr. Desjardins.

And that was all.

Later, Dickerson would tell Val that he'd asked the mother, "What happened to you and Christine after the murder?" Margaret lifted the hair at the back of her head, leaned toward Dickerson, and displayed a small scar to show where the bullet had entered. She'd remained in a coma for several months and then slowly become conscious. She was paralyzed on her right side, could barely speak, but after years of speech and physiotherapy, she'd improved, and then she and Christine had been able to live together again. She'd put it all away, the newspaper accounts of the murder, the emotions, everything; they'd never talked about it. It had been a conscious decision that had come out of the necessity to go on with their lives, go forward. Christine had done well in school, always had a lot of boyfriends, more boyfriends, in fact, than she'd known what to do with. Boys had been captivated by her. She was very popular. She'd laughed a lot—she had a wonderful sudden laugh; it just seemed to explode out of her; she loved to party and have a good time. You wouldn't have known anything terrible had taken place. It was wonderful to see the way she'd been able to get on with her life. She was gifted academically—loved to escape into the library, where she read everything; she'd gotten into several good colleges and universities, gone off to Middlebury College in Vermont.

Then in the middle of her freshman year, she'd just disappeared—this was shortly after Christmas vacation—just left everything exactly as it was in her dorm room—books, a paper half-written on her desk with notes, clothes in her dresser and hanging in her closet. The police had interviewed dozens of people: friends, teachers, people in town, in restaurants and stores. No one had seen her. No one knew anything. The police had checked bus stations, train stations, taxi records about the time of her disappearance. They'd extensively interviewed a boy she'd been dating. She'd never mentioned leaving. Or going to meet someone. Nothing. The only thing the police had found was an empty bottle of Clairol—black—in the bathroom trash. None of the other girls, when questioned, had dyed her hair black. That, and that alone, had given Margaret hope that she had not been abducted, or raped and murdered, but that Christine might be out there somewhere. And for that reason, Margaret had never given up hope or stopped looking for her. It had been almost twenty years.

Dickerson looked at the articles and then studied Margaret Desjardins. He looked at the booking photo that she had brought from the *Philadelphia Inquirer* with the caption beneath: "Who is she?"

He said, "You think this woman, Lee Anne Wilder, is your daughter? Christine? Christine Desjardins?"

Margaret said, "I think. I believe it is. I'm all but certain." She pushed several more photographs of her daughter toward Dickerson: high-school snapshots; yearbook.

Dickerson looked at Margaret Desjardins, weighing the plausibility, the actual possibility, against the woman's need to find her daughter. He wondered how many times and in how many places she had come forward in similar situations, wondered if it wasn't part of the trauma of her husband's murder, her own physical and psychological trauma. With an uneasy feeling, he placed everything back in the manila envelope. He said, "You think you'll know?"

Margaret nodded. "I think I will."

Dickerson stood. "Then let's go over to the jail and find out."

All of this Dickerson would later tell Val, who had just opened the door to his motel room and been about to take a shower when the phone rang.

"...and so," Dickerson went on, "we went over to the jail and had Lee Anne brought into a room with a one-way mirror, Margaret Desjardins on the other side, and without any hesitation Margaret just started nodding yes, yes, it's her." Dickerson had let Margaret into the room with Lee Anne, and Lee Anne had turned and looked at the woman and then walked over to her and said, "Mom," said it without a trace of a Southern accent, and let the woman hug her, Lee Anne looking both enormously relieved and agonized to be letting something go. She couldn't put her arms around her mother because she was handcuffed.

Dickerson said, "It was like, at that moment, like one person stepping into someone else, Lee Anne Wilder became Christine Desjardins from Philadelphia right before my eyes."

Val couldn't speak. Always: someone else with Lee Anne, half a step behind. He'd sensed it, hadn't he? Which was why she kept coming back... she had been hoping to find a way to reveal herself to him....

"And," Val hesitated, "Christine never lived in the South when she was growing up...didn't grow up in Florida?" He was surprised at something quavery he heard in his voice, a feeling rising as if there were a hole opening in him, something falling away, filling with, what was it? pain, disorientation?

"No, according to her mother she grew up in Philadelphia."

Val heard himself. It was almost a protest, "But she has a Southern accent."

"No. Not now. Her mother walked into the room and that was it. 'Mom. I've been trying to find my way back to you.'"

"What does she sound like?"

Dickerson hesitated. "An educated girl from Philadelphia." Then he said,

"Yeah, over twenty years missing. What a way to find your daughter: A Jane Doe booking photo in the newspaper; in custody and about to be indicted for killing her husband."

Trying to focus, Val held the receiver in silence. A man, a psychiatric patient, had killed her father. She knew, but didn't know. Moving silently within, it had driven Lee Anne—Christine—to disappear on a freezing day in January in Vermont, head blindly south, reinvent herself as someone else. On one level, the mere facts of the murder seemed so…so mundane. No, not mundane; extraordinary, yet ordinary—or rather, perhaps, the common coin of what happened only to other people, seemed to have been placed in the world with the express purpose of being a daily item in a local newspaper, the singular monstrosity, which occurred and recurred endlessly to someone else. But then, Val realized the same might have been said of Davis overboard—a freak fishing accident, as the local paper had referred to it.

"Was there a piano in the room where Paul Freivogel shot her father?"

"I have no idea."

"Can you ask her mother?"

"If you insist."

"Can you check one other thing?"

"What's that?"

"Can you find out if she was—my brother, Davis, and she—married in Miami in March or April of 1984?"

"I'll see what I can do. Enjoy your shower."

"Shower? How'd you know?"

Dickerson just laughed and hung up. Val remained holding the receiver.

In the half-light of the partly drawn curtains, he looked at the two made beds, the TV and dresser. He could still smell the jail, the closeness of bodies in the day room, cafeteria food, the stainless steel toilet, cigarette smoke. As if translating from a foreign language, Val ran through what Dickerson had told him. He lowered himself onto the bed. Said softly, "Margaret Desjardins. Christine Desjardins. Lee Anne Wilder is Christine Desjardins. From Philadelphia." He heard the echo of Dickerson's voice. He had, he realized, heard a piece of her story in Brooklyn. The translation of her father into a rocket scientist who'd had a nervous breakdown and just stopped talking. Mother a small town librarian in Florida, where Lee Anne had read everything.

Val remained kneeling on the bed. Then something—what?—an atmosphere rose on his skin, engulfed him: Davis in North Carolina, Lee Anne bringing something with her, a polarization starting between himself and Davis…

And, the atmosphere in Brent's house, Lee Anne, Brent, himself, a charge seeming to build up moment by moment, and then, even before he saw Brent, the feeling in Val of his back coming alive, a man there at the edge of his vision. Brent's sudden movements as he came across the floor, his manic rage.

Val heard Lee Anne whispering, *please, please, please…*

Saw her sinking onto the sofa, placing her hands together in her lap like an exhausted schoolgirl.

Heard her last words to him in the jail: "I killed him, but I saved your life."

Was it too much to see it now as a situation in which Lee Anne, no, Christine, had recreated a struggle that had taken place over thirty years before? But now she would intervene to change the outcome, to save his life. Then Lee Anne could let the cops have him for whatever her reasons: money, property. And revenge. Hadn't her last card said *I forgive you nothing*?

As if coming awake, but still dreaming, Val heard Dickerson's voice: she disappeared from her dorm, took nothing, left everything as it was; all they found was an empty bottle of black hair dye. Out of that single empty bottle, Val saw Lee Anne inventing herself, remembered the first time he'd seen her, cross-currents of color and hairstyles growing out; and, that day in the bar in Brooklyn, unknown to him, pregnant, the platinum beehive, the spurting match, her hair burning white in the sunlight; and, afterward; the apartment sinking into darkness and her cutting away the burned hair herself, the terrible smell, the arid rasp of the scissors in the silence, her fingers blindly groping behind her head each time to gather once more another tuft of hair, cut it…. Next morning, the incandescent shimmer of her will in the stillness. The distinct sense Val had at times that there was something both crazy and yet heroic about her, and that the craziness and heroism were indistinguishable; and that, whatever they were, he'd felt the relentless pull of them.

He turned on his side and glanced at the light coming in the half-drawn curtains. Maybe, too, it was not an accident that she'd chosen to be a hairdresser, altering appearances, her own, others; it was a way to stay safe, not to be recognized by whomever was one day going to be coming back to your front door. But who? How could you ever know it was him? And when? Inevitably that return would have to happen because another part of her, perfectly concealed, was somehow working to make it happen. In fact, it had been in the man she'd married, perhaps as carefully chosen for reasons unknown to her as she had chosen her career. Another Davis. Fabulously handsome. Often charming, as he, according to Dickerson, had been reputed to be. Rich. But poisonous. The thoughts muddled as Val couldn't take them any farther.

He sat up and took off his shirt. In the bathroom, he started the shower, adjusting the hot and cold, watching the water swirling in the drain. He smelled the skin of his arm: the close smell of the jail? He avoided himself in the mirror as he turned to find soap and shampoo by the sink. Those unsigned postcards of hers, which went back to…he now suddenly understood, went back to what would have been her starting someplace years ago, someplace cold, Vermont in January. The sense that there was a room, a place…. That terrible place she mentioned in Brooklyn that she feared coming back to. The terrible feeling in Brent's house that night. All the time, she had been, in Brooklyn, in those postcards, he suddenly knew, telling him the story of the murder, perhaps its aftermath, which she had never forgotten—knew the fact of, but no longer remembered. "You know, but don't know." She had been talking about herself. She had changed her name, changed her identity, traveled as far away as she could from that moment, only to find that she had recreated it, had never left it, had traveled back to it.

The phone rang, and without turning off the shower, Val walked naked into the other room. Crouching down, and then standing back from the half-drawn blinds, he answered the phone. At first, he didn't recognize the voice. She had to tell him who she was; she was Kazz. She was calling him back. She'd just finished making travel arrangements. She'd be flying to New York. She'd just gotten off the phone with Stan Miller, and Stan would be phoning him to coordinate. Val could barely take his mind off the sound of the shower still running in the next room to answer her.

On the phone to Val, Dickerson was brief and to the point. He'd asked Lee Anne if there'd been a piano in the room where her father was murdered. She wouldn't answer, just shook her head.

"Shook her head no?"

"Hard to say. Shook her head."

"Did she have a little smile when she did it."

"She might have. Maybe. But I'm not sure."

"Because if she had a kind of half smile, it could mean she knows something more, maybe something she herself isn't aware of..." Val heard himself. "I mean, she used to say to me about Davis, 'You know, but don't know.'" He knew he couldn't make sense of it for Dickerson, who went on to say that the mother's memories of that time were gone.

He took a deep breath, let it out slowly. "What about a record of the marriage between Davis and Lee Anne?"

"We didn't find anything in Miami."

"So they hadn't been married. Another one of Lee Anne's fabrications. Or maybe they were married somewhere else."

"Maybe." Dickerson said quietly, "Let it go, Val."

Dickerson said that he had something he wanted to show Val, but wouldn't say more. He'd pick him up at the hotel around eleven.

He came by in an unmarked white Crown Victoria. Together they'd driven in near silence to the Montauk Harbor. Dickerson pulled into a parking lot behind a boat shed and turned off the engine, and Val sat looking out across the harbor at the dozens of masts and flying bridges. It was the last week of August, boating season. An incandescent water light rose up to meet a radiance of sky.

As they got out of the car, Dickerson reached around into the back seat, and this time Val saw that he'd remembered his hat, a long-billed fisherman's cap. He placed it on his head and indicated the way. Val followed him through a boatyard and then down a wide industrial pier. Ahead he saw the top of a flying bridge and tuna tower riding below the dock. At the end, side by side, they looked down on the big Bertram floating beside the dock.

Val said, "Brent's boat."

And Dickerson nodded. "Brent's Bertram. The Sun Tracker."

Val looked down at her, her windows obscured with caked bottom mud, silt and growth, the bow pulpit, the lifelines and stanchions and cleats and hatches and portholes, the fighting chair in the big cockpit, the tuna tower, all enshrouded in muck, now baked dry in the sun. Val slowly paced off her length. When he reached the bow, he looked back and noticed the boat's soft rhythmic movement against the pier's bumpers. He wrapped his hand around the thick bowline, felt the heartbeat tremor of the hull afloat. Again he saw the cut dock line in his hand as he stepped up onto Brent's dock, turned and looked up at the house, Brent's house. Now he breathed in the smell of tar and diesel, tide, caught wayward currents of summer heat, asphalt, grass, marshes. He thought of the airless cells this morning in the county jail, the day room thick with smoke. Overhead, gulls hung motionless in their glide.

He closed his eyes and felt the August sun warm on his face, and for a moment, no time had gone by, it was the same, the same as it had always been, he was a boy standing on a dock, his father beside him, above him, holding his hand, and it was so for another instant even when Val opened his eyes as if waking from a dream and Dickerson started to explain how after the salvage team picked up something on sonar, they'd returned with a team of divers, who'd gone down and found the boat sitting upright on the bottom with the hull settled into the mud up to the boat stripe on the transom. They had confirmed that the registration numbers were those of Brent's boat, then come back with a full salvage crew—five boats, including a tug with a 125-foot-long deck barge carrying an eighty-ton crane. The divers went back down and spent the next two days strapping the hull into seven slings. Then the crane slowly brought the Sun Tracker back up to the surface, where six pumps emptied the water out. Dickerson paused. "The salvage team found three main breakers for the bilge pumps turned off, a raw water intake hose disconnected on the port engine and a diesel generator exhaust hose pulled off the muffler in the lazarette; the work of someone who knew what he was doing. Once they put together all the hoses that had been taken apart, she floated fine." Dickerson held out his hand to the Bertram riding at the dock. "Just fine."

Val watched a gust silently darken the water out in the channel; a Lightning tacked higher upwind, suddenly came about with a flutter of the mainsail, which wafted loud downwind. A moment later, he felt the wind raise his hair, flutter his shirt. Dickerson reached up just in time to catch his hat. Again, Val let the sun close his eyes, felt his father close.

Dickerson pointed at the salvaged Bertram. "We know Lee Anne—Christine—did it somehow. We're sure she had to have had a partner. Maybe she followed him out in a boat and took him off after he opened up the Bertram. Maybe he came ashore in an inflatable and she met him. Maybe she just hired him and he worked alone. There are a lot of possibilities. She's not talking."

Val opened his eyes and looked down through the harbor to where the channel opened out to the Atlantic and thought of the Bertram lying silent down there in the freezing darkness beyond the reach of sunlight; he saw her slowly rising out of the bottom muck, the first silvery light reaching her tuna tower and bridge and hull as she inched toward the surface, of her hanging in her slings beside the barge as they pumped her out until she floated

Dickerson pointed at a red police tag attached to one of her handrails. "It's in evidence. A little big to bring into a courtroom. Pictures will have to do. But there it is. Insurance fraud. Grand larceny. This will make it impossible for her attorneys to get the lesser beef, murder two. It's almost a good circumstantial case on this alone; anyway, it will lock down her murder one indictment and she'll have a tough time beating it." Dickerson nodded. "Of course, now it's all going to start with the expert psychiatric witnesses: if she's crazy; if she can go to trial." Dickerson tugged on one of the spring lines, let it go. "Take it from me, she ain't crazy." Before Val could get it out, Dickerson said, "If and when they do get a conviction, all of this about her father will add up to a ton of mitigation. Still my take is she knew exactly what she was doing."

Dickerson gazed with satisfaction at the raised Bertram and then they turned and started walking back up the dock toward the car.

Val lay on the bed; outside the motel room, the sound of vacationers getting an early start on the day—breakfast, a trip to the beach, fishing. Car doors slammed. Neither rising nor falling, the Bertram hung in the thin silvery water light above him as Val saw Lee Anne in North Carolina, in Brooklyn. A hundred gestures, postures, glances. Her Southern accent. He saw her standing dressed by the bed one morning in Brooklyn. She had been trying, he now understood, to work up the courage to come out from behind her mask and tell him who she really was. But first she had to see something in him, get some signal, which would tell her that she'd be safe in doing so. Of course she couldn't. Her reasons were insurmountable. But, in almost a plea, she'd said in passing, *part of you wants me to be this way.*

More than by the betrayal of her brilliant deception, Val felt stung by the now undeniable truth of this. He'd heard the protest in his voice when he'd said to Dickerson, "But she has a Southern accent." As though it were something lost to him. He remembered the sound of her voice, how when she told him about her father being a scientist with the space program at

Canaveral, she'd whispered, in response to his question of where her father was from, "Philadelphia." That much true. Everything had been a transmutation of some fragments of her life, some knowable, guessable, others not, including dozens in the postcards; perhaps the ultimate irony was that the single fact driving her inventions remained suspended, there, but not there: a blank space, her father's murder.

Still, she'd tried to break out from the behind her mask: the pregnancy. Let her body do it if she couldn't confess. If nothing else, then together they had Davis. Together they'd keep Davis, but go somewhere else, new. Would she have then finally told him the truth that she was someone else? Had that been Christine Desjardins trying to reach through? Or Lee Anne? Or were they inseparable? Did it even matter?

*Part of you wants me to be this way.*

Is that what he'd felt from Lee Anne, the bright gleam of her will to invent herself? Heroic. Cowardly. She'd gone miles beyond anything he'd ever imagined, much less attempted, when he'd dropped out of law school and gone south, looking for something, a new self. She had succeeded brilliantly. But he also remembered her saying she feared being walled up in something if she let it go on too long. He'd gone back to law school. She'd married Brent. Walled herself in as Brent's wife, Lee Anne.

But she had gone on writing him. They'd remained connected. And he'd felt the pull of her...of her lie? Was it the illusion itself, or the lie of it, which kept drawing him back one more time?

And all the time, the thing in her, known, not known, had been choreographing her back to the start of her journey, to the thing forgotten.

Finally, what she had or hadn't done—or why—seemed, in a way, beside the point. It was about him. Had he loved her lies? Or been moved to know the truth? He had no idea, just knew that she had held him tight.

She was in the women's wing. He hadn't counted on his return to the jail freaking him out—its closeness, the smell of disinfectant, the buzz and click of its security systems. He hadn't imagined Lee Anne—Christine—in a red jumpsuit or handcuffs. Or that there might not be anything to say.

He'd never been able to make small talk with her—something in her had never allowed it—and now, after a moment, he gave it up, and there was an awkward silence. She stared past him. She seemed slightly amused at his self-consciousness, which is the way it had been from the beginning.

She still hadn't said anything. He was vaguely aware that he was waiting for something, though he didn't know what; he was sure that she was aware of this. She looked past him at the corrections officer at the door. He surprised himself and said tentatively, "Christine. Christine Desjardins."

She didn't answer. He realized he was trying to see where—or even if— Lee Anne was there—or how she was there—and where Lee Anne ended and Christine Desjardins began. He said, "Lee Anne…" She didn't answer, but smiled slightly. "I didn't know what I'd feel, but I'm not happy to see you like this."

She shrugged, as though she were beyond caring about anything he could possibly say or think.

He said, "I understand now what happened to you. Why at least some of it had to happen the way it did with us, and…." He didn't know what he was going to say. "I think I forgive you." He was surprised. "I forgive you." He said again, as if to hear himself correctly. He nodded.

She smiled vaguely, ironically, raised an eyebrow slightly, and as always with her, he felt foolish, that his every gesture or offering or effort was wrong, merely self-serving, or bad drama, that it was never right. Perhaps, he thought, that had been her true genius, to read that in him, to know how to make him feel false to himself. That, and simply that her presence, even here, overwhelmed everything for him. It was also as if she were saying she was beyond his forgiveness, receiving it, caring about it, needing it.

Trying to hide a sudden flash of anger, he saw her satisfaction now as she detected it; had she once more brought that out in him, a spurt of anger even as he was forgiving her, to make him betray himself? How could he forgive her, and yet be furious at her for her lack of caring about his offering of that forgiveness? He stood. "Well, I think that's all, that's all." It was still the same battle of wills over something neither of them understood. He thought about the Bertram and whoever her partner in stealing it had been, and that Dickerson was going to try to get that name, and he thought almost with satisfaction that he'd never get her cooperation. He realized that he might finally win this battle now—of the held and withheld—by his ability to simply walk out of jail.

She watched him. He wanted to go, but he still felt a pull from her. With a determination not to meet her eyes again, he walked toward the door.

Behind him, she said, "Val." He stopped, but didn't turn. "Is this what you've been waiting for?" He looked back at her. "To hear me speak without a Southern accent—isn't that what's it's really been about, the visit?"

He realized she was right. "No, but part of it."

"And how do I sound, Val?"

"Like Dickerson said you did." ·

"And how's that?"

"Like an educated girl from Philadelphia. Like a girl who read her way through a library after her father stopped talking to her."

He started walking quickly toward the guard shack and the parking lot beyond. With each step, he felt off balance. She had been there for seventeen years as Lee Anne; yet all of that time, it was as if someone or something were just a half step behind her, something coming out of a distance. Now he knew what was there—it had been this necessary invention of hers. She'd opened the front door and delivered her father to the man who killed him and shot her mother. Unbearable. He had been held by the brilliant fabrication, the shining lie and fierce will of it. A few minutes ago he'd heard her speak, her Southern accent gone—just like that. He'd loved her, Lee Anne, but she was gone. Hearing her voice seemed to be the final release. Lee Anne, herself, was out of Lee Anne. And he, Val suddenly realized, was out of whatever he'd needed from her as Lee Anne, whatever had been holding and suffocating him.

He walked unsteadily toward the waiting taxi. Now, he saw that his father, too, had been so driven by a similar kind of fabrication—his version of American success—that he killed a large part of himself to make it work; when Davis hadn't been able to meet that narrow, meticulous standard, desperate, enraged, he'd denied Davis, whom he'd loved more than anyone. Yet Davis had gotten his message completely, and when he no longer had a football field, a baseball diamond, a track, a pole-vaulting pit, he'd started living out his father's vision of success upside down and backward—Val shook his head at the grotesque irony—in a kind of dyslexia of action; he'd re-invented himself as a thief, and in the process, poisoned himself; he'd traded his father's vision for the cheap thrills of being a crook, of getting over, getting one up, kicking ass, of proving his father wrong, a kind of suicide by spite and revenge.

Halfway to the taxi, Val stopped. He became aware of himself just standing there. When he'd married Kazzie, he'd made a choice to go to the sane world. Kazzie had been his first step. Living far away in Arizona, another.

But he'd been carrying them—his father, Lee Anne, Davis—inside all this time, living within their craziness. They'd continued to hold him tight. He'd been trying to get out when he'd taken the picture of Davis and gone to see Lee Anne. He was, he realized, out now, all the way out.

# VAL

## *His Father's Voice*

Running out of air, Val swam hard for the surface, gasped awake, panting and disoriented.... Where was he? Slowly, his hard breathing started to subside. He noticed a blanket had been laid over him.... Remembered that Kazz had gone to bed early and that he and Michael had been watching TV.

Since he'd returned home, several weeks now, Michael had been asking him questions, one, two at a time; he asked them almost in passing, incidentally, barely seeming to pay attention to Val's answers, often walking out of the room when Val least expected it. Val answered everything he asked: what Davis had really been doing in Miami; and how he'd gotten kicked out of Clemson; and how he'd showed up in North Carolina alone and how his girlfriend had followed. He told Michael how they had had a misunderstanding over Lee Anne—was that the right word?—the night before Davis had gone overboard. He told how she had come to find him in Brooklyn, and how angry she'd been when Val left her—she'd wanted something from him, more than he'd understood or was possible to give, and how the last day he saw her she gave him that picture of Davis driving the boat, but wouldn't say more about it—which was why Val hadn't ever been able to answer Michael's questions about Davis.

Val told Michael that he had been afraid of doing what his father had done with Davis, and that he needed to find out exactly what had happened if he wasn't going to repeat it with Michael, "...and I thought Lee Anne knew." To all of his answers, Michael had stared blankly at Val, sometimes nodded once or twice, then seemed to disappear; Val would look out and Michael would be rocketing up from the trampoline, upside down against the burning, desert sky, golden hair exploding around his head; later, he'd reappear, silent, distant, ask more questions. Val held back nothing—the unsigned postcards, how he'd panicked in Lee Anne's house, how terrified he been when the boat had rolled over ten miles off shore in the dark.

Val turned on his side, stared across the living room. Earlier, they'd been watching *The X-Files*. As he'd leaned across Michael to get a pillow, he sniffed toward him for the odor of cigarettes, marijuana, a kind of poisonous variation on a kiss which Val had developed with Michael in the last couple of years and which he hated in himself; he hated the distrust. He'd said, "Michael, by now you've figured out there's really nothing I can do to stop you from doing drugs, or whatever you're doing with your friends." Michael gave no indication that he'd heard; his face remained closed. "Our seeing a counselor didn't seem to change it, and if we see him again…" Val shrugged. They watched Mulder put on rubber gloves and pick up something with tweezers, hold it up to the light. Goddamnit, was Michael listening to him or not? "I can't stop you if you don't want to be stopped. So just talk to me. Are you…" he trailed off. This was impossible…. The baggie of white pills he'd taken out of Michael's pocket. Mulder put whatever he'd found into some kind of specimen bag. Val forced himself. "Michael, are you using drugs? Still using them?"

Michael stared at the TV. His face was hard, impenetrable.

Val said, "Michael, I can't stop you. I can't even really punish you. I mean, I can forbid you to do this or that, but I know it's not going to have any real effect, and it'll make things awful. I'm not going to have a war with you until you're out of reach. We've just got to try to do something different." Michael still didn't answer. "Michael, did you hear me?"

When he thought Michael wasn't going to answer, Val gathered himself to walk out of the room in sullen protest. Michael said, "Yeah, I've been doing some shit, but it's all like, kind of, whatever, but…yeah."

"Do you know why you're doing it?"

Almost as if considering this for the first time, Michael remained silent. Val said, "Beside the fact that sometimes it's fun…"

Michael shifted, crossed his huge bare feet. "No, can't say. Not really."

"Thank you for answering me. Really." Michael still didn't take his eyes from the TV. "Can you just keep talking to me? I told you. I can't punish you. I can't stop you. So if you'll just talk to me...."

Michael seemed to consider that. Then, without answering, he said, "Are you going back to being a lawyer?"

"I've got some offers to go into private practice, but I'm not sure. Sometimes it seems that you like the idea of my being a lawyer a lot better than being an art teacher."

"You could make more money."

"Right, that's true."

"I mean, like, why'd you go to law school it if you didn't want to do it? Like, that's fucked."

"Sometimes people just change. Back when I started I was just going along with something. Maybe I was afraid to do what I really wanted."

When Val was absolutely certain that Michael hadn't heard him—he checked a sudden urge to turn off the tube—Michael said, "Like what?

"Like building or designing boats. My father discouraged me from it. I was just starting to head back in that direction when Davis had his accident." Annoyed with himself for his veiled reference, he said more emphatically, "When Davis was pulled overboard. After that, I didn't want to be near boats."

Michael didn't reply. He watched the commercial. God, why couldn't Michael just look directly at him? Then Val realized that Michael was listening to every word, but couldn't show that he cared so much. "Michael, what do you want?"

Michael said suddenly, "I want you to stop making that *gabacho* face when I don't do something you, like, want."

"What face?"

"The one you just made. This one." Michael showed him.

Val recognized it, an expression his father used to make him feel bad, show that he'd hurt him. Val's first reaction was to deny it, that *couldn't* be him, but then he nodded. "Okay. I will. Help me. Tell me when I do it."

They drifted into watching *The X-Files*, neither of them saying more, and after a while, Val slid down on the sofa, the sound of the music and voices fading.... Far away, Michael, towering above, spread a blanket over him. Now Val noticed, felt it gathered around him. Michael hadn't done anything like that before. Then Val remembered he thought he'd been awakened by the front door closing. Whenever Michael had been kind or considerate with him in the past, it was to set up a deception, his sneaking out with friends. The next thing would be a phone call from the cops, the drive to some twenty-four-hour, Circle K parking lot, the blue strobe lights, the electrostatic sound of cop radios.... Val took a deep breath, lay quietly listening into the house, fighting back his distrust, his fear.

Val threw back the blanket and walked down the hall to Michael's room. He hesitated, heart pounding, before the closed door, bracing himself for the hall light across the empty bed. Then it would be the hours of waiting, hoping the phone would ring, dreading its ringing in the silence of the late night. He pushed open the door.

Cereal bowls dried up, spoons still in them. Piles of clothes everywhere. Lights on the stereo and CD player. An unidentifiable part of an engine lying in the middle of the floor where it had been for days, twists of wire coming out of it. The results of an EKG under his foot, the spider-leg weave across the graph paper from when Michael had gone in for a physical. Val listened to the rise and fall of Michael's breathing, looked down at him huge in the bed, blond hair spread across the pillow, his hand across his chest as if he were an after-dinner speaker rising to face an audience. His hand was covered with ink. Val leaned closer. An interwoven tangle of names and phone numbers, single words. Val tipped his head, trying to make them out, but they remained an indecipherable weave of smudged numbers, names, doodles. And, Val realized, he was going to leave them that way—undeciphered. He would have to trust that Michael could go out the door each day and return, and that each day Val was not going to be fighting a battle to keep him from suddenly disappearing. He understood that he had to have been sending that message to Michael, terrifying him with his own terror, that the world was sudden, deadly and arbitrary. Val would trust that he could act without being his own father with Davis, that things could be all right. He'd have to let Michael go. Val gently picked up his hand, kissed it, placed it back on Michael's chest. Sighing, Michael turned on his side and pulled his knees up to his chest.

In the living room, Val walked back and forth, picking things up, putting them down. He realized that he believed that his father had never really forgiven him for losing Davis, but now he understood that in his own way, he had never forgiven his father for being so hurt, so destroyed, so mortally wounded. He was beginning to remember things long forgotten, the sound of his father's voice when he'd asked him how he was doing, the love and tenderness in it, which seemed to be flowing into a new fragile love he and Kazz were feeling.

He noticed a letter that had come earlier in the day. Kazz had frowned with apprehension at its legal letterhead. Val said, "Don't worry. It's not trouble. It's an invitation to talk about joining Aaron Brown's law firm."

"How great. And?"

"I'm thinking about it. For the first time in my life, I don't feel a pressure, like I have to do something, make a decision."

Maybe he'd go back to being a defense attorney; he still had a real sympathy for the Tom Jacksons, for the Val Martins—ordinary guys who were driven to do something that seemed inexplicable, destructive and stupid. Maybe he'd continue teaching art a while more; he was interested in what happened with kids, how they came to be who they were, but now, if he went on, he wouldn't feel that he was failing by not doing something else he was supposed to be doing—his father's vision of success. He'd be doing it for its own sake.

Kazz set the letter down and put her arm around him.

Now he caught some movement across the room, which flooded him with adrenaline before he realized it was his reflection in the sliding glass door. He drifted toward it until his face was almost touching the glass. At times he could still feel the Atlantic freezing in his marrow as he'd hung on to the boat through the night, feeling the terrifying infinity of the black ocean. He could still hear Lee Anne's voice as he kept trying to separate out the pieces of what she'd told him from what he thought he knew or understood. Had she actually been married to Davis? It wasn't, finally, knowable. Dickerson had not turned up any record of it. Still, he heard her voice, her Southern accent, heard her say, "Part of you wants me to be this way"; he had to keep reminding himself that there had never actually been a Lee Anne.

Val pressed his face to the glass and cupped his hands around his eyes and looked out into the dark. He flicked the switch and the pool light came on. He remained motionless staring at the water light trembling silver into the underside of the olive tree.

# LEE ANNE

### *Clairol Black*

…sweltering in here, I run the tap into my cupped palm, remain motionless as I'm caught by a glint of light, the lines of my palm magnified through the lens of water, drops seeping between my fingers and trickling from my knuckles, and then as I lean forward and close my eyes, as I touch my forehead to the water, I think of a bird swooping to a puddle…

I'm just getting back to my cell after another visit with the shrink, and I'm filled with the echoes of voices…. I talk to so many different people now. I talk to the cop, Dickerson; I talk to my mother; I talk to people who are not here. I go on talking to Val, who, along with Dickerson, conned me with the wire though maybe a little part of me knew something was up; and, like, of course, the shrink, mistress of after-the-fact perception, has suggested that yes, some small part of me knew something was fucked and went ahead anyway and maybe even wanted to get caught, though that just tells me what she knows about getting taken down; and of course, in her world, whatever I did, it's not for up-front reasons, like I just fucked up, or even guilt; no, her world isn't like that, but it's more like once Lee Anne was caught, I could become myself again, that I wanted to become myself again, Christine Desjardins…. And how else could that happen, but that I get forced into the light? She has been slowly constructing an obvious little theory, and I'm just rolling with it, and, like, I can't stop her, anyway. And who can ever know anything for sure, so I talk and I let her play or rather she just does…

And whatever it is, it's done now and there's no going back or second-guessing it. Except for the fact that he took me down on it, part of me kind of loves Val for his conning me and pulling it off. And however it plays out, though the law is using the word *murder* for what's happened with Brent, what they say I did, *murder*, I never once really saw it that way.... It just happened a step at a time, it led, I followed, and whatever I did or did not do, whatever else can be said, however it is put together or taken apart, I saved Val's life that night. He knows it and I know it. Strangely, I talk to Brent... or more, maybe I see Brent, feel the thing he always brought with him, a kind of terror, or maybe just a suddenness. Hard to know exactly how to put that, though I think it's important. I keep seeing the newspaper photo of his body on the deck of the trawler in the snarl of anchor line, arms and legs torn ragged by sharks, teeth marks.... Just now, I'm not sure about the man who comes to the door, where he is, where he's gone, but I can feel him there. In a way, I have no real recollection of him, of his having been there, but still I sense something different now. I talk to Dickerson, even when he's not here. When he comes in, I watch him traveling in his narrowing concentric circles; sometimes it makes me want to laugh; he says things like, *we know you had help on the Bertram, give us the names of the boat thieves, cooperate with us, help yourself, a lot of things will be taken into consideration before this plays out.* He makes me want to laugh. A lot of things will be taken into consideration. I just look right through him. Give him a few names and get help when you're going to trial.... Sometimes I just want to laugh.

But right now I'm back here in my cell and I'm alone again. Today the shrink got me talking about Lee Anne and that time just before I left school and how I became Lee Anne and it was all just practical, is all, an accident, something that came to me in a toilet stall, Lee Anne happened to be the name on the driver's license. When I said that, the shrink sat up like, oh, this is going to be significant, and I just laughed because I knew I wasn't going to be able to get her to take the psychology out of what I'd just said, make her see that it was practical, the plain real world, funny, how else can I say it?

She said, "Well, before Lee Anne, you just disappeared...your mother said that you went back to school freshman year, Middlebury College, this was right after the Christmas vacation, but then a few weeks later you suddenly left, left everything as it was, even your 3" x 5" cards arranged in order. What happened that day?

"It was 'The Pardoner's Tale.' Chaucer."

"The only thing the police found that even remotely suggested that you might have had a plan was a bottle of Clairol hair coloring. Was it yours?"

I don't answer. Stupid question. Of course it was mine…. It was my one mistake. Maybe I'm a perfectionist. How dumb of me to leave that empty bottle. I always wondered what I'd been thinking about. Maybe some small part of me wanted it as a goodbye…or as a way back. Maybe.

I say, "I was trying to get that paper going and decided to take a break. I put on my coat and went out for a walk. Everything was frozen. January. Vermont. The river through the middle of town was frozen into silence. I followed the river a ways and then made my way down the bank and walked out onto the ice; the ice was crying and groaning in the freezing air, letting out these sudden dry explosions, I can still hear them; kneeling, I put my face to the ice, I cupped my hands around my eyes, and looking down I thought I could make out something down below, a car; I think it was a wreck down there in the freezing water; I could feel that black water going somewhere under the ice and then it was simple. I realized I didn't have to be here, stay here, and maybe it was as I was standing or coming up the riverbank, I already knew, the beginning, what next, I went into the drugstore and bought a candy bar, but really I went in to steal a bottle of hair dye; I knew it had to be stolen, because I already knew I'd be getting on a bus and sooner or later the cops would come asking questions, the girl at the register, *do you remember seeing someone who looked like this?* and I didn't want to give her anything to remember, *oh, yeah, she came in and bought a bottle of hair dye* and then, like, maybe they'd kind of know, like, she's out there, so I stole it and that way nobody would know anything…. I just knew to do that, always knew to do that, I was born with it, knew that there would always be someone coming after me or coming back to find me, cops, someone, and that I had to make myself invisible, hide, keep moving, watch out…. All this time, on and off, I thought about the one stupid thing, which was to leave that empty Clairol bottle in the trash in the dorm bathroom.

"The hardest part was my mother, leaving her like without a word, it's not easy to explain about my mother…that it was all there between us everything that could be said and not said, everything forgotten, half-remembered, always there and not there. Right before I went back to school in January she married Dwight. Of course I was there at the wedding, and I had warned her that he is after the settlement money. She thought that I wasn't adjusting, that naturally she understood my feelings, my complex, difficult feelings, as she liked to say, she tried to talk to me, I didn't tell her that this wasn't about my *complex difficult feelings*. But it was. What I really knew in my heart is that much as I couldn't stand her, her limp and her funny slur, she was mine, and I was hers, we were there that day, and she was the one who knew how it had been before on all the other days, and then, the days after, we had lived, together, we had lived, I had her, and she had me, and I couldn't have Dwight there, he was a fuck.... Anyway, she went ahead and remarried and part of me said okay I am going to do what I'm going to do; I didn't know yet what that was until I came up that frozen riverbank and even then didn't know any more than dye my hair and leave. I had absolutely no idea how long I'd be gone. None. If you'd told me that it would be years, half my life, I wouldn't have believed it."

"Your mother took a second husband and you were going to take on being Lee Anne.... If she could do this, then you could do that."

Half the time I never know if she is asking me a question or making a statement. Tricky inflections. I just shook my head.

I said, "Lee Anne didn't exist yet...how could she have? I didn't know where I was going. I hadn't reached Miami. I didn't know about Lee Anne yet. Can I state this any more clearly? I do not have multiple personalities. None of this will fit into a theory or a psych book. Hey, I read, too. Let me make that good and fucking clear to you. Lee Anne was an actual person. I had not met her yet. Are we together here?"

She doesn't answer me, as in, like, *yes, I understand*. She has her agenda. I know what that is about.

"But you *had* dyed your hair so you could get out of town and disappear for good..."

"I didn't know how long it was going to be. *For a while* was all I knew."

"You did it very well—disappeared—you became Lee Anne and were gone for years."

"I just told you, I had no idea it would be years. None. One afternoon I just left."

I shrugged. It's easy to say anything after the fact. But not right. At the time I was just... I just did things, what I had to do, the next thing, each step led me to Lee Anne. It was like that with Brent. Now Dickerson calls it murder...it wasn't like that...it was just one thing and the next thing until someone calls it something, Lee Anne, murder and it kind of startles you, that's not me...

Anyway, I told her I went back to the dorm, locked the bathroom door, and dyed my hair from my natural honey blond to black—that was one of my favorite colors, black, and I looked in the mirror and I did not recognize myself, it was like I was still waiting for myself to arrive even while I was looking at myself and then I knew it would work and wearing a scarf and glasses and weird cheap lipstick and nail polish, I got on the bus…. I was still Christine Desjardins, but not; didn't look like her, wasn't going to do whatever she did, be where she was, had been, anymore; knew that much; I was in motion, going somewhere, waiting to find out where. I was in limbo. I was sleepwalking.

We talk some more, Lee Anne, Lee Anne in Miami, and then we run out of time and end the session there and I am taken back to my cell.

But the echo of my voice to the shrink has me seeing and hearing things I've forgotten…getting off a train in Philadelphia in the middle of the day— was it the next day?—and I'm not sure how I got there—maybe a cab—but then I was standing in front of our old house, the one we'd lived in before my mother was taken to the hospital and I went to live with my aunt—I hadn't been back there since—I didn't know the way or even knew I remembered, but there I was and I just stood in front of it, a simple white two-story house with a lawn and shrubs, still white, still the same—was it? It had snowed a few days before, a thin white covering—and I stood in the street looking at the house, the bare branches of the trees rising and falling against the blue sky; I paced back and forth, stopped and stood, paced, and then I walked up to the front door and stood looking at it; I peeked in the sidelight windows, down the front hall toward the back of the house. I cupped my hands around my eyes and saw a door off to one side, but I couldn't really see much so I stepped back and came around and slid behind the evergreen shrubs, almost to my shoulders, and looked in the window. There was a sofa and a TV and an easy chair and some built-in bookshelves; even though I didn't know any of it, I still felt like there was something missing, something that I had once known very well….

Then I pushed through the shrubs and followed along the side of the house and I came around into the backyard and there were flowerbeds—had they been there before? If so, were they the same or different? It was hard to tell because they were covered with snow, and I think I remembered flowers glowing in the sun; as I crossed the yard, here was a trellis, with bare vines wrapped around it, arching over a backyard walk. Did I know that? Looking at the house I started wondering if it was the right house and what exactly I was doing here.

I walked to the back patio crusted with snow, and then up to the French doors and peered down the hall and saw the front door from the inside. Again, I cupped my hands around my eyes and I could see the lower half of the banister and staircase, which rose up and disappeared from view. I closed my eyes and felt myself going up those stairs, turning at the landing, reaching the second floor, then turning again, left, and going down the hall. I tried the handle on the back door, shook the door. I stepped back from the house, looked up and found my old bedroom window on the second floor—it was, wasn't it? Springs and summers I'd lie on the bed and look through the thick heavy branches that grew right up to the house, look through the leaves at the garden—or was I just telling myself that?—the tree, bare now, would be huge and green and grown right up over the window, it was like you were in a tree house.... I could watch the squirrels darting on the branches. I looked over at the tree, the branches etched with snow, and saw several of the thick lower branches amputated at the trunk, for a second I had the sensation of something rising and moving through the air or in a mirror and light suddenly flooding the space around me, something splintering, and I looked down at my boots in the snow and thought of my mother, newly remarried in her house somewhere on the other side of town...

I close my eyes and when I open them I see someone standing in the window in the house, a woman, my mother, she's frozen, she's staring at me, she is picking something up, I see her starting to dial, and I realize from the look on her face that she is terrified and is calling 911, and I turn and start to run across the yard toward the street...

Then I am on the bus, and brown fields are rolling by outside the windows as we move south, the sunlight changing, brightening, deepening, no longer the hard, piano-key white of snow and ice, and I see water flowing, water in rivers, catching the blue sky, water in ponds and lakes, and I unbutton my thick winter jacket and open it some, I'm listening to people talking in Southern accents, it is like the sun deepening, the ice melting, the bus moves in and out of bus stations and I can smell things, the ground, it is as if I'm waking up and following a current flowing in the air and it is drawing me somewhere, the bus keeps rolling and I drift in and out of sleep, morning, afternoon, early evening, a sailor sleeping across the aisle, then the sailor gone and a woman reading a Golden Book to a kid on her lap in a beam of light, drifting off, again I'm in that snowy backyard looking up at the tree with its amputated branches and the woman inside picking up the phone, 911, and I'm starting to run, and I wake with a start, it is morning, I open my eyes and the light is blinding and brilliant outside the window, and there are green palm trees—I'd seen them in pictures—and the buildings are white and then I'm walking through the Greyhound station in Miami carrying my heavy winter coat, all these people in sports shirts and summer dresses, so I just lay it on a bench, and I, like, turn and walk away and just leave it there.

...I'm just standing, people walking by, and I'm thinking about going into the bathroom to wash up when I see a woman coming toward me and something about her surprises me, I can't take my eyes off her, and in another second I see what it is, she looks just like me except she has bleached blond hair, I hear her call to someone I don't see in a thick Southern accent, "Jesus H. Christ, just fucking hold your fucking horses, Freddie, I'll be right back, or like, better yet, if you don't like it, you can just kiss my ass!" and something about the way she says that makes me laugh, the cockiness of it, and she walks right by so close I can almost touch her, I turn and watch her a moment, and then I follow her into the ladies' room, she stops in front of the mirror, takes a brush out of a purse, starts to brush her hair, and then, shaking her head, she sighs and gives up and heads into one of the stalls, and I slip into the stall next to her, I've got nothing in mind, I'm sitting there and I hear her on her side, people are coming in and going out, there's a big commotion, toilets flushing, water running, a couple of black girls laughing and joking, I look down and notice she's put her purse on the floor I can see it in the space under the metal partition between us, the brush handle sticking out, and then I hear her toilet flush, I see her get up and walk out, the purse still there, my first impulse is to call her, *hey, you forgot your purse*, but I don't, I slide it toward me, I catch the brush as I lift it, this brush thick with bleached blond hair, I look at it, raise the hair to my nose—thick perfumed animal smell—I push the brush back inside, notice her wallet, several twenties sticking out of the top, I'm completely broke now, but I'm not sure, still, maybe just the money, but then I think she looks exactly like me, I take the wallet, and I close the purse and slide it back under the partition; a second later, she's back in the stall, she grabs the purse, I hear her, "Sonavabitch!" in that Southern accent, and I sit there a moment scared shitless, her wallet on my lap, thinking what can I do? I can always say, if she notices it's gone and comes after me, *oh, this fell out, I was just going to finish in here and give it to you*, I wait a few minutes and she doesn't come back and then I decide the best thing to do is get out of here quick, I jam the wallet into my pocket and when I come out of the stall a woman is mopping the floor and she stops and gives me a long look like what the fuck but I don't think she really knows anything, I don't wait to find out, I just get out of there as quick as I can, bolt out of that bus station, and I'm about three blocks away before I slow up, turn around and I think I expected to see the girl and about fifty cops after me, but there was no one, just people walking around, and so I ducked into a store, opened the wallet, my hands were shaking, and I couldn't believe it, there were a couple of hundred dollars and a bunch of tickets from the dog track, some credit cards, and her driver's license, it was a picture ID, a University of Florida ID, and a couple of blank checks, and I see her ID pictures, it's like looking back at myself, and underneath, her name, Lee Anne Wilder, and I look at my watch and figure, okay, don't get greedy, you've got maybe an hour or two before she notices and can do anything, I went out, charged some new clothes, a bag, some cosmetics, found a branch of her bank and wrote a check for a couple of hundred more dollars—I didn't want it to be too big and call attention to myself. When the teller asked for my ID, I gave her Lee Anne's driver's license and the UF ID, my hands were shaking, she studied me hard, I was just turning to run when she said, "I think I like you better as you were, a blond, you know?" I couldn't make sense of it and then I remembered my hair dyed black, nodded, I thought of Lee Anne's accent, didn't think I could do it yet, and just in time I remembered to nod and smile and she counted out the money. I got out of there and dumped the wallet, kept the ID and credit cards, I had a few hundred dollars now, I just wanted the cards long enough to get something going for myself here, get some breathing room, and then I'd get rid of them, see what's next. I looked down at the photograph, I heard her, what'd she say? "Jesus H. Christ, just fucking hold your fucking horses, Freddie, I'll be right back, or like, better yet, if you don't like it, you can just kiss my ass!" in her Southern accent, I heard her voice, the cockiness, the will and the fire in it, and I said it just like she said it, said it out loud and loved it and laughed.

Using the cash, I got a one-room studio apartment, found a job waiting tables in a bar... I went to the beach, in no time I was tan; started putting together how it was going to be for Lee Anne, like translating myself from one language into another. I would think, this might be good for Lee Anne. I'd overhear someone talking and think, yes, that. I'd see a dress in the back of a Goodwill or Salvation Army and pull it off the rack and hold it in front of me in the mirror and I'd know right away, yes, like, yes, or else, nothing, there'd be no hit, and I'd put it back. I'd think, would Lee Anne say that, do that? But after a while I didn't have to wonder, I'd just know it and do it. Second nature. I'd see something, a bracelet, shoes, I'd know, get those for Lee Anne. I was inventing myself out of two picture IDs, a name, a thirty-second glimpse I'd caught of a woman, and twenty words I'd overheard in a Southern accent at the Greyhound station. *Kiss my ass.* I could hear her talking in me. *Kiss my ass.*

Sometimes I had to fight the urge to call and talk with the real Lee Anne, find out who or what she really was, if she were anything like my Lee Anne, but of course I couldn't, though I did think seriously about at least going to find her and just follow her around for a while and see what she was like inside her life, find out about Freddie and the dog track and the courses she'd been taking and if she ever finished at UF and where she came from, like, originally, if it was Florida or Georgia or, like, where, and what her natural hair color was and I don't know what all else, where she got her clothes and worked and things like that, but, like, I couldn't, I was too busy being her, and anyway, I'd stolen from her, I mean, her money, I just couldn't do it, though sometimes I thought she might have been the kind of chick who could have invited me in and had a big laugh with me over it all—well, if I paid her back—though you can never tell, she might have just called the cops…it was just a thought that would come and go…me and the real Lee Anne.

My Lee Anne…. It was scary, but at the same time it was like being high, stoned, surprised yet sure of the next thing. I just got more and more confident as Lee Anne got smarter and more sure of herself in every situation. Every once in a while I'd have a kind of blackout, panic, it would be like just like hold on, where am I? what am I doing? and at times it seemed like, okay, like, stop, I want out, it felt like I was building something around me… like I could reach out and feel something silently wrapping itself tighter and tighter around me, I wasn't sure, but if I wanted to, could I get out of it, what would it take? At times in Brooklyn I was so close with Val, I knew if I could do it with anyone, it would be with him, it was just on my tongue, in the next breath, but I couldn't quite do it, I saw it in his face, he had to have me like this, once when I knew I was driving him crazy I told him just

that, *part of you wants me to be this way*, part of it, was his fault, I think—
wasn't it? I was so close, but then, too, she kept holding on to me, I mean,
I needed to know what else she would do, where she was going, and then,
too, I kept thinking, what happens once I stop, and all the time Christine
Desjardins was still there, I knew that, though I couldn't say exactly how,
I never stopped caring about myself, Christine, I'd think of my mother,
hear her slurred speech, her fragile voice sliding, groping for vowels, for the
shapes of words, and then I'd be standing in the snow in the backyard looking up at the tree, the heavy lower limbs amputated, I'd heard something
far off coming toward me in the air, turn suddenly a flash of light above
or behind me in the mirror, see *The Pardoner's Tale* still open on my desk
and the words I was going to write in my notes at the bottom of the page
still turning over in my mind as I cupped my hands around my eyes and
looked down through the ice on the river.... Christine was always there,
maybe always waiting, I wasn't sure what, exactly, Christine was doing. Just,
like, maybe that I knew I'd always liked her, wanted to see her again, knew
somehow, someday, sooner or later, I'd get back to her or she'd find a way
to come back to me.... I was never sure when, it was never the right time,
and beyond Lee Anne, beyond Christine, I could feel someone or something
else there and always waiting....

In the meantime, I was just fascinated day by day watching and waiting
to see what would happen with Lee Anne, what I'd do with her, or she with
me. And, like, I met Davis as Lee Anne at the Allure College of Beauty. I
think part of me always kind of hoped to tell Davis about the Lee Anne
thing, all of it, how it happened, and to come out of it and be myself and
have him still love me, but I never got to do it, Davis just disappeared before
I could, first we fought, then we stopped talking, then he disappeared, never
came back, and sometimes just that one thing bothers me, that he never
knew me any other way but Lee Anne.

The shrink constructs her theory, like I invented Lee Anne until I could
become Christine again.... She makes me laugh. I wasn't the one who forgot
that purse under the toilet stall that morning in Miami. It was the real Lee
Anne did. Forget it. Forgot. The purse. I wasn't trying to be broke and find
a wallet with picture ID, money, credit cards.... I mean, it was like real life,
what I had to do.... I had cut it off with everyone and everything. I needed
her money, her credit cards, her ID. The rest just started happening a step
at a time.

But she goes on from there, the shrink. And what it is, like, is I think she is suggesting that I was trying to recreate the worst event of my life—maybe even over and over—by pitting two men against each other, but like make it come out right this time, the right man lives, and I'm kind of rolling with it as it is my ass on the line, and I'm not sure how my lawyer uses it in my defense, maybe help with leveraging a plea, maybe use it for mitigation in the penalty phase if I'm convicted, the crazier they make me, the better off I am, I don't know, I just let them go on with it, can't stop them anyway, but like, if anyone bothered to ask me, I'd tell them I think I knew exactly what I was doing, or how can I say this? it knew exactly what it was doing; that day on the Orient Point ferry, I could feel that water below, hear the engines moaning, my purse fat with cash, craps and blackjack, my midsection still watery and falsely menstrual from the miscarriage, *damage* the doctor said, and that damage came out of Val and me in Brooklyn; it was all real life; later I dreamed Val came by water, I saw him in the house where he actually came to stand, silvery flash of sky and horizon off that ashen mirror on the ferry, something I suddenly knew, always knew, all of it, water, I knew exactly what I was doing, it was coming back and I was going out…

I said to the shrink, "Hey, if you know so much, tell me, am I more Lee Anne than Christine?" and she just looked at me and smiled like she knew better or maybe better than to answer; they love to turn your questions around on you with smiles, raising an eyebrow, blank expressions. She didn't answer. I said, "Like, let me put it this way, which one do you think you're talking to now, Lee Anne or Christine?" and she said, "Are you testing me?" and I said, "No I'm asking you," but she still didn't answer, then she said, "Well you're not talking in a Southern accent now, I do know that much," and I thought, that really doesn't matter, but we both laughed, though that hardly told anyone anything…

…like now the shrink has her theory, and I think my lawyer wants it all played out, thinks it might help, but hey, what kind of theory would there be if my mother hadn't turned up, she was the one who got this whole thing going when she saw my picture in the paper and went to Dickerson with those old newspaper clippings about my father…. But, like, if it weren't for that, I know there'd be no shrink theory about recreating the event or my pitting two men against each other, and if Val hadn't come in on the deck of that trawler with Brent's body, then there'd be none of this, no theory, no psychological opportunism, how about someone just calling it bad fucking luck, and I'd have the money and property and all the rest of it, there wouldn't be all these questions about how much I remember, and the fact is, it's always been a blank, is still a blank, though I could feel funny things I couldn't explain moving inside me.

But since it's all happened and the shrink started talking to me and asking me questions I keep kind of feeling myself more and more back in this place where part of it is me standing out in the snow behind the house looking up at my old bedroom window—it was, wasn't it?—part of it is my looking in that front window and knowing something was no longer there.... And I guess what I realize is that I don't want to go inside.... That's all I know. Voices. Echoes. Questions as I come back to my cell from seeing the shrink. Christine. Lee Anne....

## ...please, please, please...

That night I wake up moaning, no idea where I am, caught in the crack between waking and sleeping, yet I am inside, too, I look up from the piano keys, I hear the piece, "Für Elise," I see a flash in the mirror above the piano, a sudden change in the light, someone behind me cutting across the front lawn, and I stop for a second, then go on playing, I see him float close by the front window, I stop when I hear the doorbell, and I get up and go to the front door and open it, a man standing there, beautiful eyes, uneven blue some parts like slate others bright and large dark pupils and he smiles at me, he has gentle eyes, but at the same time I have a funny feeling about his eyes, something pleading pulls me toward them. He is wearing a blue suit jacket, has his hands pushed down into his side pockets, and he's like my dad on Sunday mornings when he hasn't shaved, whiskers...gentle, but there's something about him.

He has the softest, gentlest voice to go with his eyes, says, "I heard your playing just now. Beethoven. "Für Elise." It was lovely, your playing." I think he is very shy because his voice trembles. Still held by his gaze, I nod. "May I ask you if your father is home?" He smiles, but I notice his lips quiver. Though it's spring, maybe he's cold.

I nod again.

"Could you tell him I'm here?"

I close the door, then come back.

"Who should I say it is?"

"Tell him…" He smiled, "Tell him it's me. He'll know."

Dad will know, it's all right, and I find him outside in the back garden. He is on his knees weeding among the flowers and there is the warm smell of sun and the earth and he looks up at me, each tulip glowing, reds, blacks, whites. He smiles and I tell him there is someone at the door and he asks who and I tell him what the man told me, that he said he'd know, he said, *tell him it's me*, and then Dad looks uncertain and stands and brushes off his pants and goes toward the house, wiping his feet at the French doors. I see him walking down the hall. I am behind him he opens the front door and I see the man with the gentle blue eyes waiting and the second he sees my father his eyes change, a suddenness, they brighten, come to points like nails his whole face changes he becomes another person he pulls his hands out of his pockets something in his hand my father grabs that hand and staggers backward they spin and jam just inside the front door my mother hears the noise and calls out I see her run into the hall just as there is a shot my father stumbles backward there is another shot he stiffens and falls another shot my mother falls in front of me.… he walks toward me I can't move he puts his hand on me holds the gun to my forehead, I hear someone whispering, *please, please, please*, he looks down at me, he seems startled to notice me even recognize or remember me suddenly he turns he steps over my mother and father as he walks back down the hall runs out the front door…

…then he is gone the front door wide open and I hear someone still saying, *please, please, please*…over and over, I have the phone in my hand when I look up there are people running in, neighbors, men in uniforms, I run upstairs to my room, turn the key, lock the door, push my bed against it, my dresser, pile everything up in front of it, outside people are calling my name, *Christine, Christine*, they stop calling, they go away and it is silent, and then I sense something moving in my dresser mirror, I whirl and see a man rising through the air he stops in midair he floats and I hear an engine start loud, I run to the window, I see the first of the heavy branches that grow up to the side of the house crashing down below into the yard, white sky light pours into my bedroom, another branch crashes down there is more light, I lock the window, then it is quiet, the chain saw is gone, I see the man standing in the basket as his hands work the levers in front of him, he floats toward the house until he fills my window huge in his thick black coat he waves at me, he shouts, *it's okay, Christine, I'm a fireman, no one's going to hurt you, I'm here to help you*; he pulls up on the window, it doesn't open, now he has something in his hand, a crowbar, he fits it to the bottom of the window; he yells, *get back from the window*, I back up, the window frame gives a loud crack, the glass splinters and flies all over the floor, the lock pulls apart; he slides open the window and steps into my bedroom broken glass shining everywhere like ice, all the time he is talking quietly he is crunching across the glass, I keep backing up he comes walking toward me in his big boots then he kneels down in front of me and slowly puts out his hands for me the sweet smell of gas and cut green wood on his big hands.... He reaches up and pulls a piece of broken glass, bloody, out of my hair.

I hear myself moaning, where am I? The jail cell though I couldn't remember I know I've always been here those eyes the piano the shots the bodies in the hall...

At my aunt's house I am free, happy even, here I am someone, it's wrong but it's my secret, I am a new person, I can do what I want, be who I want, a new school, too, there is something in the voices of the teachers that tells me they know I am different, I am always startled by the suddenness of my laugh, it sounds like someone else, not me, everyone invites me everywhere, and I go to everything, and I have to admit, it is my small secret, I love it, all the time it is almost as if I breathe a certain way or perhaps hold my breath then things are fine...later, I'm not sure when, maybe it's already a few years later, I can't be sure, I dance close with boys, first one, then the next, they know there is something different about me, the suddenness of my laugh, the way it surprises even me, the suddenness, it is part of the way I am special in my aunt's house, in my new school, in a few years they will dance with me, first one, then the next, then the first, something passing between us, and I know that I can make them do anything, though I don't know why, or even what I will make them do, just that I will, something about the way I come into a room, I just do what I want, make myself up...

Then my mother is back from the hospital and rehab, it's a long time, years, it feels like, and we are in a new house, there is money from insurance and a settlement, and truth be told I liked it better at my aunt's, I'm not so thrilled to be living with my mother again though that is not the way it sounds, I love her so much, too much, but there is part of me that just can't stand being with her, having her see me, seeing her, and it was always there, all those things that we never said, could never say are always there between us, I hate to see her with her stiff orthopedic shoe, the right one, the way she sometimes had to tug the back of her right knee with both hands to get her leg positioned so she could stand up, the background murmur of people saying her recovery is a kind of miracle, she is back from the dead, the brightness of her blond hair the way it says look at me, I'm alive, I'm not dead, and with her funny limp I think everyone is watching us, I hate being seen with her, and I hate myself for that, whenever we go out, I kind of linger too far behind her so people won't know she's mine, I'm hers, yet I am the only one who completely understands her slurred speech, waitresses and clerks and shopkeepers look at her baffled as if she is from a foreign country, and I translate for her, quick nervous breathless before she gets frustrated and starts raising her voice trying to be understood and everyone turns to look at us, I think everyone is watching us and I want to get away and hate myself for it because I love her too much…

They say my mother lost a lot of her memory—words, names, what happened, who she was, it's hard to tell, or even put into words, and I can never be sure how much and in what places, or how those places—her places—aren't my lost places…for me it's like what she's forgotten is like a place I once knew and now can't get back to, and I just let it be there however it is…the absences, hers, mine, there is something terrible that no one speaks about…it's in the absence…and her absence seems to be my absence… at times I can feel something moving in there, almost as if it is traveling, migrating, waking, sleeping, it is like the slur in her speech when she tries to bring up a word where nothing takes hold…

When I first heard Dickerson used the word *murder* for what had happened, I was stunned, as *murderer* is a word I never would apply to myself. And the shrink, the way she thinks I recreated a situation, the way she theorizes that I liked violent men, a certain kind of man, that they always made me feel on the edge of something, and something I would set right…. The shrink, Dickerson, they both do it, they take something after the fact and make it something different…. What is that? Dickerson says, the evidence speaks for itself. Knowingly and intentionally. The trip to Tucson to assess Val. The theft and scuttling of the Bertram for the insurance. The hotel receipts and airline tickets. More, to make Brent feel destroyed. And that Brent's death was my only profitable way out of a hopeless prenuptial agreement…. He says that I planned it meticulously, even artfully, that it was uncanny the way I knew I could bring Val back after all that time and use him…. Yet, though I see how it looks, none of it was clear to me, it was more that each step led to the next, was there and waiting, that I knew, but didn't know. I can see they don't believe me.

Even now I look down into it and it keeps changing. I don't remember killing Brent, but then I am looking down at him on the floor and there is the sense that I am here at last, that I'd been coming toward it and going away from it my whole life, or it had been coming toward me, and perhaps everything else I had done or lived or had been was a disguise, an invention and reinvention, myself inventing myself to reach it, or it hiding itself within my life until it reached me, and that sooner or later I had to get here.

I see what Dickerson says. I follow his reconstruction. I do. That I'd set Val up. All the steps I took. Yet once Val was there, I think I fought it, I wanted him to get away, get out of there…. I remember telling him to leave…. Maybe he'll say that in trial. I told him. *Go.* But he didn't. Go. Or didn't leave in time. I did save his life.

I see that newspaper photo, Brent's body tangled in the snarl of anchor line on the deck…. And that's when it took another turn. When Val came back in on the trawler, I saw clearly that it was going to be him or me, and I just said what I had to say, did what I had to do. They say I wanted to become Christine Desjardins again. Maybe so. Maybe that was the rest of it. Maybe not. Maybe I just got caught. I'd happily still be Lee Anne with Brent's estate and no one the wiser.

I lie here with my hand on my heart and think how I'll be going to trial soon. The prosecution will present its case and I'll be listening. The defense will present its case and I'll be listening. I hear the echo of myself talking in a Southern accent as I fight off sleep, feel the Earth and moon, the way the moon is a stone hanging in a void, cold and silent, and I wonder at their invisible attraction….

I remember in Brooklyn I asked Val to describe it, I couldn't say fish or marlin, we couldn't say anything to each other then, but I knew he knew what I meant, I thought he didn't hear because he didn't answer, but then I suspected he'd heard me, but wouldn't answer, was too pissed at me for asking, all the time we were together we never once could say a word about Davis though he was there every second as he's been since; finally, without actually turning toward me in the dark, he said in a dry faraway voice, *it was like something swimming out of the sunlight itself.…* His voice faded and I never asked anything more though I still see those beautiful blue marlin hanging at the weigh station the day before, their round black eyes staring, their perfect scythe blade tails and ribbed sails, terrible, terrible those huge marlin hanging up in the sun...

*Like something swimming out of the sunlight....* His voice fades, and Val says nothing more, but in his dreams at night in all the time we were together I could feel him sweating and moaning, could feel the fish swimming below him, Davis wired tight to it, I feel Davis' shirt go in and out of Val's hands, then Davis and the marlin are far below on the edge of blue sunlight, and then gone into darkness, and I can feel the fish pulling Val this way and that as he sweats and moans until I shake him awake...

I lie here with my hand on my heart. I'm sleepy, yet I hold off sleep. It is not sleep that I dislike so much, but that first moment when the solid world softens, liquefies, things begin to rise and float, drift and swirl on currents, table, chairs, beds, the windows fill up, it is like a boat going down, and I begin to sink into water, the sunlight fades, weakens, dies into darkness, I look up and see the hull already tiny, and I can feel the marlin taking me down into black water...

## Acknowledgments

I'd like to thank early readers and encouragers: Michael Harwin, Chris Burke, and Ann-Eve Pederson. Pete Eckerstrom clarified legal matters, and in his stories and conversations imparted the spirit of his days in the Pima County Public Defenders Office.

Marshal Gibson and Marty Cutler have been supportive friends since we've been kids and continued that support with their belief in this novel.

I'd like to acknowledge the article by Peter Wright, "Overboard," in the September 1994 issue of *Motor Boating & Sailing:* the fact of the incident, itself. My characters do not in any way resemble those in the article; they are fictional.

Special thanks to Greg Weiss for his belief in this book and his gracious support.

Tom Farber has been there with his calm, steady guidance throughout.

I have appreciated Kit Duane for her astute editing, patience, and generous spirit; greater than the sum of these parts, she has been an angel on my shoulder.

Liz Sisco read the novel, read my mind, and translated both into her cover images: just right.

And lastly, thanks to my children, Dana and Marisa, who have been my teachers, and to Linda, who read and reread this novel more than anyone ever should have had to, offered clear, incisive comments, and was gracious in doing so, as she has been in all things.

## ABOUT THE AUTHOR

C. E. Poverman's first book of stories, *The Black Velvet Girl,* won the Iowa School of Letters Award for Short Fiction. His second, *Skin,* was nominated for the *Los Angeles Times* Book Prize. His stories have appeared in the *O'Henry, Pushcart,* and other anthologies. His previous novels are *Susan, Solomon's Daughter, My Father in Dreams,* and *On the Edge.* Visit cepoverman.com